PRAISE FOR DAVID SOSNOWSKI

VAMPED

"Sosnowski's wholly original mythology explains everything from the ideal vampire vacation spot to why their strip clubs keep the heat cranked up."

—*Washington Post*

"*Vamped* is not an outright spoof of vampire fiction—it has too much respect for its subject for that. But it does smuggle some welcome modernity and comic irreverence into the form. . . . The chief pleasure of *Vamped* is in its rich imagination of the small details of modern vampire life."

—*New York Times Book Review*

"This darkly comic tale . . . provides intriguingly offbeat insights."

—*Entertainment Weekly*

"Few writers have taken as good advantage of the comic potential in vampiric metaphor as David Sosnowski does in his new novel *Vamped* . . . Audacious . . . unexpected and delightful."

—*U.S. News & World Report*

"Smart and funny . . . it's high time for a dark vampiric comedy."

—*Hollywood Reporter*

"Sosnowski's gleefully wicked sense of humor . . . and spot-on pop-culture references make *Vamped* a giddy page-turner. But at its core is a decidedly human tale."

—*Time Out New York*

"With wry wit and deft turns of phrase, David Sosnowski has penned a darkly humorous tale . . . A fresh breeze on a genre that can all too often be as stale as a dusty crypt. A fun read."
—Christopher Moore, author of *Noir*, *Lamb*, and *Bloodsucking Fiends*

"Inventive . . . intriguing . . . fun."
—*Publishers Weekly*

"Full of wit and charm, Sosnowski's fast-paced second novel . . . offers delightfully quirky characters and plenty of hilarious scenes."
—*Library Journal* (starred review)

"Sosnowski's easy mixture of warmth and humor makes for a winning, original tale about love in the unlikeliest of worlds."
—*Booklist*

RAPTURE

"Sosnowski has staked out a patch of turf somewhere between Franz Kafka and Douglas Adams, and made it all his own."
—*Detroit Free Press*

"A delightfully fresh book . . . an imaginative, uplifting tale."
—*Ann Arbor News*

"A hilarious, knowing, and, yes, *uplifting* treatise on the possibilities of being."
—*New Age Journal*

"Spinning an inventive, new riff on contemporary angel mania, Sosnowski's first novel is a fanciful zeitgeist satire."
—*Publishers Weekly*

Happy Doomsday

ALSO BY
DAVID SOSNOWSKI

Vamped

Rapture

Happy Doomsday

DAVID SOSNOWSKI

Published by 47North, Seattle

www.apub.com

Amazon, the Amazon logo, and 47North are trademarks of Amazon.com, Inc., or its affiliates.

ISBN-13: 9781503901308 (hardcover)
ISBN-10: 1503901300 (hardcover)
ISBN-13: 9781503901292 (paperback)
ISBN-10: 1503901297 (paperback)

Cover design by Faceout Studio, Tim Green

Printed in the United States of America

First edition

*In memory of Mark Schemanske,
friend, first reader, fellow writer—
and gone far too soon.*

PROLOGUE

He heard the tune in his sleep: "Pop Goes the Weasel" looping over loudspeakers as an ice cream truck circled the neighborhood, pied-pipering kids out of their homes, money out of their parents. Only in the dream, it wasn't children chasing the truck but actual weasels. Dev stood on his front porch, watching as the rodential flow streamed through the red dot of his laser sight, humming along as he tightened his finger around the trigger, timing his shot to the word *Pop!* when his eyes flew open.

Bits of the dream floated away, but not the song. It was still playing a handful of blocks away and getting closer. The gun in the dream was real too—a sniper's rifle with telescopic sight, laser targeting, a silencer. Dev kept it next to the couch where he slept, fully loaded and just in case. He'd hoped to never have to use it on people, proving yet again what a fat lot of good hoping does. Threading his arm through the shoulder strap, he ninja-ed his way to the wall next to the picture window and teased the drapes open just as the truck rounded the corner.

"Crap," Dev said, ducking under the sill.

He could just keep quiet and wait for them to drive away. But how likely was that? There were only so many doors to kick in, revealing immediately how unoccupied the houses behind them were. Whoever was in that truck would know his place was different once the doorknob punched a hole in the drywall, exposing all the evidence he'd left lying around, from fresh embers in the fireplace to the unmoldy dishes he hadn't washed to the still-warm dent from his body on the couch. Even if he hid in the attic, all they'd have to do was wait for the predictable betrayal of his stomach or bladder.

For a second, the truck seemed like it might drive by, but then it stopped and backed up, the music still playing. Nosing the curtain apart again with the silencer, Dev squeezed one eye closed as he lined up the crosshairs with the passenger door that was just then opening.

"Crap," Dev muttered as the door in the crosshairs closed, leaving a pregnant girl his age standing there, crucified, the laser's red dot resting on her belly button, an outie pressed against the stretched fabric of a *Walking Dead* T-shirt. All Dev had to do was squeeze the trigger to exchange one red dot for another not made of light.

But then the other invader emerged from the ice cream truck—a guy also around Dev's age, but bigger, with football shoulders carried in a way that suggested a future of beatings, especially if Dev shot the waddling body bag next to him.

"Crap, crap, crap—*double* crap . . ."

Until that point, things had been going reasonably well for Dev. Sure, it had been a little rough in the beginning, but he'd adapted, made do, developed a couple of life-preserving routines. It didn't hurt that he'd always preferred his own company to that of others. But now, all of a sudden, out of nowhere, bang, here comes this, what, couple, he guessed. They looked like a couple, anyway, stepping out of an ice cream truck, the same one that woke him by playing "Pop Goes the Weasel" as it prowled the streets he'd claimed as his, having done all the hard work of clearing out the bodies. But here came these two—soon to be three, apparently—just in time to ruin everything.

Thus, the question: Should he, or shouldn't he?

"Shit," Marcus, the football-player-looking guy, said, thereby confirming the day's excremental turn. Simply put, he didn't want to be here. The only reason he'd come was because *she* wanted to. He'd tagged along because, well, it wasn't like girls were growing on trees nowadays. Plus, he bore a certain responsibility for whoever was growing inside that beach-ball belly of hers. Marcus claimed it was a he while she insisted it was a she, so whatever it was, it was basically a he-said-she-said situation.

He probably should have explained earlier why he didn't want to come here, but that would have meant going into a bunch of other stuff he hadn't mentioned. So he'd kept quiet while she prattled on about "the future," leaving him to do most of the driving and worrying.

The reason for Marcus's expletive was the red dot he'd noticed trained on the baby's head or tail, whichever way it happened to be floating at the moment. The possibility that they'd wind up with red dots trained on them was why Marcus hadn't wanted to come. Noticing it now, he would have loved to say, "I told you so," but then again, he hadn't told her anything, so instead he stepped in front of his baby mama, turning sideways so the red dot fell on his arm—the one he didn't write with, not that he'd been doing a lot of writing lately. As acts of chivalry went, it was decidedly qualified. He was ready to lose an arm or a leg to being noble, but he wasn't ready to go full martyr just yet. For a guy who'd once been known as Mo (short for Mohammad), martyrdom was a touchy subject, especially considering some of those things he hadn't told her about.

"'Shit'?" This time the fecal epithet was voiced by the pregnant girl, Lucy. "What are you shitting about?" she continued. "And why are you doing that?" Meaning Marcus's stepping in front of her before scrunching his eyes shut, like they'd agreed she should kick him in the groin and he was bracing for it.

"Nothing," Marcus said, eyes still scrunched. "I was just hoping not to get shot today."

That's when Lucy saw the red dot on his forearm. "Oh, for heaven's sake," she said, like he was some little kid cowering because of some itsy-bitsy spider. Pushing him aside, she stepped back into the path of the laser.

"What the TF are you doing?" Marcus demanded, taking hold of her shoulders and trying to change places again. But everywhere he moved, she parried, making him think she'd make a pretty good offensive lineman—if she wasn't pregnant, that is, and there were enough people left to make two football teams.

"Saving your life," Lucy said.

"But *I'm* trying to save the *baby's*," Marcus insisted, and then, as an afterthought, "And yours." Pause. "Too."

"Listen," Lucy said, having done the survival-of-the-species math a while ago, "nobody's shooting a mother-to-be. Not nowadays."

"What about when President Pro-Life bombed Iraq?" Marcus begged to differ. "News flash: there were pregnant women under a lot of those bombs."

"I said, 'nowadays,'" Lucy said. "I distinctly remember qualifying my statement."

"Are we *seriously* arguing about this?"

Lucy didn't answer. Instead, she braced her back with one hand and cupped the other next to her mouth. *"We come in peace!"* she shouted before crossing her arms and daring the laser-dot aimer to prove her wrong.

PART ONE

1

If he had to pick someone to be the last person on earth, Dev Brinkman would pick himself—and not just for the obvious reason of wanting to stay alive. Constitutionally—*neurologically*—he was either in a perpetual state of PTSD or Teflon-coated against it. The artful euphemism placed him somewhere "on the spectrum," as if he were trying out for a role in *The Wizard of Oz*. Or the Wizard of Odd, as his stepfather had described him, much less artfully.

If he'd lived before Dr. Asperger bequeathed his name to a spectrum disorder, Dev probably would have been considered shy, possibly accruing other labels along the way: peculiar, stuck in his ways, eccentric. They'd skip retarded altogether because Dev clearly wasn't, as demonstrated by his talent for becoming an expert in anything he put his mind to. He had no doubt he'd have made an excellent jack-of-all-trades, grumbling to himself but nevertheless in high demand because "that Brinkman boy can fix anything."

"Even better than new, sometimes," the village folks would grudgingly admit.

But Dev lived in a time with a diagnostic box waiting for him, which his stepfather placed him in on a lazy afternoon while reading the *New York Times Sunday Magazine*. "Asperger's syndrome," he pronounced, letting the magazine flop inward so he could stare over the tops of his glasses at the child he'd inherited from his dead brother. "What they call 'on the spectrum' anyway," he continued. "It all fits."

This was when Dev was four, before he'd started school, which he'd been dreading—wisely, as it turned out—because there'd be a lot of people there and he didn't like people, especially when they came in "lots." At the moment, though, he was laser focused on the word his mom's husband just used. "What's *spectrum*?" he asked.

Fortunately, it was raining while Dev's replacement dad was mentally ticking off yeses next to the symptoms that led to a diagnosis like the one he was preparing to make. Also fortunately, the rain had stopped sometime between his pronouncement and his stepson's question. So Mr. Brinkman tapped the boy on the head with the rolled-up magazine and indicated he should follow him out onto the porch. Towering over the little boy, he shielded his eyes and scanned the sky from one end to the next.

"*There,*" he said, pointing out the ribbon of Life Savers colors arcing across the sky. "*That's* the spectrum," he said.

Dev tried connecting his stepfather's claim that he, Dev, was "on the spectrum" to the rainbow in the sky. He remembered that rainbows had something to do with people even littler than him who dressed in green, which, in turn, connected to four-leaf clovers, a breakfast cereal that turned milk funny colors, and gold like the fillings in his mom's teeth.

"Is being colored good or bad?" he asked, there being too many interlinking variables for Dev to decide for himself.

The boy's fill-in father nearly spat out the coffee he'd just sipped, having lost track of how their conversation started in favor of his little science lecture. Remembering, he waggled a finger as if Dev were trying to pull a fast one. "Touché," he said before going off to look for his wife, to tell her what her son said, leaving Dev to contemplate the candied sky just the way he liked to: alone.

After helpfully diagnosing her son, Mr. Brinkman handed Mrs. Brinkman the *New York Times Sunday Magazine* he'd annotated with insightful marginalia. "It fits," he said, making it sound like all they were discussing was a pair of shoes. And the way he handed over the magazine reminded her of something else: the way he used to hand off the two-year-old Dev whenever his diaper was full. "Here," the gesture said, "all yours."

Flash cards—that was her original intervention: a series of smiley faces displaying exaggerated emotions like the emoji that would become popular later, when people let their thumbs do the talking. Once Dev seemed to get the hang of them, nodding when she asked leading questions like, "Is that a smile?" she followed up with actual faces she'd clipped from magazines and compiled in a binder she called (but unfortunately did not trademark) his "face book."

"Look here," she'd said the first time she switched from cartoon emotions to the real thing. "What do you see?"

"A head," Dev said.

"Yes, but what's *on* the head?"

"Hair."

"I mean in front of the head."

Dev looked puzzled before answering, "A camera?"

His mom blinked. Not the answer she was looking for, but ingenious in its way. Of course, her son's problem wasn't thinking outside the box; it was understanding there was a box in the first place and learning to live comfortably inside it. So:

"A face," she corrected. "It's a face, Dev."

"Okay."

"Now, what's on the face?"

"A mouth," he tried. "A nose," he tried again. He didn't mention the eyes.

"An expression," she said, cutting to the chase. "People's faces have *expressions* that tell you what they're feeling." Pause. "What does this picture say about how she's feeling?"

Dev's face said nothing, a word he proceeded to say aloud, followed by a shrug.

"Look at her lips," his mother continued. "See how they're going up, here and here?"

Her son nodded.

"That's a smile," she said. "The lady in the picture has a smile on her face. She's smiling. Why would she be smiling?"

He answered the way she knew he would. "A prism," he said, this being shortly after his stepfather had placed him on the spectrum and right around the time he'd developed an obsession with all things optical: lenses, mirrors, DVDs with their shimmering rainbows, and, of course, prisms.

"Okay," his mother said, playing along. She'd already learned that seventy percent of her job was going to be just that: playing along. The other thirty percent? Playing by ear. "A prism would make *you* smile, wouldn't it?"

Dev nodded, overdoing it. Whenever he was uncomfortable, she'd noticed, he found peace by moving: rocking or flapping or jumping up and down. So once he had an excuse to move his head, he did it like he was a cartoon character who'd just been boinged and was still vibrating.

"And why would you smile?" she asked, resisting the urge to hold his head still, as if a cure were as simple as a laying on of hands. "What does a prism make you feel?"

She wondered if he'd remember her telling her husband how *h*-word the prism had made Dev. She watched as the connection clicked together like Legos in his head.

"Happy," he said, as her face did the same thing the face in the picture was doing.

And so they practiced, and Dev seemed to get better, calling out "Happy" or "Sad" or "Angry" correctly seventy-five percent of the time, before she realized he'd just memorized the sequence. After rearranging the pages, she went back to coaxing his random guesses into the neighborhood of the right answers, the words "Close, but . . ." the most often heard combination issuing from her lips during these sessions.

And even as she persisted, she knew the face book was a half step at best. In real life, people don't hold their expressions until you call out an answer. In real life, people's faces are constantly changing. Reading them can be like trying to read cards in the middle of a shuffle. And so it was on to phase III: the portable DVD player.

Dev could now practice on fully animated faces—she thought—except he didn't. Instead, she found him hitting pause repeatedly, playing the faces back, virtual frame by virtual frame, watching as the world's slowest smiles blossomed or the world's heaviest grief came crashing down. Released into the first grade with this new kind of practice under his belt, Dev did no better than before. A little worse, actually. He'd developed a twitch in his right hand from pressing an invisible remote, trying to make the faces go slower, so he could catch up.

Dev hadn't always been diagnostically shy. Freshly born to an older couple who'd thought—mistakenly—they were past their childbearing years, Dev seemed as normal as any other baby: playing catch with his feet; giggling when he broke wind; opening and closing his hands like starfish when it was time to nurse.

"He's perfect," his mother declared back then, and his still-living father agreed—or so Dev had been told.

He could still remember the last adult eyes he looked into, back when he was a toddler of two and his real dad was still alive to agree about Dev's postnatal perfection. He'd been flying at the time, with an assist from his god, a.k.a. his real dad, while his other god, a.k.a. his mom, was off doing mom stuff. His belly was balanced on huge upturned palms as his own palms stretched out and down while he giggled so hard he nearly rolled off.

"Careful there, Lucky Lindy," his dad said. "Paris is in our sights. This is no time to get careless . . ."

Dev looked down at his dad's eyes. He liked looking at them when his father spoke, because his eyes spoke too. This time—that last time—they winked, and then crossed as his dad exaggerated how difficult it was holding him up.

Giggling even harder, Dev started to roll, but didn't fall. Instead, his father's hands turned the roll into an excuse to flip him over so he faced the ceiling above the couch where his father lay, holding him aloft. With excruciating tenderness, his father then lowered him safely to his chest, where the little boy could feel the booming of his father's heart knocking between his wing bones.

"Whoa," his father said, and Dev remembered how cool and damp his father's hands felt. He tried ruffling the boy's hair only to leave it wet and clinging to his forehead. "You are *such* a big boy," his father said, an arm wrapped around Dev's middle like a seat belt.

His father stopped talking and just breathed after that. Heavy, hard breaths the boy's body rode like a boat rising and falling with the waves rushing to shore. He looked at the ceiling. The cracks reminded him of the lightning his dad pointed out, rocking him after the thunder made him cry.

"God's fixing a crack in the sky," he'd said. "That's just the sound of his hammer . . ."

Dev was still looking at the cracked ceiling when his father's seat-belt arm grew heavy, and cold. And when his mother returned, she found the two of them, still on the couch, one of them trying not to move, the other not having to try.

Before the funeral, Dev's mom hadn't spoken to her husband's brother since her wedding. And though the boy never asked, the pair nevertheless went to the trouble of making light of the circumstances behind their becoming a couple.

"Less paperwork," they'd say together and laugh, as if they hadn't collaborated on this self-consciously offhand remark. What they meant was that mother and child didn't need to change names, it being a lateral, Brinkman-to-Brinkman move. Plus, his dad and uncle looked like what they were—brothers—meaning Dev looked like both. Most people had no idea there'd been a bait and switch until the uncle was introduced with the *step* word, after which their eyes would wander to the awkward sets of wedding photos: the first with his mom, his dad, and his dad's brother as best man, and the second shot in a government office somewhere, plus toddler Dev, minus his dad.

Separately, and less glibly, his mother had tried explaining—again, not that Dev had asked. "He was such a help, after," she said. "I fell apart and he stepped up. Met with the funeral people. Picked out the suit. I just had to show up and be the widow."

The adjective she was leaving out before *widow* was *medicated*. Her brother-in-law and future husband was a failed doctor who donned a pharmacist's white coat as a consolation prize. As such, the consolation he offered his sister-in-law and future wife included 0.25 milligrams of Xanax, repeated as needed. Dev had seen the amber bottle with his mother's name on it in the medicine cabinet. The pills inside were the same his fake dad would eventually use to manage Dev's symptoms, postdiagnosis.

"And after that," his mother continued, "he just kept helping . . . and just stopped going back home."

They were in the boy's room when she told him this, his mother sitting sideways in a chair next to his desk, Dev on the floor, dismantling a vacuum cleaner. Doomsday was still eight months in the future, Dev was a sophomore, and his mother worried sex would soon be an issue, if it wasn't already. And so she tried explaining the complicated nature of her relationship to her latest husband. The boy didn't look up once during her entire explanation, busying himself instead with the removal of screws and the setting down of parts, positioned exactly like the exploded diagram resting on the floor next to him.

"And so that's why," his mother said finally, resting her hands on her knees.

"Okay," Dev said into the yawning pause that opened afterward.

His mother waited for more, watching the top of her son's head as he removed a cover plate and set it down carefully next to the screws that had once held it in place.

"Okay," she said, getting up to leave. "I'm glad we had this conversation," she added, as if they'd actually had one.

According to his mother, the change was like a switch. One day, he was a two-year-old bag of giggles whenever she tickled him, and the next, all the Tickle Monster got was a glare and a body like a fist. He stopped using the few words he'd been using, and his eyes began wandering away whenever she tried to catch them.

Two things happened just before the change: her husband died, and Dev got his scheduled dose of the pneumococcal conjugate vaccine. The coincidence didn't turn his mother into an anti-vaxxer, per se; she just didn't like how people made fun of that one anti-vaxxer who happened to be an ex–porn star. For Mrs. Brinkman, the ridicule wasn't about the woman's lack of a science degree so much as her having ovaries. The pro-vaxxers were just patriarchal supporters of Big Pharma—an ironic stance for a woman with a professional pill dispenser for a husband.

"Love's not logical" was all she'd say.

Her son—who suspected emotions fell somewhere between Santa and the Easter Bunny on the logic scale—didn't disagree.

But after his stepfather's diagnosis, Dev stopped going to "so-called doctors." There was no search for support, no treatment options considered. As far as the boy's symptoms went—like obsessive-compulsive disorder, panic attacks, the occasional trancelike state that may or may not be a seizure—lucky Dev had a pharmacist in the family.

"Bottoms up," he said, handing out Xanax like Flintstones vitamins from a supply he skimmed from his customers' legitimate scripts.

In retrospect, it was probably a convenient condition for a stepson to have, at least to the man who'd married his dead brother's wife. After all, Dev stayed in his room, entertained himself, kept out of the way. He was like a puppy that happily trotted into its crate and pulled the door closed behind. Except Dev was even better than a puppy; he was potty-trained and, once he was older, could be given chores he completed with breathtaking single-mindedness.

Aimed at the bathroom, not only did he scrub every speck of mold and mildew from the grout, but he buffed clean the individual sockets of the toothbrush holder and the gummy underside of the mounted soap dish before removing the aerating screen from the faucet and poking a toothpick through each clogged opening.

"Maybe we should rent you out to the neighbors," his stepfather said before insisting to his wife that he was only joking.

At school, Dev's eccentricities were less . . . appreciated.

"Ass burgers? Is that, like, what homos eat for lunch?"

Each year, at least one of Dev's classmates imagined this anal malapropism was the height of wit. And each year, he corrected the would-be comedian's pronunciation—Az-*per*-gers—inadvertently adding comedic fuel. Occasionally, a jokester might double down, insisting that Dev answer the question. "Which homos did you mean?" he'd ask before listing the evolutionary possibilities in ascending order. The crowd invariably lost it when he got to *Homo erectus*, though Dev never saw what was so funny. Instead, he dismissed the reaction as some neurotypical thing he'd never understand and frankly didn't care to.

As for those things Dev *did* care about—he averaged about one per year, a single, all-consuming fascination he dubbed his *topique du annum à la* soup du jour, using a precocious combination of faux French and faux Latin. Each new school year came with a new *topique*, and his teachers knew what to expect the rest of the year after he'd raised his hand with such urgency that not calling on him could be considered child abuse. After ten seconds of not being recognized, he'd start waving. Twenty seconds of un-responded-to waving would then be followed by adding his free hand to prop up the already-raised one, which went limp with fatigue at the wrist—a dramatic fatigue that slumped through his skeleton until he was halfway to cracking his skull on the floor. Fortunately, a simple "Yes, Mr. Brinkman?" was all it took to avoid a liability suit.

Called on, Dev snapped back into an upright and locked position as his piping voice delivered whatever urgent proclamation weighed on his poor bones. "Did you know . . . ?" was then followed by some piece of trivia about his latest, special subject, thus introducing it to one and all.

One year it was optics, thanks to the gift of a prism, so the boy on the spectrum could cast his own. From optics to microscopes, then telescopes, from microbiology to astronomy. One year, out of the blue, World War I aircraft fascinated him, followed by World War II paratroopers and the stuff they carried with them. This, in turn, became an obsession with camping gear and camping-gear catalogs, though, predictably for a budding agoraphobic, *not* camping itself. Next: survivalist websites. Next: disasters of all kinds, in history and fiction, including the biblical and/or zombie apocalyptical kind. And lastly, just before he got distracted by the actual apocalypse, another giant leap for Dev-kind: vacuum cleaners.

That other kids considered him weird didn't bother Dev; being weird was just synonymous with being smarter than they were, a point of pride purchased at the cost of one measly diagnosis. And so he sailed on through grades and *topiques*, blissfully clueless about his social cluelessness, thanks to a fortunate absence of friends to make him feel stupid by pointing it out.

But then came fifth grade—astronomy—and a boy named Leonard Slovitz, whose father got a promotion and was transferred to Ford World Headquarters in Dearborn, Michigan. Their friendship began on the playground one recess, where Dev had kept to himself for the first four years of grade school—an arrangement reached by mutual agreement between Dev and everybody else. Leo, as the new kid, didn't know any better—something he proved by walking right up, a hand out, a greeting on his lips.

Dev was into spitting back then—a dangerous but effective way of maximizing his personal space. So as Leo approached, Dev began hoarding saliva, which he let fly once a line he was waiting to be crossed was. The gob hit the newcomer right between stunned eyes before sliding down the bridge of his nose. Dev turned his back then, mission—he assumed—accomplished.

"D-d-do you know how many g-g-germs are in human saliva?" Leo stammered.

"Yes," Dev said, turning back around and proceeding to list them, starting with his favorites from the *annum* of microbiology: the ones ending in -occus.

"You left out *E. coli*," Leo said, once the spitting boy had finished.

Dev flinched as if he'd been slapped. The new kid was right. He'd forgotten perhaps the most ubiquitous germ of all. "You're correct," he said, a phrase, in retrospect, he could not recall ever using with a so-called peer.

"Leonard Slovitz," Leo said, reextending his hand.

"Dev Brinkman," the other admitted, his own hands remaining clasped behind his back.

And so they became friends—the weird kid and the slightly less weird kid—spending their days trying to out-nerd each other. For example: "Galileo didn't invent the telescope," Dev announced one recess.

"Well, certainly not the Newtonian reflector," Leo said back. "*That* was invented by Sir Isaac Newton." Pause. "Of course."

"Yes, yes," Dev said, the tone in his voice sounding a little irritated, which he frequently was during these nerd-offs, but a good kind of irritated—like he'd met his match and had to fight for what once came easy. "I mean the refracting telescope that most people think

Galileo invented, but didn't. It was a Dutch optometrist named Hans Lippershey."

"Hmmm," Leo mused, "don't you mean Sacharias Jansen or perhaps Jacob Metius?"

Leo liked to argue like a pool shark playing a mark, flailing about right up until he sank three balls with one impossible shot.

But then puberty came, Leo changed, and Dev didn't. Oh, the latter's voice cracked, and hair started growing where it hadn't before, but he remained steadfastly immune to fashion while Leo got contacts and started caring about hair products and what was and wasn't in. And spoiler alert: Dev was not and never had been "in." But according to Leo, Dev wasn't just not in; he was so out there it was like he was from *outer space*, yo.

Yes, Leo, once articulate, had suffered a lobotomy by hormones that left him saying things like, "Yo." And apparently convinced that outer space was a bad thing—a sad reversal for a once-promising astronomer.

And it wasn't just Leo. Everything seemed to be changing. Take the teachers. They'd stopped letting him bend their assignments to incorporate his latest *topique*. "You need to stretch, Dev," they said. "Get outside your comfort zone."

And what did stretching to the point of discomfort suggest, outside medieval torture? Group projects, the very thought of which made him physically ill. Why should he have to water down his grade with the inferior contributions of others? The first few times he just had the others sign his work between texting their friends and playing rounds of *Candy Crush*. But then the teachers got wise and started talking about stretching and comfort zones again. Dev complained to Leo, and what happened? He sided with the comfort stretchers!

"Just take a breath, already," Leo advised, sounding worn-out by his onetime friend.

"Okay," Dev said, sucking in a quick one before blowing it out and resuming his litany of injustices until Leo threw up a hand and said, "Stop.

"You want to know a comfort zone you can stretch out of?"

Dev prepared to say no, but was cut off.

"Your mom's car," Leo said. "We're in high school and your mom still drives you to school. Why don't you walk the last block, at least?"

"Why?" Dev asked. "The car's warmed up by then. The additional air pollution created by driving an extra block once the catalyst lights off is negligible at best. And that's assuming my mom just turned right around and drove back home, as opposed to doing errands that take her past the front of the school anyway."

Leo responded with a face-palm.

"Doesn't that hurt?" Dev asked.

"Not as much as this conversation," Leo replied.

The reason his mom drove was simple: the bus took the freeway at freeway speeds. Dev wasn't good with either of those. Riding along on residential roads already meant lying on his stomach in the back seat. Try that on the school bus and see how fast Leo changed his mind about Dev's riding with his mom . . .

The problem was data. Hurtling through the world at highway speeds involved too much processing. Even standing still, new surroundings had Dev flirting with overload as he tried to mentally map every square inch of the given space. To the lizard inside his Aspergerian brain, newness meant danger. He didn't know what was important, and so everything was and needed to be mapped like so:

- Number of doors, windows, and objects in the way;
- Ceiling height, flooring type, the distance between him and each wall in steps;
- Objects that could kill him; and
- Objects he could defend himself with.

If he could touch things—walls, other surfaces—that sometimes helped, but it was also what made being outside even worse. There were no walls to touch outside, and the catalog of things out there was as good as infinite. That's why Dramamine didn't help. The problem wasn't motion sickness; it was insufficient bandwidth. The medication he needed was Adderall, which was contraindicated because of his anxiety issues, hence the Xanax. It was a classic pharmaceutical catch-22: the pill to increase his bandwidth would crank his anxiety up to eleven.

All things being equal, the luxury of riding the bus like everybody without their own car didn't seem worth it. Or as Dev boiled it down for Leo: "My mom doesn't mind."

"Maybe she'd like to sleep in for once," his friend countered.

"Nope," Dev said confidently. "She'd get up anyway, so she can get to the good stuff at the thrift store."

"You mean like the She-Ra backpack?"

Dev adjusted said backpack. As far as he was concerned, his support of a female superhero—dated though she may be—should impress teenaged girls, suggesting as it did his attitude toward female equality, even though said attitude was largely fueled by his inability to see the advantage of subdividing mankind any further than neurotypicals versus whatever he was. So: "What's wrong with She-Ra?"

"Other than farting dust?"

"Huh?"

"Never mind."

But Dev couldn't let it go. How was it possible that his mom's driving him to school and/or his She-Ra backpack should so offend neurotypicals that ostracism was warranted? To the best of his knowledge, all the people mocking him had mothers. And how was the She-Ra backpack any worse than anything else bearing pictures with no known connection to their actual function? Was Quaker Oats full of ground-up Quakers? Did buying the stuff famous people endorsed make you famous too? Or was it the fact that Dev's backpack happened to be used?

"It's new to you," his mother always said whenever she got him something from the thrift store, and Dev was fine with that. In the case of the infamous backpack, there'd been no holes, no stains, no funny smells, and his textbooks fit perfectly, a necessity for someone predisposed to OCD. So that meant the picture of She-Ra was the only "defect," which Dev didn't consider a defect at all, just like he didn't consider Asperger's a defect. To the contrary, being on the spectrum was the source of his secret power: being smarter than everybody else. Even his once-worthy rival, Leo.

2

Some weird kids are born that way, and others are made by their circumstances. Lucy Abernathy fell into the latter category by not conforming to certain biological ratios considered attractive—and she resented the hell out of it. This resentment didn't manifest itself until she'd had her first period, but once it arrived—her resentment, not her period—it led her to embrace the beastly side of the beauty/beast divide. And not just beasts, but monsters and zombies and the horror genre in general, along with a certain gothic sensibility in her fashion choices.

Despite living in the brutally sunlit land of Atlanta, where white before and after Labor Day was not only de rigueur but heat-index mandated, Lucy opted to go black and never went back.

"Ern't y'all hawt in that?" someone asked her the first time she appeared fully gothed-out in public.

"In my humble opinion," Lucy said, "yes," leaving the sizzle-ass punch line where it belonged: in her head.

But once *The Walking Dead* started filming in her backyard, Lucy found herself coming dangerously close to being trendy, a bullet she dodged by hanging out with the second-least trendy member of Atlanta's burgeoning horror scene, her gay buddy Max. Though born in the same land of peaches, kudzu, and R.E.M., Max considered himself miles above anything below—as he called it—the Mason-Dumbass Line.

"If it weren't for you," he said, meaning Lucy, "I'd be outta here like—" and he slapped his hands before sending one flying, presumably to some place beyond the Mason-Dumbass Line, though the sound effect he chose for said departure was more gunshot than jet or even Greyhound bus.

Lucy hugged him the first time he expressed the sentiment but immediately backed off on Max's advice that she "contain" herself, "young lady."

"My bad," Lucy apologized to her BFF, the (unfortunately) gay Max.

It all went south—literally as well as metaphorically—during the Days of the Dead convention at the Atlanta Sheraton off Peachtree something and Peachtree something else. Lucy and Max met at the Buckhead MARTA station and rode down together, both already in full DotD regalia. For Lucy, this meant a zombie-goth cheerleader she'd assembled from a thrift store skirt she'd razor slit before suturing back together with safety pins, followed by water-damaged pom-poms, a skull-and-crossbones lunchbox purse, and black-and-white makeup.

"You like?" Lucy said, striking an ironic pose to give her friend a better view of what Max called her on-som-bla, making it sound like a mash-up of *Les Mis* and NAMBLA.

"You? Mos' def', BFF," Max said. "Your on-som-bla, on the other hand . . ."

"Say it."

"It's a tad, well, *impressionistic*, no?"

Max was being polite. What he really meant was that Lucy's costume screamed exactly what it was: Maybelline for mimes with a touch of resale improv. She was bound to be blown out of the proverbial water by the ultrarealistic prosthetics the other cosplayers could be counted on wearing. Max, for his part, hadn't even tried to compete with those

TWD audition reels, opting for a satanic clown/court jester, complete with bell cap and a pair of high-tech stilts with spring blades like Olympic amputees used to run in. The result was that he towered two feet over Lucy, which was all well and good—until they had to board the train for downtown.

"Um," Max said, eying the too-short sliding doors that had just gasped open.

Lucy surveilled the situation before saying, "Get down on your knees."

"I thought you'd never ask . . ."

Ignoring him, Lucy explained her plan to ride him aboard like they were playing horsey.

"How is *that* an answer?"

"It makes it looked planned," Lucy said. "Like it's part of the act. Everybody else thinks we're crazy anyway. Why not act like it?"

"Why not, indeed?" gay Max said, getting down on all fours.

"We look like Laurel and Hardy," Max said as they passed a mirrored wall at the Sheraton, "painted by Salvador Dali."

Was that a crack about my weight? Lucy wondered. Because if it was, well, it wasn't appreciated, especially not from Max, who was gay, after all, making weight on her part strictly academic on his. Plus, Lucy wasn't even fat. She was slightly—*slightly*—overweight. Healthy, really. Baseline American: what you got from following all those daily recommendations. Nothing crazy like McDonald's every meal. The main culprit was ice cream. Ice cream, and her mom.

Mrs. (*not* Ms.) Abernathy was nonconfrontational. Involved in an argument, she caved more often than not. Witness to an argument, her primary instinct was to deflect. And her go-to line when it came to deflecting? "Who wants ice cream?"

Lucy, personally, had been deflected a size or two bigger than a girl her height and bone structure should be, assuming you were judging by the unreasonable standards of Hollywood, but also, maybe, by those from the American Medical Association. Lucy couldn't help it; she'd been trained to associate ice cream with domestic stability. Plus, she liked how it tasted, the mouthfeel of it, all that silky smooth cold. She even got used to the brain freeze, romanticizing it as what it must feel like to do cocaine. She and her brother used to fight sometimes just so their mother would break out the Häagen-Dazs, their mom being stone-cold serious when it came to deflecting.

Max, for his part, used humor instead of Good Humor to do his deflecting. Like when it came to the cold-as-a-crypt shoulder Lucy had begun giving him ever since his Daliesque weight crack. He kept trying to take it back without actually acknowledging he'd said it, maintaining a stream of stand-up-ready commentary as they roamed the halls, suites, and auditoriums of the con, flipping through fanzines, gazing at the galleries of fan art, posing for photographs Lucy darted out of the frame of just before the click, not wanting to memorialize their surrealistic Laurel-and-Hardy routine.

And he kept trying, all the way up to the room they were sharing because, well, what part of "gay Max" didn't you get?

For Lucy—as it turned out—the answer was: none.

She got all the parts of gay Max, even the apparently not-so-gay private one. He'd grown so desperate to see her smile he'd stooped to doing impressions. And the one that got her smiling, then laughing, then laughing so hard she lost her breath, pleading, "Stop, stop, stop," so hard a little pee came out was one Max had timed so perfectly that it caught her off guard and landed smack-dab in the middle of that part of her soul still capable of laughing so hard she peed.

And what was that killer impression? This: Max, absolutely deadpan, talk-singing "Zip-a-Dee-Doo-Dah" as Rod Serling, each set of four to five syllables punctuated by a pregnant pause full of sardonic foreboding. By the time Mr. Bluebird was perched on Mr. Serling's shoulder, Lucy's sides were cramping, so her laughter came out interspersed with little cries of pain so incongruous they made her—ironically, perversely, painfully—laugh even harder.

Why she was laughing, she couldn't say. Was it the disconnect between Mr. *Twilight Zone* and all those bluebirds and sunshine? Was it the political incorrectitude of a gay man from Atlanta singing a song from Disney's transparently racist *Song of the South*? Did he even know about that movie, which hadn't been released from Disney's infamous "vault" for decades, or was he just familiar with its rehabilitated incarnation as part of the soundtrack for Splash Mountain in Disney World? The only reason she knew about the song's original background was because she'd heard rumors about this Disney flick that was set in Atlanta and was so racist it'd make your jaw drop. So, of course, she had to track down some scratchy clips on YouTube, after which her jaw did exactly that.

But whatever the reasons, Lucy needed Max to stop. And so she kissed him—to shock him—to make him stop making her laugh. But then he kissed her back, and Lucy knew they were screwed. So they did.

Afterward, in the unprotected afterglow, Lucy said, almost as an afterthought: "Wow, that got serious fast."

"Yeah," Max agreed. "Like a . . ." but he didn't say heart attack. Instead, he just said, "Yeah," again.

A few missed periods later . . .

"Merde," Lucy said, sitting on a toilet in the girls' room, staring at the blue cross on the pee stick. This was the third such cross on the third such stick, all from the shoplifted boxes stacked next to her on the toilet paper dispenser.

"*Shite* and onions," she added, using the euphemism her father routinely used around her mother, but nowhere else, which was how she knew he was just talking shit. Which seemed appropriate, sitting in the stall, alone with her pee sticks, trying to imagine the truckload of ice cream it'd take to deflect being pregnant. Because there was going to be some big-time confrontation once *that* news got out. Not from her mom. Her mom might manage an "oh my" before making a beeline for the fridge. But her *dad*—the man who'd married a woman who didn't like to argue because he did, especially the winning part—her dad would call down the wrath of God. And she already knew the words that would crush her: "You ungrateful shit." He'd use the *s*-word right in front of her mother—the both of them—just to show how serious he was.

He'd never used any of those words with her before—other than *you*, of course. But still they lay there like bricks in her stomach, right next to that catastrophe that would make him hurl them. "You ungrateful shit . . ." She could hear them in her head. And she had nothing to counter them with. But then she did: "Who wants ice cream?" she'd ask.

Her brother might laugh. Her mom would already be crying between scoopfuls. And her dad—her dad would be holding the door for her. Hostile la viva, baby.

Well, it was obvious what she needed to do. The good Catholic girl her mom hoped she'd be one day, *that* girl would make it up to Jesus later, when she was older and ready. And married, of course. Can't forget that: definitely married. Then she'd have legitimate kids coming out of her eyes. Or you know, where they normally came out.

Fortunately, abortion on demand was still the law of the land, even in the land of peaches and Republicans. Or so Lucy assumed—until she actually needed one.

It started with trying to find a place that did them. Local providers wouldn't even use the word. She knew. When she googled "Atlanta abortion clinic," all she got were euphemisms: family planning, women's crisis counseling, women's care clinic. Lucy settled for a place called Women's Health Planning, an interesting combination of words that at least *implied* a connection to Planned Parenthood. They even turned the *o* in "Women's" into one of those circly crossy things for *woman*.

The lady at reception seemed as pleasant as a warm slice of peach pie, just there to help. "Hi y'all doing?" she asked, hybridizing her "hi" and "how" together with her "y'all," getting two greetings for the price of one.

"Not great," Lucy admitted.

She'd not worn her zombie-goth cheerleading costume she'd been impregnated within proximity of during "that Mexican Halloween," as her mom insisted on calling the Days of the Dead convention—not that her mom had a clue about the tricks or treats Max and she had gotten themselves into. Instead, Lucy dressed in a mom-approved plaid skirt, white blouse, and matching knee socks. Mrs. Abernathy wasn't just clinging to her own past in choosing these outfits, but Lucy's too—from before they had to pull her out of Catholic school, thanks to a "downturn" in the economy. If her parents ever found out about her current predicament, she figured she'd plead a busted moral compass, thanks to being dumped among the heathens. Spread the blame.

If Lucy saw the silver cross around the receptionist's neck, it didn't register; knee-jerk Christianity was, after all, the Southern way. Plus, she was too busy filling out forms that seemed to ask a lot more questions than seemed strictly necessary for what she understood to be a simple medical procedure, especially this early on.

Suddenly, a woman in scrubs opened the door next to the receptionist's desk, bearing a clipboard of her own. "Smith?" she said, making the quotes nearly visible.

Lucy waited to see if any of the other girls fidgeting in chairs next to her made a move before raising her hand. "Here," she finally said, hand over head, head hanging low.

Unfortunately, the people naming Georgia's women's health providers weren't the only ones disinclined to use the *a*-word. The "counselor" Lucy was handed off to was equally reticent, preferring to use a different *a*-word: adoption.

"There are so many couples—I can't tell you how many couples—praying for a miracle like the one y'all got growing inside you" was the way she prefaced it. "There's just not enough babies," she continued, "to adopt," presumably because they'd all been gobbled up by the other *a*-word. "That's why y'all got people going to *Russia*, for heaven's sake."

Lucy suspected the word missing in this conversation was *white*. There weren't enough *white* babies for *white* couples to adopt. And bingo, here Lucy was, carrying one. Praise Jesus!

They'd already shown her the usual pro-life splatter porn: the ground-up fetuses of late-term abortions, not the featureless clump of cells the thing inside her was at the moment. But it did its job. It made her sick. It made her feel guilty. But it didn't change how out-of-the-question adoption was.

"I," Lucy started, stopped. "Adoption," she finally declared. *"No,"* she added, signaling that the counselor could stop talking about it, but the counselor didn't. Not as long as she had a "but . . ." still in her and interjected it before Lucy could make herself even clearer. Finally: "I don't want my parents to find out," she shouted.

There, *that* was done. But not quite. "Oh dear," the but-lady said. "Surely you know Georgia has a parental notification requirement for underage . . ." She didn't finish the sentence.

No, Lucy thought. *I was not so aware. Who thought* that *was a good idea? No, wait, don't tell me: a bunch of white, male, Cracker Barrel Republicans . . .*

"But," she said, borrowing it from the but-lady.

"But nothing," the but-lady said, taking Lucy's clipboard away. "You'll need to get the proper form signed and notarized with a copy of at least one parent's state-issued photo ID."

"And where do I get a copy of the 'proper form'?" Lucy asked.

"At one of those *other* places," the but-lady said, her peaches and cream having apparently curdled.

There was a reason her mom couldn't handle conflicts very well. She'd been abandoned herself. Raised in foster care, a part of her life she claimed not to remember. All she could recall were the parents who adopted her and sent her to Catholic school. The only problem with the story: she was twelve when she was adopted. Still, as far as her kids were concerned, she had no past before that: their mother was born at the age of twelve.

Lucy's arriving home now, pregnant and wanting to put the kid up for adoption? Other than being a personal affront to her mother's past, who knew what might happen? For all the time she'd known her, her mom seemed like she was perched on a ledge an overloud voice might startle her off of. What was *this* going to do? Lucy, for one, didn't want to be around to find out.

So what were her options? She could throw herself down the stairs and hope for a miscarriage, she guessed. But if she wound up in the hospital, they'd find out then. She could google the rules on abortion in surrounding states but already suspected she'd need to go all the way up north somewhere before she could get what the Supreme Court said she had a right to—red-meat politics notwithstanding. But then how was she supposed to explain disappearing for the couple of days it'd take to get someplace sane?

RU-486 was an option—not from any place local, of course, but online, sure. She could have FedEx deliver her abortion pills just like the Adderall Max'd scored for finals. But they'd want a credit card or PayPal to pay for the stuff, which came down to the same thing, statement-wise, and her mom had been opening her credit card bills before Lucy could ever since all those credit bureaus started getting hacked. Max's parents were apparently less vigilant or—more likely—afraid they'd find a bunch of gay-related charges, confirming what they weren't asking and Max wasn't telling.

So maybe she could work it through Max. Except . . . Max didn't know about the id-kay, and this was no way to find out, especially since he'd been avoiding her ever since, well, you know. So who else did she know who might be willing to help? Hell, who else did she know to even talk to about all this?

3

There was a reason Marcus didn't go by his first name (Mohammad) or his last name (Haddad) anymore. His reason, and his name change, both happened right around the same time as the whatever-it-was. He hadn't changed them in an attempt to pass in a part of the world where Muslims didn't happen to be the majority; when he changed them, he'd already become a majority of one—could start his own caliphate if he wanted to. He just didn't want to anymore.

It started back when Mohammad Haddad went by Mo, wearing his faith so lightly he could pull a football jersey over it. Despite living in a state full of cowboys and cowboy wannabes, he was popular in school because he was good at something more important than skin color or what direction he chose to pray in. He was a good quarterback—a winning one, which was the best kind.

He was also popular, partly because of the football, partly because he was handsome, but mainly because he listened, and not just so he'd know when his next turn to speak was. Mo mirrored people—a world-class pro tip if you want to be popular. Pay attention to what people say, and reflect them back to themselves. It'll either scare the shit out of them or make them fall in love with you—sometimes both.

One of the reasons Mo was good at reflecting other people was because when he looked inside himself, he didn't see a lot there. It didn't help that he was unclear on what kind of Muslim he was. His parents were mixed in that regard—one Sunni, the other Shia, earning Mohammad the label of Su-Shi—or it would have, if there'd been another Muslim family within criticizing distance of the Haddads. His parents believed this distance from fellow Muslims was good; no one to dredge up their respective sects' deeper divisions. Instead, they teased one another about the proper number of times to pray a day, whether to use the word *amen* after *namaste*, whether their heads touched the floor or a wooden plank while praying with their arms folded or not. What neither parent fully appreciated, however, was that by raising him as a hyphenate, they'd left Mohammad feeling like nothing so much as what the label Su-Shi implied: a fish out of water.

They'd purposely left him in the dark about which was which, focusing instead on the five (or six) pillars that all Muslims had in common: the belief that only God is God, that Mohammad was his last messenger, and that daily prayers were required, as was fasting during Ramadan, giving alms to the poor, and making the hajj to Mecca before they died. The theory was Mo could choose for himself when he was ready without being biased by loyalty to one or the other parent. In practice, though, his parents' sectarian détente left Mo feeling like nothing, like neither Su nor Shi, and even more out of water than he already was.

Which might explain his attraction to zero.

Mo had learned in a world history class that the number zero was an Arabic invention. Until then, he'd just assumed that all numbers had always existed. Yes, he knew they got written differently sometimes—Roman versus the kind they used nowadays, which were, yes, Arabic. And come to think of it, his entire knowledge of the Roman numbering system started with I, for one. So he decided to google it, prepared to be ethnically fascinated into a career in mathematics—teaching, maybe, or accounting. After all, people were starting to ask him what he wanted to be when he grew up. His joke answer—taller—had played well in the beginning, but more recently was being countered with "No, seriously . . ."

So Mo typed, "Did Arabs invent the zero?" into the search bar. And that got it started. Through some perverse combination of cookies, personal information, data farming, Russian attempts to hack Western civilization down to size, and targeted advertising algorithms—all those you-might-also-likes—Mo, a.k.a. Mohammad Haddad, was routed to exactly the wrong websites for someone named Mohammad Haddad. Sure, he didn't have to take the clickbait presented to him—clickbait tailor-made to trigger the index finger of a male Su-Shi first-generation Arabic American between the ages of fifteen and twenty within the 405 area code whose interests included football, porn, the history of Arabic numerals, and careers in mathematics—but what good's clickbait if it can't hook a fish already out of water?

And so, like Alice, Mo tumbled down the rabbit hole, clicking and also liking, chatting with bots, and watching video recs until he found himself snapping with someone somewhere who started out their chat—quaintly and ever-so-politely—using the first-person plural pronoun to make the addressee feel like he was already part of a group:

"May we call you Mo?"

They started by making Mo think the world he lived in was in a state of upheaval, not just spiritually, but physically—geologically, even. This wasn't too hard, especially for a boy living in Oklahoma, in the epicenter of the state's petroleum extraction industry.

"The only thing okay about where you live is the state abbreviation," they typed.

"What's so wrong with it?" Mo typed back.

"Man-made earthquakes. Tap water catching fire."

"The state says those are natural."

"A natural result of injecting billions of gallons of wastewater into basement rock—yes. Earthquakes are 'natural' when you do that."

"There's no scientific proof," Mo tried.

"Do you know how many earthquakes there were in your state before they started disposing of wastewater in injection wells?"

"How many?"

"One to two per year. Now? Over a thousand in Stillwater this year alone."

Mohammad didn't type a response. He didn't have one. He'd been woken up by a lot of those quakes. And thus the first hook was set.

"After the Cuyahoga River caught fire in 1969, your President Nixon started the EPA," the other side continued. "Now, when tap water catches fire, they tell you to buy the bottled kind."

Mo looked at his own bottle of Ice Mountain, sweating next to him.

"Bottles made out of plastic. Plastic made out of—do we need to go on?"

"No," Mo typed.

"Have you ever seen that ad where everything made out of plastic disappears? You can find it on YouTube. You know what that's about?"

"Advertising?" Mo guessed.

"No," the other side typed. "Blackmail."

Mohammad's eyes widened; it was like they were sitting across from him at the Haddad dinner table. He'd heard his own father make similar threats about what the petroleum industry could do to teach those eco brats with their iPods a lesson. "Don't like oil? Okay, no more oil!" Mohammad Senior had worked as a control-valve technician for Saudi Aramco before coming to the States to work on something the rumor mill predicted was going to be big—just as soon as the "right people" were in charge. All it was going to take was a little change in energy policy to outlaw suing over silly things like poisoned groundwater or man-made earthquakes.

By the time Mo was little, the "right people" were apparently in charge. There was also a Bush/Cheney magnet on their refrigerator, used to hold up a drawing of a Thanksgiving turkey the size of Mohammad's first-grade hand.

"The founders of our feast," his dad said whenever he went to the fridge, tapping a knuckle on the magnet. There was also a picture of W holding hands with a sheikh, like they were going to prom together even though the 9/11 hijackers who forced his dad to stop wearing his skullcap to work had been Saudis, mostly.

The yellowed turkey, the magnet, and the photo were all still on the family's refrigerator when Mo struck up his online conversation with the handlers hoping to convert him. He'd asked his new snap buddies about these connections between his family's way of life and what it all meant. But the people on the other end were observing radio silence, perhaps letting him think about what he'd learned, letting him go online to find out more.

Then one Saturday while Mo was sleeping in, an earthquake tossed him out of bed and cracked the foundation of their house. Later that afternoon, he saw uniformed men in his backyard. He thought maybe his dad had already called somebody about the foundation.

Nope.

They hadn't knocked. They hadn't left a doorknob sign. They were just there, with a surveyor's tripod, a measuring tape, a bunch of little flags on plastic poles they planted around Mo's childhood swing set based upon a series of mysterious hand signals from the guy squinting next to the tripod.

Mohammad broke open his father's shotgun to make sure it was loaded before snapping it shut and stepping out the door, prepared to fire one warning shot to get them off his family's property.

"Put that away, son," one of the uniforms said. "You don't want that kind of trouble."

"Get off my land," Mo shouted.

"It's not really your land," the man who called him son said before doing it again. "Not what's underneath this lawn, at least."

"Do you have a warrant?" Mo asked, not knowing what else to say.

"We're not cops," the talking uniform said. "Here. Try this." He handed him a pamphlet from the American Petroleum Institute. There was a derrick in silhouette, over which ran the title, "Know Your Mineral Rights." The *n* and *o* in *Know* were a different color from the rest—red instead of blue—and the word *rights* was surrounded by one of those slashed circles, also red.

According to the pamphlet, the uniforms were in the right and Mo wasn't. Turned out they didn't need to ask permission to come onto someone's property and start drilling. They used to, but the state legislature took care of that.

"That swing set's gonna need to come down," the talking uniform said. "We can do it, but then there's gonna be a charge."

There used to be a joke during one of the Bushes' Gulf Wars: "How'd all our oil get under all that sand?" Two days later, when the people on the other end of the internet broke their silence to tell Mo that "joke," their timing couldn't have been better. When their snap snapped, he was ready to agree with them about whatever they had to say about how not-okay Oklahoma was. But after taking his temperature about the nefarious ways of the fossil fuels cabal, it turned out they had a different topic in mind: Mo. Just like the state he was living in, Mohammad himself was pretty messed up. They introduced their new topic this way: "Congratulations on being beloved by infidels." It was like they'd reached through his phone and slapped him.

"What do you mean?" he thumb typed, the beeping of construction equipment cutting through his bedroom window, the rumbling of its digging shaking the whole house—assuming it was the machines, that is, and not another earthquake.

"You're popular. A popular boy. You play with the skin of swine, and other swine cheer you on."

"You mean football?"

"We mean a game. You play games that mean nothing and are beloved for it."

"My dad thinks I can get a scholarship."

"Because it costs money in America not to be stupid. That freedom they speak of—it means you're free to be dumb; everything else costs money. Jesus saves; Moses invests. In America, even prophets must profit. But what about the Prophet, little Mohammad who plays football?"

This time, the discussion—a lecture, really—was cutting much closer to the bone. His parents were devout, he just wasn't clear on which flavor was which. Mo himself was first-generation, Su-Shi devout, meaning he was embarrassed when his mother went out in public wearing her burka. Even so-called friends teased him about his mom being "one of those beekeepers." But when he pleaded with her to "act more American," she compromised precisely once, going outside to tend her garden in a burka and cowboy hat. The neighbors who saw her were deeply offended, and she was offended by their taking offense.

"That's how compromise works," she explained. "Both sides are angry."

Other than having to apologize for his parents, it was true about Mo's being popular. He was, especially among the other students, "the Americans," as his father put it, distinguishing them from "*our* American,*" as both parents referred to their son. They didn't say it sneeringly, but rather as a point of pride—as immigrant parents have from back when the Statue of Liberty still welcomed them.

What made Mo popular was the opposite of what made Dev a weirdo: empathy. Mohammad had too much. If the recording computer in the sky ran an analysis on the words Mo used most often, the phrase "I know what you mean" would come out right on top. And he meant them, every time he used those words, proving it often with an anecdote from his past that showed he'd heard, he'd understood, had been there too.

There are, of course, some people one shouldn't empathize with if one can help it. Unfortunately, Mo couldn't. Once his head started nodding, it became like one of those toy dogs with the bobbing head: it would keep going until somebody stopped it. And it was even worse when the people demanding your empathy beat you to the punch.

"You feel like a fraud, yes?" they typed.

"Yes," Mo typed back.

"We can help you with that."

It's not hard making someone living with their parents feel pampered. And it's not hard turning someone who feels pampered hard, especially when you pose it as a challenge they're too soft to face. And once the hardening starts, it can become diamond-like, common coal squeezed to a matrix of molecular perfection. Mo's football coaches knew this and used it to make him worthy of scholarships. And his other coaches used it, too, though the muscle that needed work was spiritual. And so Mohammad read the Koran for the first time, absorbing the words of the Prophet—the one not spelled with an *F*. His internet coaches helped decode what Allah through his last Prophet meant by this and that, correcting any misunderstandings, especially with regard to the issues of killing others and martyrdom. Allah, it seemed, could be tricky sometimes—almost sarcastic—meaning the opposite of what his words seemed to say on the page.

Mo's parents noticed the change and secretly approved, though they had no idea what they were approving. That he was showing a greater interest in the practice of Islam seemed like a good thing; the same went for attending mosque and eliminating Western temptations, one after the other. He even surpassed his father, who wore a shirt and tie to work, once Mohammad adopted more traditional Islamic dress at the cost of several so-called friends.

Stung by a case of spiritual one-upsmanship with his own son, Mo Senior quipped to his wife that "We're never as ideologically pure as when someone else is paying the bill."

To which his wife responded, "When a prayer is answered, don't ask to see its teeth."

Unfortunately, Mo's parents really should have asked to see the teeth, getting set to bite the hand that fed them. Not that he'd already decided to become a suicide bomber; he just hadn't ruled it out. And while he wasn't ruling it out, he assembled what he needed, should the calling come. Parts like PVC pipe and endcaps from Home Depot, a hunting vest and shotgun shells from the Walmart sporting-goods section. Plans for a dead-man's switch and pipe bomb off the interwebs. The prayers to say for guidance. The prayers to say just before.

Meanwhile, his invisible coaches started adding PowerPoint slides to the pitch: waist-high shots of fat-gutted SUV drivers standing next to gas pumps; dead Iraqi children lying in rubble, their faces clowned in dust and their own blood; open-carry ammosexuals parading with their guns in Walmart; more dead kids that could have been Mohammad; Bush playing golf; Cheney telling Congress to f-off; more dead kids; gas pumps; Donald Trump showing his signature on one or another Muslim ban; dead kids; and finally, the last slide, ISIS members clad in black, looking like ninjas, no voice-over, saying, "We're the Islamic State and we approve of this message." But it really didn't need it, now, did it?

Still deciding, Mohammad asked, "Why a high school in the middle of nowhere?"

"So they know," his coaches typed, "that there's nowhere to hide."

"Are your parents' papers in order?" they asked.

"What papers?"

"The ones that prove they're legal, little Mohammad." And before he could reply, they snapped in again. "Oh, but what does it matter? Their skin—your skin—is all the proof they'll need."

"They who?" Mo typed, though he already knew. He just didn't want to believe it.

"The ones making your country great again."

"They're saying we should give him a chance."

"For what, little Mohammad? To preheat the ovens?"

Mo didn't respond right away. He was too busy throwing up—as he explained once he was able to type again. "That shows it's working," their words came back, followed by the barfing emoji.

At school, they were experiencing an "uptick" in swastikas and chants of "build the wall." And Mo was spending more and more time in the bathroom, to lose breakfast, then lunch. Even the sip of water he'd had to wash the bad taste out of his mouth came back up. He thought about changing his clothes back, to make him less of a target. The thought stopped him from doing it, made him feel ashamed for the shallowness of his commitment. And that—that shame—that showed it was working too.

PART TWO

4

As it turned out, Dev wasn't smarter than anybody—Leo least of all. Becoming friends had been a strategic mistake. The only smart thing he'd done was not telling Leo about the bunker he'd found sophomore year. Deep down inside, he must have known that he'd need someplace at school where he could be completely alone—including and especially from Leo.

And he'd found it, behind an unmarked door that led to the basement and another set of stairs leading even farther down. At the bottom, he found stacks of textbooks still in their boxes and good as new—except for being printed in an America with only forty-eight states. Behind the farthest pile, Dev noticed something attached to the wall, wiped it with his sleeve, and found a tin sign with a circle in the center containing three inverted yellow triangles—one on top, two at the base—and the words "Fallout Shelter" in black. Next to it was a door, and behind that: paradise for an Aspie needing a little me (and *only me*) time.

Everything was there, still waiting for the bombs to fall. The cases of canned food were covered in dust, shredded cardboard, and mouse pellets, some cans rusted, others bulging. The cases of canned water had suffered a similar fate, minus the bulging, plus warped cardboard, the cans oranged by the rust of what they'd lost. Some aluminum-and-vinyl folding chairs were still waiting for their 1950s vacation from irradiation while the Geiger counter probably hadn't worked since Sputnik. Other than that, there were bed rolls and simple plank beds that folded out from the wall like shelves for storing bodies, a hand-cranked ventilation system (jammed), iodine tablets fused into a fist, and one hermetically sealed door that gasped when Dev shut it, leaving the rest of the world on the other side.

Despite the wonky ventilation, this was where Dev came to breathe, free from people and their distracting emotions. While his contemporaries were busy breaking hearts and/or impregnating one another, Dev drank Gatorade, chewed on 7-Eleven jerky, and imagined a postpeople world where he and his fellow Aspies survived to become the next step in human evolution—one where the species would be free from the irrationality that called down the cleansing fire in the first place.

But then, a week before It happened, a smaller it happened, and Dev discovered that—just like his Aspergerian hero, Mr. Spock—he had an all-too-human side, after all. Which is why, on the day of the bigger It, Dev was in his bunker, eyeing a noose he'd tied in between glances at his phone. He'd downloaded the video a week earlier and had been replaying it ever since, a singular YouTube upload he was determined to study until he got it or it got him.

Content-wise, it wasn't much, but then again, neither are most last straws. Just a vid of a kid with his head down, walking toward the kid recording him, as the latter makes comments about the way the first kid walks. It wasn't so much walking, really, as tripping in slow motion before catching himself and loping on, his head jutting forward like the prow of a ship on rough seas.

"It's McGruff the Crime Dog, ladies and gentlemen," the videographer says before advising his audience to "Google it."

Dev recognized the voice of his best friend, confirmed when Leo turned the phone around so he could talk to its camera, the kid still loping just over his shoulder. And it *was* pretty funny, the way the kid walked. For a fleeting moment, Dev thought maybe this was how Leo and he could be a team again, by making fun of some loser who wasn't them. But then the kid passed the camera, which started shooting from behind.

"She-Ra," Leo boomed. "Princess of power." Pause. "Google it."

Which was exactly how Dev found the video in the first place—by googling She-Ra in an attempt to figure out what made a stupid used backpack worthy of ridicule. After watching it the first twenty times in his bedroom, he asked his mother if she thought he walked funny.

"You have a *determined* walk," she said, "like Sherlock Holmes when the case is afoot." She paused, warming to the subject before informing him that "they" thought Sherlock might be modeled after someone with Asperger's, and wasn't that interesting?

In other words: "Yes, Dev, you walk funny."

On the day It happened, his mother drove him to school, as usual. And Dev lay facedown on the back seat, as usual. The infamous backpack had been left in his locker because Dev wasn't planning on going to class. He'd hide out in the bunker all day like he had the day before and the day before that.

It had been a week since he'd discovered the YouTube video of Leo's betrayal. It had been a week of feeling like what he'd hoped to never feel: stupid. Not being stupid was his compensation for having Asperger's. But then along comes stupid yo-saying Leo to take away even that. Because what do you call someone who's fooled by an idiot?

Right.

And then Dev heard the tires squeal, felt his body ricochet off the backrest and onto the floorboard, heard his mother cursing, followed by: "It's a stop sign, idiot. That means you stop . . ."

Stop, Dev thought, still lying where he'd landed, on his back and looking up.

Wouldn't that be a relief, he thought, watching the reflections and shadows of their tree-lined street play across the car's ceiling as his mother drove on.

Of course, Aspies are too logical to commit suicide, right? The act, at its core, is all about emotions. And just because he couldn't stop thinking about making everything stop, that didn't . . .

Dev stopped. Heard Leo's voice saying, "Google it."

So Dev did. Turns out that not only did Aspies commit suicide, it was the second-leading cause of death after accidents among high-functioning adolescents on the autism spectrum. Suicide among Aspies was as much about emotion as ulcers were about stress. They'd learned long ago that the cause of ulcers was viral, and suicide among his cohort was largely due to glitches in their neural anatomy and chemistry. Take the amygdala, for example—the fight/flight/freeze part of the brain. In Aspies, it was ten to fifteen percent larger than in neurotypicals. That meant that a stressor of one for everyone else was a ten for someone like Dev, leading to what clinicians referred to as "depression attacks," in which the experiencer goes from feeling fine to suicidal in a matter of seconds. It also contributed to a tendency known as "catastrophizing," in which every conceivable scenario suddenly morphs into the worst possible outcome—a tendency that went a long way toward explaining his own fascination with doomsday scenarios a few *topiques* ago . . .

All of which meant Dev didn't *just* have a diagnosis; he had an excuse too. Which made it okay to do what his brain kept telling him to do. It wasn't even a decision; it was a symptom. And a pretty foolproof way to stop feeling like crap all the time.

Well, almost. It wasn't until he decided on the ultimate painkiller that Dev realized how unprepared he really was. That's when he started noticing things about the bomb shelter he hadn't before, despite having mapped it.

For starters, the whole room was capsule shaped, having been repurposed from an underground storage tank of the type used at gas stations but with what looked like a surplus submarine hatch for a door. The walls curved smoothly up and over on all sides to the ceiling, leaving no need for rafters because the structure's strength came from its shape. There were also no water pipes, or gas pipes either—or, for that matter, enough headroom for someone Dev's height to hang himself.

But what if he tucked in his knees? Dev looked at the length of his leg below his knee and compared it with the ceiling overhead. Nope. The extra drop space still wouldn't be enough to break his neck—and strangling to death was a nonstarter, especially since his autonomic nervous system would probably veto him the second he blacked out. He'd have better luck trying to hold his breath until he died. Just testing, he grabbed the free end of the noose and pulled with both hands.

Nope.

So Dev dropped the untied end and watched it swing back and forth two-point-five times before coming to rest. It looked like the world's worst necktie. He thought about emerging from the basement with the noose still dangling, inviting all the abuse that didn't need to be asked for twice: a victim embracing his victimization.

He'd begun reaching for the hatch when an idea stopped him. Perhaps if he closed the door on the free end and just *fell* horizontally. It'd be like walking, but more conclusive. And so he measured the hypotenuse from the hatch to the floor, darkly amused that his geometry teachers were right: it really had come in handy in the end. All he had to do was subtract a foot or so from the overall length so he'd stop short of hitting the floor, hopefully with a good, sharp snap. He tied a knot at the sweet spot, ensuring the cord wouldn't just slip through the door's rubber gasket when he fell.

But once Dev opened the hatch to insert the rope, he stopped cold. It was too quiet. He checked the time on his phone. The bell should have rung; everybody should be in the hall between classes.

There should be lockers banging, feet drumming, an assortment of stupid teenage noises. Instead: *nothing*. Just nonhuman noises: the boiler; the wind outside the basement windows; dogs from the surrounding neighborhood, howling like it was the end of the world . . .

Emerging from the fallout shelter, Dev followed the silence like he was following a prowler trying not to be heard. That was the quality of the silence that hit him—the silence of a breath held. Or really, a thousand breaths, all being held at once. It was the sound of a sudden, heavy absence, and Dev needed to know where it was coming from—or *not* coming from.

This sudden need to know was like how he felt about his *topiques*. And maybe that made sense, because stepping out of the fallout shelter was like stepping into a vacuum—not the floor-cleaning but outer-space kind. The kind that creates suction through absence, pulling everything inside out, just as the silence pulled Dev back up the stairways from the fallout shelter to the basement and from the basement to the first floor, just through that unmarked door . . .

But when he tried to open it, the door stuck. There was something blocking it. So he pushed harder. And harder. And harder still until he heard something crack like a broomstick wrapped in a towel. He looked through the wedge of half-opened door and saw an arm lying on the floor, its hand twisted the wrong way, the fingers pointing painfully backward, its owner not making a peep to disturb the sucking silence.

Dev worked a shoe through the opening and kicked the arm out of the way, then pushed again until he hit another body part. He'd gotten leverage by that point, and so he kept on pushing as into the silence came the sound of a belt buckle, muffled underneath a body, scraping as it slid across linoleum, clicking when it crossed the seam between tiles: sssshhhh, click, sssshhhh, click, sssshhhh, click. It stopped when Dev stopped, started up again when he did, until the door was open wide enough to step through.

And so he did.

5

She decided to tell Max. He might be avoiding her—had the sex really been that bad?—but she needed to talk to him. She needed to talk to somebody, and being sans friends as she was, that made Max it, like it or not. Plus, she missed him. They weren't just BFFs; they were BAOFs—best and only friends, with an option now, apparently, on the forever part. And it wasn't like she was going to ask him to marry her or help raise it or anything. His contribution would be as short-lived as the part that had gotten them into this mess. Just let her use his credit card and she'd take care of the rest.

So she called him. Voice mail, no answer. Texted him. No answer. Snapchat. Facebook Messenger. Email, for Pete's sake.

No answer.

Okay, IRL. She'd go to his house. In real life. Knock on his real door and confront him with their real problem.

The boxes of his stuff packed up on the curb for Goodwill were not a good sign. Sure, she hadn't seen him in weeks, but she just assumed he'd been avoiding her out of embarrassment. Maybe he'd used her as much as she'd used him, only he wasn't doing it to lose his virginity so much as to confirm his gayness—maybe. They were both sixteen—the time biologically and socially ordained to be confused, or so she'd heard. So maybe their thing at the Sheraton cleared up any confusion—or maybe confused him more.

Whatever.

But those boxes . . .

Had he finally done it? Had he clap-hands-gunshot split for more LGBT-friendly climes somewhere beyond the rainbow or (you know) the Mason-Dumbass Line? He'd always told her she was the only reason he hadn't already . . .

So she knocked. They had no idea who she was, but his life had always been a mystery to them anyway. "Had?" Lucy squeaked.

"Oh, child," they said, making Lucy wish she still were one, instead of one *with* one.

"Oh, child," they repeated, the monsters she'd heard about but never met, touching her, sans claws, as her shoulders shook.

Well, that got serious real quick. And not like a heart attack, but worse, like a heart impossibly broken. He'd been her best friend and she missed it. She was carrying his child, and had tried to kill it while he was off killing himself for reasons she'd never know but could maddeningly guess—invent—until her own time came. Why? Why not?

Shit.

She was trapped. She was trapped worse than when she thought she was trapped and that Max held the key to getting out. No Max; no key; no way out. She still couldn't tell her parents, but now, even if McDonald's started doing drive-through abortions, she couldn't get one, not with the last unburned-up piece of Max's DNA multiplying inside her. Doing what she needed to do would be like killing Max all over again and . . .

. . . and then the panic attacks started, and everything seemed to be a trigger. Ads in magazines and on TV for Pampers, baby food, the maxi pads she didn't need at the moment, even passing an artfully stacked display for Pepsi Max at the grocery store—they all caused her cortisol levels to skyrocket while her sense of self just kept falling. The attacks turned her heart—her *breathing*—into a ratchet pushing her, inch by inch, breath by breath, heartbeat by heartbeat, through layers of earth, not even giving her the courtesy of digging it, just pushing her down into the dirt of her own grave. And there was no fighting her way back up; that's not how a ratchet works. Once the direction has been set, that's where it goes, the other way blocked, and blocked again, down, and down, and farther down . . .

She'd eat a bullet, she decided—fight the triggers with an actual trigger. An unusual choice for a girl, she knew, but this wasn't going to be some girly suicide attempt. If gay Max had the balls to do it, so did Lucy. She just wanted to die, instead of feeling like she was dying all the time.

She didn't have a gun but got one easily enough. After all, what's the point of living down south if you can't get a gun out of a vending machine, practically? She'd do it in the girls' bathroom at school, which was still in session in June thanks to a series of not-at-all-climate-change-related snow days earlier in the year. But that was okay. School was the better choice of venue. Spare her family, let the taxpayers pay for cleanup. And let all the jerks who'd ever called her weirdo wonder the rest of their useless lives whether they'd been the last straw. Consider it a twofer—no more panic attacks, plus revenge.

The gun was in her locker, and she was headed toward it—dead girl walking—her books for her next class pressed against her stomach, as if a separate side of her was trying to protect itself while she plotted against the two of them. She was looking down when it happened: the soft thunder of bodies falling all around.

Everywhere she looked, people just *stopped being alive*. For a second, she thought—*hoped*—it might be some sort of flash mob, except it was too disorganized for that, not to mention painful-looking. Heads gonging into lockers; legs buckling before kneecaps slammed into the tiled floor, making this horrible double-pop noise. A fellow student, now dead, fell right into her, knocking the books from her hands before she stepped aside so he and his face could fall the rest of the way to the floor. The sound of his nose and cheekbones breaking, muffled by the surrounding head, made Lucy's pregnant stomach flip upside down. Before she could stop herself, she coughed out a blast of vomit that hit the back of her dead classmate's head.

"I'm so sorry," she spluttered, but then stopped as a pool of red spread outward from her classmate's head, mixed with the vomit, and then began crawling ever closer toward her shoes.

She couldn't tell by looking at the ones who'd landed faceup whether there was any recognition of what was happening. She couldn't tell if there had been any pain. They just stopped in the middle of a breath, a word, a heartbeat, a gesture. A foot that went up through an act of will came down again thanks only to gravity, the ankle buckling before bringing down the rest.

The suddenness of it was like hearing about Max's suicide standing outside his front door; he was there and then he wasn't and there was nothing she could do about it. And somehow she hadn't made the leap from that to what she'd been planning to do to her own family. She thought she'd be sparing them shame and herself pain; instead, she'd bequeath them this yawning ache. This, now, all of this felt like a punishment for what she'd been planning—a punishment she'd been spared specifically to feel its ripples . . .

Her body flooded with chemicals, and Lucy thought she was going to have another attack, but instead of feeling like she was dying, she just felt numb. *She's in shock,* a remote part of her thought. Her eyes were somehow behind her, pitched just slightly, like she was watching a movie over the back of her own head. She wanted to reach out, touch her shoulder, ask if she'd mind scrunching down, but was afraid if she did, she'd feel her own fingers tapping from behind.

Shock. Definitely shock . . .

Which was a good thing. Being self-anesthetized was the only thing allowing her to move from the spot she was in, stepping between the bodies until she reached the exit and left. Outside, there were more bodies and leashed animals minus their owners, running about. She could smell smoke from crashed cars burning nearby and was knocked to the ground by the concussion of a jet in free fall hitting the ground several miles short of Hartsfield-Jackson Airport. Still in shock, Lucy got back up and continued walking. Where she was going, she had no idea. But the fact that she could still walk suggested she should. And so she did.

She didn't realize she'd miscarried for the longest time, not until she noticed her robot legs getting itchy and saw the blood now dried down either thigh. The cell clump she'd been so worried about had died right along with everyone else. Which was sad, but Lucy was too busy to mourn. She had walking to do—that, and staying what she was for now: not dead.

6

Though he'd renounced many Western temptations, there was one Mo couldn't shake: Twinkies. His mother had barred them at home, believing they were haram. She'd heard the creamy filling was confectioners' sugar whipped with some kind of animal fat, undisclosed as an industry secret, so of course she suspected pork. Mo figured he could google the answer but didn't; on the subject of Twinkies, ignorance was bliss.

He'd discovered the devil's yellow cake in grade school during lunch. Everyone's mother but his had packed their little Americans off to school with these cellophane-wrapped loaves of gold. All Mo ever got was an apple he'd snap into with an envious eye turned toward all those face holes stuffed with sun-colored cake.

Finally, one day, his future best friend took mercy on him and offered a lopsided trade: an apple for one of the two Twinkies the other's mother had packed. "Deal," Mo said, having to remind himself to remove the plastic before inhaling all that cakey goodness. The other kid became his dealer after that, accepting milk money instead of an apple, which he'd accepted only so that first taste didn't come off as charity. It hadn't been, of course; bait was more like it.

As Mo grew older and learned to ride a bike, he found himself riding by the local 7-Eleven, where, it seemed, he could buy a two-pack of Twinkies for what he'd been paying for one. He got into a fight with his best friend the dealer over it, but unlike fights between girls, theirs didn't last. They went back to being friends once the other kid turned over a stack of comic books to Mo in reimbursement for the overpayment.

Afterward, Mo prided himself on not being anyone's fool—ignoring the common wisdom about what happens to pride just before a fall.

Though Mo had his driver's permit by the time he was being recruited for martyrdom, what he didn't have was a car. That was okay; school was a bike-able distance away, and there was a 7-Eleven between there and home. He'd long been in the habit of stopping to feed his Twinkie addiction before pedaling the rest of the way—to home, to school. At this particular 7-Eleven, the bike rack was right next to the large picture windows out front, the ones advertising new Slurpee flavors, Big Gulps, or specials on those scary hotdogs rolling in their own grease in the glass case next to the register. Mo was pretty sure the roller dogs were not halal, but if they were, he wouldn't have touched them, not even with those glove boxes used for handling plutonium.

On the day he decided, he'd stopped for a Twinkie fix and had just clicked his bike lock when all the bikes tipped to the left. *Earthquake,* he thought—punctuating it with a period, not some amateur's exclamation point. Just, *earthquake,* as in, *oh yeah,* as his legs struck the stance they usually did in these situations—a kind of bowlegged half crouch with his free arms horizontal to the ground, to provide extra stability as he rode the rocking earth. He looked like a cowboy at high noon or maybe a sailor on shore leave trying to get his land legs back.

It was a "good-un," as the Okies would say—a respectable 5.1 magnitude that lasted about twenty-five seconds, during which the window Mo was standing closest to split from top to bottom. In the slow-motion way these things usually go, he could see the crack spread, hear the splintery squeak of it until it hit the bottom of the frame, and the single pane became two, separating at the crack, one half tipping into the store, the other tumbling out.

Seeing what was going to happen and not having time to get away, Mo squatted further into his earthquake-surfer's stance, raising his arms to shield his head just before the large pane shattered over his crouching body. Shards flew everywhere, including one long sliver that found its way into the hand of a kid who'd just stepped out with a lemon-lime Slurpee, now a plop of yellow-green slush, blood drops from the wound making brown polka dots in the colored ice. Mo blinked as the kid screamed bloody murder but with the sound turned down. All he could hear was the crash, stuck in a loop, playing over and over.

The world returned only after the cashier's hand—red specked, lacerated—touched his shoulder. That's when Mo could hear things again: the screaming kid, mainly, but also the cashier's softer, "Are you okay?"

Mo had no idea what he was, other than still crouching, still waiting for the crash, now a minute or two in the past. He tried standing and found he could. He checked his hands, arms: nothing, just the cashier's bloody handprint on the shoulder of his tunic. He touched his face, looked at his fingers: nothing. The top of his head, still stinging from the crown where the pane made first contact: nothing. Nothing leaking through his skullcap or underneath it either.

When the cashier realized that Mo, a regular, was okay, he darted back inside and out again with a pack of Twinkies. "Here," he said, pushing them into Mo's unstained hands with his own bloodied ones, "on the house."

At home, in his bedroom, he sat at his desk, his phone plugged into its charger. The uneaten Twinkies sat next to him. The blood on the cellophane was sticky but still red. The light from a desk lamp passed through it, drawing spots of orange against the unnaturally yellow cake. Orange, like the perma-tan of the Muslim-hating president, the one who *hadn't* dropped any bombs on the Middle East—yet. Still looking at the Twinkies, Mo was remembering what he'd read about how Bush the younger used widely discredited claims that Iraq was seeking "yellowcake" uranium as a front for bombing a bunch of innocent civilians, when his phone issued two quick tones, letting him know they were reaching out through Snapchat again.

"So?" it read.

It felt like they'd been reading his mind. "O," Mohammad typed, slowly, deliberately, his index finger stabbing the virtual keyboard, "K."

Mo had filled PVC pipes with black powder, fashioned triggers from instructions online, wired batteries, and made a dead-man's switch from a clothespin and a strip of copper. He fitted the device into a vest designed to carry it underneath his clothes and tried it on to feel the weight of it. It was heavier than his football gear; it pulled down on him harder.

The time, place, and date had been set. All that remained was writing his martyr's statement. This, even more than blowing himself up, was the part he'd been dreading. Part will, part obituary, part apology to those left behind, his martyr's statement was to be a declaration of faith, a condemnation of its opponents, and his last words for all time. As such, they weighed much more than ordinary words, and Mo hadn't been a fan of writing essays before, when the stakes were much lower. Very soon, he'd talked himself into a writer's block he could have built a nuclear bunker out of. Twice he had to postpone what his coaches referred to euphemistically as "the event." The grounds: "personal reasons."

"Your personal reasons sound like feet that are insufficiently warm," they told him, their hang of idiomatic English a little weak in spots.

"Do you mean cold feet?" Mo typed back.

"Yes."

So Mohammad confessed the problem he was having, composing his martyr's statement. Their reply came moments later in the form of two Microsoft Word documents, one .doc and the other .docx, "In case you haven't upgraded."

They had boilerplate, it seemed.

After filling in the blanks, printing it out, and sealing it in an envelope to be left behind just before, Mohammed prepared for his last night on earth. He'd read that several of the 9/11 martyrs had spent the evening of September 10 at strip clubs, which sounded great—except that pedaling up to valet parking would probably be a dead giveaway that he was underage. Unlike many of his contemporaries, he'd been too busy being devout to get a fake ID. He could always steal a car, he guessed. Or borrow his parents'—if they'd let him—but they were kind of sticklers about obeying the laws of their adopted country, and Mo had only his learner's permit.

And so he decided to bike around his neighborhood instead, mentally saying goodbye to—well, *everything*. He picked his favorite time of day, just as the sun was setting, painting the sky to the west miraculous colors: pinkish purples sliced through with clouds, up-lit yellow and dark on top. Faced from the other directions, the world turned golden, shimmering leaves lit with lemony light, their branches outlined in it, shadows stretching to their breaking point.

As dusk became twilight became night, the windows of the neighborhood clicked on, yellowed through draperies, silhouettes of domesticity passing over them, while others, un-blinded, let the world peek in as they watched their big-screen TVs, some tuned so loud he could hear the cheering of crowds for one sporting event or another as he rode by. Or maybe he was just remembering the cheers—from his own days on the other end of them, those days like all the rest, filed down to this last handful of hours, minutes, seconds . . .

Mo found himself pedaling faster, the rushing air making the skin of his cheeks tighten as the tear tracks dried. With his knees and heart pumping, he could feel his contempt leaking away as something else took its place. Something unproductive: his empathy.

They—his handlers on the other end of the internet—had used his empathy against him, directing it first at the scores of dead children they showed him before weaponizing it. He even empathized with their using him like this—understood that in conflicts as asymmetrical as the one they were in, fighting dirty was their only hope. Mohammad just happened to be the dirty bomb du jour.

Eventually, his pedaling carried him past the houses and their humans to the land of parking lots and strip malls and gas stations on each of the four corners at intersections. He passed a Walgreens and a CVS and a Rite Aid. He heard his handlers' haptic typing:

"So many drugs for such a sick civilization . . ."

And there. He could feel it coming back, and just in time: his contempt.

Mo was wearing the vest at a pep rally the day everything changed. All morning he'd been saying goodbye to things in his head: his locker, his teachers, his supposed infidel friends, his footsteps echoing down the empty hallway as he carried his bathroom pass to the boys' lavatory to throw up.

After rinsing his mouth in the sink, he made his way to the gym, took a seat in the bleachers. It was early June, and the school year was finally ending after being extended to accommodate a series of wholly non-fracking-related building repairs. There were no more games, away or at home, but they were still having a pep rally—perhaps as a pep booster shot to carry them through the long, pepless summer. Mo tried cheering along but mainly just watched, trying to imagine the bodies after the blast, trying to imagine paradise. It was easier with his eyes closed, and so he shut them tight, as all around him his fellow students stomped and clapped the intro to Queen's "We Will Rock

You." Mohammad, meanwhile, prayed silently, asking for guidance on whether he should say "God is great" or "Allahu Akbar" before doing what he'd come to do.

Suddenly, everybody—the whole gym-full of people—skipped a beat, followed by a stomp so thunderous it was a miracle the bleachers didn't collapse. Mo's eyes snapped open, and there they were: all the bodies he'd imagined and more, well beyond even the most optimistic blast range. But these weren't torn apart and bleeding. These bodies were just suddenly, cleanly dead.

He elbowed the body to his right that had slouched into him, and the rest of the bodies on that side followed suit, dominoing until they reached the bleacher's end, followed by the sickening thud of a body hitting the gym floor. He nudged the corpse to his left, and it was the same thing: tilt, tilt, tilt, tilt, thud. And there was Mo, the only one in his row, sitting upright—an exclamation point with back slashes and forward slashes on either side of him. But why?

7

Before, Dev liked sneaking out to ride his bike around the neighborhood while the rest of the world was asleep and the place was his. He liked how quiet the streets were, the only sounds coming from him and nature: the wind, the insects, the circle-sounding sound of his bicycle tires turning on pavement, a sizzle if it had rained, a whisper if it hadn't, punctuated regularly by the seams in the pavement, bonkity-bonk, bonkity-bonk, bonkity-bonk . . .

So the feeling he experienced crossing that threshold from the school's basement wasn't necessarily new. It was just like the world at 3:00 a.m., but with dead bodies everywhere he looked. Cheerleader bodies, jock bodies, bullies, burnouts, dweebs, teachers, one traitor he thought was a friend . . . people in style and out, people who gave a crap and didn't, lying tumbled down in the hallway, facing up, sideways, down, as randomly arranged as if a bulldozer had dumped a bucketful of mannequins.

For the most part, the bodies seemed peaceful, as if suddenly overcome by an irresistible need to sleep. Seemed, but what did Dev know? He'd never been that good with people's faces, and their being dead didn't change that. All it did was stop them from changing so fast, as if he'd finally gotten that pause button his hand kept imagining. That they were dead and not just faking was apparent only from the unnatural poses some of them struck—a head at a ninety-degree angle from its neck or crashed through the window in a just-opened door.

To be sure, Dev pried an iPhone from the closest limp hand and checked to see if the screen fogged when he placed it under a random selection of noses. It didn't. He checked foreheads, necks, wrists, but it was the same story each time: nothing. Nothing to the power of nothing . . .

Tiptoeing between them and over them and around them, Dev made his way down the hall, his handkerchief out and pressed to his face, in case whatever killed everybody was still in the air. It was only after he saw a blind kid's dog nuzzling its late master, trying to wake him up, that Dev decided the whatever-it-was probably wasn't airborne.

Seeing the dog also reminded him of what Principal Butler said when his mom and stepdad asked about getting him a comfort animal to help with the stress of high school: "Why don't you just get him a teddy bear?"

Dev whistled for the dog and clapped his knees. "Here, boy," he said. And the dog, as spooked as any living thing would be around so much sudden death, ran, tongue flagging, toward the human voice calling him. "Good boy," Dev said, grabbing hold of the dog's lead. "There's someone I want you to meet."

Standing outside the office door, like he had so many times before, the victim as the accused, Dev poked his head in to confirm Principal Butler's untimely but warranted demise. Releasing his hold on the leader dog, he shooed it inside before closing and locking the door.

Whatever-it-was had happened between classes; doors were open all up and down the corridor, sunlight from windows spilling across the floor as slanting white rectangles, lighting up specks of dust still adrift from the violence of all those bodies dropping at once. Continuing down the hallway—stepping over ex-classmates, dropped books, the coughed-out contents of backpacks and purses—Dev wondered what to call this particular tableau. Neurotypicals, no doubt, would call it hell, but his Aspie sensibilities begged to differ. For one thing, Dev didn't believe in an afterlife, be it heaven or hell, having been raised by a not-particularly-practicing Anglican of Indo-American descent by way of the Church of England and a not-particularly-practicing Jew by way of Bloomfield Hills. But if heaven was like this, he just might have to change his mind.

Regarding those who hadn't survived, Dev looked into the faces he could see, once so inscrutable, rendered meaningless once the muscles that animated them stopped. He wondered if the nothingness he felt toward them now was the same nothingness he'd felt before, or if it was something new, like shock.

Am I in shock? he wondered before following it almost immediately with: *And so what if I am?* Because if he was in shock, it felt like he'd felt most of his life. And so Dev shrugged. Moved on. Waded back into the Jell-O of his previous life, emotions a rumor, going through the motions, including walking to the bus stop, where he waited for his mother to pick him up.

It was hardly the only rote thing he did, immediately afterward. He'd also gone all the way back to his locker, tripping over bodies along the way, having to slide one aside so he could get the door open, before wrestling his She-Ra backpack out and on, and then stepping over bodies again to the bus stop, where he waited. There was no one else waiting, of course, and so he set his backpack beside him on the bench and stretched his arms along the back. Letting his head drop back, he looked up at the sky to see what it was doing.

Nothing especially doomsdayish at first glance. Brittle blue, birds still flying in it—probably good. But there were also oily black clouds churning up from the direction of the interstate—which probably wasn't. Otherwise, the scene outside was the same as the scene inside: humans sprawled here and there, with the exception that there were more animals to investigate the nonliving, meaning birds and squirrels and a few stray dogs licking here, test nibbling there.

He wondered how long the guide dog in Mr. Butler's office would wait without food. Not long, he hoped.

The fact that there were dead people outside helped confirm that whatever-it-was wasn't limited to the building, wasn't a gas leak or carbon monoxide, though the leader dog's surviving had suggested as much. The question remained, however: How far did all of this go?

He could walk from the school grounds and go house to house, he guessed, but then he had another idea. Getting off the bench, Dev found a chunk of concrete from a crumbled parking berm and threw it as hard as he could into the grille of a car that had "Please don't steal me" written all over it. And just like that, the tranquility of birdsong and whispering leaves yielded to flashing lights and the whoop, whoop, whoop of a car alarm, sliding up in pitch and decibel before sliding down and starting all over again.

He waited.

Dev waited to see if the car's bleating called anyone else out of the woodwork. The sound carried for blocks, at least. If there was anyone within hearing, Dev imagined them stumbling out of their nearby houses . . . only to be attacked by the scattered dead, suddenly rearing up again and shambling after the still living, cannibalism the only thing on what was left of their minds.

Dev watched from the sidelines of this fantasy, willfully impervious to the impending buzz-saw gore. His premise: zombies were attracted by the smell of the emotions he lacked. *Interesting theory, Brinkman,* he thought. *Interesting theory . . .*

But as long as Dev waited, nobody else came from anywhere, and the dead did not rise to feast upon them. Instead, the animals that had been startled away came ambling back once they got used to the noise of the car alarm.

Well, that settles that, Dev thought. Whatever-it-was was at least as big as the several blocks surrounding Edsel Ford High School. Did it extend to the other school districts, the names of which he'd seen scrolling across the TV screen on snow days? To the post offices, libraries, parks, and municipal airports that sometimes also closed? To the Upper Peninsula? Other states? The European Union? To other, less Caucasian parts of the world?

Did it stretch all the way back to the house where he lived with his mom and stepfather? Which reminded him, he needed to let his mom know to pick him up early. He checked his phone; it still seemed to be working. Dialed home. Listened to the ringing. She'd usually be home from the thrift store by now. Not that she needed to be home. She had a smartphone too. So he called that. Same nothing. She wouldn't be coming early. By the looks of it, she might not be coming at all.

And so Dev looked at the parking lot, where the zombies weren't, but where a lot of unclaimed personal transportation was. He hadn't bothered with driver's ed—hadn't seen the point. Though not being able to drive in Michigan rendered him pretty much an invalid, regardless of his position on the spectrum, Dev knew he'd never be able to drive. Moving through an ever-changing landscape at twenty-five miles or more per hour was just too much data for his brain to process. He knew this because it had been too much for him to handle just being a passenger, which had been his argument to Leo some time ago. If his parents and he ever had to go anywhere that involved getting on the freeway, his stepdad slipped him a Xanax, and then Dev would stretch out on the back seat, eyes closed, facedown. More than once, they'd been stopped while going through customs at the Ambassador Bridge that connected Detroit to Windsor, Ontario, the agents insisting that Dev get out and prove he wasn't dead or a hostage. Maybe give him a chance to blink "help me" in Morse code or something.

But now he needed to get home, and neither the bus nor his mom was coming. On the plus side, he figured, there was no law against going too slowly—not anymore, at least. Plus, his phone was still good for googling, and so he did, bringing up a host of YouTube videos in response to the search string "how to drive a car," followed by "how to hot-wire a car," and then finally on to Google Maps for the route home. After that, it was just a matter of picking a car, using another busted piece of concrete for his key.

Except the windows didn't explode like they did on TV. Instead, the concrete bounced off, taking out a thumbnail-sized chip, but that was all. He tried again, and got another chip bounce. By the third attempt, he had to admit (1) this was going to take all day and (2) the car he'd picked didn't have an ignition like the ones in the how-to videos, just a button on the dash. And so it was back to googling, this time to learn how to start a car with just a button for the ignition, which is how he learned about the antitheft benefits of the wireless key fob.

It was obvious what he needed to do, both to get into a vehicle and to start it: he needed to choose a car whose owner he knew, go back inside, and get the keys and/or fob. It'd be easy. As easy as, well, taking keys off a dead guy. He'd already decided he wouldn't be going through any girl's purse, partly because he was a little afraid to, but mainly because he couldn't remember what any of the women he knew drove. Trying to picture them in vehicles, it was always with some guy who wasn't Dev, the ride always something sleek and red or big, black, and combat ready.

In the end, he picked a cherry-red Mazda Miata belonging to a kid named Kevin, a Beavis-and-Butt-Head yes-man to the latest leader of the We-Hate-Dev Club. This one had distinguished himself by using Dev's tie with Dev still attached to buff away an accidental fingerprint on the car's paint job. Dev found him pinched between the door and jamb to the boys' restroom, the key ring making a bulge the size of a fist in his hip pocket. He tried extracting them, first by dipping his index and f-you fingers, tweezer style, inside the pocket. But then he wondered what he was being so careful for. Straightening back up, he proceeded to kick at the pocket bulge repeatedly until the key ring came rocketing out before landing on the floor with a clatter. Scooping it up, he looked back at Kevin. Nothing. Not a blink. Not a flinch. Dead, dead.

He threw the key fist in the air and caught it. It felt good, and so he did it again, and kept doing it, all the way back to the parking lot—where he hit the wrong button. Once again, his peaceful doomsday gave way to a frantic whoop, whoop, whoop as he fumbled, clicking randomly before remembering there was no peace left to disturb. So he stopped. Composed himself. Let a few more whoops go before locating the alarm button and tapping it off. The next button he hit popped the doors.

After reviewing the owner's manual he'd found in the glove compartment and assuring himself he knew where all the important controls were located on this particular make and model, Dev adjusted the mirrors, pulled on his seat belt, and checked the mirrors again. He put his foot on the brake and made sure the car was in park before turning the key. His skin tingled. The sound the engine made, *made* his skin tingle. It also made the hair on the back of his neck stand up. If he didn't know any better, he'd say he felt excited—as opposed to the feeling he'd been expecting, namely a Pavlovian urge to vomit. But no. He did a literal gut check; whatever else his bile was doing, it wasn't rising. His skin, meanwhile, was still tingling.

What was different? He looked around at his suddenly—miraculously—de-peopled world. And it was as if, by dying, they'd taken his anxiety with them. He had a couple of emergency Xanax from his stepfather in the coin pocket of his jeans. He thought about taking one but really didn't seem to need it. Because, what was different?

Everything is different, Dev decided. *Including me.*

He was in the driver's seat. He wasn't a hostage with no control over where he was going, every bump a surprise. He was in control, and it made a bigger difference than he could have imagined. Tapping the gas, still in park, he tingled all over again.

His top speed while riding his bike was about ten miles an hour. Dev didn't get sick while riding his bike, especially when he mapped the route ahead of time using Google Street View. So driving at ten miles an hour seemed safe for starters, especially after previewing every five hundred feet or so ahead of him, shrunk down and manageable by definition, seeing as it fit on his smartphone, which, in turn, fit into his hand.

Balancing his phone where he could see it on the dash, Dev took hold of the steering wheel, placed his foot on the brake, and kerchunked the shift into drive. Easing his foot off the brake without touching the gas, he held his breath as the car started rolling. He listened to the slow grind and pop of the tires as they crawled out of the parking space, rolling over pebbles and other parking-lot confetti.

He could feel the gentle but persistent pull of forward momentum. He imagined himself an astronaut, strapped in during liftoff, the g-forces rippling his cheeks, stretching his lips into a teeth-baring grimace. He looked down at the speedometer, the needle wobbling midway between zero and ten.

Tapping the gas the slightest bit humanly possible, he wound up bumping over a dead classmate—but so slowly he could hear the bones breaking individually. Again, they sounded like broomsticks, wrapped in towels, cracking one after the other. Dev tapped the gas again, harder this time, just to make the sound stop faster.

The needle now flirted with twenty, while the car, only marginally steered by Dev, left the asphalt parking lot. A sidewalk appeared, and the tires rolled over it, onto the grassy green space on the other side. Unlike the noisy asphalt, the grass was practically silent, the only sounds being the engine and the wind shaking the trees, a sound like the ocean rushing to shore or a chorus of librarians, all shushing at once. It was peaceful—*calming*—like the sound of his mother vacuuming outside his bedroom door.

If this is what driving is like, Dev thought, *I wish I'd known sooner . . .*

But it wasn't, of course. Driving—at least, driving before—was nothing like this. *But it is now,* Dev thought. *Why?*

Because I said so.

Finding the cruise control, Dev set it at twenty-five and watched the world go by from the driver's seat, the self-appointed king of doomsday, returning in triumph. He took the route Google Maps suggested—or rather a route of his own, mostly next to the roads unfurling ever so slowly on the screen. And so onward he rolled, across manicured lawns and overgrown lots where dandelion seeds shook loose and hung in the air like snow in a globe. It was good being king.

One way to find out how far "it" went was to keep driving the red Miata until Dev either met other survivors or ran out of land, at which point he could switch to a boat. Assuming the water he hit was an ocean and not just the Detroit River, wouldn't that be an adequate sample size? Couldn't he just decide, "The whole world's dead," and spare himself months of seasickness?

Or if he *really* wanted to be efficient, maybe he could just turn on the radio, hit scan, and watch it weave back and forth across the dial, like some FM version of *Pong*. Robot stations without DJs wouldn't count. Ditto anything prerecorded. But how would he know if what he was listening to was prerecorded? Unfortunately, this wasn't Dev's first national disaster; if whatever he hit wasn't nonstop coverage of the whatever-it-was, it was prerecorded.

And so he pushed the button and waited for a station that wasn't there anymore. Which was adequate for the time being. No need to drive to either of the two oceans bookending the country. The broadcasting area around Metro Detroit and Windsor was a big enough sample size for him to call it. And so, at around noon, 12:30 p.m. eastern daylight time on a Monday in early June, in the second decade of the twenty-first century, the world—or at least the world of people, at least mostly—had come to an end. Cause of death: whatever.

There was a bridge over I-94 along the route his mom took to and from school, perhaps to remind him of the trauma she was sparing him. But even if it weren't, he would have wound up here anyway, to confirm with his own eyes what the empty radio dial already told him. Standing next to the Miata on the otherwise empty overpass, Dev surveyed the aftermath of whatever-it-was, cars whose drivers suddenly stopped being alive still moving until they hit something, usually another car or truck or wall. Amazingly, the center lane was clear, as if Moses had raised his staff, parting the interstate down the middle. This was no miracle, though—just the result of neglected roads and bad alignments, cars that tugged left crashing left, right, right. If he was one for political metaphors, he would have said this was a good one for the way the country had divided itself since just before he was born. But the closest thing he had to an interest in politics was vacuum cleaners. The thing they had in common? According to his stepfather, they both sucked.

It must have been something to see when it was still happening, the vehicles piling up, steel and rubber, glass and combustible fluids, shrieking, squealing, imploding, exploding, compacting into denser and denser polarized clots of destruction as wave after driverless wave kept coming, kept crashing, kept coming, kept crashing, out, out, out, reaching toward the horizon. Now, quiet except for natural noises—wind, shaking leaves, the guttering flames of those vehicles that were burning—punctuated occasionally by an exploding gas tank.

And then Dev saw it: a singular car, sticking to the center lane, performing evasive maneuvers around the occasional sheared-off tire or far-flung fender. He was halfway back inside the Miata, ready to start honking, when he noticed the GPS globe on top. Whose it was—Uber, Google, GM—he couldn't tell, though he admired how well its sensors and programming were calling the shots, considering the unlikelihood that its designers had thought ahead to an apocalypse mode.

Dev wondered what the Little Autonomous Vehicle That Could would do when it reached one of the broken planes that had dropped out of the sky shortly after takeoff from Metro Airport, this one leaving debris spanning both lanes of the freeway. Others had gotten farther in their doomed journeys, dropping out of the blue to incinerate whole neighborhoods, the blue-black crematory smoke billowing up like rough drafts of mushroom clouds. As best he could tell from his phone, none of the fires seemed to be coming from his neighborhood, though that was just luck; the entire area seemed to be under one flight path or another, judging from the grid of contrails thinning in the wind.

If the Underwear Bomber had succeeded however many Christmases ago, Dev wouldn't be standing here, watching what could have been back then playing out in front of him now. People at the time joked— what else could they do?—resorting to gallows humor, wondering what sort of terrorist would pick Metro Detroit for a target. Didn't they teach that in Terrorist Targeting 101? When picking your target, make sure it's somewhere where the damage will be noticed. Dev hadn't thought it was funny back then, and still didn't.

As he drove out of the business district and into the surrounding neighborhoods, Dev noticed a return of the sound he'd heard outside school: the unrelenting howling of dogs. The sound followed him the rest of the way home, their guttural cacophony becoming his background music as he drove. It was the sound of humanity's shirked responsibilities. As a shirked responsibility himself, he identified more with the dogs than the ones they were howling for. And so he let out an *ow-ooo* himself, sounding like Warren Zevon in "Werewolves of London," a golden oldie his stepfather played often, sitting in the dark, ice clinking, sipping the evening away.

"Warren f-ing Zevon," he'd announce, as if Dev didn't already know that from the dozens of times before. "You know what he said before he died?"

"Enjoy every sandwich," Dev thought, each and every time after that first time when he hadn't known the answer. Still, he'd shake his head anyway. He'd learned that when his fake dad asked certain questions, not answering was the answer.

"'Enjoy every sandwich,'" the older Brinkman would say, right after a sip, delivering the line like it was something from centuries ago, perhaps carved in stone. Dev—an avid consumer of the food his faux father was forever reminding him he'd paid for—nodded, like he was thinking about it. And he was, kind of.

What does dying taste like? he'd wonder. *And how do you get it between bread?*

Getting closer to home, he saw smaller versions of what he'd seen on the freeway: man's machines, suddenly unmanned, continuing on until something got in their way. Taking the green lane through one neighborhood, he noticed a self-propelled mower with its dead handler sprawled across a half-shaved lawn at one end, connected to the other end by a clean swath that jumped the neighbor's driveway and continued on, cutting a path through neighboring lawns, steered by the ground underneath, its bumps and dips having caused the mower to go right, left, swerve, zigzag until it had finally jumped a curb and slammed into the passenger side of an SUV, where it was still chugging blue exhaust, stuck between the truck's chassis and the pavement. Elsewhere, smoke whispered from under front doors or coughed out open windows, signaling the locations of unattended irons, frying pans, cigarettes, while from under other doorways rolled steady streams over porches and sidewalks to pool darkly around the nearest storm drains.

Dev wondered about his own house as he approached the neighborhood he'd grown up in. Had anybody—meaning his real mom or fake dad—left anything going that had run amok in their absence? Probably not; *hopefully* not. They were both fairly careful about that sort of thing, mainly because leaving stuff running cost money and they'd been on the economy plan ever since Dev's unexpected entrance into the picture, just months short of his mom going through menopause.

According to his replacement dad, quoting his own dead brother, what followed was "a real joy," though it didn't sound like it: postpartum depression punctuated by hot flashes. And if that wasn't enough, while Dev was still a baby, his dad—his uncle's brother—died of a sudden heart attack. Of course, his uncle (now stepfather) stepped up and did the right thing, but the right thing wasn't cheap, buddy boy—a hard reality Dev could hardly make it through the day without being reminded of.

So yeah, they were old and cheap but also both out of the house the day it happened—at least he hoped so, because love lost or not, he didn't want to come home to a dead parent, meaning his mom. As for what's his name, finding him dead would be a drag too—as in, he'd have to drag him out before he stunk up the place any further. The actual sight of his dead body? Yeah, Dev wasn't the emotional kind—in case his fake dad hadn't heard.

Before getting home, he drove by his sign, the one that had gone up shortly after his stepfather's diagnosis. "See that?" his fake dad had said. "That's your sign. That sign's just for you."

The way he said it made Dev feel special—*privileged*—back before he could read. Afterward, though, it was a different story. "Slow," the sign advised, "Autistic Child in Area."

There were other signs as well, signs for other children. "Caution Deaf Child Area," "Watch for Blind Child," "Children at Play." Only the last didn't seem to pass judgment on the children it warned about. But the one that warned people about him seemed most judgmental of all, because of that word: *slow*. Was it an admonition not to speed? Or an adjective? Either way, but especially the latter, hurt the feelings he supposedly didn't have.

And so he stopped the red Miata and put it in reverse. Fast. Or fastish. Fast enough to bend the pole the sign was attached to, for the sign itself to gong against the trunk. Shifting into drive, he jerked forward, and the sign slid off, hitting the ground like a cymbal. Reversing again, Dev looked over his shoulder as the car's passenger side drive tire rolled onto the painted sheet metal. He pressed the foot brake and yanked up the emergency, put the car in drive, and punched the gas, hard. And there went his sign, flung skyward by the spinning tire before sailing back down and wedging itself—thunk!—deep into a tree trunk where the wobbling from its final impact sounded like thunder.

Satisfied, Dev released the brake and drove the rest of the way home, one long-overdue task checked off his to-do list.

Pulling into the driveway, he noted the absence of their cars, as well as of smoke, water, and/or flames. So that was good. His mom and the other guy both likely did their dying at the thrift store or at work, respectively, which is where they usually were while Dev was serving time at school.

But for all the dead bodies lying around and the fact that he'd driven himself home, the latest return to base camp wasn't a whole lot different from all the other times. He let himself in with his key and headed for his room, where he locked the door. This time, though, he added a step: a pit stop in the kitchen. The whatever-it-was happened before he'd had lunch, and surviving the apocalypse had kicked his hunger into overdrive.

So Dev opened the fridge and removed a package of cold cuts, two different kinds of cheese, and an assortment of condiments in chilled, squeezable bottles. These, he laid out on the counter along with a carton of milk like the props in a religious ceremony. From the rolltop bread box, he fished out half a loaf, spun it open counterclockwise, set aside the twist tie, dealt out two slices, and closed it again with a clockwise spin. The roll top slid shut with a satisfying thunk and clatter as Dev turned to assemble his sandwich, pour milk, and unclip a bag of chips from the top of the fridge, which he shook out in a kind of nest around the rim of the paper plate on which the aforementioned sandwich rested like a bull's-eye. Satisfactorily provisioned, he proceeded to his bedroom—more out of habit than necessity—closed the door, and proceeded to enjoy his sandwich in a fashion he was sure Warren Zevon would approve of.

8

Until she found herself surrounded by them, Lucy had never seen an actual dead person in person. She'd seen thousands on TV and in movies, where dead bodies were like parsley—a garnish that came with pretty much everything. Even when her grandparents died and she went to their viewings, she hadn't *really* seen dead bodies. What she saw was the plastic fruit equivalent of dead bodies: close, but a little too idealized. They looked like they'd been airbrushed in 3-D. The only real thing about their posed deadness was how cold they felt when she brushed their hands, saying goodbye. The thingness of their bodies came through in that touch. It resonated on her fingertips long after, like the ghost of a camera flash, but one she could feel instead of see: the phantom limb effect using someone else's limbs.

Is this what people mean when they say they're keeping someone's memory alive? she'd wondered.

The corpses all around her now hadn't been pumped full of antifreeze, gussied up, had their hair sprayed hard. They were death au naturel, their hair doing the wind's bidding, unable to lift a finger to brush it out of their eyes. When she first started walking through the valley of death, a part of her wanted to do it for them, reach over, there, that's better. But then she stopped feeling it. Looking at them now, she tried to think of them as the former vessels of souls. She couldn't. Even the bodies she knew, she didn't know anymore. The transformation of death turned them into human-shaped things that were just shy of real, like that CGI Tom Hanks in *The Polar Express* that gave her nightmares for weeks. And probably would again, now that she remembered it. *Shite . . .*

Of course, CGI Tom would have plenty of competition when it came to poisoning her dreams after all that happened the day It happened. To keep things manageable, Lucy placed the day's events into two boxes: (1) the miscarriage and (2) the . . . rest of it. She started with the miscarriage because she'd been living longer with the need to do something about her condition, and in a way, she'd caught a lucky break, seeing as ever since she'd lost the cell clump, she hadn't had a panic attack.

Which brought her to the other box: the . . . rest of it. As boxes went, it was pretty big because it had to be. There was no other way for her finite brain to cope with the enormity of the enormousness she'd witnessed. Even summarized into those three monosyllabic words, the box in question was too heavy to lift without hurting her brain stem.

And the more Lucy walked, the heavier the box got, as more stuff went into it. Crushed cars placed next to the geysering fire hydrants they'd decapitated, followed by snapped power poles turned into hypotenuses by straining wires and geometry. A traffic light lay crashed in the bull's-eye of an intersection, shocking her with how huge it seemed up close. Elsewhere, a car had jumped a curb into the plate-glass window of the non–abortion clinic she'd stomped out of, earning itself a very special place in Lucy's . . . rest of it box.

She noticed that the traffic lights that hadn't come crashing down into intersections still seemed to be working, cycling through their parfait lights. She also noticed that the space inside her—only recently vacated by the cell clump—was growling something powerful. Whether it was a stress growl, a miscarriage growl, or a growl of hunger, she knew what the answer was—"Who wants ice cream?"—phrased like they did on *Jeopardy!*, in the form of a question.

Me, Lucy thought, *I could eat a whole freaking Baskin-Robbins after a day like today* . . .

She decided to settle for the freezer section of the Walgreens up ahead, a pint of Häagen-Dazs white chocolate raspberry truffle. The working air-conditioning blasted dry the sweat from all her walking. It felt good.

What didn't feel good was stepping over the dead customers along her way to chilly solace. She'd started noticing how the bodies didn't seem so bad anymore. Dead, not talking, not posing any threat, they kind of grew on her in a way the living never had. They were all so soft and vulnerable, postmortem. Take the pharmacist with the bad toupee, lying facedown in aisle three, his toupee lying next to him like a hairy pancake, the peach-fuzzy wisps on his skull playthings for the AC. And right next to him, like the dictionary illustration for *irony,* the underage shoplifter the pharmacist had stopped everything to stop—or so it seemed to Lucy—the pack of Trojans still clutched by fingers starting to go rigid with rigor mortis. Two sad people, photographed forever together by death . . .

It was almost enough to make her feel sorry for them—a little too little, a little too late—but still, it was progress. Empathetically speaking.

The thing about the end of the world—that is, when it's ended for everyone but you—is the melancholy that sort of creeps up on you. Granted, Lucy was neither the warmest nor fuzziest person alive when there were others to compare her with; the world had kicked all the warmth and fuzz out of her, along with any sense of self-worth she might have had. To the extent she had a chip on her shoulder, though, it had been nailed there by others, using one of those nail guns that uses shotgun shells. To say she was bitter fell a wee bit short, like calling sulfuric acid tangy.

But then everybody else died, leaving their stuff behind to find when she kicked open the door of some house she'd always wondered about from the outside. It turned out all that stuff had become infused with little bits of sadness she never knew anything about but could suddenly feel now, in the weight of a knickknack hefted in the palm of her hand.

Huh, she'd think, over some worthless piece of kitsch from under a bell jar on somebody's mantel. *What was the story,* she'd wonder, and then . . .

. . . she'd find herself supplying it, before getting sad for no reason, because ownerless things gravitate that way: toward sorrow for all the absence they represent.

Pretty sappy, Abernathy, she thought, grateful there were no witnesses left to call her on it.

9

The weird thing about seeing all the dead bodies, it didn't bother Mo as much as he imagined—in part because he already had. Imagined it, that is. He'd had help, what with the PowerPoint parade of war casualties they kept sending his way, most no doubt chosen for him, specifically, so many of the bodies seeming to be around his age or younger. The purpose—in addition to working up his righteous rage—was to disabuse him of the comfortable American myth that he was too young to die. "Here you go," the slides implied. "Someone your own age and complexion: dead. And another. And another. We can do this all day.

"Shall we?"

Thus when it actually happened, it was very much a case of been there done that, became a jihadi and expected to die one. So the things Mohammad saw afterward weren't the stuff of nightmares so much as dreams of paradise, suddenly exposed for all the many shades of stupid they really were.

Shade of Stupid Number One: Imagining He'd Been Betrayed

Clearly, they'd been grooming someone else in case he chickened out. They'd given this "understudy" Mo's time, his place, *and* his date. Maybe he'd postponed too many times because of his "insufficiently warm" feet. Maybe his handlers figured a ricin attack—so much deadlier and farther spreading—would creep out the cowboys even more.

Except—yeah: Mo wasn't dead. So scratch the whole backup-martyr-with-ricin idea, and start feeling stupid for having had it.

Shade of Stupid Number Two: Not Quibbling with the Method of Deployment

They'd asked him to strap on a bomb, walk into a packed gymnasium, and blow himself up. And what did Mo say? "Sign me up, my brothers." Why? Why not buy a cheap clock, make a timer, stay home sick? Why not buy a burner phone, turn it into a remote detonator, and live to terrorize another day? Was Mo's life so cheap it wasn't worth the price of a TracFone? Or were his handlers just showing off—letting the world know they had martyrs to burn? So Mo felt stupid about that too.

Shade of Stupid Number Three: Believing a Straight-Up Murder-Suicide Could Be Called Martyrdom

Yeah, about that: How was picking the time and place and then doing it to yourself *martyrdom*? Didn't that take paradise and turn it into just another thing you bought like groceries, but with your earthly life? Oh, he knew what his handlers would say, if they were still alive. "Allah knows what's in your heart. Allah knows when your motives are pure . . ." Why did Allah suddenly sound like the heathens' Santa Claus? "He knows when you've been bad or good, so be good for goodness' sake . . ." Plus, what if Mo's motives *weren't* pure? What if the 9/11 hijackers getting lap dances were thinking how they wouldn't have to *pay* for that kind of treatment when they got all those virgins? Was that martyrdom—or just an exchange of services?

He'd tried resolving his parents' ambiguous Su-Shi Islam by embracing a weaponized variety made attractive by his handlers' world-cleaving certainties. The world was simple; it was just a game of sides, believers versus heathens, with the latter one extreme haircut away from the damnation they deserved. Pick a side—they demanded—and Mo had. Now he'd just as soon not play the game at all. And so, the former terrorist stood up and carefully made his way to the center aisle. The bleachers squeaked as he headed down to the gym floor, littered now with dead cheerleaders and other pep-related corpses.

Before leaving, no-longer-Mo walked up to the school's mascot, a giant plush badger. The head of the costume had been separated by gravity and the floor from the cartoonish body in red sweatshirt and no pants, the body itself now topped by a normal-sized head framed by a growing halo of red against the honey-blond floorboards. The bomb vest under his clothes would have left the same punch line, if whatever this was hadn't beaten Mohammad to the punch. And it occurred to him that the bomb he was still wearing was every bit as much of a costume as a giant, pantless badger—and even more ridiculous, given the deadly seriousness of its intent.

And so he pulled his tunic over his head and off. He ripped the Velcro straps of his suicide vest, removed it, and slung it over his shoulder, like a sport coat too warm for the change in weather. He worked his tennis shoe into the opening at the base of the badger head, kicked up, and caught it as it came down. He tried it on; it was the perfect, imperfect fit, making the world outside echo around its inside.

"Hello down there, Marcus," he said, remembering the mascot's real name and realizing he liked the sound of it. "Hello, Marcus," he said again, this time to his reflection in the gym door's window.

Yes, he thought. As names went, Marcus had a nice, nonterroristy ring to it. And seeing as the badger wasn't using it . . .

But no. That was too glib. Choosing a new name was something one did—he tried to remember that phrase he'd liked—in "the smithy of his soul." Mo—now Marcus—had run across it in an English class while reading an anthologized excerpt from James Joyce's A Portrait of the Artist as a Young Man. He'd had to look up smithy and discovered it was another word for blacksmith. The smithy of the soul was apparently where an artist made things. Feeling a bit empty inside, Mo fell in love with the image of the soul as a workshop where things were made of iron, pounded red-hot on an anvil, metal on metal, clang after sparking clang. And now the phrase came back to him as he melted down his old self and prepared to make of it something new.

"And he would be called Marcus," the ex-Mo intoned inside the giant, hollow head, making the words sound vaguely godlike. And then he realized he should probably change his surname too. "Smith," he decided with a smile, seeing not the motel anonymity of the name, but that maker he'd imagined, making metal sing.

Now that he was Marcus Smith, the boy formerly known as Mo ditched the extra head and borrowed a T-shirt from a classmate who hadn't managed to bloody it while dying. The skullcap was a loss already, having been used to wipe the other Marcus's blood from his hands. The vest, which he was still carrying, didn't go with anything else he was wearing. And so he set it off in the middle of the football field long-distance, thanks to a match and a long line of gasoline between himself and it. The explosion left a crater the size of a Volkswagen Beetle and a concussion he could feel reverberating through his skin. Car alarms were still going off in the parking lot, and dogs howled pretty much everywhere as he grabbed his bike from the rack and headed back home.

10

When Dev was still on autopilot, it hadn't occurred to him to wonder about things like utilities. He'd come home from school, gone to his bedroom, and shut the door, just like the school day before, and all the school days before that. But on the day everything changed, his routine did too. He'd been hungry after missing lunch, and so he'd taken a detour to the kitchen, opened the fridge, and assembled a quick snack before continuing on his way, not having noticed what he hadn't been looking for.

That had been a few hours ago, and now he was looking at an empty glass on his desk, and a fly that had taken an interest in it. There was a milky film dulling the inside of the glass, and the fly was walking through the souring dregs at the bottom, its proboscis probing, its wings twitching.

Glad you waited, Dev thought, directing it at the fly as he set the glass off to the side so he wouldn't reach for the last few drops while preoccupied with something else. No point getting food poisoning now that . . .

And that's when the fingers in Dev's head snapped: the refrigerator's light had come on! The cold cuts and bottles of condiments had been cold. The traffic lights he'd passed on the way back home had dutifully directed the nonexistent traffic, those that hadn't been downed in the immediate aftermath by cars jumping the curb into the poles they'd been suspended from. Even the wind dancers in front of the car dealer-ships had continued dancing. Sure, his phone still worked and so did Google, but that was often the case in blackouts before; that's what allowed him to check the DTE maps to see how widespread the outage was and what the estimated time of restoration was.

So Dev got up and began flipping switches; yep, he had light all over the house. Not so much as a circuit breaker had broken the flow of electricity from the outside world. Back in the kitchen, more good news: there was water and gas too. Even without anyone to run it, the local infrastructure was chugging along all by itself. *Thank you, robot overlords,* he thought, grateful to see that even the router in the corner was still blinking so he could use Wi-Fi instead of his phone's data plan—not that he was expecting a bill anytime soon.

Logging on, Dev found the Google suite of services still hum-ming along—they'd gotten him home, after all—but was pleased to find several other sites still gathering and spitting back data on their users. Amazon, Twitter, and Facebook all came when he summoned them, though the last was minus its updates, likes, and comments now that the updaters, likers, and commenters were dead. Even doomsday hadn't stopped the automated clickbait and pop-ups from mining Dev's electronic cookie crumbs for fodder, informing him of the availability of women over fifty who weren't into games, as well as steep discounts on Viagra and hair-replacement therapies. Apparently, his electronic self was a balding middle-aged man with ED who couldn't find a date. Which was reasonably close, based on his social calendar—especially now—though the reason had nothing to do with needing hair plugs or boner pills. As unbiased a source as his own mother had informed Dev that he was handsome, and he'd even been approached by female members of the species who didn't know any better. But then, as the story goes, he opened his mouth . . .

And that was another good thing about doomsday: the whole dat-ing thing was off the table—a definite plus for someone who couldn't stand being touched. But back to the interwebs—those parts that still worked, post-whatever. Skipping through banner ads and 401 error messages, Dev had a hunch about how to determine the extent of the whatever-it-was that didn't involve leaving the comfort of his keyboard. And so he went to Google and started typing: "Why is everyone . . ." If Google's predictive search algorithm filled in the word *dead*, Dev figured that would mean—ironically—that everyone *wasn't* dead, because others were consulting the oracle of Google to figure out what happened. Instead, the top choices for completing his phrase were:

- . . . so mean
- . . . depressed
- . . . happier than me
- . . . taking up zumba

Even when he forced the issue and typed in the word *dead*, the predictor guessed beyond what he was looking for:

- . . . on the walking dead
- . . . on the last man on earth
- . . . at the end of hamlet

So there was his answer; he was it: the sole survivor. Or at least the sole survivor who did Google searches in English. And had internet access. And who—before searching for loved ones or their remains—decided to check Google instead. And if not sole, among too few to skew Google's infamous ranking algorithm.

The next stop on his tech tour of assurance was TV. And bingo, even live TV was still there, though "live" really needed quotes. Surfing the channels, Dev found a combination of local stations broadcasting a variety of static scenes: a news desk with anchor and sidekick, one slumped back, mouth agape, sharp-knotted tie acting like a tourniquet, stopping the gerbil of his Adam's apple from further passage down the digestive tract; the other slumped forward, a mop of spray-hardened hair split open from the force of her head hitting the particleboard desktop, her carapace sprouting a few blond strands, stirred upward by the studio's still-functioning air-conditioning. On another station, a basketball game had gone into sudden death—so to speak—tiers of dead fans having avalanched out of their seats into body piles here and there, while the players on both sides lay splayed across the hardwood, in and out of the paint, the basketball having long ago rolled to a stop where it would wait forever—or at least until a dozen freeze-thaw cycles opened up the roof to let the rain in, after which the ball would slowly bob and rise as the arena became a watery graveyard. Another channel was a rainbow with a black box along the bottom with the words "Sat Feed" in white and a whirling countdown marking the hours, minutes, seconds, tenths of seconds since the whatever-it-was happened—or the pretaped soap opera that had been running at the time ran out. Followed by snow, snow, "Please stand by," snow, "We are experiencing technical difficulty," a *Twilight Zone* marathon, snow, a close-up of floor tile, snow . . .

Dev took the clicker and clicked back a few channels to where the *Twilight Zone* episode was reaching its punch line, that "To Serve Man" is the title of a cookbook. In the next, the future Captain Kirk freaked out big-time on a plane, followed by the pig faces, followed by the one with Burgess Meredith as the last bookworm on earth who winds up breaking his glasses.

Even though Dev knew the ironic twist was coming, still a kind of cold wind blew through him. If he didn't know any better, he'd say he was feeling creeped out by the parallels between his own experience and the one he was watching on TV. But that was the beauty of having what Dev had, especially postapocalyptically: he didn't creep out—at least not easily. He did respond to physical stimuli, however, often in a spectrum-enhanced fashion, but abstractions leading to a physical reaction like goose bumps? Not really. And so he checked the windows and doors, trying to track down the source of this strictly nonmetaphorical chill, only to find he'd left the refrigerator open as he'd darted around the house, switching things on.

He pushed against the enameled door now until it gasped, confirming its seal, and then thought about the fallout shelter where he almost died. The shelter had a door just like the fridge, a rubber gasket sealing it hermetically against human stupidity. He wondered whether the shelter saved him. Thought: probably. Thought: good. Because the odds against anybody else being in an abandoned fallout shelter at precisely the same time seemed pretty slim. At least he hoped so. After all, now that Dev had the world to himself, he wasn't exactly eager to share.

To kill time before the sun set, Dev downloaded everything on the web he could find that might come in handy once things like the web disappeared. After sunset, the plan was to kill something else: streetlights, specifically. Dev had been an amateur astronomer, after all, and had been repeatedly thwarted in the practice of his hobby by clouds, daylight saving time, neighbors who thought he was spying on them, and—even when everything else cooperated—light pollution. Doomsday—he figured—provided a certain leeway for addressing the last of these.

The neighbor he borrowed the rifle from was—had been—a deer hunter, as advertised by the buck head decal on the rear window of the pickup's cab. In the bed of the truck lay a blanketed lump in the shape of an assault rifle, concealing—of course—an assault rifle, fully loaded with laser sight and silencer for catching the deer by surprise. If he'd had a pole that reached, Dev could have gone after the streetlights like so many glowing piñatas, but shooting would work too. Plus, it probably wasn't a bad idea to learn how to use a gun, given everything he didn't know about what might be coming next.

He'd known about his neighbor's hobby even before finding the gun—had gone looking for it, specifically. He'd known because he'd found actual deer hooves in his neighbor's trash once. Unfortunately, his parents had been feeding him the whole Santa story at the time, sanitized of any religious affiliation, and solely as a behavior modification technique.

"If you don't stop that," they took turns warning him, "Santa's not going to . . . ," etc.

Looking at the hooves, he wasn't sure what they were at first. The actual hoof part looked like it was made of some heavy black plastic, the tawny fur like paintbrush bristles. He'd made the mistake of pulling one out, and that's when he saw the bone knob and caked blood, dropped it, and just stared. Having finally realized what it was and where it had come from, Dev felt his moral universe collapse. What was the point of being good anymore? How was Santa supposed to bring him anything with the reindeer equivalent of a flat tire?

And so he started acting up until his fake dad made his diagnosis and began treating his stepson accordingly: under-the-counter by shorting the prescriptions of other kids with official diagnoses.

Now, with the stock nestled against his right shoulder and his finger poised on the trigger, Dev the first-time sniper prepared to return the universe (moral or otherwise) to its pre-Edison glory. Steadying the barrel with his free hand, he drew the laser's bright-red dot up the lamp pole until it disappeared in the glow of the mercury vapor light. He pulled in a breath, held it for a heartbeat, and then squeezed the trigger. The silencer dampened the sound to that of a watermelon seed being spat away. But the recoil—the *recoil* put Dev on his back, staring up at the few stars he could see in the night's milky gray, his hand already blistering, his target's aluminum hood bullet-creased but with its bulb still shining.

Crap . . .

Staying where he dropped to avoid any reruns, Dev raised the gun again, testing the barrel with his finger until he found a spot to hold that wouldn't burn him after firing. He squinted through the rifle's telescopic sight, noting that the crosshairs and laser dot did not strictly agree, lowered his aim a tick, and braced for the kickback. He let out his breath like a tire losing air and then squeezed the trigger. *Thwip! Pop!* Glass shards tinkled against the pavement like wind chimes as the street grew dimmer by a few lumens. A dozen more misses and twice as many bullets cleared the street.

Though Dev knew what to expect when he finally stopped shooting and looked up, he didn't *really* know what to expect. There'd be more, he understood, but actually *seeing* them was on a whole other level. It didn't seem possible the night sky could hold so many. There were the usual suspects, of course. The bears, major and minor; Polaris; a few other connect-the-dot constellations he'd made up on his own, changing their names as his obsessions changed, his latest sky including such notables as the Dyson, the Hoover, and the constellation Electrolux. But there were so many others, not even counting the Milky Way spilled like a pail of pale light crawling across the sky, every dust speck in that incandescent cloud a star like the sun, with worlds maybe, some peopled, maybe some peopled wholly by people like Dev . . .

The thought made him feel tiny and light, the burden of being the only person like himself wherever he went suddenly lifting as if in zero g, floating off his shoulders and away. Under all those would-be worlds, he'd be too tiny to be anyone's target. And he could feel them—muscles he never knew he had—unwinding.

And then came the long-overdue breathing out. Until he did it, Dev never realized how much of his breath he'd been holding back. But now there was no reason to. No more crosshairs to avoid. No one left to disappoint. No one to compare himself with, or love, whether he wanted to or not. The indifference of the stars was positively Aspergerian. Maybe that's why Dev liked them so much.

11

The animal came bounding up to her while Lucy was shooting up the bait-and-switch clinic. She'd found a gun shop just a few doors down, and it seemed like kismet—or at least a good excuse for venting a little, semiautomatically. After all, what good was doomsday if you couldn't raise a little hell—as gratuitous as that might be under the circumstances? She did it mainly for the sound and feel—she told herself—the thunk of a shell hitting reinforced wood, the tinkle of the casing hitting concrete, the shoulder shove of the stock kicking back like Max joshing her, trying to make her drop her books.

"Quit it," she'd always told him—willing to pay almost anything now for him to do it one more time.

And it was in this mix of mayhem and melancholy that she heard the thing yipping toward her: a little dog came from out of the . . . rest of it, demanding her full attention as its nails clicked across the sidewalk, the clicking stopping every few seconds as the animal leaped over another body and kept coming. It was still collared and leashed but otherwise ownerless. It seemed as needy as Lucy was determined not to be.

A determination, alas, that did not last.

"Okay, okay," she said, squatting to scratch behind its ears. "Chill, you little SOB . . ."

The dog responded in a decidedly unchill manner, licking her hands, face, and hands again. *Apparently*, she thought, *I'm being adopted.* And so, because she could, she slipped her hand through the loop at the other end of the leash and took charge. She didn't have any dog food back home, which—now that she had a dog—was where she decided she was going. The Abernathys had never gotten one because both her dad and brother were allergic. But pretty much anything could be dog food—Lucy figured—just so long as it wasn't chicken bones or chocolate.

"You like steak?"

The dog, one of those dust mops with legs, yipped.

"Thought so," she said, stepping over another body and letting the dust mop lead the way.

By the time they reached home, she'd dubbed him Sir Sheds-a-Lot because he looked like he would, judging from the staticky strands of white hair all over her fingertips. Try as she might, she couldn't seem to flick them away. And as for brushing them off against her gothic black apparel—yeah, she wasn't making *that* mistake again.

Before turning up the front walk, Lucy stopped and bent down to explain the situation to her traveling companion. "Now, I know you don't seem like an outside dog," she said. "But you're going to have to give it a try. I've got some peeps ain't exactly down with dog dander, so . . ." She paused to tie the leash to the mailbox post. "But hey, there's a steak in it for you, so keep your eyes on the prize."

Sir Sheds whimpered as she mounted the porch steps with her back to him. Turning, she aimed a warning finger. "You know, you've got a lot of nerve trying to make me feel sorry for you, considering . . ." She didn't add, "the . . . rest of it," but that's what she was thinking.

Why she didn't let him into the house, considering the . . . rest of it—well, there was part of the . . . rest of it she didn't quite believe just yet. A part she didn't want to make come true by acting as if it was. No, as far as Lucy was concerned, she still lived with her father and brother who were *still* allergic to pet dandruff. It wasn't Sir Sheds-a-Lot's fault, but she wasn't going to let him and his allergens jinx it. Plus, you know, there was a steak in it for him.

Sir Sheds got his steak and Lucy got a pint of rocky road, the former wrestling with his, slapped down on a paper plate and placed in front of him next to where he'd been leashed while his new owner sat down on the lawn with a plastic spoon, eating out of the carton. Ever since the . . . rest of it happened, she'd had a nursery rhyme stuck in her head:

> Ring around the rosie
> A pocket full of posey
> Ashes, ashes
> We all fall down.

Max had told her it was about the Black Death, that the rosie was a rash, the posey medicinal herbs, that "ashes" was a corruption of "achoo," and the "all fall down" was, of course, a good chunk of Europe dying during the Middle Ages. Snopes, on the other hand, said it was all BS, but she liked Max's explanation better. That's what made them resonate, the way nursery rhymes and fairy tales blended innocence and morbidity—the real ones, at least, as opposed to the Disneyfied versions.

She wondered if there'd ever be others, a couple of hundred years in the future, chanting nursery rhymes about what happened, whatever that turned out to be. "What do you think there, Sir? What rhymes with 'final judgment'? Spinal something? Vinyl, maybe?"

The tiny dog snarled into his slab of meat.

"Good point," Lucy said, looking at the sky for any clues about what was coming next.

The two spent the next few days bonding, mourning, and planning their next move, though the last of these was pretty much Lucy's doing. She still hadn't let the dog inside, was still telling herself that the late members of her family were just late. The only time it was any problem for Sir Sheds was when it rained one day. Lucy had rushed out with apologies and two umbrellas, one for him, one for her. The only other time he needed rescuing was when she found he'd manage to lash himself to the mail post, having circled it too many times, chasing his rumor of a tail under all that teased-out fur. Inexplicably, she found herself crying as she carefully unwound him, the poor thing whining all the while.

"Don't you say it," she said, mad at herself, mad at her too-late tears. "Don't you say *anything*..."

What she imagined Sir Sheds might say, even Lucy didn't know. Non sequiturs, she'd found, were easier than trying to stay coherent all the time. And when you got down to it, the only thing the dog really cared about was the tone. And another one of those steaks the Abernathys seemed to have a freezer full of.

To prevent further attempts at canine bondage, Lucy redid Sir Sheds's leash, unclipping it from his collar so she could feed the clip end through the loop at the human end with the hitching post in the middle. No longer knotted in place, the new arrangement slid around the pole with Sir Sheds-a-Lot as he circled, instead of wrapping itself around the pole until it ran out.

Ring around the posty, she thought. *A pocket dog, well mostly...*

"There," she said, shaking her head. "Now you can keep moving without any mishaps." She'd already told the dog how important it was to keep moving in this part of Georgia, lest the omnipresent kudzu snatch him up in its green tendrils like Seymour from *Little Shop of Horrors.* "And wouldn't that be a fine howdy do," she'd said, "finding nothing left of you but a few hairs and a tiny little pile of poo?"

12

Dev's goal re what came next was to preserve as much of his pre-whatever routine as possible, minus the parts he didn't care for, like going to school and being picked on. He figured a good place to start was where daily routines generally began: with waking up. So after he'd had his fill of the night sky, he wound and set an alarm clock for seven the next morning, just in case the infrastructure crashed in his sleep. Fortunately, he'd had this particular, ancient timekeeper since he was a toddler, when his mother discovered the calming effect its ticking had on the young Dev.

Before closing his eyes and slipping away under the clock's metronomic ticking, Dev wrote a note to remind himself what was going on: "Happy Doomsday, Day One." He placed the note so it would be the first thing he saw when he woke and then settled back for a long . . .

Stopped. Got back up. Yes, routine was one thing, but the mattress in his bedroom had come from the same place all his other stuff did: the thrift store. Every night, he could feel the ghost dents of the mattress's previous owners like a dozen different peas, his Asperger's skin as good as a princess's when it came to finding each and every one. The only reason he had spent so much time in his room wasn't the bed; it was the door—and the way it kept the world on the other side of it.

Looking at the front door, just off the living room, and his bedroom door, just off the hallway to the bathroom, it struck Dev as overkill, putting up with a mattress he didn't like just to place an additional door between him and the people who weren't around to bother him anymore. Trying to recall the last time he'd felt comfortable horizontally, what surfaced was the memory of lying on his father's chest as they lay on the living room couch together, taking a break from flying.

What he remembered was his dad's steady hand on his back, keeping him safe, the waterbed lullaby of his breathing growing shallower as Dev grew sleepier. Even the way the warmth had left his father's body was tranquilizing, like finding the cool spot on a pillow. He hadn't woken up until his mother had opened the front door. And even after he had, he hadn't moved, not wanting to wake his dad. It was the last good sleep Dev got for a while, thanks to his mother's suddenly crying all the time.

He looked at the couch now, as full of ghost dents as his second-hand mattress. The difference was he loved the ghost who'd first made those dents, the last person he could remember to whom the word *love* truly applied. And so Dev grabbed the blanket and pillows from his room and took them to the couch. He placed the clock on the coffee table, and his head on the pillow, scrunched up next to the arm of the couch where his father—his real father—had died with him in his arms. That—and not having a target on his back anymore—made a world of difference when it came to sleeping, which Dev proceeded to do—just like a baby.

"Priorities."

Under the happy-doomsday note, he'd written a reminder for the day: he needed to set priorities. Like most invalids (and those treated like invalids), Dev hadn't had to worry about setting priorities before the whatever-it-was. His parents—the real one and the fake—had set priorities for him, leaving Dev to focus obsessively on trivia and vacuum cleaners. But now that his caretakers had taken their leave, well, Dev had better get busy deciding what needed to be decided. He hoped he'd do a better job of it than he had picking friends.

"First things first," he said out loud, raking a hand through his hair before giving his tangled mane a shake. He could feel the previous day on his fingers, rubbed two together, felt the oiliness, sniffed it too. Yep. "Shower," he announced to the nobody who cared whether he took one or not.

Dev knew that a lot of Aspies don't care for showers. The drops hitting their skin either tickle like feathers, feel like someone trying to get their attention, or pelt them like hail the size of golf balls. This aversion to showering often leads to a side benefit only an Aspie could appreciate: a significant increase in personal space. And Dev appreciated this—he did—except that smell was one of his amped-up senses, one that didn't distinguish between his stench and that of others when it came to being offended.

Not that he didn't have showering issues. There'd been a lot of experimenting with water pressure and showerheads before they found the Goldilocks combination that was *just right*. First, no interruptions in flow—no syncopation or strobe effects like with most shower massagers. For Dev, the sudden on-off pressure was like an anxiety machine gun, his body tensing between each pulse until he either jumped out of the shower, threw up, or both. Second, the stream couldn't be too misty or too tight. The former felt like someone blowing, the latter like being poked by broom handles. Heavy rain was what he needed—a downpour. He had to not feel the individual drops, but instead a constant, wet embrace.

Once they'd found the right combination, his parents had noted that keeping Dev clean wasn't a problem anymore; keeping him dry was. "Again?" his stepfather would ask as Dev walked from his bedroom to the bathroom wearing nothing but boxers.

"Panic attack," he'd learned to reply, a justification that caused his stepfather to shoo him on, throwing in the proverbial towel.

Taking a shower that first post-whatever morning, Dev's enjoyment was tainted by the realization that it couldn't last. Sooner or later, the taps would tap out, the spigots squeak with nothing to show for it. He had no doubt about getting enough water; it fell from the sky, after all. Purification? He had downloaded instructions from the internet while he still had it. But what about water pressure? Would gravity and acceleration be enough? Could he hoist a bucket so that when he dumped the water over himself, the effect would be the same as that of the showers to which he'd grown not only accustomed, but depended upon for mental as well as physical hygiene? Seemed it would have to be an awfully short shower, or an awfully big bucket. And getting it high enough so it came down hard enough meant he couldn't do it in the house, so winter was going to be a problem. Plus, for all he knew, just waiting for that quick hit of water might produce more anxiety than the dousing could possibly alleviate.

"Okay," Dev said to his reflection after wiping away the steam, "Project Number One: The Shower Situation."

The problem with establishing priorities based upon projecting how much you're going to miss something is this: that's not how priorities work. Set one, and as you move through your day, you quickly realize how interconnected everything is. Take the shower project. Getting a decent shower would mean using all three of the utilities currently on life support: water, gas, and electricity—the first for obvious reasons, the second for heat, and the third to create enough pressure. Rain could replace the faucet, the fireplace would serve as water heater, and he'd heard enough generators put-putting around the neighborhood whenever there was a blackout to know where to get the electricity. The last puzzle piece was a pump of some sort to create pressure.

Fortunately, Dev was familiar with something that worked a lot like a pump, thanks to his obsession with vacuum cleaners, including the subset of wet/dry Shop-Vacs. The average such machine had two ports for attaching a hose: one for suction, the other for blowing. His stepfather had used theirs to drain the laundry room after a blocked sink left it flooded. Dev could just fill the collection drum with hot water, fit the hose with a showerhead, and instead of sucking water into the drum, flush it out. Use a dimmer switch to adjust how fast the water pumped, which would translate into pressure on Dev's end.

But then priority creep settled in. Generators need gasoline. Fine. Dev could get it from the SUVs parked all over the neighborhood. Except something happened to gasoline when it lay around too long— something his stepfather always remembered too late, the first time each season he went to use the snowblower or lawnmower. Presumably, gas stations had something to keep the gas from settling, but gas station pumps ran on electricity. To get a decent shower, Dev was going to need gasoline to get electricity, and electricity to get gasoline.

So he'd need to ration the energy situation. What else couldn't he live without that needed electricity? Most of his gadgets ran on rechargeable batteries, meaning he could run the generator, charge them, and then turn it off. Light? There were candles, kerosene lamps, the fireplace, those solar-powered path lights everybody seemed to have nowadays. So what else?

As if in answer, the refrigerator's compressor switched on and started cycling.

Crap, Dev thought.

A freezer seemed obvious, at least for the warmer months, to keep frozen however much frozen meat he managed to rescue from the world's last and longest blackout. As far as how much meat that might amount to, the hunter next door had a dedicated freezer in his garage for storing venison. It was empty at the moment, he'd heard his neighbor tell his stepfather, thanks to two missed deer-hunting seasons: the first because his neighbor had accidentally shot himself, and the second because his neighbor's hunting buddies wouldn't let it drop.

As far as the fuel situation went, he wouldn't have to run the freezer constantly. Once it got down to freezing, he'd work out a schedule, limiting the times it was opened to keep the cold in. Dev remembered his mother and her husband having the same argument whenever the power went out.

"Just keep the door shut and we'll be fine," his stepdad would insist.

"But what about food pois—"

"The last time you defrosted," he'd cut her off. "Remind me again, how long did that take?"

These arguments invariably ended with his mom telling the step that nobody liked a know-it-all, followed by said step reminding her she'd married two.

But did he need a refrigerator too? Dev opened his own to see what needed to be kept cold that he couldn't live without. Ketchup, mustard, salad dressing, lunch meat, a six-pack of beer minus two, orange juice, milk, cheese, cottage cheese, mayonnaise, some diet pop, the last batch of his mother's chicken soup (ever), an aluminum foil brick he knew to contain emergency cash intended to fool burglars if they ever got robbed, and that was about it. Dev was all ready to move on, when he bumped aside a tub of butter and his heart sank.

Crap, Dev thought.

Eggs were what Dev had for breakfast, the most important meal of the day. Cereal? Not breakfast. Breakfast bars? False advertising. Pop-Tarts? Be healthier smoking a pack of cigarettes. As far as he was concerned, all such breakfast impersonators were stomach occupiers that left him feeling bloated and vaguely depressed.

"But it's fiber," his own mother had tried one day after carelessly running out of eggs and replacing them with a bran muffin.

"Fiber is for old people," Dev rebutted this lame bait and switch. "It helps them poop. I don't have *any problem* pooping."

Dev looked inside the carton—complete, minus the two for breakfast the morning before. Assuming two eggs per day, that meant he had five days of breakfast left—well within the carton's expiration date, but far short of Dev's own. Even if he raided his neighbors' refrigerators, the expiration dates wouldn't be much more than a month on either side of the one he was staring at now like the second set of numbers on a tombstone: his.

Was that overdoing it? Dev didn't think so and had learned he could blame his amygdala. The catastrophe in this situation? It was simple. Breakfast was the most important meal of the day, but without eggs, he'd have to skip it. But without the most important meal of the day, how could said day begin? It couldn't, clearly. He might as well stay in bed. And if his day never started, how was he supposed to get to lunch, and from lunch to dinner? That was equally obvious; he couldn't. So: no eggs, no food; no food, no Dev; ipso facto, egglessness equaled Devlessness.

Even with all the gasoline in the world and a refrigerator full of eggs, eating them for every meal with hard-boiled snacks in between until he looked like he might start laying his own, eventually he'd run out or they'd go bad. Meaning Dev was a goner unless . . .

Exiting the house and walking the street, Dev picked the biggest pickup he could find, the owner of which was still seated inside, keys in the ignition, engine off, forehead resting on the dash. It was impossible to tell if he'd just returned or was just heading out. In either case, he was dead now and so Dev unbuckled the body, pulled it out, and hoisted himself up behind the steering wheel. He'd already raided the unlocked garages in the neighborhood for some of the supplies he might need, including: the rifle from last night, ammunition, a pair of leather work gloves, bolt cutters, a sledgehammer, duct tape, bungee cords, three empty pet carriers, rope, an ax, a machete, a chain saw, a case of water, and a roll of chicken wire, mainly because of the name. All of these were piled into the bed of the pickup truck, after which Dev pickpocketed a few of his neighbors' credit cards, in case he needed more gas and the pumps' card readers still worked.

To chart his route to farm country, he resorted once again to his phone and Google Maps, figuring he should take advantage while he still could. He drove toward the relatively unroaded parts of the map, where the grids of cities yielded to solitary offshoots snaking through large areas of gray or green but not blue, to avoid driving into one of the state's eleven thousand lakes, not counting the great ones surrounding it. Along the way, Dev made use of side streets, gravel and mud roads, parking lots, sidewalks, lawns, and vacant fields—pretty much anything reasonably flat and body-free. But he drove so slowly that after an hour, he was still passing through retail areas interspersed with suburban neighborhoods and industrial stretches sporting tank farms and smokestacks that had stopped staining the sky around them, before repeating the pattern all over again. The only thing that changed, and not by much, was the street signs, alternating between dead presidents and trees that didn't grow there anymore, with a little unpronounceable French in between.

Eventually, this sense of déjà vu started working in Dev's favor, overwhelming his need to map with sheer monotony, kind of like how a file-compression utility minimizes the need for disk space. And so he pushed it up to thirty, didn't puke, and goosed it to thirty-five. Still puke-free, thirty-five became forty, became forty-five, then fifty. Thus Dev discovered the attraction of speed: it made the boring stuff go by faster. Soon, the strip malls, tract homes, and "Coming Soon" signs yielded to open stretches of grassland, then woodland, then billboards for outlet stores, antiques, bait shops, and truck stops. Dev was doing fifty-five (still fifteen miles below the limit) when he noticed an interesting thing about driving several tons of metal at that velocity: smaller stuff lost, every time. As long as he avoided trees and brick walls, it was smooth sailing, with the occasional glance in the rearview for flying fur or feathers.

Another hour in and Dev was passing signs for pick-your-own farms, followed by vast stubble fields dotted with rolled bales of hay, collapsing barns, and horses posing for postcards. Everywhere else, vast green, leafy swaths of corn, the stalks about thirty inches high, in rows miles long. Turning down a stretch passing between fields of the stuff, Dev started seeing signs posted on telephone poles, trees, stop signs. Some were little more than cardboard and Magic Marker, others laser printed on fancy, colored stock, while one was just a paper plate with the bottom sliced into phone-number tags for ripping off. Each sign was an advertisement for the local lifestyle: tractor repairs, tractor for sale, tractor for parts, the name of a lawyer who specialized in tractor accidents. And then, on a scrap of lumber nailed to a tree and painted in whitewash white—"Fresh Eggs"—followed by an arrow pointing up.

Turning from pavement, Dev drove down a dirt road flanked on either side by fields of stunted green corn stalks that appeared to be shaking with more than the breeze. It seemed like cows that had been grazing elsewhere when the whatever-it-was happened had wandered wherever their bovine curiosity took them, which for some was the cornfields he was just now driving between, broken stalks tipping into the dirt road before being smacked out of the way by the truck's bumper. From the cab, Dev could see the cows drawing nearer, their legs eclipsed by leaves and shadow, their big heads and shoulders hovering above the green, looking like hippos wading through swamp. The cattle seemed curious but unhurried, ambling amiably his way, exuding the animal confidence that comes with hauling around a ton of beef packed to your bones.

Dev stopped to let one cow pass, only to be ambushed by another, its black-and-white head gliding through the field until the corn parted and there was the whole thing, its barrel-muscled chest intimidating just by being there, its tongue pressing obscenely against the driver-side window. Yelping like a stepped-on poodle, Dev began pounding on the car's horn to scare the animal away—stopping only when he felt the earth rumbling underneath him.

He wasn't sure how many charging cows constituted a stampede but figured even one, aimed unfortunately, was too much. And so he went back to the horn, hammering away at it, creating, he hoped, enough of a deterrent so the leaderless cattle drive heading his way would take however many cloven steps were needed to avoid a head-on collision with the source of all that racket. Just in case, he hit the alarm, his high beams, and the hazard lights too. And the wave of cattle parted around him, judging by the sound of it, the gonging of vegetable matter against metal sliding into a gentle swish. In all, it was perhaps a minute of pure terror; Dev couldn't be sure because even after the ground stopped shaking, his body kept going, his eyes closed, his pulse sounding like the ocean in his ears. Why his brain didn't hit "Ctrl-Alt-Del," he didn't know, but he was grateful it hadn't, especially since there was no one left to make sure he rebooted with all his files.

When Dev finally opened his eyes, all he could see was the haze of settled pesticide dusting the windshield followed by leaves and crippled stalks once he flicked on the wipers. And then something he hadn't seen before, but could now that the cows had mowed down all the carefully planted rows stretching to the horizon on either side of him. In the distance off to his right, a farmhouse stood, visible through his passenger-side window, asterisked with corn spatter. Next to the house sat a tractor that had stopped in the middle of some tractor business, now playing roost to a bunch of crows. Set a little ways farther back from the house and idle tractor, a barn and, next to that, a white building on stilts with a pair of gangplanks leading up on either side. The building was covered by an extended roof like a front porch and screened in, appropriately enough, by chicken wire.

"Bingo," Dev whispered, as if the sound of his voice, even this far away, might make it all disappear.

He'd googled raising chickens before setting out on his quest for the sustainable breakfast. The math suggested he needed about four hens and a rooster. That way, he could set aside some eggs for food and the rest for future generations. While chickens can live for eight to ten years, he had no way of knowing how much of that time the grown specimens he'd be starting with had already burned through. So it would be prudent to get started on that next generation sooner rather than later—especially since he had no intention of coming out this way again, even if there was a chance there'd be anything left when he did.

He thought about getting two roosters, one for backup, not wanting to put all his egg fertilizers in one basket. But when he entered the coop, he found it was actually two coops, each with about ten hens and one rooster, each feathered harem walled off from the other. In retrospect, those walls should have been a hint, as should the fact that cockfighting was still a thing in some of the world's more savage places. But the phenomenon of cockfighting had never really crossed his radar. And so, after picking his four hens and packing them away in two of the pet carriers following the recommended handling instructions he'd googled, Dev returned to the divided coop with his third and last carrier.

The hens hadn't minded each having a roommate; considering the coop situation, sharing space with just one other bird instead of nine must have seemed almost like a private room. Dev saw no reason why the roosters should be any different. Sure, the first had put up a squawk—literally—when Dev entered his territory, but those YouTube videos on how to hypnotize a chicken had come in handy. Wearing work gloves, he'd scooped the bird up, pressed its head to the floor, and then drew a line with his finger, starting at the bird's beak and drawing it out until the rooster's eyes crossed and it went limp. He'd then set him aside until it was the rooster's turn for crating, when he snapped out of it and resumed his angry, but now pointless clucking.

The plan for the backup rooster was to repeat the same steps used with number one. Unfortunately, while his human stink had proved an annoyance to the first rooster, introducing a direct breeding competitor (albeit caged) into another bird's territory proved utterly unacceptable. He hadn't even gotten the crated rooster all the way through the door when the backup bird cocked its head one way, then the other, its comb flopping like a bad comb-over, while at the same time, the carrier began jerking wildly as the other ball of territorial feathers thumped about every compass point in his shrunk-down world. Looking down, Dev saw talons hooked through the carrier's grate. A stabbing beak followed, and it was all he could do, just holding on, as the uncrated bird came at him—*them*—claws first and crowing like dawn hadn't just broken but exploded into a million pieces.

Backing away, Dev slipped and dropped the carrier, which proceeded to scoot and rumble around the hay-and-excrement-strewn floor, the uncrated bantam riding it, half fighting, half trying to breed. And for a moment, all Dev could do was watch, amazed by the unimaginable sordidness that went into a protein-dense breakfast.

In the end, he broke up the cockfight by sliding the pet carrier back through the doorway and then pulling the plywood sheet after it, so the rooster riding had to decide whether to keep hump fighting with broken legs or just give up and let go.

"I think I'll call you Lucky," Dev said to the crated rooster after draping a towel over the cage to simulate night and then strapping it into the passenger seat. "That goes for all of you," he added, looking at the rearview mirror reflecting the two carriers he'd strapped into the back. Along with the chickens, he'd raided the barn for bags of feed, a bale of hay, an incubator, and several years' worth of the *Farmers' Almanac*. As for the inevitable, there was an ax and a foot-driven sharpening wheel. But even this eventual fate was better than what waited for the ones he was leaving behind. The local predators might be fooled by habit into leaving the untended chickens and cattle and horses alone, but eventually they'd figure it out. The darkened farmhouse at night, the overgrown fields, no more smell of diesel in the air or the sound of farm equipment. Or maybe they'd just catch a whiff of rot on the wind and follow it back to dead farmhands . . .

"Yep," Dev said, steadying the rooster's crate while he eyed the hens in back, "I'm calling all of you Lucky." He paused before adding, "It'll be easier that way."

13

After getting home from not blowing himself up, Mo-now-Marcus found to his surprise that there was still some electricity and most of the internet left, which he decided to celebrate by downloading and playing some of the loudest, head-banging-est, Satan-loving-est death metal he could find, the sort that could make a teenage boy's heart feel its most alive because that's what Marcus still was: *alive!* The bass made the windows wobble and hit him in the chest like the explosion from his suicide vest. Looking at his reflection bowing in and out, he flashed devil horns with both fists, because this Marcus guy never did anything halfway, including apostasy.

The thing with head banging, though—after a while, that's what it feels like: like you're banging your head against a wall. And though Marcus had his reasons for doing so—first to knock some sense in, and next to justify with physical pain the tears that kept coming for all he'd lost—after about a week, he could tell it was time to stop and did so. The problem was, even once the music stopped, the windows still wobbled while the floor underneath his feet kept on shaking.

Earthquake, he thought, in the blasé way he affected, though it had been harder since nearly becoming collateral damage outside the 7-Eleven. But blasé or not, Marcus knew he shouldn't be in his bedroom where the floor could collapse out from under him. He should be at ground level, under the arched doorway between the living room and kitchen. The wall it was in was load bearing, and the arch itself provided additional, structural strength, should things start falling down around him, as they occasionally did ever since the frackers came, along with informational pamphlets about the importance of load-bearing walls and standing under archways during an earthquake. So Marcus took the steps two at a time to the living room, which was surprisingly dark for the middle of the day.

He'd thrown open the curtains after getting home from not blowing himself up, seeing as there were no neighbors to see anything anymore. And he'd left the curtains open ever since, getting a certain thrill, walking in front of them naked just because he could. The point was, at this time of day, on a day like this, the living room should be bright and cheery, not buried in gloom.

But then he saw them, blocking the ground floor windows on all sides of the house. Pigs, both domesticated and feral, their squeals pitched high and hanging over the heavy bass of their hooves. Oklahoma's neighbor state Texas had been breeding the sausage kind since the mid-1800s, according to his ag studies teacher, an antikosher and/or halal neo-Nazi aptly named Bücher but pronounced *butcher* behind his back. The fanged kind—per the same source—had been imported as Eurasian wild boar in the 1930s by Texas sportsmen for target practice. But then "nature kinda ran away with itself—you boys know what I mean—and lo and behold: hogpocalypse." The Butcher had gone on to explain that the feral pig population in the US had exploded to around six million or roughly one pig for every fifty people, and they'd spread to nearly every southern state, including Oklahoma and as far east as Florida and up through Georgia into the Carolinas, causing approximately $2 billion in damage and control costs per year.

"And you're probably wondering why I'm yammering on about this," Mr. Bücher said, preparing to bring his lecture in for a landing. "It's because swine eradication's gonna be the next growth industry, boys. Once this fracking thing taps out, it's all gonna be about hunting hogs." He closed by doing his Porky Pig impersonation, waving the class out with a "Th-th-that's all, folks!"

That lecture had left Mo-now-Marcus with a greater appreciation for religious prohibitions against eating pork—a sentiment only strengthened by his current predicament. He'd taken the class only because all the football players took the class, an easy GPA booster for those who might need the buffer. Who knew a blow-off class for jocks might actually come in handy—if only for explaining his current predicament.

Speaking of which: there had to be about twenty pigs out there, a half-dozen domesticated monsters lumbering about, bumping into the side of the house, making the walls shake, and the rest, these smaller but scarier fanged variety, covered in wiry hair and rooting up clods of lawn with their preternaturally long snouts. Both varieties of pigs were omnivores, he remembered from the lecture, but didn't need to; he could see it for himself, especially after he tried to scare a path through them with his father's shotgun and watched them cannibalize the one pig he'd made a lesson of. After that, there was really nothing to do but wait them out as the pigs ate their way through whatever parts of the local landscape they found tasty.

Lucy hadn't heard Sir Sheds when he wrapped himself in his leash, the dog's reaction to that particular humiliation being an embarrassed whimper. But she heard him this time, a full-throated bark that sounded like it was coming from a much larger animal. Going to the window, she saw what warranted so much noise from such a little dog: rats. Dozens of them, skittering in waves down the street like something out of the Pied Piper story, minus the flute.

Lucy was appalled. She hated rats deep down in her DNA. She hated the way the sun stretched out their shadows, making them look even bigger, more hunchbacked. And she hated watching Sir Sheds straining at his leash, each bark propelling him upward like he'd fly if he could. She felt like darting out and snatching him inside, safe and away from the steady, rodential flow polluting her once-decent neighborhood. But there'd be the hassle of undoing the leash, the possibility of Sir Sheds bounding out of her arms to join the rats because there was no way he was beating them, stupid dog. Under all that fur, he probably wasn't much bigger than they were. Fortunately, the actual rodents didn't seem to notice the yapping mutt attempting to fly in their direction. They were too busy getting to where they were going—a destination Lucy could guess: the bodies, of course.

The bodies had spent about a week in the Georgia sun by then, plenty of time to get fragrant. Lucy herself had started using her hair like a wind vane, letting her know where to point her face if she didn't want to get sick every time she went outside. She kept telling herself to go to the army surplus downtown, get herself a gas mask, one with charcoal canisters for capturing sarin or whatever. Except every time she went out, her plans and thoughts scattered, replaced by one overriding need: getting back inside.

So: rats.

Of course.

They had rotting flesh to get to. And once their numbers dwindled to a few then none, Lucy figured she'd seen the worst when it came to unwelcome critters parading through her designated comfort zone—an uncharacteristically upbeat thought for a girl whose chosen color was black. It just never occurred to her that instead of running toward something, it was equally likely they were running away.

Marcus went back to his room on the second floor to get a better idea of how many there were only to realize that they were still gathering. In the distance he could see several more of the domesticated variety, likely escaped from family farms and petting zoos, huffing and hoofing after their fleeter cousins, eager to get in on the everything buffet the avant-garde of the species had found to its delight, finally and completely unguarded.

Mr. Bücher had said that pigs were incredibly smart animals, and here they were in the process of proving it, by consolidating, by seeking out more of their number and joining the strength those numbers offered. His handlers had pitched jihad and the new caliphate to him in much the same way—conveniently ignoring how counterproductive it was to encourage new members to blow themselves up. Looking now at these porcine inheritors of earth, he couldn't imagine any of them being stupid enough to put on a suicide vest. Nope, it took the pigheaded—not pigs—to do something like that.

Abandoning his attempts at conducting a local pig census—it was a moving target, after all—Mo moved on to the view from his parents' bedroom window, to better survey the damage from whence they'd come. There, across the street, his neighbor's lawn was completely gone, replaced by trampled mud and bits of bushes tossed off to the side like parsley. It had gone worse for the neighbor herself: the wife. She'd died in the driveway, car door still open, groceries dropped. Now there was no evidence of her or the groceries. The car's door had been bumped off its hinges, the car itself, knocked partway onto another neighbor's lawn, one tire rubbed till it blew out, the lack of clearance the only thing that spared the grass underneath the chassis, resting there unmolested like the car's dark-green shadow.

The pigs had buzz cut the earth, mowing everything down to the dirt. Moving back to his bedroom window, Marcus watched as the growing herd finished up with his yard before moving on to the next-door neighbor's, the one he shared a fence with—the fence the herd made short work of, the chain link sprung and unraveling. He looked down with a certain grim satisfaction at where the uniforms that had charged his family to tear down his swing set had been working before. They'd died like everybody else, leaving their bodies in the backyard for him to look at when he'd gotten back from school. He'd not thought much of them, other than thinking a silent, *Good riddance*, in their direction. And now that the pigs had been through, the only things left were metal buckles, key rings, hard hats . . .

"Good riddance," Marcus said aloud, imagining the foreman's passage through pig guts, regretting only that it hadn't happened sooner, before the swing set came down. Though he hadn't used it in years, he thought he might like to hear the old chains squeak a few more times before going to wherever the pigs weren't.

When Lucy woke to noise in the middle of the night, she took it for thunder or a passing train. Groggily, she had to remind herself that the second wasn't likely anymore, occupying her brain just enough so she didn't stop to wonder where the lightning was if that really was thunder. Instead, she pulled a pillow over her head and dreamed she was on a train, rocking her to sleep in both the dream and the real world too.

In the morning, she saw how mistaken she was about the sound from the night before. In her defense, however, she'd never personally heard a herd of pigs stampede before. She'd heard about the feral pig problem on the radio farm report as she scanned through stations, trying to find something other than right-wing bloviators and pulpit-pounding preachers. But that was the closest they'd ever gotten to the Buckhead region of Atlanta. Perhaps the smell of still-living humans had kept them at bay; perhaps it was just the traffic-choked freeways. But now that both those perhaps had been rendered nonapplicable . . .

That's when she realized the rats hadn't been running to but from. Good for you, rats. Smart. Not like . . .

Lucy stopped. Thought: *Sir Sheds!* Ran to the front door, opened it, saw not just the mess the pigs had left behind, but also what they hadn't. As inadvertently foretold, all that was left were a few hairs and a plop of dog poop. They'd also left some blood spatters, the metal clip from the leash, the buckle from the collar, and part of an ear, presumably Sir Sheds's, though she'd never seen one before, just felt them here and there, under his fur.

She wanted to cry, but didn't, realizing she hadn't before—not for all the people who, she now admitted, must have included her family. The loss hit her through a complicated combination shot by way of Sir Sheds: she wanted to tell her mother what had happened to her dog. And that's when it all came crashing down: the . . . rest of it was made out of people, like Soylent Green, including all the people she'd ever known and loved. There was no one left to talk to about it or anything else, ever. No shoulders left to cry on—ever—not anymore.

She hadn't cried back then—*couldn't*—because she was too stunned. And the passage of time hadn't lessened the yawning nothingness she felt whenever she tried to feel something. If anything, she was even more stunned now.

Stunned: as she kicked in the door of her neighbor's house, the one with the car in the drive. Stunned: as she plucked his keys out of the ashtray on the coffee table next to the couch where the owner had been napping before his nap was extended indefinitely. Stunned: as she revved the engine and drove away from the lawns and flower beds of her neighborhood, all turned over, dirt-side up. Stunned: as she drove—stunned block after stunned block—until she came to a place it seemed like the pigs hadn't gotten to yet and then kept driving, thataway: stunned.

14

Dev set the chickens up in the attached garage, splitting up the floor space with strewn hay, potting soil for dirt baths, and laundry baskets lined with his parents' old clothes for nesting. Water was delivered via the plastic tub his stepfather used to soak his aching feet after standing all day, washed thoroughly to remove any lingering traces of Epsom salt, while feed was delivered through the same handheld broadcast spreader his stepdad had used during the winter to salt the sidewalk. As chicken coops went, sure, it was on the minimalist side, but what it lacked in accommodations, it made up for in space—at least compared with the coop they'd come from.

It was while he stood over the kitchen sink by the window, rinsing feathers and hay out of his stepdad's footbath, that Dev spotted him: the neighbor's dog, a black Lab named Diablo, waiting to be let in the door just off his owner's back porch. He wasn't howling; he wasn't scratching at the door, just sitting at attention. He'd been locked out for about a week since the whatever-it-was, and in all that time, Dev hadn't heard him bark, even though his food bowl and water dish were both empty. What he'd subsisted on during that time—rats, rabbits, birds?—Dev didn't know, but one thing was clear: all told, the dog seemed to be handling doomsday exceptionally well.

Dev's stepdad had hated Diablo—used to say Diablo was a good name for a hellhound. The feeling was apparently mutual. The only time Dev could remember the dog making any noise was when his stepfather crossed through their backyard, wearing his pharmacy jacket. "Maybe you remind him of the vet," his mom had tried, which angered the pharmacist even more, as if such a misunderstanding was a willful affront to the profession of pill dispensation.

Personally, Dev never had any trouble with the dog. Back in the days of the comfort animal debate, he'd decided he wanted a black Lab, just like Diablo. Before getting distracted by the end of the world, he'd looked forward to seeing his neighbor's dog when he left for school in the morning and returned in the afternoon. Diablo was always there, the only creature on the planet visibly happy to see him.

Unlike the moods of humans, Diablo's weren't subtle; they shouted themselves with every muscle of the dog's body. They were so loud even Dev understood them. Sometimes, doing the dishes at the kitchen sink, looking out at Diablo's run, he'd wave to the dog, imagining they could read each other's minds, the dog's thoughts being in type large enough even an Aspie could read them.

Bolting through the back door and up to the fence line, Dev reached over to pet his animal buddy. "Hey there, devil dog," he said, scratching behind a big, floppy black ear. "You're a good dog, aren't you, huh? Such a good dog. How'd I forget about such a good dog?"

Judging from Diablo's tongue, lapping away at his free hand through the chain-link fence, his forgetting was already forgotten. Instead, the dog's eyes just angled up at him, full of animal adoration. Seeing the look, Dev stopped scratching. "Listen, buddy," he began—redundantly, seeing as the dog was obviously all ears to whatever his human had to say. "I've got some bad news . . ."

All in all, Diablo took the news that his owners were never coming home reasonably well, especially since Dev leavened it with the news that he had decided to adopt the devil dog.

"Would you like that?" he asked, cheating by asking it after he'd returned from the kitchen with two Tupperware bowls, one full of water, the other a can of Campbell's Chunky beef stew. Afterward, wherever his boy went, Diablo went too.

And that's how Dev figured he avoided talking to a soccer ball named Wilson—not that he really believed he was capable of such a thing, dog or no dog. Dev was an aficionado of aloneness—always had been. In a position to serve it, he'd have done solitary confinement on his head. A dog-less postapocalyptic world would be a piece of cake. But having a dog was nice, even if his need for a comfort animal seemed largely to go away—along with all the people who'd made him uncomfortable.

For having spent most of his life outside, Diablo adjusted to the indoors pretty quickly. After dinner and a little stargazing, during which Dev felt compelled to point out Sirius, the Dog Star, the two settled in for a good night's sleep: the human on the living room couch and Diablo . . . also on the couch, on top of Dev. At first, he tried pushing the animal off, but then noticed how the dog's weight pressing down on him actually felt good. It was Dev's paradoxical relationship with being touched: light touches freaked him out, while being squeezed calmed him down, just like those high-pressure showers of his.

"You know what," he said, addressing Diablo, whose nose was conveniently close to his own. "On second thought, stay. This is good. You're good where you're at."

Dev yanked the chain on the little lamp next to the couch on the end table, and the house went dark. He could feel Diablo lowering his head to his chest and had a fleeting moment of déjà vu, back to when he'd fallen asleep as his father held him, only the roles were flipped this time—Diablo was Dev, and Dev was his father. His *real* father—the one who visited him in a dream that night, for the first time in a long time.

"How's the ticker?" his dream dad asked.

"The what?"

"Ticker," his dad said. "Your heart."

"Kind of heavy," Dev said in the dream, feeling the weight of Diablo pressing down on him through the fog of sleep. "Like it's full of something."

"That's responsibility," his dream dad said. "And love."

"I thought love was supposed to be like fireworks," the boy said.

"Nope," his dream dad said. "It's like a lump in your throat. But in your heart."

"Oh," Dev said in the dream, thinking it sounded more like a blood clot than love, but not quibbling for once.

The next day was perfect. It should have been a school day but wasn't and never would be again. Dev and Diablo woke at the same time, to the same sound: the rooster in the garage, crowing. Though Dev had closed the overhead door against any wandering critters with a taste for poultry, there were windows in the front through which the rising sun made itself known, knifing through the dark, igniting the rooster's spidey senses. With a reinforced door and insulated walls between the rooster and them, the noise of its crowing was muffled just enough so that it woke them without causing Diablo to bark wildly or Dev to want to break things.

"Morning, devil dog," he said, opening his eyes to the big, wet eyes of his buddy and blanket. Diablo's big paws were resting, sphinxlike in front of him, one on each of his human's shoulders. At the sound of Dev's voice, the dog proceeded to lick the Labrador crap out of him until the boy just had to laugh—something he'd almost never *had* to do before. As it turned out, he liked it. The way his insides jiggled felt good—like exercise, but without boring him to death.

Of course, there were limits.

"Okay, okay," he finally protested. "I'm getting pruney already."

Feeling Dev push up ever so slightly, Diablo took the hint and relocated himself to the floor with a quick clatter of dog nails on hardwood.

"Guess I should have warned you about the roommates," he said, his head tilted toward the garage. "And"—reaching for the still-wound alarm clock—"guess we won't be needing this." After unsetting the alarm, he rested his hands on his knees and rubbed them, back and forth, contemplatively.

"So," he announced, "got any plans for the day?"

Dev did. Several, actually. Plenty for both of them. Having plans was one of the things that would make the day perfect. Because nothing beat nothing like something, and now that Dev was on his own, he had plenty of somethings to do. Like locating the Shop-Vac for when the shower went out. Like making breakfast with eggs fresh from his own chickens. Like setting the neighbor's lawn on fire . . .

Not that arson was the original plan. He'd started the way he assumed he should, with a shovel, rake, hoe, and the bag of feed corn he planned to plant to ensure a supply of chicken feed into the foreseeable (and sustainable) future. But it was a big yard, and cultivating was hard, turning the soil over a shovelful at a time. After picking through the first few clumps, sifting and inspecting to make sure there was no grass or grass roots that'd take hold again, Dev looked around and realized that the combination of the yard's square footage and his OCD would mean he'd still be at it by the time the first flakes fell.

But then he remembered a show on PBS his mom watched, about the history of agriculture and something called "slash-and-burn" farming. It wasn't necessarily the most environmentally friendly form of farming, especially not when practiced in the Amazon rain forest, but Dev figured that nothing he could do would reverse the environmental boon of everyone else being dead.

And so he took the gallon of gasoline his neighbor had set aside for his lawn mower, dumped it into a sprinkling can, and sprinkled the lawn from corner to corner, before stepping back to his side of the fence and flicking a match. Diablo woofed as his old world was swallowed up by a circle of flame spreading outward from where the match landed, like ripples running away from a stone. The fire was pale in the sunlight, manifesting itself more as heat shimmers, as the grass itself darkened, then lightened, becoming a thousand tiny embers before blowing away and turning to ash as they cooled: an early, gray snow. Eventually, the fire died as its fuel did, leaving dirt above, dead, compost-ready roots below.

A pick, a hoe, a rake—lots of sweat, but laughing in spite of it—Diablo playing foreman (or foredog) while Dev did all the work. "We're getting there," he said, mopping his brow with his sleeve before removing his shirt. The early-summer breeze on his sweaty skin felt like a miracle. Why hadn't anyone ever told him about this? To hear his stepfather tell it, any work that involved sweating might as well be done by an ape. To hear the television tell it, the very act of sweating was something embarrassing and in need of chemical prevention. Apparently, sweating was just another one of those things the neurotypicals got wrong.

"I'd invite you to join me," Dev said, addressing his furry friend. "But dogs don't sweat; they pant." He paused. "Which you're free to continue doing, by the way." Diablo, as if waiting for the permission, panted even harder, like watching his human work was pretty hard work itself.

Once the corn was planted, Dev showered again because he could—still, for the time being, without needing gasoline for a generator to run a Shop-Vac backward. After dressing, it was time for lunch, some soup and a sandwich from what remained of the refrigerator's lunch meat and a can from the kitchen cabinet. Diablo got some kind of stew again, which seemed to be his favorite stew, i.e., some kind. Dev, meanwhile, read the cans' labels while he ate, a habit going back as far as he could remember.

This time was different, however. This time, Dev didn't look at the labels as exercise for his eyes or something to kill time while he chewed.

This time, he actually looked at the ingredients and their percentages with an eye toward actually living off the stuff. "I'm going to have a heart attack before I'm twenty," he announced to Diablo. "The sodium alone is off the charts. My head will literally explode."

Diablo looked up from his some kind of stew.

"We're going to have to do something about this," Dev said, and after lunch, they did.

Just like he'd read the labels with fresh, postapocalyptic eyes, Dev toured his neighborhood after lunch, looking at how much of it he could eat. And to those new eyes, the world suddenly seemed like a Jewish mother in a sitcom; it wanted him to "Eat, eat . . ." Food didn't rain down like manna, per se; it sprang up like dandelions, mushrooms, rhubarb, wild strawberries, blueberries, raspberries, sunflowers—all already there with no effort on his part but partaking. Food also came hopping in and flying over and swimming by. Sure, it'd be a while before he trusted the Ecorse River as a food source, but eventually even it would provide a meal or two a week, the catch fresher than anything he could have gotten at Kroger's before the whatever-it-was.

There was, of course, a certain amount of skill required to differentiate food from poison when it came to flora and fungus. Fortunately, his stepfather, the cheapskate, had several books on foraging and freeganism he'd bought for pennies at yard sales, determined to stretch the family's food dollar by means of free salad that he'd scavenge and prepare but never partake of, being a devout carnivore. He'd forage a T-bone if he could, he'd said, but hunting in residential areas was frowned upon, at least back then. Not to say that he didn't come close. He once fought over the ownership of some roadkill, pulling off to the shoulder while the driver who'd grilled it was still stunned from being punched in the face by his airbag. When he'd returned home, the blood in his stepdad's trunk attested to how close they'd come to eating free venison, while the blind sockets where his headlights had been attested to the persuasive power of a tire iron.

The point was Dev's little corner of the world was a bountiful place, despite the suburban kitsch of lawn gnomes, fake geese, or waterless bird baths topped with colorfully mirrored gazing balls. The tackiness of these did not suck the world dry of its eagerness to please the belly or parched throat. Before he went looking, Dev figured his one option for staying hydrated, once the taps ran dry and he'd emptied the neighborhood of its bottled water, was to start treating rainwater. Worried about losing the internet, he made a point of downloading plans for making his own water treatment system. It wasn't as bad as he thought; gravel, sand, and activated charcoal seemed to be the main ingredients. He wasn't sure what the difference was between regular barbecue charcoal and the active kind but learned it was pretty basic chemistry. All he needed was some heat and that other bulk staple of suburban garages, at least in the Midwest: rock salt.

But there was a far easier and time-honored way for purifying water, called photosynthesis. Sunlight, dirt, and biology would do the hard part, and all Dev had to do was squeeze. His neighbors who couldn't afford privacy fences had bequeathed everything he needed by growing grapes to obscure each other's views. A good half-dozen chain-link fences in the neighborhood had been taken over, the vines growing explosively, twining and winding in, out, and around the wire diamonds, replacing the see-through chain-link fences with walls of shivering green. The grapes did the rest, filling with water, sunshine, and sugar, testing their skins, pulling down their vines with fist-sized clusters, weighted and waiting to become juice or wine or vinegar or all three.

Elsewhere in the neighborhood, there were apple trees for cider, cherry trees for cherry juice, every kind of berry you could think of, and even tomatoes if Dev had a hankering for a virgin Bloody Mary. So even after the last bottle of Ice Mountain was sucked dry, he wouldn't die from dehydration—a nice thing to know, especially since discovering the joys of sweating.

In the evening of that perfect day, Dev and Diablo dined on roast beef. He'd found it in the freezer and thawed it out in the kitchen sink during the day. He originally planned to just stick it in the oven, prepared like his mother always prepared it, meaning overcooked and thus dry. But overcooked roast beef is hardly any way to celebrate a perfect day.

The temperature had dropped sharply later in the day as clouds moved in and it began to rain. But even the rain was perfect—just enough to be entertaining without being scary. Dev left the front door open so he could hear the pattering rain falling through leaves and lit a fire in the fireplace to counteract the slight chill of having the door open. Watching the fire, listening to the rain, Dev had a moment of inspiration and stepped out to the garage, returning with the motor and spit his stepdad used for making rotisserie chicken during the one or two summer weekends when he took over cooking duty from his wife. After seasoning the meat with salt and pepper, Dev drove the spit through it and transported the skewered roast to the fireplace, where he'd set up the rest of the rotisserie.

"This is going to be better than watching the laundry," Dev told Diablo. As it turned out, a rotisserie in the fireplace was Dev's equivalent of the most virulently mesmerizing of viral videos. He loved watching the gears turn, the teeth meshing neatly and predictably, their turning translated to the meat on the spit, turning slowly from white or red to golden and brown, rivulets of fat and juice drizzling down, the meat basting itself, the drops hissing against orange embers, sizzling and flaring up, the light in the living room reminding him of the light outside, now that the sun was setting—one of those golden moments cinematographers called the magic hour.

Diablo, a remarkably patient dog—or maybe just wary of being burned—sat next to Dev, seeming to sense that his patience would be rewarded, once the meat was removed from the flame and Dev took out the carving tools. "Here, boy," the other boy said, flinging the first slice like a meat Frisbee, one half crust, the other juicy protein, as the dog made an expert leap and caught it in midair. Landing, Diablo tossed his head back, and the meat disappeared down his throat in a single gulp. And then he watched Dev as the latter raised and chewed his own slice of meat, seeing how long the dog's patience would last before giving in and sending another meat Frisbee Diablo's way.

Later, happily groggy with roast, listening to the pop of the dying fire, the steady beat of the falling rain, Dev read from one of his favorite, nonzombie survival stories, *My Side of the Mountain*, about a boy who runs away from civilization to live in the Catskills, where he trains a falcon and has adventures. He began by reading to himself at first, silently by the firelight, but noticed Diablo watching him, his eyes heavy with sleep, but still guarding his human.

"You wanna hear a story?" he asked.

Diablo didn't say no.

And so Dev read, aloud, and Diablo listened or seemed to, until their perfect day came to its perfect end.

"Night, Diablo," Dev said, his hand on the dog's back, rising and falling as their breathing synced up, carrying them wherever boys and dogs go in their dreams.

15

As she drove, Lucy listened to the radio—or rather *for* the radio—for anything suggesting there was someone still out there. Set on perpetual scan, the station numbers counted up, dropped back, counted up again, while the world's most earnest listener became an aficionado of static. AM was different from FM, top of the dial different from the bottom. In the first few days, she'd catch the occasional live mic broadcasting dead air— literally. She'd stop on these stations, pull over, crank up the volume, and then listen as hard as she'd ever listened to anything: the hum of lights; an air-handling system switching on; ions from solar storms sizzling through the carbon and crystal of microphones. One studio must have caught fire. She could hear the alarm going off, the tapping of the sprinkler system on the hot mic. But no voices. No living human noise. No bodies banging into obstacles as they fled. And then, a loud, staticky pop followed by another dead line in the electromagnetic spectrum.

Lucy continued scanning even as it became obvious that the electrical grid, which had been on autopilot since the whatever-it-was, was catching up with the population it once served. As the islands of light toward which she drove grew farther and fewer, Lucy thought about an old VHS cassette of an even older comedian whose name always reminded her of Halloween: Red Skelton. Her father had shown the tape to her, which was about right, because the guy specialized in what she considered old-people humor: funny voices, funny hats, mussed-up hair, crossed eyes. Except he'd get serious, too, sometimes. You could tell when he was, because the act would be silent, the stage minimally lit. The one she remembered as she drove through the night featured the comic with a broom, sweeping up circles of spotlight, like a janitor, until all the spotlights were one big circle of light. And that's when he'd sweep it into his dustpan and *click*: the screen went black.

That punch line hadn't happened yet in the world she drove through, but would. And when it did, she'd still listen to the radio, ping-ponging from empty station to empty station. She'd already found a few survivors too late to actually hang out with, their having died of something else between the thing that happened and Lucy's finding what remained of them. In one heartbreaking case, she'd heard the shot and found a boy her age, the gun still warm as the body cooled. She figured that if there were other survivors who hadn't gone on to kill themselves, intentionally or otherwise, they'd come in two varieties: searchers, like her, looking for others, and broadcasters signaling for others to come to them. The latter would find a radio station, take it over, and keep it going, by generator, most likely. If she'd known anything about running a radio station, that's what she would have done.

And so she drove, listening, hoping for a break in the static that would mean others. Other humans, she hurriedly specified. As opposed to alien overlords or something, letting the stragglers know their vacating the premises would be greatly appreciated.

The thing about listening to the ebb and flow of static day after day—it could make a person appreciate the complexity of country-western music. Not that she didn't have musical options. She had a phone full of MP3s and the stolen car she was driving had Bluetooth, so she was good when it came to tunes for the road. Plus, she should probably stagger the radio monitoring—break it into shifts. Listen to dead air for an hour, cover the local bandwidth a couple times, listen to Nine Inch Nails, go back for another hour of *Radio-Free Doomsday*, take a break with some old-school Alice Cooper, "I Love the Dead," especially, on repeat and extra loud—let the ex-populace of the latest necropolis know she cared.

"I'm on your side, dead heads!" she screamed after dropping her window. "Dead lives matter, woo-hoo!" Followed by a power fist before hastily shutting the window again. She'd closed the outside vent a few days ago and forgotten just how bad it had gotten. Now she remembered. Dead lives mattered, all right, but more importantly, dead matter stank. Hard. Like a-pie-tin-full-of-crap-in-your-face hard.

She'd finally gotten that army surplus gas mask she'd promised herself—a sweet little two-barrel number with replacement canisters—but didn't want to wear it while driving because the lenses tended to fog up in the southern heat and humidity, which was also aiding and abetting all that decomposition out there.

"That's a catch-22 or something," she said to the mask, lying on the passenger seat next to her. "That's what that is."

And there—that was another good reason to play some tunes. Because singing along wouldn't make her question her sanity like talking to herself did, and she'd been doing it . . .

". . . a lot," Lucy said to herself, completing the thought aloud.

The thing was, she didn't trust her luck. She'd also become convinced that if she started listening to music, she'd get lost in it and miss something. Back before, driving around with her brother and a learner's permit, she'd turn on some tunes and promptly miss the exit he'd told her was coming up "three freaking times . . ."

"Pay attention," he'd snap, turning off the radio before changing his mind and switching it back on—but tuned to NPR, to teach her a lesson.

"I hate you," she'd say, not knowing how soon she'd come to regret those words.

"Right back atcha, sis-boom-bah," he'd say, grinning his older-brother goofball grin.

Listening to static for hours, hoping for signs of life, was a little like floating in an isolation tank. Deprived of the stimulation it sought, the brain started making stuff up. Or maybe it was like hearing the landline every time she stepped into a shower. Or like feeling her phone buzz against her leg, even though she could see it right there in the cup holder. Phantom ring effect: every time it happened those first few days, her heart would race, and every time, it was a false alarm. Even after the phone totally bricked on her and she tossed it into the back seat, she could *still* feel it vibrating against her thigh.

And that's what did it, finally: growling at her leg to "Stop it!" That was the gateway to talking to herself. Eventually, the phantom phone stopped ringing, but Lucy kept on talking to herself. Eventually, she started hearing answers in the static.

The first time it happened, she slammed on the brakes, cranked up the volume, and shouted, "Hello, hello," as if the radio worked both ways. But it was just like when she showered and stepped out naked for a phone that hadn't rung or somebody who'd just hung up. And unlike with the phone, the car stereo didn't come with caller ID.

It wasn't voices she heard, in her head or over the radio; it was dots and dashes. Her father had been a radio operator a million years ago in the peacetime navy, back when it wasn't just a job, but a wholesale relinquishing of your civil rights. He'd taught her the Morse code that meant (secularly) "save our ship," but which her dad, a devout Catholic, always translated as "save our souls." Long after she'd stopped hearing ringing phones, she heard patterns in the static, waves of sound that ebbed and swelled in what she swore was a series of three threes: dits, dahs, dits.

SOS, SOS, SOS, she thought.

"SOS, SOS, SOS," she said, aloud.

16

Waking to the sound of crowing, Dev extricated himself from under Diablo before the two headed to the kitchen, where the human opened the refrigerator to darkness. He waved his hand through the unlit space. It was still cool but not cold. Certainly not cold enough to keep its contents from smelling, Diablo already nosing at the spoils destined to be his.

"Well," Dev said, pressing the door closed until the gasket gasped, making it airtight like the upright coffin it now was, "it was fun while it lasted."

And then he went from room to room, confirming that all the things that didn't work anymore, didn't work anymore. The lights, yes, obviously. The TV—not that there was anything to watch, but yes. The burners on the stove neither hissed nor ticked—so the gas was gone too. The little timers all around the house that always blinked midnight or noon when the power came back on after a blackout weren't blinking at all, a little like Dev as a baby, or so he'd been told. He tried the faucet and hit the trifecta: all his utilities had died peacefully while he slept.

Well, he'd gambled. He'd gone with eggs in the "What comes first?" debate: eggs versus electricity. Which was fine; at least breakfast was locked down. The other meals he'd planned, using all that now-thawing meat? The clock was ticking—or would be if he'd remembered to wind it, which he hadn't, defaulting to the organic alarm clock in his garage.

Not that his point needed literal ticking. It needed electricity, which meant he needed gas, pronto. He also needed to relocate a neighbor's generator or two.

But even considering all the SUVs in the neighborhood waiting to be siphoned, how long could he keep a generator puttering along? Certainly not the sixty or so years he planned to keep living. How many swimming pools would a supply like that take? And would the smell of it alone make the place uninhabitable?

Dev decided to take the chicken-run truck, the bed full of garbage cans, lids, and bungee cords to make sure they stayed on. He'd trace the streets he'd driven earlier, repeating the same clusters of franchises on infinite loop until he hit an intersection that was still lit, with a gas station on each corner, the neon open signs still burning bright. He'd pull up to a pump, hope the card readers worked, enter his zip code if asked, seeing as the credit cards all came from the pockets of neighbors.

And if there weren't any islands of light left? Well, that's why he loaded the smallest generator into the back of the pickup: gas, for electricity, for gas. Newton was right, after all: energy could be neither created nor destroyed, merely changed from form to form. And that was the good news, for this doomsday week two, and counting.

The last time he'd been through this part of town, he'd taken the greenway at about twenty-five miles an hour, which had been fine at the time, but gas stations were built to be accessed from the road, not by crossing somebody's front lawn. So Dev had to take a real road this time, surrounded by stuff, as opposed to the two-lane ribbons running through nowhere he'd practically flown over during his trip through farm country. In this case, the real road was named Telegraph, and doomsday had not been kind. Everywhere he looked, there were clusters and clutches of twisted metal, plowed-over traffic signs, crashed-into trees, storefronts with the rear ends of cars and trucks sticking out of them. He zigged and zagged, driving down this obstacle course, looking for that island of light he'd promised himself, along with pumps that worked, and a fifteen-horsepower plan B if they didn't.

But then he saw it.

It wasn't an island of light, not even a peninsula. And he wouldn't be needing plan B. It was a Sunoco station with an eighteen-wheeled tanker truck that looked like it was just getting ready to fill up the underground storage tanks when the whatever-it-was happened. The door to the tanker truck was wide open, the driver dead on the pavement, a clipboard lying where it had clattered to rest, the wind flipping through its pages like a student caught napping when the teacher asked a question.

Dev turned the steering wheel so fast two tires left the ground, the pickup tilted, and the empty trash barrels went bouncing as he braced himself for the roll he hoped wouldn't stop with the driver's side pinned against the pavement. It didn't. The truck landed and wobbled on the roof of the cab, neither door pinned, all four tires spinning in the air, like the legs of a turtle flipped on its back, pedaling frantically. Dev had just enough time to unbuckle, drop to the ceiling, and wiggle out through his kicked-open door before the truck's cab—rendered structurally unsound once the door was open—gave way, spraying safety glass like rock salt in all directions. Belatedly, the airbags thumped and gasped inside the now considerably smaller cabin, followed by a bunch of pointless binging, warning alternately of unfastened seat belts and doors ajar.

Shaking glass from his hair, Dev proceeded to the ride he'd just upgraded to, his future several thousand gallons brighter, after just one pit stop.

After patching the biggest generator he could find into the main circuit box in the basement, Dev ran a length of duct-taped extension cords over to his neighbor's garage. The air inside the empty chest was still cold but no longer freezing, judging from the lingering aroma of dead deer that rose out of it when he checked. The fact of its being empty no doubt contributed to its rapid loss of cold once the power cut out. It would take a few hours to get down to freezing again, and in the meantime, he left the neighborhood's freezers full, closed, and cold—the fuller, the colder, at least for the time being.

Diablo had followed him to the basement, a little skittish after his new human disappeared earlier only to return wholly unlickable thanks to Dev's smelling like gasoline. With the air conditioner dead and the temperature outside rising with an extra shot of humidity, the basement was now the coolest place in the house—one that stopped smelling like gas as soon as Dev left it. And so Diablo stayed downstairs while his human returned to the first floor, where he rebooted the router to check on how the internet was doing.

Not well.

His first attempt—Google—came back with the dreaded 404: site not found. He tried Bing, and bingo: same nada. Yahoo!, too, had gone missing, which was hardly a surprise; Dev was pretty sure they'd gone missing even before the whatever-it-was. The inexhaustible internet had finally died from exhaustion, the almighty cloud, so much vaporware.

Too bad, because Dev wanted to check how long a fully stocked freezer would stay cold after the power goes out. Based on past outages, a day didn't seem unreasonable, but beyond that—he couldn't remember any blackouts that lasted longer than twenty-four hours. He'd been a toddler during the Northeast blackout of 2003 and couldn't trust his memory of the time, which was secondhand from his secondhand father and mainly involved complaints about getting charged twenty-five dollars for a gallon of gas.

And so once again, he was on the clock, suddenly second-guessing his plan to rescue whatever was in his neighbors' freezers. It now seemed like a good way to waste a lot of time. What if his neighbors all turned out to be vegans, with freezers full of frozen broccoli and harvest burgers? Plus, he'd have to break in, mentally map a bunch of new places, try not to trip over any dead bodies, *and* get past all the spiders. Not that Dev was arachnophobic, but . . .

He'd first noticed them that morning before leaving to find gas: webs everywhere, like the internet's nickname turned literal. Silky threads strung from porch railing to porch railing like crime-scene tape, but dazzling, too, every thread beaded in dew and lit by the rising sun. Clearly, the arachnid community had gotten the message that humans weren't storming around all over the place anymore, wrecking their hard-spun traps.

The spiders responsible were brown and humpback, a species he'd nicknamed, collectively, Quasimodi. He was reluctant to disturb their handiwork—or leggy work, he guessed—in equal measures out of respect and fear of getting some on him. Because even though he wasn't arachnophobic, he could not abide the feathery touch of anything against his skin.

All in all, the better plan was to go looking for that island of light again—this time with a grocery store in it, preferably a Kroger whose floor plan he'd already mapped. He'd make quick work of it, having already decided that this trip "out there" would be his last. He'd stock up on stuff from the pharmacy first—first aid supplies, medications previously available only through prescription, like antibiotics, mainly, some painkillers, Xanax in case his symptoms returned, as they threatened to with each new, unavoidable trip "out there." He'd grab some luxuries, too, like toilet paper, toothpaste, lots of peanut butter—because, well, it was peanut butter—some proper dog food for Diablo, and then enough frozen meat to fill his neighbor's game locker.

Meanwhile, the spiders did a little stocking up themselves. Unlike Dev, however, all they had to do was wait to get what they needed delivered, as if Amazon had finally gotten that whole drone delivery thing off the ground. By the time he returned with the tanker truck, he couldn't help but notice that the morning's chandeliers had become dotted with countless flies, some still struggling, others already mummified in silk. One web was so weighted down with insect death it had torn away and now hung off to one side like a parted curtain.

"There are an awful lot of flies out there," Dev announced, calling down to Diablo, who was still camped out in the basement. "I wonder what that's all about," he said, worried that he might already know, wondering if perhaps Diablo had simply gotten the olfactory news before . . .

"Oh, jeez . . ."

The wind changed, blowing through the house's open windows, and there it was: what had drawn the flies that drew the spiders. Out came the handkerchief, clamped to his face, trying to block the nasal assailants eager to take advantage of the tiniest space between fingers.

Dev knew all about decomposition, having studied it as an auxiliary *topique* during the zombie period of his apocalypse phase. But he'd been in denial, at least partially enabled by the actual pace at which his local doomsday seemed to be unfolding. For example, Dev knew that normally, decomposition happens at a very predictable rate because death itself happens at a very predictable rate. In the insurance and funereal industries, they referred to it as the CDR—crude death rate—or the number of people out of a thousand expected to die in any given year. Before, in Dev's corner of the world, that rate had been 8.4. This year, the rate would be 999. And next year? Next year, with any luck, the CDR would be zero, or so he hoped.

For bodies left out in the open, in a temperate climate experiencing moderate temperatures, the flies will show up within ten minutes to lay thousands of eggs in the mouth, nose, and eyes. Twelve hours later, those eggs hatch and the maggots begin feeding on tissue surrounding their writhing numbers. Twenty-four to thirty-six hours later, beetles show up to eat the dry skin. And two days after dying out in the open, the corpse is approached by spiders, mites, and millipedes, drawn to dine on the earlier arrivals. Three days after death, gas begins to form inside the body as bacteria digest the muscles, tendons, and organs. Two- to three-inch blisters form on the skin, and the body's various orifices begin to leak. And on the grisly countdown goes, until flesh and bone become just bone.

But then there was that caveat: *normally.* There was nothing "normal" about the post-whatever-it-was world. It suddenly dawned on Dev that with nearly every human being dropping dead at once—a lot of them outside—the insect kingdom had been momentarily overwhelmed. Suddenly, the job of insect-facilitated decomposition became just like any other job in the modern economy: twice the work, half the workers, all of whom were expected to do more with less. It was Econ 101, supply and demand—or something like that. The point was, after the whatever-it-was, the bugs were working overtime and a little behind schedule.

So Dev had gotten lucky, for a while. Despite an unusually high number of his neighbors dying out in the open, he'd been granted a little over a week's worth of time-outs to enjoy this pause in the natural course of things. The dead were just dead, minding their own business while he was otherwise occupied. But now the insect facilitators had arrived, and Dev had another job to do, basically the same one the bugs were doing, but much too slowly by the smell of it.

17

Marcus found a car with the keys in the ignition, its owner still behind the wheel, getting ready to go somewhere he'd never get to. The oily sheen on the driver-side window did not bode well, despite the pine air freshener hanging from the rearview mirror, and sure enough, once Marcus opened the door, he stepped back as if slapped. Pulling up his T-shirt to mask his nose and mouth, he reached in and grabbed hold of the driver's belt, tugged, and then tugged some more until, like a stubborn cork, the tugging and sloshing of the inside contents found their tipping point and the body fell sideways, after which Marcus let gravity take it the rest of the way to the lawn next to the driveway. Where he planned to go with his stolen car, he didn't know at the moment; he just wanted to be going. He'd almost died twice within the last year—once by accident, the other time on purpose—and missed out on number three for reasons he couldn't imagine. What mattered was that he'd been reborn a shark—one that had to keep moving or die. And when his fins got tired, there was always that ever-growing pig stampede to get him going again.

He made himself a promise as he drove. He'd see how far this went, this everybody-but-him-being-dead business. He'd keep moving until he found others alive like himself. He'd embrace them, call them brother, or sister, and confess what he'd almost done and ask if they forgave him. He hoped they would, but if they wouldn't or couldn't, he'd understand. If whatever this was, was strictly local, he'd work with the authorities to track down the monsters who'd recruited him. He'd serve whatever sentence he had to serve. And he'd atone. He'd atone like his life depended on it, which, as far as he knew, it did.

He'd drive toward light at night; he decided that after his first sunset on the move. That's what the others would do, he figured. He'd—*they'd*—be like moths drawn to the flame of electricity, for as long as it lasted. Each night began the same way after that, the visible world funneled down to whatever his headlights cut through, until the starry darkness above turned gray, meaning either the sun was coming up or he was getting closer to another flickering vestige of civilization. Once there, he'd beep his horn and see if anyone emerged for him to confess to. If not, it was on to plan B: breaking into someplace nice to spend the evening.

So far, every evening had ended in plan B. But that didn't stop him from practicing his confession. "There's something I need to tell you," he'd say. "Something you need to know about the person I was." He'd pause before adding, "*Almost* was."

He'd confess so he wouldn't have to go around with this secret splitting him in two—into the inside Mo and the outside Marcus. He didn't want to worry about sleeping in another person's company, having realized—now that he had no one to ask—that he didn't know if he talked in his sleep. Total, brutal honesty would be his policy from here on out—theoretically, at least, until he found someone to be honest with, other than himself.

He hadn't packed before hitting the road, and so he gathered supplies along the way, switching vehicles when they ran out of gas. But as his collection of essentials grew, Marcus came to appreciate the inefficiency of constantly moving his supplies from one ride to another. And so he began looking for something a little more "apocalypse ready," which turned out to be a Good Humor truck, of all things.

In homage to his newborn apostasy, he edited the signage with spray paint to read, "God's a Rumor." The message seemed about right, given the lack of heavenly announcements regarding recent events. Plus, Marcus was probably the only one left to be offended, and he wasn't, so why not?

The other nice thing about the truck was the loudspeaker, broadcasting his survival to any who might hear, to the tune of "Pop Goes the Weasel." This was much better than just driving toward light and beeping when he got there; the weasel covered both darkness and light, in case any of the survivors were afraid of their fellow survivors and were avoiding the islands of light for the same reason Marcus drove toward them.

A dirge may have been the more appropriate soundtrack under the circumstances, but Marcus was okay with a little discordant peppiness. Counterprogramming—he thought they called it. It's what all the cool kids were doing—assuming there were any cool kids left.

The beauty of an ice cream truck as one's vehicle of choice for surviving the apocalypse was this: on-board refrigeration and a generator to power it. Plus sinks, a porta potty, and a soft-serve machine that could be easily disconnected and left at the side of the road—after opening the rear doors and rocking gears back and forth until the unhooked unit walked itself out. An air mattress fit neatly into the vacated space, for when the shark needed a little shut-eye.

A mobile home might have been even better, but the ones Marcus checked out along the way were more "home" than "mobile," meaning they were designed to be parked somewhere with hookups for electricity and sanitation. Plus the Good Humor truck (with edited signage) made him smile in a way a Winnebago wouldn't: perversely. It'd be a conversation piece too—if he ever found anybody to converse with.

"Ice cream, eh?" he imagined this hypothetical human saying.

"I sure did," he imagined saying back. "Didn't you?"

His itinerary was pretty simple: someplace else, preferably with fewer earthquakes and pigs and more survivors. Once that was settled, it was just a matter of eliminating compass points he didn't want to travel toward. North got eliminated from the start because things just got colder the farther north you went. South, too, was dismissed because things just got hotter until you either hit the Gulf of Mexico or Mexicans. Not that Marcus had any problems with Mexicans, seeing as they had a common enemy in the Orange One, but all he knew was English and a smattering of Arabic that was mainly about holidays, food, and swearing. Going west looked like sand, sand, and more sand, which might seem perfect for the descendant of a desert-dwelling people except, yeah, no thanks. Oklahoma was wasteland enough for one lifetime. And so east it was. Or eastish, depending on the condition of the roads and/or what looked interesting on the horizon.

As he drove, Marcus became a broadcaster *and* a seeker, both, playing the truck's loudspeaker full blast while on his dash rested two scanners, one police, one CB. He didn't bother with commercial frequencies, mainly because of his personal bias for movement versus standing still. Sure, a commercial signal could cover more ground, but you couldn't see what was on that ground as the radio waves passed over it. Listening for other mobile broadcasts as he sent out his own low-tech signal and scanned the world rolling past his windshield for any other signs of human activity seemed the most effective way to go. Plus, if any other humans started squawking on one of his scanners, he'd know they were relatively close. Also, he could talk back to them anonymously, just in case they weren't as happy to hear from him as their shared humanity and survivorship might suggest—an attitude toward others Marcus was starting to think wiser than not.

Because that was the thing about being without people to reflect back to themselves: all Marcus had was Marcus, and this Marcus, left to his own devices, got increasingly paranoid about others the longer he drove with no sign of them. Take the idea of driving toward a commercial signal without being able to interact with the signaler at a safe distance first. Once there were no more islands of light to drive toward anymore, he started seeing what he hadn't before: that showing up after being called was a good way to get ambushed. As a son of immigrants, Marcus had too much secondhand paranoia to leave any room for naïveté like that. So even if all the Whos in Whoville started shouting, "We are here," as far as the ex-terrorist was concerned, it was, "Proceed with caution." That, and a shotgun.

18

Dev did the outside bodies first, seeing as they were the most immediate affront to his olfactory senses, which—contrary to popular belief—were *not* limited to the nose but included the tongue and, to a lesser extent, skin. Regarding the last, it was almost as if he could *feel* the rot molecules wafting over him from the scattered jigsaw of crime-scene bodies. He could *feel* the oily, pestilential specks alighting on his skin, making him look intently at, say, his bare arm just above the wrist, at the tiny hairs bristling there, imagining little drops of death hanging on their tips, like dew on blades of grass.

It was amazing how many there were, above and beyond the fact of their being dead. Doomsday had come on a Monday, in the middle of the day, toward the end of the school year. It was the sort of day that made people complain about having to go to school or work—about being *trapped inside* when there was *all that* (indicated by a hand thrust dramatically toward the nearest window) *out there*.

So what were they all doing outside, where they could die, leaving their rotting bodies behind for Dev to clean up? Had they called in sick, not knowing how prescient the lie would prove to be? No, they were just laid off. Again. At the time it happened, Michigan was in the middle of its latest cycle of rebound and bust, triggered once again by the price of keeping a gas tank full.

To get even with Russia, or Iran, or whomever, the Saudis had cranked open the spigots, gas dropped below two dollars, and his neighbors exchanged gas sippers for guzzlers, parking up the driveways and side streets with shiny new pickups and SUVs. Suddenly, MPG was out and towing capacity was in. To satisfy the public's schizophrenic taste in personal transportation, the Big Three had shut down their assembly lines to retool from subcompacts to behemoths with tanks measured not in gallons, but Gulf wars. And that was why so many of his neighbors were outside the day it happened, making the best of their unemployment, washing the brand-new trucks they'd no longer be able to fuel, once the oil derricks swung in the opposite direction.

Not that Dev minded all the trucks with their extra-large gas tanks. They'd come in handy given the chore at hand—one he'd already put off for too long, judging from the way his skin tingled with all those pestilential molecules clinging like dew to all those tiny hairs.

He left Diablo at home while he collected the bodies—not that the dog seemed especially eager to join him. Having seen a dog eat its own poop once, he was worried that once the black Lab got used to the smell, it might not be too great a leap to that first nibble. Though he had no idea whether rot-tenderized flesh would tempt a well-fed dog, he figured it best not to find out. Not only was it a bad idea letting him know what humans tasted like, but Dev heard once that a dog's mouth is cleaner than a human's. The thought had gotten him through Diablo's tongue-based displays of appreciation with a minimum of flinching. He wasn't sure he could keep it up if he started wondering not *what* the animal had been eating but *whom*.

Speaking of, it was a pity none of his neighbors had a hazmat suit. Instead, Dev had to make do with a raincoat, duct tape, gloves, boots, a painter's respirator augmented with a couple of pine-scented air fresheners, and a pair of goggles. He'd already made the rookie mistake of trying to grab a body by its hand, only to have the skin strip off like a glove. A surprising amount of stench and spatter followed the skin off, along with a sound that sounded like Velcro pulling apart. After that, Dev grabbed whatever they were wearing that was handy—belts, mainly; waistbands; something equatorial body-wise so the deadweight balanced on either side as he lifted or dragged or pushed.

He propped a plywood sheet against the open tailgate of the vehicle he was loading and rolled the bodies up the incline, using either gloved hands or booted feet, depending on how heavy the body was. It was a little like riding on a flat tire, but still better for his back than trying to clean jerk one of these gut tubs. Plus, after the first one, the skids were greased, so to speak, every new body laying down a fresh trail of leaking lipids and generic dead-person goo, so their movement up the impromptu ramp was part rolling, but mainly sliding.

Kids—and there were some, the ones too young for school—these he lifted like rolled rugs, their bruised faces turned toward the earth, where he didn't have to look at them before loading their bodies onto the truck. This face thing with kids was a total reversal from how things had been before. Back then, kid faces had been the only human ones Dev could look at. Their palette of emotions was so limited, their needs so elemental, their eyes so lacking in the need to judge that he'd found no reason to look at his shoes in their presence. Quite the contrary, he'd played hours of peekaboo, standing behind some frazzled parent with a child slung over their shoulder, the kid facing him as they all waited in line. The eyes of children were almost as good as dogs' eyes, meaning Dev could look at them without feeling stupid or judged like he was taking some all-or-nothing quiz. He could just look at them, hide one eye behind a palm, hide the other, unmask both, and get a giggle. He'd do it again, and it was like the first time, a little kid shaking full of little-kid delight. And on and on and so on, until the groceries were bagged, the check deposited, the package mailed. And there went that little hand, reaching out for him, its little fingers opening and closing: bye-bye, bye-bye . . .

"Bye-bye," Dev echoed now, placing another precious, limp bundle ever so gently upon the latest pile.

Now that he was up to his goggles in viscera, Dev looked back at all the doomsday fiction he'd read, back when that had been his latest obsession. And the thing that struck him now was how they'd cheated. Whether nuclear or viral, through asteroid collision or climate change, those would-be apocalypses almost always left the world conveniently unpeopled. It was like there'd been some kind of rapture that made all the decomposable bodies disappear, leaving the last remaining protagonist to pursue his make-believe adventures safe from the mundane danger of tripping over corpses.

The only exceptions Dev could think of were the zombie apocalypses, which were pretty much wall-to-wall dead bodies in various stages of decomposition, shambling about, looking for brains or brainless humans to infect. But even in the zombie apocalypses, the problem of body disposal was largely ignored. Decapitation, skull cleaving, rotten bodies exploding across windshields and speeding grillwork, or just heads getting blown off by shotguns: yes, plenty of that. But as far as cleaning up afterward, they didn't, despite the tripping hazard created by leaving a headless body lying around.

Dev wasn't going to make that mistake, filling up another SUV, driving to the perimeter he was slowly creating, shoving a rag in the gas tank, striking a match, and standing back as the greasy black smoke turned another nice day to soot and ash. Looking back, it occurred to Dev that they'd all been pretty nice days lately, with the exception of the corpse burning, of course. He hardly ever flinched anymore and hadn't needed his meds at all. With the exception of the smoke, which was strictly local to the latest torched SUV, the air was clearer than it had been in years, replacing even the noise pollution with the rustling of leaves, the chirping of birds, the tick, tick, tick of an acorn pinballing through branches. The temperature anywhere but the immediate vicinity of the fire was a pleasant seventy-two degrees, balanced on a dew point that actually *felt* like seventy-two degrees.

Not too far away, lawns like green carpeting fronted a Tetris pack of working- to middle-class houses, the streets dividing them featuring fewer and fewer bodies, thanks to Dev, his nose and mouth covered with a respirator, his face shimmering through heat ripples. The hard part done, he supervised the flames as they un-skinned his ex-neighbors, the white parts blackening, the black parts glowing orange, almost festively, like Halloween decorations, except for the fact that they were real ex-people burning away in there.

He'd not burned them before now out of an abundance of caution, he decided after the fact. Given the lack of any adequate explanation like a plague or smoldering ruins, maybe they weren't really dead, just stunned or hibernating or something. Sure, the phone hadn't fogged when he placed it under a sampling of noses, but what if they'd been congested or mouth breathers or something? What if the screens came with some antismudge, antifog technology? Sure, he couldn't feel a pulse in the handful of necks he'd checked, but he wasn't sure he'd checked in the right place, or how to distinguish the pulse in a neck from his own heartbeat, which he could sometimes feel all the way down to his fingertips.

It had been so sudden, so switch-like, efficient, and strange. Dev didn't want to rush to any conclusions, especially if it hadn't yet. Concluded, that is. So he'd waited, subconsciously, just in case the bodies started getting up again. While before he would have dismissed such magical thinking, he couldn't anymore. Not once everybody dropping dead was added to the list of things that could just happen.

So Dev waited and his neighbors rotted, not changing into anything but stinkier versions of what they'd been. And even then, he held back, until the flies came and the stench rose to human-detectable levels. Left unaddressed, the flies would yield to whatever fed on them in addition to the spiders, followed by the creatures that dined on those, until the party grew to include beasts of the Dev-eating kind, which he wasn't too keen on meeting. So:

He looked at the bodies left to go, still lying in the street, across lawns, bent over porch railings, and next to toppled bicycles. These were just the tip of the iceberg. Behind all those doors up and down the block, there were more, dropped where they were when the whatever-it-was happened, leaving Dev to clean up the mess.

It wouldn't be so bad if they'd died politely like they did on TV, their looking-at-nothing eyes closed and their gas-venting mouths zipped tight. The real dead didn't die like that. The real dead let it all hang out, mouths slack, lips pulled back, eyes bugged out. Blood did a funny thing once the heart stopped pumping; it pooled and bruised whatever part was closest to the ground, the bodies frozen in their last poses until rot beat out rigor mortis and they got bendable again. That actually made things worse, though, as he discovered while shouldering a midsized body, only to be rewarded with a pair of dead hands slapping his rear end, making him turn, only to get slapped again.

When there was no room left, Dev paused to consider what had to be the world's grisliest clown car. Its soon-to-be driver would fit right in, judging from his reflection in the side-view mirror. His goggles and goo-smeared raincoat had turned him into a giant bug like the one named Gregor they'd read about in English class. Dev wondered if that was the job of fiction, to test-drive the impossible, to loosen our grip on conventional reality. He guessed that's probably what fiction writers would claim—if there were any left, that is.

Stepping into the driver's seat of his latest mobile crematorium, Dev checked his rearview mirror, even though the view was blocked with another batch of ex-neighbors. Which was okay. He'd taken to watching them in his mirrors as he drove hardly faster than walking. Whenever he'd hit a pothole the arms would jerk and flop, like they were waving goodbye, which seemed appropriate.

Sometimes, Dev would wave back, and other times, he just waved to clear the air. Because the dead weren't polite, as previously noted. They weren't quiet either. One or two in every batch would make some kind of noise as the gases building up inside found a way out. The latest load was no different.

Gagging as the pestilential molecules slipped past the fibers of the respirator's filter, Dev squeezed the mask more tightly about his nose and mouth. It didn't help. The stench was impervious to a whole forest of pine trees. "Light a match," he said finally, resorting to his stepfather's fart humor. And then he thought about it.

"Oh yeah," he said. "I guess that's *my* job."

19

For the first several evenings when it was time to stop for the night, Lucy would break into a home within the island of light she'd driven toward. Once inside, she'd take advantage of the air-conditioning and ice makers, raid the refrigerators, roll up any dead bodies in the nearest rugs and slide them out before sleeping like a baby in a full-sized bed. And between the splintering door frames and squeaking bed springs, she'd wander through the rooms of these borrowed lives, going through other people's stuff, trying to CSI what the dead must have been like.

Lucy was perversely fond of the survivalists she found. There seemed to be a lot of them below the M-D. She wondered what they'd make of this unimagined version of their dream: the end that left so much stuff behind, with so little competition for it. Most seemed to have been prepping for the Obama apocalypse, the one with FEMA storm trooping in, black helicopters dispatched by the first black president, come to seize their guns, hustling them off to camps where they'd be forced to read the Koran, eat kale, who knew what, while they waited to be dragged before death panels. Scary, scary stuff—that's what they'd been prepping for—all of it squat patties at least partially endorsed by the Cheetos-tinted successor to the White House, the one who'd convinced the liberal end of the political spectrum that the end was indeed nigh. Craigslist missed an opportunity, Lucy figured, not setting up a matchmaking service for right- and left-wing preppers to sell their stuff back and forth to each other with each swing of the political pendulum. In the end, none of it mattered, all the vacuum-packed MREs, iodine tablets, fire-starter kits, and firepower had been bequeathed to, well, her.

Thanks, she thought, tipping back a fresh-cracked bottle of fluoride-free water distilled from the runoff of melting glaciers. *You really shouldn't have . . .*

During his home stays, Marcus kept an eye out for pornography, which was always hidden, though with a sort of consensus on cleverness that made it easy enough to find: in underwear drawers, in toilet tanks inside Ziploc bags, clipped into family-friendly DVD clamshells unlikely to be viewed anytime soon (see *Swiss Family Robinson, Gentle Ben, Flipper,* et al.). Props to the guy—he assumed it was a guy—who squirreled his stash away in the refrigerator, under a false bottom of the lunch-meat drawer.

Of course, when it came to hard-core voyeurism, nothing beat the financial porn of their filing cabinets: the bank statements, tax information, pay stubs. Marcus—the onetime future accountant—was amazed by how many people had been living so close to ruin. One unexpected health emergency would wipe most of them out, and as far as retirement, they seemed to have settled on one of two options: hitting the lottery or dying on the job. In a way, it made the catastrophe of what happened seem less catastrophic. The whatever-it-was spared so many people a future of saltines and cat-food pâté. That was the lesson he took away from these amateur audits; it helped assuage any guilt Marcus might feel for using all these dead people's stuff. Because, all things being equal, they hadn't paid for it either. Not with money, at least.

And then one night, there was just night: no islands of light to drive toward. Lucy decided to go west, partly because of the famous advice regarding young men, whom she wouldn't mind meeting. As far as deserts went, this is what she knew: at least it was a *dry* heat. Not like Hotlanta, where the humidity was so thick just breathing seemed like being waterboarded. Plus, California was the place to head to find others, assuming the more people you started with, the more likely some would have survived. Worst-case scenario—she figured—the Day of the Dead souvenirs got more authentic the farther west you went.

But after a few days of traveling in her chosen direction, Lucy decided she needed something a little more planned. Or plannedish. It wasn't lost on her that all it took was a few detours for her to have no idea where she was. And all it took was a few evenings spent driving through woodland and/or farm country that didn't seem to end to convince her that heading for the bigger dots on a map would make sense.

When the lights disappeared in Marcus's neck of the woods, he knew it was time for an old-fashioned, foldable map. But even the search for directions meant more detours. He had tried several chain gas stations, hoping to find a map of wherever he was, preferably one with all the side streets and intersections labeled, so he could check the nearest cross street and get his bearings. But paper maps were even rarer than pay phones and record stores in the years just before; they'd all been replaced with the convenience of an iSomething, tucked neatly into one's hip pocket.

Marcus had started his journey with his pocket-sized world, still functional but becoming less so as the internet died along with the cell networks to connect him to it. Even stuff he thought he owned—music, e-books—disappeared. Turned out all that stuff needed an okay from the cloud to work. Unfortunately, said cloud was about as substantial as smoke on a windy day; it disappeared when the older-tech grid that supported it did likewise.

The atlases he found—pages yellowed, colors discolored—lay dust covered in little independent gas-n-go convenience stores whose main convenience seemed to be drug paraphernalia: rolling papers, bud vases that doubled as crack pipes, incense, potpourri, bath salts, Whip-Its—all helpfully labeled to inform the consumer that using them in a manner other than intended (undefined) was strictly illegal. The atlases themselves were better than nothing but hardly the turn-by-turn convenience of Google Maps he'd gotten used to. Afterward, he wound up driving pretty much as randomly as before, just with fewer stops looking for atlases.

For Lucy, the loss of electricity meant more than just no lights; it quickly turned into a lack of overnight housing. Found atlases got her to where the houses were, but minus electricity, those houses became inhospitable in the extreme. Take air-conditioning, for example, which was pretty much the only thing that made the South bearable during the summer. Without it, foam mattresses weren't the only things with memories. Once the unrelenting southern heat bore down on all those hermetically sealed boxes of domesticity, they filled with memories—of all the smells building up inside.

Dead bodies were the worst of it, of course, but not the only things to rot and stink, permeating anything porous, from carpets to curtains to the aforementioned mattresses of memory foam. Every organic thing contributed to the general stench: fruit in fruit bowls clouded by flies, garbage in garbage cans leaking black ooze, sewers backed up into basements. Man-made products pitched in too: urethanes, synthetic fibers, and plastics, all shedding their toxic molecules when the temperature inside broke ninety. Even an empty cereal bowl, left in the sink before going to school for the last time, was enough to perfume an entire house with the dregs of unslurped milk left ringing the bottom.

Marcus was in denial about the lack of livable housing once the world went dark until his shoes squished after stepping on some stranger's shag carpeting. A huge water stain on the living room ceiling had dropped paint and plaster like clumps of cottage cheese spattering the place's 1970s bachelor-pad decor. The ceiling was still dripping when Marcus broke and entered, and the carpet squished all the way up to the second-floor bathroom.

Standing outside, he knew he shouldn't open the door, but did anyway. And there it was: a body in the tub, lavender candles burned down to wax pancakes along the rim, a large rubber sex toy lying on the tiled floor, surrounded by a puddle that had skinned over green. The body seemed to be made of rubber too—a person-shaped balloon inflated until it took on the shape of the tub: SpongeBob SquareBody, minus the animation, and with a ball gag in its mouth.

Marcus tried hard not to judge. He'd made progress, after not blowing himself up. Tolerance would be his middle name—he'd vowed—belatedly forgiving the late of the world, but . . .

The world had ended before noon on a Monday. And this here—this was Saturday-night-after-midnight-grade kink. Being open-minded was one thing; having a little self-restraint was another. And then Marcus looked at the toilet next to the tub.

On top of the tank, a half-eaten sandwich was still plated, turfed thickly in mold, but with a dollop of congealed mayo still weeping out through multiple layers of bacon, maybe a half-inch thick. Apparently, Tub Boy wanted something for every orifice. Which begged the question: ball gag? Which forced the ex-terrorist to imagine the guy, lifting the gag to take a bite, his no-doubt yellowed and ill-fitting teeth splintering through strips of fried swine, squirting mayonnaise like ersatz ejaculate before lowering it again and . . .

Marcus felt a bolus of bile rise hotly up his throat, choked it back, and decided: *karma.* That's what caused all of this, meaning not just the guy in the tub, but *all of it.* Mankind had gone too far and had gotten what it deserved.

Good, Marcus thought, and thinking it, found he felt better. All things being equal, at least he wasn't some pervert, rising like a loaf of bread out of a bathtub. He was just an ex-terrorist, accent on the "ex-."

Lucy's home stays ended when she entered the house with the baby. She found it, dead in its crib, thumb still corking its mouth, skin robin's-egg blue, flies at its lashes. Its stomach, full of gas, had inflated to the size of a soccer ball, stretching its onesie tight, rolling the body just enough so she could see the side of its face it had fallen asleep on before its life just tiptoed away. The heart stopped, its blood had pooled wherever gravity pulled it, staining its once-pink cheek, first blue, then bruised, then black as an eggplant. And there went her leading theory about what had happened and what caused it:

Karma.

What kind of karmic debt could a baby chalk up? She knew what her mom would say: original sin. She'd bought it herself—in the abstract. But here, served up in a bassinet: no.

And then a very different thought crossed her mind. Was she really alive, or had she gone through with it? Was everyone's being dead just her point of view? Were they only dead *to her?* And had she ended up where she worried she might? The world she found herself in was decidedly hellish, especially lately, with the putrefaction, the isolation, the disappearance of all the conveniences she'd taken for granted before, even the finding of other survivors who'd stopped surviving before she got to them. And things were only getting worse. The bodies were stinkier, the sense of aloneness more profound. And then this last straw: the baby, worse than any of the pro-life splatter porn they'd shown her at the clinic. One look and she felt a tug behind her belly button as something whispered: "Am I yours?"

Running from the house, Lucy clawed the gas mask from her face and coughed out her last two meals: canned peaches for breakfast, pea soup for lunch. Afterward, when there was nothing left, she just stood there, bent at the waist, hands still bracing knees, staring at peach parts and bile lying there in the dying grass. She was looking for something else, some clue to her true fate, but didn't find anything else she recognized— except that she wasn't finished throwing up just yet.

After that, Lucy slept in her ride, windows rolled tight, engine idling, the white noise of AC and internal combustion lulling her to sleep through the now-useless nights. From then on, adventures under other roofs were reserved for emergency supply runs, and only with something to hide her nose.

During the day, Marcus resumed his search for others like a cowboy on a mission remounting his horse. Minus the glow of light bulbs to signal civilization's bright ideas, he found himself looking for smoke instead. Where there was smoke, there was fire—the saying went—and hopefully the people who set it.

But the longer he drove, the pickier he became about the kind of smoke that warranted detours. He'd been fooled too many times by spontaneous combustion at untended landfills, lightning strikes, and downed power lines. He'd mistaken the clouds of carrion eaters over factory farms as something that needed investigating, only to have the clouds pixilate in front of him while the wind brought rumors of the stench to come.

In the end, he learned to ignore the angrier black plumes pumping their way into the sky like wannabe mushroom clouds. These were almost always petrochemical in nature, too toxic and too fast to get close to, useless for cooking, dangerous for heating—or even breathing near. White smoke was still investigated, even though his experiences with it thus far had been as wild and goose-like as the darker stuff he now steered clear of. White smoke meant something organic was burning, like a campfire doused before moving on to the next site. That was the theory, at least—the one that kept him chasing every white wisp he saw on the horizon, with a heart full of hope and the safety off.

20

Dev hadn't planned on building a wall; it just grew out of a need to get rid of the bodies the world's ending left behind. He'd filled, parked, and torched the first of his dead clown cars and was backing in the second when one of his passengers farted, he jerked his head, and bam! His rear bumper buckled the bed of the charred pickup truck behind it, scooting said vehicle a few sparking feet across the pavement. The tires that melted during the fire now scraped away to bare rims before the latter crumpled, followed by the truck's much-abused struts giving out.

Dev stepped down from the cab and looked at the result: one brand-new truck, collision-welded to the rear end of a charred truck full of blackened bones. The exhaust system was pancaked so the chassis lay flat, while the crash and skid had ground the rest flush with the pavement. There wasn't enough space for even a squirrel to squeeze through.

Dev touched the charred metal; it was cool. He wrenched open the driver-side door, where he'd rolled down the window so he could breathe while driving. He'd parked the pickup on the wrong side of the street because he could, but also so that the driver's side faced home while the passenger's side, still rolled up, faced everything else. Thus vented, the vehicle's windows survived the fire without imploding.

Reaching across a tumble of bones in the passenger seat, Dev pushed down the button to lock the side facing the whole rest of the world—the "intruder side," as he now liked to think of it. And thus the wall grew, one rear-ended truck after another, following the line of the street until it came to an intersection, turned right, and kept going, truck, truck, truck, until it came to the next intersection and turned right again.

Before, the neighborhood he was gradually boxing in didn't have a name. People lived on streets with names, in houses with numbers, but nobody ever bothered to set up gates, establish a homeowners' association, or adopt ordinances against things nobody did anymore anyway, like drying laundry on a clothesline. As collectives went, the old neighborhood was about as loose as you could get, the people there bound mainly by: (1) their complaining about the smell coming from the Ecorse River next door and (2) not being able to afford anyplace better.

Regarding the former, the river cut through the heart of Dev's block as well as several cities surrounding it, known collectively as "downriver," though the Ecorse wasn't the river they were all down from. That honor went to the much larger Detroit River, which the Ecorse drained into. As bodies of water went, the Ecorse was more like a creek, measuring mere yards across even though it ran nearly nineteen miles long and cut every riverside street in the neighborhood in half with a railing, a steep drop-off, and a bright-yellow "Dead End" sign.

The river meant that Dev had one side of his wall already taken care of. And as far as his new, gated community not having a name, he liked the sound of "Devonshire." The vote was unanimous.

Working diligently for five days straight, Dev felt safer the closer he got to finishing. Now that the local infrastructure had failed, it was just a matter of time before all sorts of exotic ways to die made their ways to Devonshire. The Detroit Zoo was the one he worried about most. All it would take was for the backup generators to fail along with the electromagnetic locks. The animals might not notice at first, waiting to be fed out of habit, like Dev waiting at the bus stop for his mom. But eventually they'd get hungry enough, or they'd scratch their butts against the bars and notice the doors swing open . . .

Plus, there was always the possibility of people.

Even though no one had shown up yet, he couldn't rule it out. And while people might fool him, the fact they'd have left the home they knew for somewhere they didn't meant they were stupid or desperate or both—none a good trait in a world without rules, and potentially fatal in combination.

Staying put: Dev had decided that as his go-to survival strategy even before the world ended. The stupidest thing people ever did—and they *always* did it in those stories—was leave where they knew what was what to go wandering, which invariably led to exciting plot complications easily avoided by staying put. So why go looking for trouble?

He'd had this very argument with Leo, back when they were both doing the doomsday thing. Leo followed the neurotypical line, assuming the survivors were just looking for others. "You know, for a sense of community."

"What does that even mean?" Dev asked.

Foolishly, Leo tried explaining. "The need humans have to be together," he said.

But young Brinkman's Aspie superpowers were immune to such reasoning. "What else?" he asked.

"Um," Leo tried. "Two heads are better than one?"

"Next."

"It's all about teamwork?"

"Are you kidding?" Dev asked. And so they continued arguing, Leo failing to convince Dev that leaving home during a zombie apocalypse made sense, while Dev wondered why the apocalypse was taking so long.

This conviction re staying put versus wandering didn't come out of nowhere. It was rooted in some sports mythology he'd learned from his stepfather—*the home-field advantage*—a term his replacement dad first used not while watching a game, but *Home Alone*.

"You see that?" he asked.

Dev nodded, because he'd been watching the TV like he was study-ing it. His stepfather had stopped admonishing him for sitting too close, instead keeping Windex handy to clean off the nose smudges. This was before his Asperger's diagnosis.

"That's the home-field advantage," his stepfather explained. "Kevin *knows* the house; the burglars *don't*. That's how one little kid gets the better of two adults. That's how important the home-field advantage is."

Dev nodded. And while most of what his fake dad said exited his opposite ear without pausing for speed bumps, this particular idea set the hand brake and stayed. It helped that his mom already called him a homebody, while his stepfather figured agoraphobia was more like it. All Dev knew was he preferred places he knew to those he didn't. So when the world offered him the home-field advantage to excuse his natural inclination, it was an offer he couldn't refuse.

After using up the outside bodies with the wall only half built, Dev took a day off because of rain. He hadn't noticed the sky darkening at first, confusing the black clouds rolling in with the smoke rolling up and away from the latest truck as it burned. Once drops started sizzling on the hot metal, though, he turned for home but then stopped. He was already wearing a raincoat; staying put meant he wouldn't have to hose it off.

And so he did. He stayed put. And as the rain fell on him, Dev remembered why walls were necessary throughout history, and probably still were. It was a seemingly innocuous sight: foam. Like from soap or detergent, bubbling on the ground, conjured up from the grease and ashes of his neighbors by the steady, pattering rain.

That's when he remembered a chemistry lesson his stepfather had taught him about man's inhumanity to man. The senior Brinkman had read about foam just like this, forming outside the crematoriums in the death camps during World War II. Eventually, the Nazis capitalized on the process. Industrialized it.

"They used our bodies to make glycerin and soap," he said. "Glycerin to make nitroglycerin to blow up more Jews." He called this the opposite of the circle of life; it was the circle of death—and mankind was still paying the karmic debt for that depravity.

"It's one thing to use every part of a whale," he continued. "It's another to use every part of a person. Cross that line, and it's worse than eating some fruit in a make-believe garden. It answers the question: Is man good or evil? Well, I'm here to tell you, any species that can turn its own into soap and bombs is *evil*. End of story."

Dev looked up at his stepfather's indictment of the human race. Finally, something the two of them agreed on.

PART THREE

21

The hardest part for Lucy and Marcus in their separate search for others wasn't the wild-goose chases or the false alarms: it was finding fellow survivors who'd succumbed to something else. The accidents were heartbreaking in every flavor: electrocution, asphyxiation, blood poisoning, animal attack, heart attack, or just thinking they could make it when they couldn't. Each new find was a thwarted hope that nevertheless kept hope alive. But the suicides—the hangings, gunshots, ODs, bloodlettings—these felt like déjà vu from the future, but-fors that were also maybe-stills . . .

But then they found each other, in spite of everything—including Marcus's decision to not chase black smoke anymore. Later, Lucy would admit she didn't know how to change or even top off the oil in a car—or, indeed, that she needed to. But this was the stroke of dumb luck that made their meeting possible. Because the reason Marcus went back on his previous decision was this: the black smoke Lucy made kept moving.

Recalling previous failures, Marcus imagined the worst: some poor animal caught on fire, running madly as the flames ate through fur, flesh, fat. Or worse, a survivor who'd chosen to stop surviving through self-immolation before having second thoughts. But the longer he watched, the more obvious it became how *un*randomly this smoke was moving. If it *was* an animal being burned alive—or some jackass human—it was an especially *focused* one, not zigzagging or running in circles but heading steadily west in a straight line without slowing down or stopping to die and smolder.

A few turns on his part and the smoke was coming straight for Marcus. He looked toward his shotgun, but let it be. He thought about turning off the loudspeaker, but left that alone too. It was easy to be paranoid when the others were strictly hypothetical. But seriously, why wouldn't they be grateful, like he was feeling now? It wasn't like they were competing for resources or anything. And so he sped up. When his tires didn't blow, he sped up even more. The smoke continued at its steady pace and so Marcus drove toward it, halving the distance and halving it again until he could see the other and then floored it.

The ice cream truck reading, "God's a Rumor," and the Hyundai Sonata with the deep-fried engine screeched to mutual halts just short of colliding. Both drivers jumped out at roughly the same time.

"I can't believe it," Lucy kept saying.

"Neither can I," Marcus kept saying back.

Their fingers reached toward each other as if toward their own reflections, or perhaps their shadow's projection against fog, tentative, waiting for the resistance of glass, the passing through of a figment of their own longing. Instead, warm skin met warm skin.

"Thank God," she exclaimed, temporarily forgetting she'd given up on religion.

"Allahu Akbar," he said, likewise.

They both paused.

"This is going to be interesting," they said together, before laughing a nervous, tandem laugh, the harmonics of which, bouncing off the empty world, only made them laugh more nervously still.

Leaving their rides where they'd come to a stop, the two sought out the shade of a tree that looked like God himself might have planted it, during that six-day burst of creativity. Under its sprawling branches, with their backs resting against its massively contorted trunk, they told the stories of where they were when, each leaving out a few details.

Both had been at school, they learned. Lucy, in the eastern time zone, was getting ready for lunch, while Marcus, central, had been stuck in a pointless pep rally just before. Telling what they'd seen had the effect of making them relive it. Lucy shivered as if cold, despite the warmth, even in the tree's shadow. Noticing, Marcus held her to provide what comfort he could—and for something to hold on to.

"It was just terrible," she sobbed finally, her face buried in his shoulder.

"I know," he said, patting her back while his own eyes welled. "I know, I know . . ."

And as they sobbed, reliving the worst day of their lives, they kept sneaking little touches of each other: an arm, a neck, a shoulder, a face. It was practically autonomic—their bodies still needing to confirm the reality of the other. And once their bodies were satisfied, their brains and emotions got in on the action, hugging to console, and then hugging just to hug. Kissing just to kiss. Making love just to make love . . .

Over the next few days, they spilled out their selectively edited lives, organized around the dividing line of "before" and "after." The stories of their lives before, naturally, took up the most time, while the afters were short and ended the same way:

"And then I met you . . ."

Once they both finished, it seemed natural for one of them to ask, "And so now what?" So Marcus did.

"To be continued?" Lucy said, making it sound like a question as she waited for Marcus to squeeze her hand—which he also did.

They decided the ice cream truck was big enough for two with the added advantage of not having a blown engine. Plus, they both concurred with the truck's editorializing: Marcus because he'd done it, and Lucy because she'd felt it, not only after, but just before, when it seemed as if she'd been abandoned by the guy upstairs. But when it came to the vacancy their former faiths had left behind, neither wanted to talk about it. Instead, they filled said vacancy the old-fashioned way: with survival sex. Still, it was a present absence, manifesting itself euphemistically during moments of frustration.

"So who thought *this* was a good idea?" one might ask with his or her eyes cast ever so subtly skyward.

"Who knows?" the other would answer, shrugging, at a loss over whom to blame for this nondenominational apocalypse. After that, there wasn't too much left to say but:

"You wanna?"

"Sure, why not?"

Checking herself in the rearview mirror afterward, Lucy announced that she hated her smile. They were practicing with admissions, tiptoeing up to the line of confession and then chickening out last minute with benign substitutions. The latest safe category for discussion was certain attributes they didn't like about themselves. Lucy hadn't mentioned her modest weight issues, mainly because several weeks on the road away from Häagen-Dazs had worked wonders on her figure. Despite their living in a literal ice cream truck, the on-board freezer was not stocked with the stuff.

"You like Blue Bunny?" Marcus had joked when she noted the irony. "Here," he said, producing two he'd caught, skinned, and frozen. He clacked their carcasses together; they sounded like rhythm sticks.

So, no, it wasn't her body generally that Lucy hated at the moment, just her teeth. Marcus kissed the lips she'd wrung down over the offending dentition. "Think of it this way," he said. "Let's say you'd gotten braces." Pause. "Let's say you still had them."

Lucy thought about it—her jaws wired for the rest of her life, or at least until they stumbled onto somebody else who happened to be an orthodontist. She smiled, imperfectly, but smiled nevertheless. "Good point," she said. "Now you."

"I could do without my overwhelming charisma," Marcus said, even further from confessing what he needed to than Lucy was, replacing it not even with, say, crooked teeth, but with jokes. "It's quite the burden. Women constantly swooning in my presence . . ."

"Where are these women of whom you speak?"

"Before," Marcus said. "Trust me. It was crazy."

"I shall try imagining it," she said, brushing her fingers across his forehead, moving his charismatic hair out of his eyes. "You need a haircut."

"That was going to be my second thing," Marcus admitted. "This hair?" He tugged a fistful. "It just keeps on growing." He thought about the hair on the heads of his would-be victims and how some people believed it kept growing after death. It didn't. Really, as the body lost moisture, it began to shrink, including the skin around the face and head, creating the illusion that the hair was longer. Deciding to keep this fun fact to himself, Marcus turned toward Lucy, saying, "Your turn."

His de facto girlfriend shrugged. "Got nothing. You?"

Her de facto boyfriend shrugged.

"What are the odds, huh?" Lucy said. "Two perfect people hooking up in this crazy old world of ours?"

"Lucky us," Marcus agreed.

"Lucky us," said Lucy, a trace of her imperfect teeth showing through her smile.

Before this conversation, they'd been talking about a different smile, Marcus's, and its disappearance whenever the fuel gauge started flirting with *E*. With all its on-board appliances—the generator, loudspeaker, fridge—the ice cream truck was not the most fuel-efficient ride around.

Not that there wasn't plenty of fuel for the taking, even after the electricity died and the gas pumps stopped working. Everywhere they went, there were cars and SUVs and pickups with gas tanks like full udders, just waiting to be milked. And still Marcus frowned whenever faced with the prospect of milking another one.

"What's wrong?" Lucy asked, after noticing him do it a few times.

Marcus had been transfusing fuel the old-fashioned way, with a rubber hose and a pair of lips. And even though he only ever got the slightest taste before the gas started flowing from one vehicle to the other, he'd been doing it so often he joked about blowing up if he ate anything too spicy. He didn't mention the previous occasion when blowing up had been on the menu. Instead: "It's the taste," he said. "It tastes like brain damage and a side of cancer."

Lucy laughed. "Why didn't you say something sooner?" she asked, along with why he was being so careful about the other cars. "It's not like they're going to bust us for vandalism or anything."

True, Marcus thought. "True," he said.

And so they got a Rubbermaid tub from under the bed of a house they broke into looking for assorted other supplies. They dumped the horrible-looking collection of Christmas sweaters out, a handful of mothballs bouncing across the floor, rolling under the bed, crunching under Lucy's combat boots, courtesy of the same fashion depot from which she'd gotten her gas mask. The tub even had little casters underneath, which came in handy for sliding it under gas tanks. In the basement of the same house, she found a handyman's workshop, from which she rescued a claw hammer and a file. She used the latter to sharpen the former.

"Observe," she said, sliding the tub under their next pit stop, before scooting in after it with the hammer. She punctured the gas tank twice, once on the bottom and again as close to the top as she could reach. "It's like one of those old-school beer cans," she said. "The ones you needed a church key for, before pop-tops?"

"How old are you, again?"

"Dad collected," she said, sliding back out. "eBay."

Marcus nodded as they listened to the gas glugging into the tub. "Sweet," he announced. "My DNA thanks you."

"Excellent," Lucy said back. "I've got me some plans for that DNA."

They both stopped to let an uncomfortable pause go by.

Sure, they'd been having sex—a lot—but hadn't openly discussed the possible ramifications. Of course, it was easier for Marcus to not think about the *p*-word than it was for her. And Lucy, apparently, had been thinking about it—apparently ever since that first time.

Noticing Marcus's face, she waited to see if he said anything, assuming that if he didn't, that was probably her answer. He didn't and so she didn't. Instead, they rode quietly for a while, the only sound "Pop Goes the Weasel" playing over the loudspeaker. In her current mood, the lyrics struck Lucy as especially Freudian.

Eventually, realizing that quiet could become as lethal as talking about uncomfortable subjects, Lucy decided to try humor instead.

"You know what would be hee-larious?"

"What?"

"Rod Serling singing 'Zip-a-Dee-Doo-Dah.'"

Marcus looked at her. "Rod who?"

Lucy was surprised they couldn't hear the sound of her heart breaking. "Don't tell me you don't know about Rod. Not believing in God, fine. Been there, stopped believing that. But Rod? OMG! I . . ." But then she noticed the smile sneaking across Marcus's face.

"Gotcha," he said.

"True story," she agreed, knitting her fingers with his.

22

The day after the storm, Dev continued putting off doing the inside bodies. He decided to walk Diablo instead. He felt bad about leaving the dog locked up in the house while he collected bodies. But now that the streets were free of possible temptation, he decided a little stroll through their semigated community would do them both some good.

They had barely made it past the Brinkman estate when Diablo found the end of the leash and started pulling. Well, duh. The house next door belonged to his previous owner. Of course Diablo would want to investigate.

"Sorry," Dev said, giving the leash a tug. "You don't need to see whatever's in that house."

But then it happened again. And again. House after house. Could the smell of rotting flesh be *that* tempting? Could Diablo even smell it through the closed windows and doors, all the way out on the street? But then he noticed it wasn't the dog's nose but his ears that were on high alert. They perked up as the two approached the next house, followed by Diablo's head turning and the now-familiar tug on the leash. This time, though, the dog turned around again toward Dev, eyebrows asking a question in canine before actually whimpering.

"What is it, boy?" Dev asked, as if he might be spared having to check for himself. Unsurprisingly, the dog said nothing, just kept whimpering and pulling instead.

"Crap," he said before letting the black Lab lead the way to the locked door, where Diablo parked himself as if waiting for his human to do something. Dev decided the front window was the path of least resistance, a theory he proved with a lawn gnome, thrown just so. He tinked off the jagged bits still clinging to the window frame, his thumb and index finger flicking, one, two, three . . .

As suspected, there was a body in full rot, an afghan on its lap, a TV tray next to the chair, flies. He'd not brought his respirator because the walk hadn't started out as a body removal mission, not until Diablo insisted. Hastily pulling his shirt collar across his nose and mouth, Dev was prepared to leave the body for another day when he heard what the dog must have heard: the rusty-hinge squawk of a parrot, followed by the clink, clink, clink of its beak on what looked like an empty water dish.

"Oh jeez," Dev said, his shoulders slumping like somebody just cut his strings.

It never occurred to him. Even though he'd adopted his own, he hadn't thought about his neighbors' pets. Innocent animals in desperate straits behind all those doors, untended to, un–provided for, now that their owners had very inconsiderately died.

He barely had a chance to wonder how the bird had survived when it showed him. Focusing on a fly that had foolishly flown within beak's reach, the bird's head darted and snapped. A couple more and the feathered Renfield had enough juice to hazard another door-hinge squawk.

"Water," Dev supplied. "You want water, right?"

"Agua . . ."

Dev flinched. He hadn't had one of his questions answered since all of his questions became rhetorical. The response so surprised him he momentarily forgot how plumbing worked. Assuming the house's water lines were as empty as his, he checked the freezer instead and returned with a thawed ice-cube tray as the parrot began rocking its cage. Dev hesitated, seeing the talons hooked between the bars as the bird stirred the air with its green and shedding wings. "Coming," he stalled. "*Agua* is coming . . ."

"Water," the parrot translated.

Looking at the tray in his hands and the door in the cage, Dev couldn't imagine opening it without getting pecked. "I'm . . . ," he started, stopped, started again. "Wait right there," he said, placing the tray beyond Diablo's reach, even though the devil dog seemed more interested in this bird that could talk like a person than stealing its water.

After rummaging through the kitchen, Dev returned with a handful of drinking straws and poked one through the bars above the water dish, where it immediately became victim to a vicious beak attack. "Too short," he said, letting go of the first before grabbing three new straws and wedging them together. Taking a sip from the tray, he poked the straw through the bars and released a stream into the empty dish.

"Don't mind the spit," he advised, and the bird didn't seem to as its tongue darted and flicked water down its arid throat.

"Thank you," it said after a dish and a half.

"You're welcome," Dev said back, for lack of anything better to say.

There was a pause then as one survivor eyed the other two between bars. "Food?" it finally squawked, pitched perfectly so even Dev could hear the question mark at the end.

The parrot became the spokesbird for the rest, talking Dev into the totally impractical decision to take care of his neighbors' pets. And it was true what they said about pets resembling their owners. Not necessarily physically, but in terms of circumstance. That was the conclusion he'd reached after noticing that wherever he found aquariumed, bowled, or caged pets, there was also a dead caretaker who looked like they hadn't gotten out much. Two were further confined to wheelchairs, which was considerate of them, especially when it came to removing their bodies.

As imprisoned as these animals were, they had done reasonably well, all things considered. The snakes still seemed to be digesting their last meals while the reptiles with legs benefited from the clouds of flies their rotting benefactors had drawn. The birds, too, appeared to have supplemented their diets this way once their seed stashes ran out, while the fish didn't want for food or water, the latter for obvious reasons and the former because fish tended to be notoriously overfed. What the fish needed most was oxygen, once the air pumps died and the water in their tanks grew stagnant. Dev found several aquariums that had simply become slime-green monstrosities full of dead fish. Ironically, the few that had survived he thought owed thanks to thirsty, furry housemates who'd helped themselves to the tanks' water, keeping it moving and oxygenated until the water level was too low for them to reach, by which time the fish's own swimming was enough to stave off stagnation.

While the fish won Dev's admiration for the improbability of their survival, the rodents earned his ire by having resorted to cannibalism, the evidence of which consisted of little curled paws lying among their wood shavings. Dev's response to this lack of civility was feeding the offending creatures to the snakes that still had room for dessert, his acts of mercy limited to those that deserved it.

From the looks of things, some of the dogs and cats not lucky enough to bunk with a tankful of fish had either been left with the toilet seats already up or had figured it out for themselves, while also having access to bags of dried food whose chip-clips were no match for a good set of claws. The less lucky had improvised their survival, recycling their own waste and/or gnawing on anything leather. For water, they had lapped at puddles from the defrosting coils of inefficient refrigerators, air conditioners, knocked-over vases, and/or backed-up sinks.

In retrospect, Dev probably should have set them free to fend for themselves. The dogs and cats probably stood a fifty-fifty chance. The lizards, who knew? And the snakes—especially the boa constrictor—might lower the odds for the rest.

But then there were the fish.

If the parrot hadn't talked him into it, the fish would have. They'd already been through so much, had survived so improbably, he couldn't condemn them to the Ecorse River, which had been used as an industrial toilet too long for anything but Frankenfish to survive. Eventually, it would heal itself just like the air, but Dev wouldn't be dining on anything he pulled from the river at the end of his block anytime soon. He'd wait until the mayflies came back; Google said that was the sign a body of water was on the rebound—even though Google itself hadn't been so lucky.

So he'd take care of the fish until the river was ready for them. And if he was going to take care of the fish, he might as well take care of the lizards, the birds, and the snakes. And if he was going to take care of all those refugees from the Jurassic, could he really ignore the mammals with which he shared so much more DNA?

The answer in at least one case was yes; he could ignore one such animal. It had not restrained itself. It had gone the dog-eat-dog route, like the rodents he turned into snake food, though this one had dined further up the food chain. He'd already imagined as much. But imagining and seeing were two different things. Diablo tried to warn him the only way a dog could, by tugging in the opposite direction as they approached the crime scene in question.

"What is it, boy?" Dev asked, tugging on the leash and meeting canine refusal. "Pretty bad, huh?" he guessed, not having the slightest idea of how bad bad could get. The Lab sent a sort of Morse code with his eyebrows before finally resorting to a prolonged howl as Dev opened the door.

It was worse than he'd imagined. The animal in question was one of those pocket dogs and would surely have died without its owner as a ready source of protein. Said owner was—or had been—an older woman, judging from the housedress the bones wore and the tufts of gray hair scattered about the living room. Dev had dealt with a lot of bodies on their way to becoming skeletons, but this was the cleanest picked he'd seen that hadn't been cleaned by fire. He paused for a moment to admire the job when he noticed the housedress moving. The top of the dress twisted and snarled as if one breast were fighting the other.

And then, just as quickly, the dress stopped as the fattest little Chihuahua Dev had ever seen waddled out from underneath the skirt. Its round belly was just a few meals away from lifting its feet off the ground, leaving its paws paddling air. As it licked its chops, Dev stepped back out onto the porch and closed the door.

"You were right," he said, pulling Diablo away from the place.

He returned later, with a can of Alpo and a handgun. Opening the door, he whistled until the offending beast came waddling out, looking more like a pregnant wiener dog than a Chihuahua. "Here you go, fatso," Dev said, tipping the open can over a bowl and letting its contents plop out. He stepped back and sighted down the barrel as the bobbing brown head chewed its own grave.

But then he hesitated. He'd never killed anything of any appreciable size before. There were the unavoidable worms that got squished on rainy days, the mosquitoes he slapped out of instinct, and the countless other bugs, from the barely visible to the microscopic. And the gerbils he'd turned into snake food, of course, but they still fell below the threshold of what he considered murder. Protein reallocation—that's what they were. But a dog—a dog of any size was killing, no matter how justified the death might be to avoid corrupting the others.

And so he closed his eyes and then squeezed the trigger. The shot went astray, blowing out a window across the street, missing its intended target by a mile. The bang, however—the bang was like a dog whose bark was worse than its bite. Dev opened his eyes in time to see the dog complete a somersault as if it'd jerked its little rat head up at the sound and just kept going. After sticking the landing, the Chihuahua looked a little surprised to still be alive, but then bolted—or as close to bolting as it was capable of, with its low-slung belly and too-short legs.

Dev followed, firing into the air whenever the dog showed signs of tiring. "Keep going," he shouted, driving the herd of one toward the wall of SUVs. Once there, he wrenched open the driver-side door of one of the lower riding ones and popped the passenger-side door before capturing and boosting the mega mutt up to where it could bounce on the blackened springs.

"Good boy," he lied, before slamming the door shut. And then he listened. Heard springs squeaking like they were trying to make up their mind. He fired the gun one last time and thought he heard the springs sproing, though it could have been the ringing in his ears. As the echo faded and the ringing stopped, they were replaced by the unnatural thing's yipping, growing ever fainter as it waddled away to its death by other means.

Dev blew across the muzzle that had already cooled. Going to holster the gun, he realized he hadn't brought one and shrugged. And then he went home to Diablo, where the lucky dog got extra helpings of the food that may have spared the Chihuahua its fate, if only it had thumbs to work the can opener.

23

Marcus didn't notice them until the third or fourth time after they'd done it, watching Lucy get dressed. "Two watches?" he said.

"Correct," Lucy said, buckling the second one on.

"Why two?" by which he meant, really, "Why any?" It wasn't like they had to worry about missing the bus or anything.

Lucy pointed to the one on her left wrist, a cheap LCD number with the day, date, and year. "This is so I'll know the date," she said, before pointing to the old-fashioned windup one on her right. "And this is the backup."

"But why bother keeping track at all?" Marcus asked, finally.

"Because I'm a woman," Lucy said, pausing to see if he got it. To her, it was obvious: women were practically clocks themselves, and a woman's quality of life could depend on knowing what time of the month it was—something that had hit home for Lucy not too long ago.

Meanwhile, Marcus thought about it and was ready to admit he was stumped when it hit him. He palmed his face, embarrassed, before peeking at her through his fingers. "I'm an idiot," he said.

"You know," she said, neither confirming nor denying his idiocy, "I'll bet the first astronomer was a woman. An astrologer, at very least. Primitive men would have been fine with the sun going around the earth, but it takes a woman to know that life revolves around the moon."

Marcus nodded as if agreeing, hoping that by doing so they could get off the subject of women and their menstrual cycle sooner. No such luck.

"I'll bet it was a woman that got men to build Stonehenge," Lucy continued, warming to her subject—and the way it made Marcus squirm.

"Excuse me?" he said, part question, part request to be dismissed from the conversation.

Lucy, meanwhile, dramatized her thesis.

"I'd like that rock over there and that other one, just a skootch that way," she said, impersonating her designer of Stonehenge, complete with hand gestures.

"But why?" she asked, impersonating the would-be stone haulers.

"Because you don't want your women pregnant all the time, now do you?" she finished.

Marcus wondered whether Lucy's question was aimed at those ancient Stonehengian contractors or some more contemporary listener, much closer by. Just testing, he tried a pointed joke of his own.

"Yeah," he said, "I guess that's something they didn't have back then."

"What's that?"

"Biological clocks with," he began, only to be cut off by Lucy's eyes, set to stun.

"What?" she prodded.

. . . *a snooze alarm,* Marcus thought, not that he'd say it. Not anymore. Instead, sheepishly, he said, "I don't know," before picking an alternative nearly as bad. "Options, I guess."

Lucy thought about going off on him before realizing Marcus was right—just not about the birth control options he was alluding to, nor the ancients who lacked them. The options they were out of? Other partners. And so she decided to make nice until either the odds improved or one of them died.

"Cute," she said finally, not really meaning it, but not needing to, seeing as Marcus had the same number of options in the partner department as she did. So there.

When it came to getting what they needed to survive, Lucy and Marcus thought of it as shopping, minus the hassle of paying for stuff. The condition they found the stores in—unpillaged—contributed to the illusion. They'd found no evidence of roaming bands Mad Maxing through all the good stuff ahead of them. Every bit of new geography was virgin territory for the pair of ex-virgins, provided they didn't get detoured back into the land of trough and toilet.

The main downside was the whole airtight, no AC, southern thing again. Even stores that had been reasonably body-free when what came down, came down, didn't always stay that way. Stores with automatic doors had swallowed up the occasional wandering animal while the electricity still flowed—dogs, deer, a goat, skunks, a literal bull once but in an appliance store, not a china shop—only to trap them inside once the helpful electronics that had let them in died, followed by the eventual death of whatever wandered into whatever foodless business it had wandered into, after toppling shelves, shattering big-screen TVs, bashing their heads bloody against panes of shatterproof glass. Anything disturbed or destroyed in these places, post-whatever, had been disturbed or destroyed by something other than humans—either animals or some chain reaction triggered by something falling onto something else, rodents gnawing at the bottom of some stack of something that came Jenga-ing down to smash or roll or bounce to its penultimate resting place until Lucy's or Marcus's foot kicked it out of the way.

The grocery stores were the worst—even ones where no one and nothing had died. Because even without putrescent corpses and/or carcasses, there were still the formerly fresh fruits and vegetables, buzzing with flies, crawling with maggots, withered, burst, turning to mush, leaking down shelves, eyes sprouting through the mesh windows of five-pound bags, damp with the beginnings of fermentation. Eggs by the dozen, fragile bombs of stench; gallons of milk turned to watery cottage cheese; cottage cheese pushing out of its container, livid with mold; thighs and drumsticks with gangrene; raw hamburger as brown and crusty as meat loaf fully cooked; the other white meat blotched purple, orange, phosphorescent with exotic pathogens, flourishing under the plastic wrap.

Marcus had teased Lucy about her gas mask precisely once—until he went shopping with her that first time and discovered that shopping wasn't an ordeal to be gotten through with a handkerchief over your face while you grabbed what you needed and got out, preferably within the time frame of a single held breath. Nope. When Lucy shopped, she *shopped*—with two or three extra "ops" stretching it out. She *lingered*. She breathed through a double-barrel charcoal canister that stopped the fouled air from reaching her young lungs, allowing her to check labels, compare nutrients, check unit prices though they'd all been commonly denominated down to zero dollars and zero cents.

"I'm kind of wishing that was 'zero scents,'" Marcus said, green at the gills and getting greener. After that, their very next shopping trip had been to an army surplus store, to see what kind of gas masks they had in his size.

The pair stocked up on the nonperishables, nonabsorbent, undamaged. Canned goods were good; things vacuum sealed like coffee, jarred nuts, crackers if they were shelved high enough; pasta; peanut butter; dried soup mixes; raisins; cookies; potato chips in tubes; multipacks of assorted carbonated beverages; cases of bottled water. Matches were essential, along with charcoal, lighter fluid, aluminum foil, toilet paper. Paper plates were always welcome, along with plastic utensils and Solo cups because, seriously, after the end of the world, who wants to do the dishes?

Each had their favorite things to scavenge. Lucy's included button batteries for her LCD watch; feminine hygiene products; those little horoscope tubes ("for giggles"); Oreos because, well, they were Oreos. Marcus's gotta-have-its included duct tape and zip ties, especially the yard-long ones he found at certain hardware stores.

"I'd be worried about that," Lucy remarked, "if becoming a serial killer wasn't a little pointless this late in the game."

"What?" Marcus asked, exaggerating a look of innocence. "*These?* These are great. Something comes apart, a rusty bolt, whatever, you don't have to sort through a million different screws because—boom—one size fits all. Just thread one of these puppies though, yank it tight, and you're good to go."

"Was your dad an engineer?"

"Yeah, so?"

"Nothing," she said. "Just wondering if it was an inherited trait." Was that too obvious? Inheritance, genetics, reproduction . . .

"What trait?"

"Being brilliant when it comes to fixing things," she said, buttering him up like he were toast. Judging from the aw-shucks grin on his face, that's exactly what he was.

Condoms.

They weren't on either of their lists—not until after Lucy's lecture on the menstrual cycle. After that, she found herself rounding the corner just in time to see Marcus stuffing boxes of Trojans into his pockets. Their eyes met, but they didn't say anything. Instead, he deflected, as she was learning he tended to do.

"You ever use one of these as a water balloon?" he asked, holding up one of the unpocketed boxes, as if he'd just stumbled upon the display. "They hold a crazy amount of water . . ."

"I prefer not to sacrifice lambs for my water sports, thank you," Lucy said back, wondering how on earth he imagined she wouldn't notice that he was wearing a condom the next time they did it. What, was he just going to go around wearing one until—to quote the old Viagra commercials—the moment was right? That hardly seemed sanitary, especially for the party on the receiving end.

Marcus, meanwhile, showed every sign of imagining they'd moved on from the subject. She'd seen them, after all. Condoms would just be another step in their routine, one of a growing number of routines imposing order on chaos—or the illusion thereof.

And so they continued shopping—a young couple in gas masks—the first postpeople customers to enter this particular establishment and all the other establishments they'd entered thus far. It was fun, the two feeling less like survivors of an apocalypse and more like a newlywed couple with a bottomless expense account, shopping together, making inside jokes about the merchandise, everything still new to them, still funny, pulling little pranks on one another, like now, Lucy hiding behind the checkout counter, waiting to see how long it took before Marcus came looking for her.

She checked one of her two watches—the less intimidating one with hands that swept the seconds into minutes, minutes into hours, as opposed to the countdown digits of the other. She could hear the squeaky wheels of his cart, the wiry bang of things going into it. He walked right by where she squatted, hiding, deciding whether to spring out or not, until it was too late; he'd already passed. She looked at her watch. Ten minutes without his wondering where she was. Then fifteen. Finally, she conceded the game he—apparently—hadn't known they were playing. Or maybe he just didn't care. Lifting her mask, she called out to her oblivious fellow shopper:

"You still perfect over there?" she asked.

"As ever," Marcus said, surprising her by popping up from behind, smiling, or so she assumed, what with the gas mask and all. "And you?"

Lucy rose as she lowered her mask, sidestepping out from behind the counter. "Need you ask?" she said, doing a twirl right there in the middle of the aisle.

"That reminds me," she called out, still thinking about the condoms. "We need more drugs."

"Need? Or want?"

Regarding pharmaceuticals, Lucy displayed a hypochondriacal Boy Scout's desire to be prepared for anything. Every drugstore or grocery store with a pharmacy in back, she stocked up on cold medicines, bandages, antibiotics, sleeping pills, cortisone, painkillers, prenatal vitamins (which she slipped into a pocket while Marcus wasn't looking), and pretty much everything else she could think of with the exception of birth control pills. Marcus, meanwhile, stuck with iodine, hydrogen peroxide, rubbing alcohol, Aspercreme, and bottles of Absorbine Jr.

"You should get some antibiotics too," Lucy said. "I mean, you can use mine, but you can never have enough, considering all the rusty edges out there."

Marcus shook his head. "I know exactly how much is enough," he said.

"Elucidate me."

"Any," Marcus said. "For me, at least." Turned out he'd had an allergic reaction to an antibiotic he'd been given when he was five. He couldn't remember the name. One of the ones that ended in "-in," he offered.

"I think that's all of them," Lucy said. "Or just about."

"That's been my general impression," he said, "yes." To hear him tell it, that singular dose of an antibiotic ending in "-in" had been enough to almost end Marcus. "My throat swelled shut," he said. "A doctor talked my dad through doing a tracheotomy over his cell phone. There wasn't even time for an ambulance." He pointed toward a knot of scar tissue just under his Adam's apple, just above the collarbone. Lucy touched it as cautiously as Adam reaching out toward God on the ceiling of the Sistine Chapel.

"Did it hurt?"

"I was unconscious by then," Marcus said. "I just remember popping out of it once I could breathe again—like Uma Thurman in *Pulp Fiction*. My parents said it was like I'd come back from the dead."

"Sounds like you kind of did," Lucy said.

"Guess the universe just had other plans for me," he said, Lucy noting how he used "universe" to avoid invoking the *a-* or *g*-words.

"Looks like," she agreed, not making the mistake of mentioning her own plans for him or his DNA. Not again, at least.

24

Earthly remains and a gluttonous rat dog weren't the only things Dev needed to get rid of. Along with the rest of civilization, the end of the world also saw the end of routine trash pickup. Diablo and he had produced enough on their own, each day's meals adding more bones, eggshells, bottles, and cans to the steadily growing pile to be dealt with, eventually. But once he started taking care of Devonshire's other citizens, garbage production kicked up a few notches. Not only that, but he'd inherited all the rotting food in his dead neighbors' refrigerators.

He'd tried leaving those upright grocery coffins alone, counting on their hermetic seals to keep the stench contained. But the other citizens of Devonshire—those with a keener sense of smell—were less inclined to let sleeping dogs lie. They either steered clear of the aforementioned appliances or worried away at them, claws raking through enamel, leaving exposed metal and flakes of eggshell, harvest gold, olive green littering the linoleum. Eventually, one intrepid shepherd got the thing open and proceeded to sicken itself on the contents before puking them up again all over the place.

Crap, Dev thought after stepping through the door, just before stepping back out again. And then he went looking for his respirator—the one he thought he'd retired.

Plastic shopping bags stuffed with more shopping bags: every house he entered had stashes of them. Armed with these, a pair of rubber gloves, and the aforementioned respirator, Dev worked through the sarcophagi of his neighbors' refrigerators, segregating the garbage that dripped from the containers whose lids had been glued tight with dried mayo, ketchup, or the aptly named jam. These latter were bagged and deposited in the charred trucks making up the Great Wall of Devonshire. Some were used to fill in the empty spaces left behind in the cabs when their passengers went to pieces, while the rest were deposited into the truck beds to top off the crenellations formed by the sequence of cab, bed, cab . . .

The drippy-stinky stuff Dev wrapped in newspaper before bagging it. He had plenty of those too—newspapers—including one particular edition he'd been wondering what to do with. After getting home on the afternoon of the whatever-it-was, he found a still-bound bundle of the *Detroit Free Press*, the last edition of the last day before there was no more history to be the first draft of. Even though the papers were dropped off by truck early in the morning, the delivery kid always waited until getting back from school. None of the working-class subscribers complained about this deferred delivery schedule; like the paper kid, they were too busy establishing a.m. consciousness to be bothered with news of the world (or even just that of the greater Detroit metro area). Plus, those who were really eager to be depressed just checked their Facebook feeds to catch up on the latest dead celebrity or political travesty their once-sane friends were ranting about. The only reason any of them still subscribed to the *paper* paper—other than out of pure habit—was for the want ads, sale inserts, and coupons.

That bundle of pristine copies of the doomsday edition would have made a good collector's item, if there were anyone left to collect it. Dev himself—out of respect or superstition—had set it aside, away from the rain, to wait until he figured out what to do with it. Reading at least one copy might have seemed like a no-brainer, but based on what he could see of the front page above the fold, he decided to skip it. At first, everything was still too raw. And then there was too much to do. Finally, when Dev was ready, the old adage proved true: old news was no news. Nothing he'd read in that last edition could possibly hold his interest for the simple reason that he knew exactly how each and every one of the stories contained therein turned out:

". . . and then everybody died."

Dev technically didn't need to wrap the garbage in the first place, especially before placing it in a plastic bag. He'd started because that's what his mother had always done. When his mother was still alive to ask, she'd said it was because that's how *her* mother always did it. When Dev asked why, his mother called her sister, who called an aunt, who discovered that Dev's maternal grandmother—the originator of this multigenerational routine—did it because the garbage pail they used had rusted through in spots and she didn't want to attract rats, which were a big enough problem in that part of Bombay (now Mumbai). And so three generations of headlines and want ads had been used to swaddle Pranesh, then Brinkman, garbage because a rusty pail in India leaked a hundred years ago. And even though he'd eventually gotten to the root of the practice, it didn't stop him; the habit had already been set.

In a way, it seemed fitting: wrapping old food in old news for old reasons. Dev did set aside one copy—out of respect or superstition or maybe to show the aliens once they arrived, so they could see what humans were interested in just before going extinct. The rest of the copies, however, were dedicated to garbage wrapping. And when he ran out, he started using the other papers his neighbors had left behind. What was left after that could be used for toilet paper, once he ran out of the real kind, which, thanks to his neighbors' tendency to buy such things in bulk, shouldn't be for a very long time.

The plastic bags full of gift-wrapped garbage would not be added to the wall. Despite the plastic and paper, gulls, crows, and other scavengers would eventually find them, rip them open, and cry or caw or chitter their delight over what they found. And Dev wasn't having it. In addition to the inconvenience such animals posed, there was the chance their presence in numbers might attract larger animals of the Dev-eating kind.

Which left him with a problem: Now that he had all this neatly packaged garbage, what was he supposed to do with it? That it needed to be somewhere on the other side of the wall was obvious. What wasn't obvious was how he was going to get it far enough outside the wall so that it wouldn't act as bait for things he didn't want to attract. Dev was never that good at sports; given a baseball, he was as likely to space out over the red stitching x-ing itself in a kind of Möbius strip around the ball as throw it with much strength, speed, or aim. So just throwing the bags over the wall wouldn't do it. And the idea of loading up a car and driving to a dump site on a regular basis for the rest of his life seriously conflicted with his decision to stay put.

Burning was an option, but Dev got hung up on the whole respect versus superstition thing. It didn't seem right to treat the garbage like corpses or vice versa. Plus, Dev wasn't sure he'd burn the bodies now, if he had it to do over again. He'd just gotten lucky all that smoke hadn't drawn others—if there were any to draw in the first place—an unknown Dev preferred not be resolved by having them show up on his doorstep.

He'd begun imagining the construction of a kind of garbage catapult using bungee cords zip-tied into a bungee cable and attached somehow to a long-handled, big-bladed shovel when he noticed the half-hushed giggle of a far simpler solution: the river. The one flowing past at the end of his abbreviated block. All he'd have to do is lean over the railing, drop, and let the current carry it out of sight and out of Devonshire. He hesitated at the thought of polluting the already-polluted river, which he had plans for, once nature, no other people, and time cleaned up its act. But then he rationalized it. He wasn't some factory, pouring who knew what into the river. He wasn't the local sewer system, diverting its overflow there either. He was just dropping neatly buoyant bubbles of organic material on top of a moving medium that would carry it away without necessarily interacting with it. At some point, something hungry or curious would fish them out, or the tumbling current would work the knots free, as the organic stuff sank and dissolved to become fish food while the plastic bags, unknotted and unburdened, could go flying to wherever the wind wanted them . . .

Once again, out of sight, out of Devonshire.

25

As they drove, passing billboards advertising memories, a game suggested itself: What Do You Miss? This was not to be confused with *Whom* Do You Miss? They never played that game; it hurt too much. *What* was as far as they could let themselves go. Rounds were started randomly, when one of them announced some missed thing, like:

"Ice cream," Lucy said, beginning a round. It was a no-brainer but personally a little risky, seeing as it reminded her of her mom, a very big whom she missed desperately.

"Twinkies," Marcus countered, inspired by Lucy's ice cream, which itself, he assumed, was probably inspired by the truck they were driving.

Lucy was about to leapfrog to the name of a K-pop boy band that specialized in a discordantly peppy goth-jazz-steampunk fusion she liked but was also talking herself out of mentioning because, well, in her experience one of the few universal things boys her age *didn't* care about was boy bands of any ilk, followed by *Twilight* as a close second. But then she stopped. "Twinkies?" she said.

Marcus nodded behind the wheel.

"There still *are* Twinkies," she pointed out. "They literally *did* survive the apocalypse—despite *Zombieland*-ish suggestions to the contrary."

"Almost didn't," Marcus pointed out. "Hostess went bankrupt, but then the brand got bought and brought back."

"My point being," Lucy clarified, "we've seen boxes of them all over the place. You know that 'best by' date is a bunch of hooey, right?"

Actually, he hadn't known that, but that wasn't the reason. "I gave them up," Marcus said. "Just before." Which was only technically true. The earthquake at the 7-Eleven and the bloodied Twinkies had only temporarily put him off the golden cake, though at the time his abstention was expected to be permanent—given other things he'd decided to give up at the time. But after what happened—and *didn't* happen—he decided that giving up Twinkies was the least he could do, as punishment and a reminder of how easily he'd been led astray. None of which he was ready to confess to Lucy, not having stipulated a timeline on that promise to himself to come clean on the whole terrorism thing. It wasn't something you led with—he decided—when starting a new relationship, especially considering the limited number of still-breathing options he'd come across in that regard. And so when she asked him why, he lied. "Watching my weight," he said, which was just close enough to the bone for Lucy to switch topics away from food altogether.

"New episodes of *The Walking Dead*," she said for her next missed thing.

Marcus gave her a thumbs-up, impressed with a girl who didn't feign being put off by all the gore. But just in case, "Don't tell me it's 'because of the characters,'" he said.

"Nope," Lucy said. "Blood-n-guts, straight up."

Marcus let go of the wheel briefly to give her two thumbs-ups.

"Now you," Lucy said. "Your turn."

Marcus thought, hesitated, then said it: "Believing."

"In . . . ?" Lucy prompted.

Marcus leaned back to meet her eyes in the rearview mirror and then went back to staring straight ahead, at the road where they were the only thing going or coming anywhere. "You know," he said.

And she did. Though her former kind and his former kind differed on the particulars, neither had doubted that there was some bigger personal intelligence in charge of things; whether you called it God or Allah or your higher power as you understand it, it came down to the same thing, emotionally: an invisible friend who had your back and cared what happened to you. Instead of what the world they were driving through now was: indifferent.

"Domino's Pizza," Marcus said to break the gloom that had settled over the two of them.

"I thought you were watching your weight," Lucy said, eager to get off the food thing Marcus had brought them back to.

"Am," Marcus lied. "But Domino's is safe."

"How so?"

"They don't deliver anymore."

Lucy mimed a rim shot, and Marcus said, "Basketball."

"Watching or playing?"

"Both."

"Hanging out online," Lucy said.

Marcus made a face, aiming it into the rearview so she could see instead of having to guess from his profile.

"What's wrong with hanging out online?"

"What's wrong with hanging out in real space instead of cyberspace?" Marcus countered. He'd come to view the easy anonymity of the latter with a belated but healthy dose of skepticism.

"Nothing," Lucy said. "It's just, you know, convenient." She didn't mention that when it came to meeting others with her interests, staying local had resulted in basically one: Max. But in cyberspace you could connect to like-minded people you'd never bump into IRL. She had no way of knowing that those were the same reasons Marcus had for despising the web's so-called convenience.

"Some people take advantage of that convenience" was all he wanted to say on the subject.

Lucy paused, then got it, or thought she did. Said, "You landed yourself a catfish, didn't you?"

"Catfish?"

"Like some fifty-year-old creep passing himself off as a sixteen-year-old cheerleader with big boobs." She paused. "I think the name has something to do with being reeled in or bottom-feeders. Probably both."

Marcus considered the excuse she'd given him for discussing what he'd been through without really discussing what he'd been through—and took it. "Kind of," he said, eyes tentative in the rearview.

"That sucks," she said, returning his reflected gaze. "Was it, like, some total perv? Did he get you to, like, show up at some motel room and then go all pervy on you?"

"No," Marcus said, too hastily. "I mean, they took advantage of me in different ways."

"'They,'" Lucy repeated, catching it immediately. The I-don't-want-you-to-know-the-sex-of-the-person-I'm-talking-about pronoun. "Is this a he they or a she they?"

"A she they," Marcus said. "She got me to," he hesitated, then came up with a euphemism he figured he could work with, "send her money."

"How much money?"

"Almost everything I had," Marcus said, not untruthfully.

"How'd she get you to do that?"

"She played on my sympathies," he said, also not untrue. "There were all these things she wanted me to help fix."

"Like . . . ?"

"Broken car," Marcus said. "Broken tooth. Stuff kept breaking on her. I told her she must be the unluckiest person I knew—except I didn't really know her. Every time I started getting suspicious, she'd send me a picture to hook me all over again," he said, thinking of the slide shows they'd used against him.

"What, like, sexting?"

"No," Marcus said, again too hastily. "Like to make me feel sorry," pause, "for her."

"How'd she make you feel sorry," Lucy said, echoing his pause, "for her?"

Feeling cornered, Marcus went for broke. "I think someone was beating her. Her dad or somebody. She'd send pictures of bruises, blood, and stuff."

"Why didn't she go to the cops?" Lucy asked. "Why didn't *you* go to the cops?" Pause. "And how was sending money supposed to help?"

Marcus could feel the lie getting away from him and wanted to wrap it up. "She was going to run away. She needed money for a ticket, to get a place and stuff."

"Okay," Lucy said. "And then what?"

"Everybody died," he said.

To her credit, Lucy didn't make any jokes about Nigerian princes or Russian chatbots. She could tell Marcus was still pretty shaken up by the whole thing. Instead, she tried to console him with a thought that would have consoled her under similar circumstances. "Well, on the plus side, you won."

"How's that?"

"Whoever she was—if she even *was* a she—she's dead and you're not," Lucy said. "Plus, who needs money nowadays anyway?"

"Well," Marcus said. "There is that."

"And plus," she said, feeling a little cocky, "you got me." Pause. "Bonus points!"

"Bonus points, indeed," Marcus said, leaning sideways to mime a kiss in the general direction of her cheek, as if he'd actually confessed and been forgiven.

"A long, hot shower," Lucy said, initiating their next game of What Do You Miss?

"Yes," Marcus said. "Wow. Yes, yes, yes."

"It's not like I said I knew how to get one," she admitted.

"No, it's just," Marcus started, switched gears. "You win. You win What Do You Miss? forever."

"Your turn," Lucy said.

"No point," Marcus said. "You've won for all time."

"It's not really a *winning* kind of game," Lucy pointed out. "It's a time-killing one."

"Oh, okay," Marcus said before trying to win anyway. "Being ten," he said, thinking, *Take that.*

"Ten what?" she asked.

"Years old."

"That doesn't count," Lucy said. "We stopped being ten a long time before."

"I still miss it, though," Marcus said.

"Yeah," Lucy said, "me too."

Being ten. In a lot of ways, Lucy thought it was the perfect age. You were smart enough to understand most things when explained the right way, but still young enough not to care about things like your appearance, the opposite or same sex, life plans that preempted things like being an astronaut or princess or princess astronaut—back when magic wasn't just possible, but how you made it through the day, from the miracle of meals to the casual assumption that your safety was somebody else's responsibility. The only thing better than being ten was being ten during the summer, when even school couldn't interfere with your plan to read comic books all day on the porch, play video games until you discovered secret levels the conquering of which would make you famous but on your own terms, signaled by your saying, "Okay, I'm famous now," or "Time to leave me alone."

"Yeah, ten," Lucy sighed. "I think you may have won after all."

26

Dev remembered an online meme from before. The top half was a stock image of Jean-Luc Picard from *Star Trek: The Next Generation*, his mouth open, his arm out, palm up, declaiming, "Who the hell . . ." The punch line was the caption for the picture below, whatever it happened to be. In the one Dev remembered, the bottom was a still from *The Walking Dead*, the caption: ". . . is mowing lawns during the zombie apocalypse?"

He had the answer, now that the apocalypse had arrived, minus the zombies: Dev. *Dev* mowed lawns during the zombie apocalypse. Why not? He needed to do *something* now that the wall was finished. And keeping things tidy prevented Devonshire from looking quite so apocalyptic, now that the bodies had been dealt with. So Dev and Diablo did whatever yard work needed doing, which is to say, the human did it while the foredog watched.

And so Dev celebrated the one-month-ish anniversary of the whatever-it-was (his calendar may have slipped during his getting-to-know-you period with Diablo; in his experience, happiness frequently had that kind of effect on time) by mowing every lawn in Devonshire, bringing each to its pre-whatever-it-was, well-trimmed height. The work went quickly, thanks to a riding mower he borrowed from one of the neighbors, and even more quickly when he realized that by knocking down the fences separating the backyards, he could just ride straight from one end of a block to the next. And so down they came: bolt cutters for the chain link, a crowbar for the pickets, and a sledgehammer for the privacy. After the fences were down, mowing the backyards was pretty much as easy as mowing the front, especially after he made the first series of end-to-end passes, taking out whatever flowers or decorative shrubbery had been planted along the fence lines.

Dev's goal was not to keep Devonshire beautiful, per se. It never had been in the first place, a suburb being a suburb being a suburb. But keeping the wilderness at bay was what people had been doing for millennia, and that's all he was trying to do. That, and keeping himself busy.

Feeding the neighbors' pets was another way Dev kept occupied. Originally, he'd promised himself he'd set them free before he ran out of whatever food their owners had left behind. But then he got hooked on daily animal gratitude, accepting the wet tongues of appreciation, the trill, the flicked forked tongue and bubbles and blinking lizard eyes. Unlike the human variety, Dev liked looking into the eyes of his menagerie; they didn't make him feel like he was in a gunfight without any bullets. Unlike with humans, he could look long enough to note the curve and shine of their eyes, how in just the right light, he could see a little silhouette of himself staring back.

But then he ran out of pet food, or at least the stuff so called. Diablo had been eating what Dev ate all along, but if they started sharing with the rest, he'd be facing a trip out there anyway—just looking for people food. Plus, could some of them even eat people food? The fish, for example. He imagined dumping a can of sweet peas into an aquarium: yeah, no.

"They better be extra grateful is all I have to say," he said to Diablo, who wasn't and never would be part of the group known as "they." Diablo was Diablo: human's companion, first class. And no, there wasn't a second class. There was just the third-person plural for a lot of not-even-people he was taking care of: they, them, the others.

While it was debatable whether this was his first or fourth trip beyond the wall, depending on whether you counted mental walls or just the real kind, one thing was clear to Dev afterward: it would be his last. All the way to Pet Supplies Plus, he kept having to stop, swerve, back up, to make way for deer running through what had once been traffic, followed by packs of feral dogs. Elsewhere, through former neighborhoods, rats and rabbits darted into and out of foot-tall grass and weeds, busily taking over the front yards on either side of the street. The houses themselves looked like they'd been through a riot—charred shells here, busted-out windows there, the latter, no doubt, thanks to startled deer making a last-ditch attempt at not being mauled.

And then there were the bodies, the ones without a Dev to dispose of them. Left alone, their skin had been reduced to residue clotting their clothes, baggy and flapping around the remaining bones. There wasn't much left for nature to recycle, except a few hairs, barely holding on to the skulls they once covered, glued there now by crusted scalp gunk. These last human scraps made good nesting material, it seemed—judging from the birds perched on all the dead heads he could see. The wide availability of hair also explained how everywhere he looked—in tree branches, under eaves, and even in the open mouth of a skeleton, still harnessed to a utility pole, its empty sockets facing skyward—Dev saw these fantastic, bird-woven toupees of many colors. Human hair had become the seventies shag carpeting of the avian world—a questionable look destined to fade away, but comfortable underneath bare toes, or talons. And the chicks seemed to agree, peeping up a storm in their impromptu dos. Dev admired the creepy practicality of it, while also noting he should probably add a hat to his outdoor wardrobe.

Dev parked outside the store like he was just another customer, avoiding the handicap spaces out front as if someone else might still need them. Stepping down from the truck, he passed other cars that had obviously pulled in just before the whatever-it-was, passengers just getting out before dropping and cracking their skulls on the asphalt. Others had corpses still inside, the windows rolled up and clouded with the grease and gas of their decomposition, their skin turned jerky, cooked by the sun day after sunny day.

One car parked in a handicap space was particularly grisly. The driver's window was rolled down just an inch while in the front, two bodies rested, one of an elderly man, judging from the plaid sport coat and matching fedora, and the other a dog—its skeleton, really—shrunk-wrapped in fur so tight Dev could count the bones. One of the driver's hands was missing, the sleeve of the sport coat empty. Pressing against the window to get a better look, Dev noticed what looked like dice scattered about the front of the car. There were slivers of something too—splintered bone—and he realized that the "dice" were the knobby ends of finger bones, as if the driver's passenger had taken the expression knuckle sandwich literally.

Backing away, he noticed that the driver-side window, the one that had been rolled down an inch, had been scratched repeatedly from the inside. Along the top of the quarter-inch pane, the glass was chipped, while dried blood and spittle streaked either side of the glass. The fedora, meanwhile, was left unmolested, counterpointing the mess of everywhere else inside the car, some of the piles looking like they may have passed through the poor animal more than once as it starved to death just a few yards away from a fully stocked pet-food store . . .

Dev shook his head and tested the front door. It was unlocked. Of course. The world had ended during normal business hours. And so he headed for the queue of shopping carts before stopping himself. *What am I doing, parked all the way back there?* Another head shake and he returned to the truck, threw it into reverse, and drove carefully up to the front window, watching as it loomed larger in the rearview. Stopping just inches from the glass, Dev got out to check the clearance between truck bed and windowsill. Perfect. Hoisting himself back into the cab, he pulled forward a few feet, and then slammed it into reverse again as the bottom half of the window exploded, leaving the top half to drop seconds later, sending a galaxy of shattered glass everywhere. He helped himself to a dead stock boy's broom to sweep out the truck bed.

Once inside, Dev wandered the aisles, filling his cart, steering around the remains of dead customers and whatever they'd knocked from the shelves when they died. And then he remembered what the "plus" in Pet Supplies Plus stood for: pets. Or more specifically: cages of dead puppies and kittens; tanks of back-floating fish; snakes and lizards reduced to leather; dead hamsters and gerbils surrounded by fur balls, wood shavings, and the same tiny dried paws that led to an earlier batch of rodents becoming snake food. The birds were self-plucked mummies, surrounded by their colorful plumage, as if feather bombs had gone off inside their cages. An emaciated ferret looked like somebody had stretch-limo-ed a possum before letting all the air out . . .

It was the Animal Planet edition of *It's a Wonderful Life*, showing what would have happened to his neighbors' pets if there'd never been a Dev Brinkman in the world. *There*, he thought at the bullies who'd called him a waste of space. And then he moved on, down other aisles, tossing boxes, cans, shakers, and sacks into his cart a little faster than before, so he could get back to grateful wards of Dev even faster still.

27

"You don't think Babyhands pressed a button he shouldn't have, do you?" Marcus asked one day, out of the blue, not unlike the whatever-it-was he was referring to. "Like, maybe he thought he was just sending a tweet but . . ."

"There'd be mushroom clouds," Lucy said, "fallout, instant skin cancer—all that."

"Only from what we know about. What if there was something we *didn't* know about, like some secret doomsday machine."

"Like in *Dr. Strangelove*?"

"Like the neutron bomb that just kills living things but leaves buildings standing," Marcus said. "Something like that, but targeted to just people, so everything else survives."

"So, in this scenario you're suggesting," Lucy said, "the Orange One is, like, tweeting something nasty about his target du jour but launches these specializing nukes instead?"

Marcus shrugged.

"You know what the sad thing is?"

"What?"

"For as totally stupid as that sounds . . ."

"Yeah?"

"I can still kind of see it."

"I know," Marcus said. "We are *so* doomed."

"*Were,*" Lucy corrected. "Past tense. Now we're just, you know, *left.*"

"Do you remember when everybody was talking about the God particle?" Lucy asked. "That big collider they were using to find the pigs bison of something . . ."

"Higgs boson," Marcus corrected. "Yeah, it was like in Sweden or somewhere. The Hadron Collider. I had a science teacher who was all geeked about it."

"Do you remember how they were saying there was this *really slim* chance it might destroy the universe?"

Marcus nodded. "'Not impossible' was how my teacher put it."

"So maybe . . . ," Lucy began.

But Marcus was already shaking his head. "They were worried about creating a mini black hole or antimatter or something, maybe ripping apart the fabric of space-time," he said. "Nothing that would leave puppies or us behind."

"So what do you got," Lucy asked, "other than bombs with a discriminating taste in their killing?"

Marcus rubbed his fingers across his lips, thinking. "Maybe the void got mad at people always giving God credit for everything. It's like, 'Dudes, listen, there's *no God.* I'm all you've got, the cosmic goose egg, okay?'"

"Um, I think you're kind of personifying the impersonal universe, there."

Marcus shrugged. "Force of habit."

"That's what Sister Mary said," Lucy said, tapping out a rim shot on the dash.

There were at least two theories Lucy wasn't putting forward because mentioning them meant using the *s*-word. The first was that irony wasn't just a rhetorical device, but a force of nature, like gravity. Because that's what her survival had been, Lucy knew. Being saved from suicide because everybody else died? That was some big-time irony right there. And there was more where that came from. Looking back, a lot of her life seemed like it might have been written by Rod Serling. Losing her virginity to a friend she thought was gay? Getting pregnant by that same maybe-gay friend, who commits suicide before she can tell him he's the father? Being a liberal intellectual born in the heart of Dixie? A Catholic nihilist? Being a goth chick who secretly digs Hello Kitty pretty much *exclusively* because doing so is, well, ironic . . .

She'd had an English teacher who'd spent a whole class on the topic of irony, tying it back to Greek tragedy. He'd said the word came from the Greek *eyron*, which was a kind of minion that kept mankind in its place. The punishment doled out by these creatures was ironic to the brink of tragedy, using their victims' proudest qualities to bring them down. Think Achilles and his heel or Oedipus fleeing his fate only to seal it. Science class followed with a lecture on gravity, and Lucy had started thinking about irony as a force in nature, invisible but inescapable, quietly shaping the arcs of human lives. It was like Occam's razor meets Murphy's Law: faced with two equally likely outcomes, the universe was biased toward the most ironic one.

"Maybe our money should say, 'In Rod We Trust,'" Lucy said aloud, a throwback to when talking to herself was how she spent most of her time.

"Excuse me?" Marcus said, not having been privy to the stream of consciousness that led to Lucy's free-floating punch line.

Shaking her head: "Low blood sugar," she said, popping open the glove compartment for the Snickers she kept there. And so on they drove, Marcus chewing over theories, Lucy chewing chocolate, peanuts, and caramel, with occasional bites of her own tongue. And then:

"What about the Rapture, but in reverse?" Lucy tried, remembering her panic attacks and how they seemed to be driving her deeper and deeper underground with every breath. "You know, instead of getting lifted into heaven, you get sucked into the bowels of hell."

"And what would this reverse Rapture be called?"

Lucy thought about it for a moment. "The Crapture?"

"Like in, 'Holy crap! I'm dead'?"

"Exactly," Lucy said; *not*, she thought. Instead, she was thinking about the other theory she couldn't mention: the one where she'd actually killed herself and this was her punishment. Not that she'd phrase it that way. *Afterlife* would be the euphemism for polite company—especially since any company in this scenario would be part of her torment. For the most part—and especially in the beginning—Marcus's company had been so far from punitive she'd nearly abandoned the theory.

But then he started getting on her nerves . . .

"Could you *please* pee against *something* that doesn't *rattle*?" she'd had to ask like a hundred times already.

"Sure," Marcus always replied, only to make it worse the next time—peeing into standing water, for instance. And Lucy would be stuck there, listening to the long, deep gloop of his spillage while it went on forever, teased an ending, and then went on a bit longer, practically echoing all the while. "What?" he'd say, looking over his shoulder at a growling Lucy. "No rattling. I'm not rattling anything."

"No splashing either," she shouldn't have to insist, but did. "No peeing-related noises, period."

"What*ever*," he'd say, zipping up, but acting PO'd, like hearing himself when he took a leak was some personal affirmation or something.

Lucy shook her head to clear it of all urine-related thoughts and then returned to where her stream of consciousness had begun: Was she or wasn't she dead? If finding Marcus didn't necessarily disprove the "successful suicide" theory, what would?

A baby, she concluded.

If she had a healthy baby that wasn't a demon or anything, that should do it, seeing as the very notion of the dead reproducing seemed counterproductive re the whole point of dying. But just seeming to get pregnant wouldn't be enough. Hysterical pregnancies were a thing, after all, even among the living. Who knew what a postmortem pregnancy in hell might be like? Other than hellish, of course. Maybe she'd get pregnant but never deliver. Get morning sickness, forever. Mood swings, forever. Get bigger and bigger until she blew up like Mr. Creosote in *Monty Python's the Meaning of Life*, her rib cage thrown apart like an open book, but inside, where that reluctant baby should be, another her, like a nesting doll—this one already pregnant and getting bigger, the whole thing on infinite replay.

How's *that* for the *eyrons* outdoing themselves?

But if she got pregnant and had a healthy baby after only nine months? That'd mean some of the rules she'd taken for granted from before were still in play. And they'd also have a head start on the whole rebooting-the-species thing, which—sci-fi cliché or not—was pretty much obligatory, under the circumstances. Provided her peer, the happy pee-er, went along with it, of course.

Meanwhile: "Maybe the planet just got tired of us," the pee-er himself suggested, breaking the ice that had formed while Lucy mulled her unmentionable theories. "Think of it: mass extinctions, global warming, deforestation, the ozone hole . . ."

Lucy nodded, then added to the litany of anthropogenic disasters. "That giant garbage patch in the middle of the ocean," she said. "Ocean acidification, oil spills, genocide, freaking *man-made* earthquakes . . ."

It was Marcus's turn to nod. "Exactly," he said. "So maybe there are, like, ecoantibodies that planets have and when it gets bad enough, they go after the source of the disease. Maybe we're all that's left after the earth's immune response to humanity."

"But why'd we survive?" Lucy asked, because the whatever-it-was was a two-parter: (1) What happened? and (2) Why didn't it happen to them?

"Because we're perfect," he said, smiling, but not unserious, not at the moment at least.

"Oh yeah," Lucy said, playing along. "I forgot we'd already decided that."

28

Driving back with a truck full of supplies for the last surviving pets in the world, Dev kept the same careful pace he'd set before, steering around corpses, braking for deer and dog stampedes, making note of how the world beyond the wall had changed to remind him why he would not be returning. And so the driving went, peacefully enough—until Dev slammed on the brakes so hard his seat belt seized to stop him from hitting the windshield. There, in the middle of the road, the embodiment of all his reasons for building the wall: an escaped cheetah, its face bloodied as it looked up from the ripe, ripped throat of a boy about Dev's age, a fellow survivor who'd stopped surviving just minutes earlier. He'd hoped that when the zoo's locks failed, the animals would busy themselves getting even with their dead keepers, feasting on their more exotic cohabitants, or just dying because they'd forgotten how to be wild. He'd also hoped that he didn't have to worry about anyone else showing up to disturb the hard-won peace of Devonshire.

At first, Dev didn't know which dashed hope was the more terrifying. But then he remembered a fun fact about cheetahs: they can run up to seventy miles an hour. Even in data-poor farm country, he'd never driven that fast. Of course, what was data sickness compared with being mauled? Plus, he *was* driving several tons of metal with a bumper height that could decapitate a Prius like it was a speed bump. All in all, he liked his chances—even if they came with a promise of panic attacks and puking.

"Let's see what this baby can do," he said, squeezing courage from cheap movie dialogue, before executing the tightest U-turn the truck was capable of. A few mailboxes lost their heads, and some wrecked cars got wrecked further along the way, but once the big cat was centered in his rearview, Dev smashed the pedal, jumping curbs, tearing up lawns, scattering uncollected mail and shredded metal as he headed for freeway.

Dev risked another look in the rearview. The cheetah was still there, still too close, but clearly not going as fast as it could. Pounding bare pawed across sun-cooked concrete couldn't be any fun, which might explain why instead of running, the cheetah was springing like the gazelles it once chased, all four paws air cooling before hitting the hot pavement again. Even empathetically challenged Dev could practically read the animal's thoughts, which were basically one, repeated:

Hot, hot, hot . . .

And then the animal stopped. Turned. Figured: *Why bother?* Or maybe it was lured away by the smell of corpse jerky wafting from the ad hoc convection ovens collected along either side of the road. Whatever the reason, once stopped, the cheetah's reflection shrank so fast it was like clicking off an old-fashioned TV. Dev was so relieved he almost cheered—just before the TV inside his own head blipped out.

He could feel something coming away from his face and was able to breathe through his nose again—making him realize he hadn't been able to before. Doing it now hurt, along with pretty much the rest of his body. His shoulders, his chest, and neck—all ached. The pain in his neck differed depending on location: in the back, it was skeletal-muscular pain, while in front, his throat felt rug burned. Until he opened them, he hadn't realized his eyes were closed. Once opened, it took a few seconds to focus on anything, as if the fluid in his eyeballs had been stirred up and still needed to settle down.

The windshield was gone.

Even before he could focus, Dev knew this, the warm wind whipping down the artificial canyon of the freeway brushing against his face, making something in the cab rattle like a plastic grocery bag pinned against a fence. The airbag had gone off, was even now hanging out of the steering wheel—crumpled, deflated—like the steering column had puked it into his lap. Rock-salt chunks of safety glass spilled off as he brushed it aside. What had he hit? He couldn't see anything over the accordion-crumpled hood . . .

Something was inside the truck with him. He sensed its presence before he saw it, the sensation slowing his ability to turn and look. But he did. He turned—*slowly*—and looked. And there, wedged into the passenger seat next to him: an adult male deer, folded almost in half. Dev just stared at it for a moment, watching as the warm wind tumbling through the cab rustled its sandy brown fur. The fur looked soft; Dev wanted to touch it. Did.

Mistake!

The deer wasn't dead. The pressure of Dev's fingers on its fur was enough to switch it back on. The triangular head yanked up, turned, turned, craned up at the roof of the cab, ears pitched at full alert, pivoting independently of one another, seeming to lock on Dev's breathing as both ears turned in his direction, followed by the rest of the animal's head, its black marble eyes drilling through him. Snot and blood leaked from its black nose, its nostrils flaring and collapsing, its breathing labored. The thing's hooves began pedaling in the air, looking for ground to escape over, only growing more frantic when they found none. One of the hooves dangled and flopped at the end of a break, the bloody stick of a bone poking through the fur.

Dev flashed on this very image in his neighbor's garbage, pre-school, pre-Christmas, pre-disillusionment with the things his parents told him. He wanted to reach out, to pull on either side of the break, set it right before apologizing for being the cause of it. But the animal wouldn't hold still that long. One of its unbroken hooves kicked out a chunk of the padded dash before cracking the plastic lens of the odometer. Another banged against the roof of the cab, tenting the metal overhead. And all the while, it was emptying every deer hole it had, blood and vomit from its mouth, arcs of urine, blasts of deer feces and death stink.

Dev, cinched in place by his seat belt, was right within blast range of all the creature's exiting fluids. But sheer grossness was the least of it. He was also within striking distance of the dying deer's dangerous hooves, which didn't seem bent on revenge, necessarily, but not *not* either.

And that's when Dev's Aspergerian tendency to map—once debilitating—suddenly started feeling like a superpower. If this had been a movie, his POV would have overlapped with computer-generated targeting circles around the three hooves that could still do any damage, the circles doing a complicated dance in front of his eyes, our hero ducking and darting, keeping his eyes and the head that held them just a split second ahead of disaster.

Bobbing and weaving for his life, Dev felt hypnotized by the motion—his and the deer's—the chaotic dance of one dying, the other trying to stay alive, the latter suddenly on autopilot, leaving his mind free to observe. And what he observed was this:

Death.

Death with a capital *D*. Death getting ready to happen right in front of him. Death as one big, bucking muscle, covered in skin and fur, refusing to be taken alive, kicking and smashing until it cried uncle and died . . .

Death so full of crap it wasn't even funny. Because the thing was still emptying itself all over him, filling his nostrils with the pestilential stench he knew all too well, like something had crawled up somebody's butt and died. He'd thought that was a funny way to describe a fart back when Leo first said it. He'd thought about it breathing through a respirator full of air fresheners, and he thought about it now.

What crawled up your butt and died?

And then the deer did. Its limbs stopped thrashing and shuddered instead, as if it were cold despite the windblown heat filling the cab. All four limbs, including the broken one, gave in to gravity. Its ears folded back, the black marble eyes locked open, and the head dropped against a chest that was white underneath the spatter of everything that had come out. Little beads of fluid hung at the tips of the longer hairs around its black leather nose, the nostrils open, but slack, not going anywhere anytime soon.

Dev tested his luck and turned the key. The truck was seriously crunched but not dead. The battery worked, at least. He could tell from the lit dash full of warning lights. The engine didn't turn over at first, but then he checked the emergency fuel cutoff under the dash with the little fuel pump in a circle slash. He flipped it, kerchunked back into park, and turned the key. And even though the windshield was missing; even though the front end was an accordion; even though the airbag was puked out and the deer in the passenger seat was for-real dead this time—still, the truck started. It was drivable. The engine wasn't happy about starting, but it did, sending up the sound of something loose and metallic from underneath the crumpled hood. A ball of blue smoke coughed out of the tailpipe as Dev watched in his side mirror, the rearview being lost somewhere in the back, along with the rest of the windshield. Another blue ball of smoke, some more rattling, and Dev kerchunked into drive.

The exhaust drove itself clean while the busted-out windshield—mercifully—provided adequate venting against the buildup of shit-piss-puke-related smells. And as Dev brought the truck up to forty, the rattling underneath the chassis sped up too, becoming a whine that turned into a ping, followed by a chewed-up bit of sheet metal, skipping down I-94 behind him in the side view. *That was a close one,* Dev thought, assuming that the specter of death was through with him for the time being.

Wrong.

Driving back home, he noticed them in his dead passenger's fur: little black specks framed against sandy brown. At first, Dev thought they might be dried flecks of blood or vomit, maybe some other dark fluid atomized as the poor thing bellowed out its last breath. But then they moved. The deer's fur was full of ticks—literally *crawling* with them.

And even though he couldn't *see* them on his own arms, he could *feel* them. Ditto, his neck and scalp. He couldn't see those, either, but they were there, a small battalion of deer ticks, plotting their invasion of his bloodstream with any number of pathogens, though there was only one he was sure of: Lyme disease.

Pulling up outside the wall, he exited the truck, tugging at his shirt as the buttons went flying, followed by his shoes and socks. When the zipper jammed on his pants, he shimmied out of them, followed by his underwear, pulled up and over, down and off. He'd not bring a stitch of that infested fabric inside the world he'd set aside for himself and a handful of select others.

After unloading the pet food wearing nothing but the skin he was born in, Dev stuffed a sock in the gas tank, lit it, and stood back as flames like liquid spread throughout the wreckage. The buffeting heat made every hair on his body move—at least he hoped it was just the heat. He stood there, watching, making sure it was done. Once the deer's sandy brown fur had withered to black, each bristle of it melting down to a hard ball of charred keratin, Dev gathered up the pieces of his abandoned wardrobe and chucked them into the flames, one by one. Satisfied that everything that needed to be was burned, he padded home, barefoot and scratching, until blood ran.

Ignoring Diablo for the dog's own good as the animal's whimpering followed him to the bathroom, he turned, said, "Stay," and then shut the door. He filled the Shop-Vac without waiting to heat the water, stepped into the tub, and drew the curtain, poking just a finger out to flip the switch. Cold water pelted every inch of his body as he scrubbed, rinsed, and then scrubbed some more. Soap suds ran pink and gray down the drain. Clumps of hair—clawed out while working the shampoo around his scalp—collected in the trap and stopped the water from draining. Dev checked the cloudy runoff for swimmers, didn't see any, but also didn't know whether deer ticks could swim.

Still standing in the tub with the water off, he turned a white towel into a bloody candy cane from where he was still bleeding. He loaded a washcloth with hydrogen peroxide, wiping and foaming, foaming and wiping as more pink residue slid off him, bubbly this time.

Stepping onto the bath mat, he looked at himself in the full-length mirror hanging from the back of the bathroom door—the same one he could hear Diablo through, scratching and whimpering. He'd always heard the first sign of Lyme disease was a red, bull's-eye-shaped rash, but couldn't tell if he had one, thanks not only to all the scratching he'd done, but also because of the complexion he'd inherited from his mother. He tried smoothing his hands across his skin. If the rash was raised, maybe he could read it, like braille.

But everything felt wrong, his fingers dyslexic. *Was that always there? Or that?* And what about the parts of him he couldn't see in the mirror or reach around to touch?

He unlocked the bathroom door, and Diablo fell forward with a click of nails against tile. Holding him at bay with the balled-up towel,

Dev stepped around him and out, before closing the door so Diablo could scratch the other side for once.

"Sorry, boy," he said, pulling up a clean pair of pants before tugging down a clean T-shirt. "Sorry," he repeated, while rooting around his great big box of dead electronics until he found what he was looking for: his smartphone and charger. The thing couldn't call or surf, but it could still shoot, and he needed video of the dark side of the Dev. While it charged, he crossed the street to a neighbor's house where he remembered seeing a selfie stick he'd thought especially useless—until he'd found a use for it.

He thought about how he'd tell this to Leo—if he were still alive, if Dev had forgiven him. "Sounds like the world's most boring porno," his dead ex-friend might have said.

And true enough, the resulting footage was hardly titillating. In fact, if he hadn't shot it himself, he wasn't sure he'd be able to tell what it was. He'd maxed out the zoom, getting as close-in and close-up as he could without going blurry. But he could just as easily have been shooting a leather chair—one with the occasional pimple and a lot of black hair. But no red bull's-eyes or off-brown bull's-eyes or slightly raised bull's-eyes showing up as Dev lit himself like the moon going through phases—the craters always standing out best along the line separating light from dark.

Nada. Bubkes. Zilch.

He shaved his head just in case. He'd seen *The Omen*, and he could practically feel it pulsing there, hiding cleverly under his hair, just like those three sixes, which might be there as well, given the recent apocalyptic turn of events. But again: nothing. Not in the mirror, not on video, not when he went over every square inch with soapy fingertips.

He'd exchanged places with Diablo once more, and when Dev emerged from the bathroom this time, the dog held back. His human reached out a hand to pet him for the first time since the whole thing began. Any ticks that might have been hiding on his clothes, on his skin, or in his hair had probably dug themselves in so deeply by now it was unlikely they'd be able to launch a sneak attack on Diablo or any of the others.

"So?" he said, rubbing his shiny new dome. "Like it?"

Diablo seemed on the fence. And so the boy knelt and dropped his head. He could feel the dog's breath as he sniffed around this new development, inspecting it nasally. And then he felt the dog's tongue sliding across the top of his head. "You can keep doing that," he told him, finding it hard to think about dying or strangers as long as Diablo was so occupied.

29

For a girl whose previous pregnancy had led her to contemplate suicide, it was a little odd, Lucy's sudden desire to get preggers again. Timing: that's what changed her mind. Before, the pregnancy and Max's suicide had become inextricably linked, leading to those sneak previews of death known as panic attacks, triggered every time she saw anything about babies or overheard someone advise someone else to "take it to the max," which she couldn't anymore. Suicide had seemed preferable to the so-called miracle of birth because suicide introduced a certain level of conclusive certainty into her situation.

But now? There was none of that—just a father-to-be who'd come willingly on or not. Marcus might have objections—exhibit A, the condoms—but he couldn't deny the world needed more people. So she'd just have to talk him into it—or maybe burst his bubble about the effectiveness of his chosen form of birth control. A pinprick should do it, she figured. And after that, she'd be on her way to having her own little backup person in case . . .

In case . . . *what?*

In case Lucy's luck turned sucky again. Sure, Marcus *acted* like he loved her, but she'd known herself longer than he had. It would only be a matter of time before the jig was up. Or maybe Marcus would turn out to be the jerk. In her experience, statistically speaking, guys and girls were pretty much fifty-fifty when it came to being jerks. If the line between Jesus and jerk were a teeter-totter, the Messiah'd be catapulted halfway to heaven, the scales were that unevenly balanced when it came to good people versus the rest. So, a baby would either cement the relationship or expose one of them as the jerk they really were, before driving the other away. But that was the beauty of it: either way she'd have a backup person, growing inside her, waiting to keep her company. A backup person who'd force her to keep on keeping on.

She introduced her topic using the Socratic method by way of *Jeopardy!*, tiptoeing up to it with questions, beginning with, "What are we doing?"

"Doing?" Marcus asked back. "Doing when? Like, for dinner?"

"Right now."

"Um, driving?"

"But why?"

"You know why," her cosurvivor said. "We're looking for others."

"Correct," Lucy said. Paused. "But what if there aren't any?"

"That'd suck."

"And . . . ?"

"And what? It'd suck." Marcus paused, worried he'd walked into a trap—which he had, just not the one he was thinking of. Hoping to avoid a fight, he looked for the words that'd show he didn't mean being alone with her would suck. What he meant was . . . blank. He had nothing. But then Lucy surprised him by going in a totally different direction.

"I meant, *And* . . . what are we going to do about it?"

Marcus shrugged, stumped.

"If the mountain won't come to Mohammad," she said, quoting the old saw, "Mohammad must go to the mountain."

Marcus jerked the wheel, catching the shoulder and spraying gravel as he fishtailed to a stop. "What's that sup . . . ," he began, preparing excuses, though what these would be, he had no idea.

"What I'm trying to say . . . ," Lucy said, clearly flustered.

"So say it," Marcus said, cutting in.

". . . *is,*" she continued, ignoring him, holding on to the syllable for a beat or two.

"Yes?"

"Maybe we need to make the others ourselves." *Boom,* Lucy thought. *How'd you like them apples?*

Meanwhile: *This again,* Marcus thought, rubbing his brow, but then nodding, not wanting to argue. "Okay," he continued, still nodding as he pulled off the shoulder and back onto the road. "Okay," he said again, not necessarily agreeing with her, but stalling so he could weigh how being a father would cramp his style, in the event they found any others that were still breathing—women, especially. Because even though the fun had been fun, even fun gets old—a rationalization of male fickleness she'd not be getting from him, even under torture.

"Okay," he said after several miles of not talking about it. "Let's talk about it." By which he meant: "Let's see if I can talk you out of this baby nonsense."

"Okay," Lucy agreed. "Let's."

"One," Marcus said. "More mouths to feed."

"In a world full of canned goods as far as the eye can see," Lucy countered.

"Two," Marcus said. "I'm no doctor."

"You're *kidding,* right?" Lucy said, with more sarcasm than Marcus felt was strictly necessary. "Mom's going to be *soooo* disappointed."

"No talking about," he warned, not saying "others," "mothers," or "the departed"—and not needing to.

"Sorry," she said, pursing her lips, turning an invisible key. She waited for the weasel to pop once more before continuing. "Where were we?" she asked.

"Me, not being a doctor."

"Oh yeah," Lucy said before wondering aloud about how the species had managed to reproduce for millions of years without the medical-industrial complex, to which Marcus added: "And women died. In childbirth. A lot."

They'd seen proof of it together, in a Civil War–era cemetery they'd made love in because they were still alive, and there was no one to stop them. It was also (ironically) one of the few places outdoors that *didn't* stink of death—or at least not human death. When a breeze happened over where they lay in the grass, it smelled of dead flowers, the essence of their perfume condensed and distilled as the petals darkened and curled. Afterward, walking among the tombstones, enjoying the floral breeze, they noticed the family plots. There seemed to be a disturbingly high number with one old man's stone flanked by a bunch of graves for women sharing his last name, all dying in their twenties, judging from the dates that hadn't dissolved from acid rain.

"What do you think?" he asked, double-checking the gravestone math Lucy had pointed out. "Some kind of epidemic?"

She shook her head. "They were martyrs," she said, eliciting the slightest flinch from her companion, who masked it with a question. "How so?"

"They died in the cause of reproduction," she said. "They died so others might live."

Marcus was quiet for a moment, considering what to say next, the only sound in the cemetery the rustle of leaves. "Guys get off kind of easy," he said.

"In more ways than one," she said.

He figured the memory of that conversation would be enough. He should have known better. Because once a person willingly accepts that something can cost their life, trying to talk them out of it is pretty much a waste of breath. The cost—perversely—was part of the attraction.

Plus, he got it, he really did. He knew why having a kid was important to her, the emotional and literal backup it would provide. He even knew she was worried about things souring between them, might even be being especially bristly lately to test how much he'd take. Thing was, Marcus was done with being tested—on faith, on loyalty, on his level of commitment to a cause. *Take me or leave me,* he thought, *or watch me do the leaving . . .*

But the even bigger truth was simpler: he didn't want to be a parent because thinking about it made him miss his own parents all over again. The thought of being a father without having a father to call for advice seemed unimaginable. And that went double when it came to not being able to share all the baby's firsts—tooth, word, non-gas-inspired smile . . .

How was he supposed to tell Lucy the bundle of joy she wanted to inflict on him promised to be a nonstop refresher course in grief? He couldn't, obviously. And so he resorted to that time-honored male birth control method: acting like a jerk.

He started by opining aloud about the so-called equality of the sexes. He wasn't seeing it and said so. Now that it was down to one of each, the sexes couldn't be graded on a curve anymore—he said—suggesting they had been before. The sexes needed to be judged by nothing more than their individual physical abilities and circumstances—their indisputable, *biological* differences.

"All I'm saying is," he said, leaping seamlessly from the dangers of giving birth to the dangers of equal rights, "you can pass all the amendments you want, I still can't get pregnant, and you're not writing your name in the snow anytime soon."

"Wow," Lucy said, with an edge that seemed to ask how such a handsome face could hide such an ugly mind. "Way to cut your side some slack." She turned toward her window and seemed to be letting it go, but then: *"Seriously?"* she said, turning back. "Getting pregnant versus peeing standing up? *That's* what you're going with?"

Marcus nodded, feeling like a creep—as planned.

"I guess you're right," she said, actually throwing up her hands in mock surrender. "Men and women *are* different—starting with their ability to at least *act* like mature adults."

So Marcus dropped the *b*-bomb, placing the word right there in the ice cream truck between them—a trial balloon, perhaps, of just how much crap she'd be willing to take from him. A trial balloon she couldn't hit him for, unless she wanted them to crash, seeing as he was driving and had steadily increased their velocity as the argument escalated. And so:

"Fine," she said, her lips fusing shut like a vacuum sealer when they were done with the word, sucking out all the air after it. *Let the silent treatment commence . . .*

Time passed. Slowly. Like a kidney stone. Or like someone using the bathroom when you need to, making you imagine the kidney stones you're growing out there in the hallway, knees squeezed together, each tick of the clock an accident waiting to happen. Something's got to give—meaning some*one*—and it (they) does (do). Because—postapocalyptically—the shelf life on the silent treatment was *not* what it used to be, thanks to there being literally no one left to exercise her talking parts with, except herself, which, given the tightness of their quarters, Marcus would most certainly hear, real life not being a Shakespearean soliloquy, and so . . .

"I need words," Lucy announced one morning over microwave coffee.

Marcus let out a slow sigh like a pricked balloon.

She'd been thinking about their situation all the while she wasn't talking about their situation. And what she kept coming back to was Marcus's confession about how easily he'd been played by some cyber slut he'd never met, back when there were plenty to choose from. Feeling thus emboldened, she figured maybe she should exercise some of her power as the last woman on earth.

"What were we using before?" Marcus asked.

"Not *talking* words," Lucy quibbled. "*Reading* ones. I need to rub my eyes over some words on a page."

"If you're bored, we've got DV—"

"Words. On. A. Page," she clarified, a stubbed finger punctuating each word as the TV tray that was their breakfast nook shook, making both their coffee cups ring like bells as their spoons jiggled against ceramic.

"Okay," Marcus said, hands up. "Message received. We'll look for a bookstore or something."

"I think there's one next to the record store," Lucy said, hiding her smirk behind a sip.

"Right," Marcus said. "Library. Got it."

A single dead librarian lay behind the checkout desk. It may have been Lucy's imagination, but the book sorter's corpse seemed to be decomposing more neatly than others she'd seen, more like a Smithsonian mummy than the fly-clouded gut bags she was used to. She tapped Marcus's shoulder and pointed wordlessly.

They'd passed from the unrelenting heat and humidity of a southern summer into slightly drier and more reasonably heated territory, but this hadn't stopped them from wearing gas masks. As such, their conversation that followed felt a little like another argument.

"*Weird,*" Marcus shouted. "*It's like somebody just let the air out. The skin's all sucked in around the bones, like one of those suitcase space savers.*"

"*What do you think caused it?*" Lucy said back, pitched at a volume normally reserved for swearing.

Marcus of the Desert contemplated the corpse before shouting back: "*Humidity, maybe?*"

"*What about it?*"

"There doesn't seem to be much," he said. He rolled up his sleeve and fingered his arm. *"No sweat,"* he said. *"Literally,"* he added.

"Why do you . . ."

But before she could finish, he answered: *"Books,"* he said. *"Paper. I think all this paper must have acted like sponges, dehumidifying the place."*

Lucy shook her goggled head like a giant bug, still trying to figure out a world that just kept getting stranger as she headed for the shelves.

Unfortunately, all that paper couldn't wick away the moisture inside her gas mask. Trying to read the spines, her eye windows kept fogging up, making her look like some steampunk Orphan Annie. She tried holding her breath and waited for the fog to clear. And waited. Beads of fog collected into bigger beads, became drops, sliding down the glass, but still blurred the world beyond it. Finally, impatient—and needing the breath she was holding—Lucy yanked back the mask, gulped at the air, and was about to wipe the lenses clean when she noticed she wasn't gagging. She sniffed. Musty, not lilacs, but not all that bad either. The olfactory influence of the mummified librarian was limited at best.

"Hey, Marcus," she called, her tone normal, her voice unmuffled.

He turned to face her standing there, smiling, unmasked.

"What are you . . . ?"

"It's okay," she said. "The air's not bad."

Marcus looked at her, and Lucy knew he was wondering if he was being punked. She had cried "clean air" before at times when it was especially rank. It had amused her, their differing capacity for bad smells. The last time he fell for it, he'd inhaled a little bit of his own vomit and spent the rest of the day hacking up phlegm. He folded his arms. *"I can wait you out,"* he said.

"You could," she admitted. "But there's no need to. It's really not bad."

And it was true, this was what they'd given up hoping for: four walls and a roof with space to stretch, protection from the elements, and air that wasn't toxic. Slowly, he raised his mask like he was raising a cup of something hot to his lips. "Hey," he said, removing his mask the rest of the way. "It's not that bad."

Lucy thought about telling him she'd told him so, but decided to save it for something bigger.

They stayed the night and did what couples often do at night, though, being young, they did it during the day as well. Needless to say, one of the unspoken rules of the silent treatment was: no sex. And so they made up for lost time, working through Marcus's stash of prophylactics, with no mention of having babies and no mention of not having babies. They seemed to have acknowledged that one another's bodies were one another's business; one couldn't force the other into doing anything they didn't want to.

Up to a point, of course.

30

Dev contemplated the Brinkmans' liquor cabinet, the one his stepfather went to when he'd had a "hard" day. It was also, interestingly, the one he went to when he'd had a "good" day, leaving the boy to wonder what sorts of days *weren't* in need of liquid mitigation. Weekends, perhaps? Nope.

"Hey, it's the weekend," he'd say back when his wife complained about how early the cabinet's door was creaking open, followed by the clink, clink of ice hitting glass like chilly punctuation marks.

Dev didn't think his stepfather was what you'd call an alcoholic; he just drank every night. And he always drank the same amount, measured not in shots but with a graduated cylinder. Though the colors that climbed that Pyrex column changed from day to day—sometimes amber, sometimes clear, sometimes exotic hues of blue, green, red—the level to which they were poured always remained the same.

"I know my limit," he told his stepson, "to within one cc." And after that, an equally anal evening of paced sipping followed.

Perhaps it was this methodical nature that kept his stepfather from becoming one of the angry drunks on TV, bashing wives and children and cars until they found God or AA or died. Dev's stepdad sipped, loosened up, became more talkative and reflective, more complimentary of Dev and his mom. Less, well, frankly, Aspergerian. The alcohol was not merely medicinal, but surgical. At least that's what Dev gleaned, after hearing his mother tell a friend over the phone that her husband's drinking was one of the few things to remove the stick from his butt.

Come morning, Mr. Brinkman was never the worse for wear. Unplagued by hangovers, he never had to ask what he'd done the night before. Instead, he kissed his wife while pulling his arm through the sleeve of his pharmacist's jacket, snatching a triangle of toast on the way out the door for another day of filling amber bottles with the same attention to detail he used to mix his evening cocktails.

Dev had researched the symptoms for Lyme disease in a neighbor's encyclopedia and crosschecked those with a copy of the *Physicians' Desk Reference*. He wanted to know what he should be looking out for. Because not finding a bull's-eye rash didn't mean he didn't have it. He also learned that Lyme disease was a hypochondriac's dream. It mimicked all sorts of diseases it wasn't, earning the nickname the great imitator. One of the few things most sufferers shared was originally being diagnosed with something else. Confusion, fatigue, muscle soreness—those could all be symptoms of Lyme disease, or the flu, or the fact that he'd been in a car crash. Misdiagnosis was itself part of the pathology; while the patient was being treated for something he didn't have, the infection spread to more systems, leading to more symptoms to further confound proper diagnosis. Eventually, the disease took over really important stuff, like the brain and heart, leading to heart attack, dementia, Parkinson's . . .

Dev was underage for drinking, but just reading through the progression of the diseases he might or might not have made him feel like an old man. Correction: an old man who needed a drink.

And so he opened the cabinet, removed a bottle of vodka, a mixer, and his stepfather's graduated cylinder. Maybe he could make his liver an inhospitable place for parasites to settle. He couldn't see how it could possibly make things any worse. Plus, he was curious about what it felt like. Would it feel like how it felt when he was in the throes of a *topique?* Would the top of his head lift so lightly into the air, knowledge like a breeze would come whispering across the crests and valleys of his exposed cerebellum?

Dev tipped the threaded neck to the smooth rim of the graduated cylinder and let the vodka glug out halfway to his stepfather's mark. He tipped more vodka in until the surface made a silver disc level with the line his stepfather had established, back when he'd perfected his high-functioning alcoholic routine. He cracked the cap off a bottle of tonic with a gasp and topped off his first real drink-drink.

"Cheers," he said to Diablo, dragging the dog's water bowl forward so he wouldn't have to drink alone. And then he brought the glass to his lips, sipping one of his stepfather's patented hummingbird sips. He wondered what the magic would feel like once it happened.

Except it didn't. And it continued to not happen, even as Dev stepped up the pace. For his next drink, he skipped the cylinder and the tonic. Now *there* was something. Not necessarily a *good* something, but something for sure. It felt weird, this room-temperature liquid making his mouth feel cold when he inhaled afterward, followed by a warmth that traveled down his chest and felt, maybe, okay. He tested to confirm the feeling: yes. And another yes. And yes again. And still yes, until . . .

He hit maybe.

And then a string of noes and one, big *definitely not*—as he realized, too late, that everything in his stomach wanted out. *Now.* And *now.* And no please no, not . . .

Now!

And in the morning, Dev still didn't know whether he had Lyme disease, but he did know one thing: inside his own head was no longer his favorite place to be.

Once the hangover let go—one bloody talon at a time—Dev decided the only way to deal was to go on as if nothing was wrong. He should be able to, he figured. Call it the hypochondriac's paradox: if he could talk himself *into* being sick, maybe he could talk himself *out* of it as well.

And so that was the plan: to live until he stopped. Or just keep on living forever, if that was in the cards. Because he still hadn't entirely ruled out being immortal—despite his one data point to the contrary with its throat ripped out. Still, being alive when most people weren't? Who knew how badly the end had messed up the rules previously in play? Like universal mortality, for example. There were experiments Dev could use to test this hypothesis, of course. But why spoil the surprise? If Dev was immortal, he figured, he'd prefer to find out by not dying. No need to force the point.

It wasn't until late August, maybe early September (fear, like happiness, played a number on his sense of time) that Dev admitted—finally—he probably *didn't* have Lyme disease. Try as he might, he couldn't talk himself into any of the symptoms. Did he feel like he had the flu? No. Chronic fatigue? Nope, not really. Joint pain? Facial droop? Parkinsonian tremor? Nope. Nope. Nope. He couldn't even work up a decent fever.

"Well, devil dog," he announced, "looks like I'm not going to die." Pause. "Not right away anyway."

Judging from the way his tail wagged, Diablo was glad to hear it. As would be the other critters that had come to depend on him, if he'd ever confided his fear to them, which he hadn't. "This is between you and me," he told Diablo. "No telling the others."

Diablo woofed his agreement.

"No use getting them worried when there's nothing they can do."

Diablo cocked his head, as if considering the wisdom of this.

"I'll leave the door open," he concluded. "Just in case."

Diablo looked confused.

"So you won't have to," Dev said, before miming a set of jaws clamping on his throat.

Diablo responded by licking Dev's hand, a gesture his human would have found reassuring—if not for the knuckle bones at Pet Supplies Plus. Those gruesome dice just kept coming up, the fact that the animal hadn't stopped at the bone, but cracked them open, sucked out the marrow, left splinters and those bony knobs behind.

Diablo looked at his human like he was reading his mind. His eyebrows seemed especially agitated, vexed by not having the ability to speak, to plead his case. He nosed at Dev's hand, the one that had recently played the role of Diablo's own jaws. He kicked his nose up and then slid his head underneath so that Dev had two choices—slapping the back of his head or petting him. He chose the latter, and the dog seemed satisfied with that decision.

Even after he'd cleared himself of Lyme disease, however, Dev kept thinking about death. Not his: Diablo's. In many ways, he was more attached to the devil dog than he was to life itself. It was a little pointless, after all, surviving everybody else just to die anyway. But taking care of Diablo, playing with him in the backyard: those were something. They weren't pointless. And if he was being honest with himself, the only thing Dev really feared about the future was Diablo's exit from it.

And they'd reach a future like that; it was pretty much a mathematical certainty, given the human-to-dog ratio when it came to years. The only way that future *didn't* happen was if Dev died first. And so he was a little disappointed, having to admit he didn't have Lyme disease. Maybe Lyme would have been the handicap Diablo needed so the two of their biological clocks could run down together.

"But hey," he said, still patting Diablo in the here and now, "maybe I'll get something else fatal," he added, leaving the door open in more ways than one.

31

There was only one thing wrong with the library: having to decide whether to stay or go. After three months on the road, first separately and then together, they could be forgiven for finding stasis attractive. But how long before stasis became paralysis?

"This could be it," Marcus suggested. "We could live here."

It sounded like a proposal, making Lucy flinch even though her leftover Catholicism saw marriage prior to procreation as the only way to go. "Let's not get," she started. "But," she started again.

"I'm just saying it wouldn't be so bad a base camp," he said. "Send out our own smoke signals, let others find us. Why should we have to do all the work?"

"Because the earth's round," Lucy said. "Because you can only see smoke from so far away. We could end up waiting an awfully long time."

"I meant smoke metaphorically," Marcus said. "I was actually thinking about something like a bunch of helium balloons attached to a fishing line. Reel it out as high as it can go, for maximum visibility."

"Like that old song," Lucy observed.

"What old song?"

"'Ninety-Nine Red Balloons.' It was originally in German, I think. *Luftballons.* It was about accidentally starting World War III."

"Lovely."

"Speaking of," Lucy continued, "if we just signal and wait, what if the others turn out to be creeps? Or crazy? Or just plain dangerous? There's no guarantee we'll get as lucky as you got."

"Cute."

"But the point I'm making is serious," she insisted.

"Yeah," Marcus said. "In a zombie apocalypse, maybe. But it's not like there's a shortage of stuff around. No need to fight over it."

Lucy stretched out her arms. "With the exception of a good place to live," she said. "For example," she added.

They wound up taking sides in the ongoing debate over the relative desirability of finding or being found by others—just not always the same side as they'd taken before. Sometimes Lucy cheered for the family of man while Marcus pointed out the territorial nastiness of the species. Other times, it was Marcus who sang "Kumbaya," while Lucy suggested something by Wagner was really mankind's tune. Who came out where was probably an indicator of how claustrophobic one or the other found their cramped, little, four-wheeled world.

And that's why the library was such a lucky break. It offered their relationship the one thing it lacked: space. A place with a roof and space where they could get out of eyeshot of each other without worrying about being attacked by wild dogs or pigs. Give the heart a little bit of what it needed to grow fonder.

And so they started spending their days apart, while in the evenings, they'd meet like they were meeting for a date. They'd go up to the roof of the library and set off some fireworks they'd found. The green, red, and yellow blossoms of light were more romantic than flares and still sent the same message to whoever might be out there, letting them know that they were not alone. And after that, the two went back inside, where they were not alone together until one of them fell asleep while the other watched them, the light of the moon outside the window painting their skin the loveliest shades of blue.

He'd noticed the changes in her body and wanted to blame the Oreos but had his doubts about whether eating too many cookies could actually increase the size of a person's chest. Plus, she'd been "secretly" throwing up—which was difficult to pull off behind a library restroom door where the sounds of retching tended to echo.

The question of how was natural. And not the basic how, but the particular how, under the circumstances, considering his own efforts to prevent such an outcome. And so Marcus filled an unused condom with water, acting on a hunch. Dangling the bulbous thing, he frowned as a needle of liquid whizzed out.

So that's why she'd taken to prolonged bouts of cuddling afterward, not wanting to decouple right away, giving his little swimmers a shot at establishing a beachhead. He walked to where Lucy was reading a warped copy of *What to Expect When You're Expecting* (hint, hint). He let the stream hit her in the forehead before running down into the collar of her three-sizes-too-big T-shirt. Having gotten her attention, he stepped back, the condom still dangling, still tinkling as it drew a darkened slice across a page.

"Yes?" she said, looking up, a rather large drip balanced on the tip of her nose.

"Why?"

"Why not?"

"We—" Marcus began.

"If you're about to say 'can't afford another mouth to feed,'" Lucy said, "let me present to you exhibit A." A hand thrust dramatically in a broad sweep. "The whole *frickin'* world."

"But we're still kids ourselves," he insisted. "I'm not even seventeen yet."

"Me neither," Lucy said. "But news flash: that still makes us the oldest people on earth."

"Allegedly," Marcus qualified.

"You keep hanging on to that," Lucy said, returning to her reading. "In the meantime, I've decided to seize the means of reproduction."

Marcus watched the top of her head, trying to imagine how it worked. For once, his knack for empathy utterly failed him. Not that it mattered what he thought about what she thought. What mattered was whether she was or wasn't. "So?" he said, opening the door for the answer he dreaded.

"It's looking pretty good," Lucy said, pulling from her pocket a white stick with a blue cross on it.

He couldn't kill her. Well, he *could*—but he couldn't. And when it came to appeasing the universe for prior sins, giving up Twinkies was really pretty lame, Marcus had to admit. An eye for an eye, a tooth for a tooth, a life for a life: so sayeth that part of the Bible her ex-people and his ex-people agreed on.

So, atoning for planning to take life demanded he either save one or make one. Hopefully, there were others elsewhere, deciding the same, so that when their kid and his kid were old enough to start making their own kids, the species would have a shot at not being a bunch of inbred idiots—which might be a nice way of rebooting a species that had been tending toward idiocy, especially in its waning years.

"Okay," he sighed finally, like the cells already dividing inside her were just waiting for his permission.

"Okay what?" Lucy asked, clearly wanting him to say it—*needing* him to say it.

"I'm happy, I guess," he said, shrugging. "Happy?"

"Now *there's* the enthusiasm I was missing . . ."

"It's just taking a little getting used to," he said.

"We've gotten used to bigger things," she pointed out.

Their break from the road came to an end with Marcus standing on the library roof with a pair of binoculars while Lucy read inside. As usual, he was looking for signs of others. What he saw instead was a tidal wave of rats, heading right for the library.

Marcus tapped on the skylight to get Lucy's attention. "Um," he called down, "we've got a little problem here."

"What kind?" Lucy asked, looking up from the last issue of *Entertainment Weekly* in the periodicals section. It was a double issue: their summer blockbuster preview. Lucy had been silently mourning not just the movies she'd never see, but all the actors who were probably dead on the sets of the sequels, already in production, each set probably looking the same about now: like something out of *The Birds*.

"Rats," Marcus called down.

"Shoot 'em," Lucy advised.

"We don't have that many bullets," he said.

"How many are there?"

"Take a look," he said, and Lucy moved toward a nearby window. "What's your estimate?" he called down. "A bazillion?"

Lucy went quiet, just staring.

"Hello?" Marcus said, knocking on the skylight. "You still down there?"

"I don't like rats," Lucy said, backing away from the window.

"Join the club," Marcus said back before rejoining her inside the library. Outside, the rodential river kept flowing past the windows. He wrapped his arms around her, and she let him. The ice cream truck—their ride away from the worse that was coming—seemed to be parked in a vast brown lake, the muscles under all that fur making the surface ripple. A wave here and there would overtake the one in front of it, rats scrambling over rats, their squeaks of protest coming to the humans through the glass, making their skin crawl.

"I've been through this before," she said. "In Georgia. There's more coming."

"More, in like . . . ?"

"Pigs," Lucy said. "That's what I think the rats are running away from."

"I saw the pigs before leaving Oklahoma," Marcus said. "Don't remember any rats."

"Maybe you slept through them. I did with the pigs. I mean, I *heard* them. Thought it was thunder. It wasn't till morning when I saw what they left behind and put it together."

"So, like, how many rats are we talking about? In Georgia, I mean."

"This," Lucy said, gesturing toward the window. "Minus a bazillion."

"So, lots more this time."

Lucy nodded. "Way," she said. Paused. "How many pigs?"

"Two dozen. Around."

"I wonder if they're . . . ," they said together, before stopping, trying to think of the word they wanted.

"Connected?" Marcus tried while Lucy suggested, "Correlated?"

Neither was a very comforting thought. And so Marcus returned to the library roof with his binoculars and scanned the horizon. What he saw reminded him of the dust storms from his home state during the Great Depression. His English teacher had shown them a video before dragging them through *The Grapes of Wrath*.

He broke the skylight in his hurry to get down. "Yes," he shouted at Lucy, still rattled by the noise and glass shards. "They're correlated."

Pooling their educations, they decided it only made sense that the herd had gotten bigger. Herds from the southeast and herds from the southwest had probably met and merged in the middle, not unlike the humans now contemplating the future to come. Feeding, coupling, and spreading, that's all mankind's successor species had to do, now that the humans had gotten out of the way. And just like the humans before them, they were depleting the resources in one area and then moving on to the next, turning the world before them into trough and toilet. Lucy, remembering a poem from English class, riffed on T. S. Eliot re the world and its ending.

"Not a bang," she said. "Not a whimper either. Just an oink."

"Yeah, great," Marcus said, before reminding her that the domesticated and feral pigs heading their way had likely begun interbreeding, conjuring up the image of five-hundred-pound porkers with tusks in the not-too-distant future.

"Is it too late to vote for zombies?" Lucy asked, following Marcus out to the truck where the straggler rats were still straggling. Holding hands, the couple did a little run dance as they bolted so as not to be swept apart and away in a second wave, while individual rats kept skittering between, underneath, and around the humans' pumping legs like pylons.

"You didn't get bitten, did you?" Marcus asked, pulling the door shut while Lucy sat in the passenger seat, pant leg rolled up, sock rolled down, scratching.

"I don't think so," she said, moving on to the other leg, still scratching.

"So quit doing that," Marcus said. "You're making me itchy."

"Can't help it," she said. "I can just feel . . . *stuff* . . . crawling on me."

He held on to the steering wheel, dark knuckles blanching. "Don't say it," he said, not looking at her.

"Don't say what?" Lucy said back, her pale leg candy striped with nail marks.

"It."

"It?"

"Fleas."

"Fleas?" Lucy echoed. Her fingers stopped scratching as her brain filled with pen-and-ink skeletons, merrily directing plague victims with their scythes to carts heaped high with medieval bodies, most nearly skeletons themselves.

"I said not to say that," Marcus said as he started the engine and pulled forward, the truck's tires leaving bloody toupees in their wake.

32

On clear nights, Dev could see them: the satellites mankind had flung into orbit around itself, some spying, some looking toward the stars, others there to bounce signals beyond the horizon, and still others playing fortune-teller in five-day chunks. All were no doubt still beaming their data back to earth, to control rooms full of desiccated corpses.

It was the last—the weather satellites—that Dev missed the most. Though it was popular to make fun of weather reporters and their forecasts, the truth was during his lifetime, he'd grown to rely on them. A tap on his smartphone provided hourly to weekly forecasts of amazing accuracy; if danger was on its way, the weather service sent him text alerts to take cover. The same app would show him animated satellite views so he could watch a storm traveling from Romulus, to Taylor, to Dearborn Heights, with pins listing the time and speed. But all those early warnings had gone away, along with all the people to intercept the satellite data streams that made them possible. Now weather was something it had never been for Dev: a total surprise.

Take that first hard freeze post-whatever. The day before had been fall-like, but on the warmer end of the scale—light-jacket weather, probably around fifty degrees or so, precipitation best described as indecisive: mist, sometimes bigger drops, a general pain in the butt, but not committing to what type of pain it wanted to be. After sunset, the rain came down just hard enough, just long enough to make noise against the windowpanes, while leaving puddles marking the uneven collection points along the sidewalk and street. Those puddles would burn off well before noon the next day if there was any sun at all, Dev was sure.

But the next morning, the rooster's crowing sounded more miffed than usual, though neither boy nor dog mentioned it. Instead, Dev stretched and rolled Diablo off him before padding to the living room window to see what the day had to offer. Before he could focus, though, the pane fogged in front of his eyes. Diablo, standing next to his human, smudged the chilled window with his wet nose. As they stood there, the smudge turned to frost, the geometric crystals feathering outward according to their molecules and math.

Dev wiped a clean porthole and squinted before it could close up again. The puddles from the night before had turned into black ice marbled with white air pockets.

The boy clapped his hands and rubbed them in anticipation. "First ice," he observed, looking down at Diablo. "You know what that means," he added, and the dog woofed as if he did, though really, he hadn't a clue.

"Snow's on its way," he said before preparing for it, locating his hat and scarf, boots, gloves, ski mask, and parka, all smelling of mothballs from the storage tub his mom had put them away in the previous March. And most came in handy almost immediately, as Dev dressed to do his outside-going chores. His boots, however, stood sentry in the vestibule, emptily awaiting their imminent donning. And kept on waiting. And waiting.

Dev knew the transition between seasons could be a little bipolar at times, especially in Michigan, where you could sunbathe one day and freeze the next. It was just that sort of schizoid meteorology that made the TV weather report so vital before, reassuring viewers that it was just the weather, and *not* a sign of the apocalypse.

Now it was a different story, and all he had to go by was his calendar and the memory of what was and wasn't normal. But Dev hadn't been alive for a hundred years, and if Michigan was about to experience one of those once-in-a-hundred-years kind of winter—some El something, Niña, Niño, maybe even Diablo—he'd just have to wing it.

Not that Dev was complaining about the lack, thus far, of any appreciable snow. Though he loved the way it uncomplicated the outside world, he could wait. Because winter would be the first real test of his ability to survive, alone, in the world postworld.

Diablo barked suddenly, almost as if he'd read his human's mind and objected to the *a*-word. "Well, of course I'm not *alone*-alone," he reassured the animal, wondering what he should do about the snow if and when it came.

Before, it was just a given that the neighbors took care of their paved areas, the fear of getting stuck or sued real and ever-present. So out came the snowblowers and shovels, cutting troughs through the white stuff while the city's plows and salt trucks took care of the roads. Dev hadn't been crazy about this haste to unbury the neighborhood, partly because the Brinkmans' snow removal duty usually fell to him, but deeper down, he hated the way everything looked afterward. Where once great white dunes of snow blanketed his suburban homeland, afterward, it just looked like crap, all that simplicity rendered complicated by block-long gashes of exposed concrete, flanked by dirty snow and slush, the underbelly of civilization unearthed by the slide and scrape of shovels, the great roar of snow-vomiting machinery.

"People have to work, don't they? They have to get to school," his mother—the snow-ruiners' spokesperson—always justified.

"And what if someone broke his neck, slipping on our sidewalk?" his stepfather added.

Whose? Dev wanted to know, trying to imagine how the breaking of a neck that wasn't his should matter.

"Like the mailman," his stepfather added, almost as if he'd been reading Dev's mind.

Oh, Dev thought, *yeah . . .*

Not that he had any feelings for the mailman personally. He was just the means by which the stuff Dev ordered arrived, all the magazines and boxes feeding whatever the latest obsession happened to be. Properly schooled in his personal stake in snow removal, he'd reluctantly pull on his boots, zip up his jacket over layers of clothes, and mummify his head with a scarf to clear a path between his passions and front door.

But there was no more mail service, FedEx, or UPS, and as far as necks went, the only one left was his own. The unopened pouch of vintage 1930s Electrolux vacuum cleaner bags he'd ordered on eBay but never got? It was out there, somewhere, lying in some pile of boxes at the end of a conveyor belt in some mail-sorting facility or in a delivery truck, maybe, squashed between semis or upside down in a ditch.

So why not just leave it? Dev wondered, imagining the snows to come, unmarred as he stood by the window with a warm cup in his hands.

To leave something alone, of course, it has to be there in the first place. But the snow wasn't. By the beginning of December, there'd been no measurable snow, which was weird, even by Michigan standards. It was almost as if the sky had forgotten how. Everything else was on schedule: the trees got naked; the sky turned dryer-lint gray; the temperature fell below freezing while Diablo's fur thickened and Dev started wearing sweaters over sweaters whenever he went outside. Inside, they kept the fireplace going and used the generator to run a space heater in the garage for the chickens. The freezer had been shut down for the season, the unheated garage next door being plenty cold enough to keep frozen food frozen. His neighbors' warm-blooded pets began breathing fog, even inside.

Dev wished he could do something about how cold the other houses were, but what? Setting unattended fires in the houses with fireplaces? Not smart. Space heaters? Right, he was going to spend the winter keeping a dozen generators going, running around with sloshing cans of gasoline, getting it on his gloves, his clothes, risking self-immolation every time he struck a match.

Plus, they had fur coats. All those hairy mouth breathers chugging away like chain smokers? Their ancestors used to live outside *all the time*. These pampered pets had it easy—a roof and four walls keeping the wind off them and, once it started snowing, keeping that off too. Not to mention the free food they didn't have to catch for themselves. Or the couches and beds for sleeping on. No rolled-up magazines coming at them no matter where they decided to poop. All in all, it was a pretty sweet existence, even without central heating.

Meanwhile, outside, the snow continued not falling.

And Dev kept waiting, scanning the overcast sky for promising clouds. But aside from a few flurries to turn the dead lawns salt-and-pepper, there'd been nothing worth noting. The real snow—the snow measured in inches and feet—that snow, apparently, was AWOL for the time being, leaving the temperature to do what falling there was.

Unfortunately, not all degrees are equal—not in academia, not in fevers, or global warming, and not when it comes to the temperature in your living room. The difference between sixty-five and seventy on a sunny day is hardly noticeable; ditto, the difference between ten and fifteen degrees below zero. But make a one-degree difference between thirty-three and thirty-two degrees Fahrenheit, and everything changes.

That shift had already happened outside. After the first hard freeze, there'd been several freeze-thaw cycles, but now the ice stayed ice, morning, noon, and night. Inside the houses where the pets had begun chain smoking, Dev figured it was probably somewhere around forty, maybe the midthirties. It wasn't freezing, though. Every time he visited, he'd kick a water bowl and watch it jiggle before topping it off. And as far as the pets without fur, strangely, they didn't seem as bad off as the others: case in point—no visible breath. Sure, that could be a sign that they were already dead. So Dev flicked his fingernail against the glass, and watched as a coil unwound here or a tongue flicked there. Just to be sure, he emptied his neighbors' linen closets of their blankets and quilts, and alternately wrapped or draped these around the cages, bowls, and aquariums.

But then one night, what little heat was trapped by insulation inside his neighbors' walls leaked away, escaping through loose doorjambs, single-pane and steel-pan windows, up chimneys and out through the holes where gas, water, and electricity were previously piped in. And that's when the inside temperature everywhere but where Dev and Diablo lived crossed that all-important, one-degree threshold, heading down.

When they made their rounds the next morning, the boy and his dog found them: reptiles frozen in their last gestures, lying on their ridged backs, green, brown, or yellow limbs in the air; scaly black-and-green bodies wrapped around driftwood, forked tongues frozen midflick; a half-dozen burst fish bowls, their sun-orange residents decoupaged in ice; an aquarium with the safety glass splintered but holding, the fish gathered like dead leaves in a layer on top, their swimming no longer enough to aerate this kind of stagnation; a pair of parakeets, inert among the spilled seed and droppings at the bottom of their cage; the parrot who'd talked him into this folly, speechless now and forever.

In the houses of survivors—the ones with those fur coats—there was no wailing or gnashing of teeth at the passing of their less hirsute fellows. Nope. The dogs and cats left over panted and puffed, instead, licking furiously at frozen water bowls, unused to having to work so hard just to get a drink.

Dev ran from one survivor to the next, apologizing, giving each a brisk rubdown, trying to work a little of his own warmth in. He made a mental note to bring a thermos with hot water the next time they made their rounds, maybe with a splash of his stepfather's vodka, to keep it from freezing so quickly.

And still the temperature dropped, well below zero, judging from Diablo's frosty beard and Dev's own frozen nose hairs. He thought about inviting a few of the other dogs back to their place—his and Diablo's—but figured he better not. Diablo got along fine with other dogs when the pecking order was clear, but who knew what would happen if his authority was suddenly challenged? That's all he needed, a bunch of dogs marking their territory with urine like streams of caution tape, part of that territory being Dev himself. So no. When it came to dogs, the Brinkman house would remain monogamous—or whatever the right word was.

"We don't need any interlopers, do we?" Dev said, preparing the couch for bed. Ever since the change in weather, he'd inched that particular piece of furniture ever closer to the living room's primary source of heat—the fireplace—while making sure the fire screen was in place to avoid any accidental immolations.

"Two's company, right," he added, patting the dog's head, feeling like he felt most nights since the end, but especially so on cold ones, with a good fire going and a loyal dog settling in on top of him, all his doggy weight calming the boy underneath, keeping all his pieces together and in one place. And what he felt like was this:

Yes, he thought. *This will do.*

The explosions started sometime just before sunrise. Dev had been dreaming a dream that was basically him outside himself, watching as he slept with Diablo on top, the fireplace snapping, the occasional log collapsing, sending orange embers up the chimney. Except for the difference in point of view, his dreams were almost the same as his waking life—a byproduct, he assumed, of his Aspergerian literal-mindedness.

Before the first explosion, in the dream, a particularly large log cracked open, releasing a jet of pure blue flame the out-of-body Dev marveled at just before . . .

Boom!

Dev jerked out of sleep, his heart shot through with adrenaline. Another explosion went off, this time sounding like a backward bomb—the explosion coming first, followed by the long, steady hiss of a burning fuse. Another explosion followed, along with more postexplosion hissing. Then two more, right on top of each other, as if whoever was setting them off wanted to make sure he got the point.

Leaping from the couch, the maybe last boy on earth ran to the living room window and snapped open the venetian blinds, wondering who or what was attacking the neighborhood. The sun, just rising between houses, caught him right in the eye. Blinking away some tears, he made himself look again.

And that's when he finally saw it—*them*—the rivers flowing, the geysers geysering from his neighbors' houses, the water looking like blood in the streets, from all the rust after months of standing stagnant. And the frozen pipes kept bursting—boom, rattle, hiss—all up and down the block, followed by more rusty blood in the streets.

Diablo began howling, either because of the noise or in sympathy for his fellow animals. Listening hard between the devil dog's long, doggy notes, Dev finally heard it—*them*—the others, yapping, yipping, or growling, trapped in the houses surrounded by exploding pipes punching through the drywall, spraying their fur, flooding basements, kitchens, bathrooms . . .

He hadn't taken the hint after the first round of dead pets. How had he missed it? Easy: he reasoned it away. The survivors were safe; they'd survived; they'd all been wearing fur coats, blah, blah, blah. But what good was a fur coat once it got wet and there was no place to get dry before you froze to death?

For the briefest second, he thought about all the meat they'd leave behind. He'd unplugged the freezer because it had become redundant, but it was also nearly empty. There'd been plenty of cultures, before, that ate dog and cat. And cooked in a Crock-Pot, even the toughest cut . . .

One look at Diablo and his mind-reading eyebrows squashed that thinking in the middle of its being thought. "I wouldn't," he assured the dog standing ever loyal at his side. Diablo, meanwhile, had stopped howling. He stood guard with his human instead, his big, floppy ears flinching upward with each new explosion.

Eventually, the pipes stopped bursting and the water slowed to a trickle that finally froze, leaving a great bloody slick filling the street. The boy and his dog, too, were frozen. The former had pulled a kitchen chair to the living room window and just sat there, staring out, while the latter sat sphinxlike underneath, his back barely clearing the seat bottom, his big Labrador head wedged between his human's knees. Dev angled his legs inward to hug and calm the animal while his hands worked behind the dog's ears, soothing, thinking. Outside, beyond the chilled glass, the primal chorus was still at it, complaining loudly about this totally unacceptable development.

Reaching behind and bracing himself, Dev rose finally from the kitchen chair. "You can come if you want," he told Diablo. "I might need a translator."

And with that, Dev began loading up the wheelbarrow he used for making the round of pets, filled with cans of Alpo and Fancy Feast, a box of Milk-Bones, some catnip, and a thermos of water freshly nuked in the microwave. He plugged together every extension cord he'd scrounged from the neighborhood, duct taping the connections so they wouldn't pull free. After suiting up—parka, gloves, ski mask—he topped off the generator before plugging one end of his extension cord into an outlet and the other into the biggest, baddest hair dryer he could find. He looked at himself in the hallway mirror, holding the dryer like a sheriff's six-shooter. Stepping out the front door, he began unlooping yard after yard of duct-taped wire as he headed across the street.

"Anybody home?" he asked, letting himself into the first house, Diablo at his heels.

No answer.

And so the two went looking, Diablo in the lead, Dev holding his leash, calling, "Here, boy," and whistling. They heard a sad yip from behind a couch, its skirt soaked dark with standing water, its cushions sliced from seat to back, tufts of batting yawning out. There were claw marks against the wall where the couch's back once pressed—now pushed away from the wall at an awkward angle. And behind the couch, shivering out ripples in the standing water was the toy collie that lived there.

"Oh, buddy," Dev said, sloshing the couch farther away from the wall before scooping up the dog trapped behind it. He'd tried making it to higher ground, but apparently misjudged the reliability of a couch that had been set on glider pads to make vacuuming behind it easier for the long-dead housekeeper of this now-ruined house. He wrapped the animal's shivering body in a blanket and began rubbing him down from snout to tail. When he'd done all he could with the blanket and fresh towel, Dev flicked on the hair dryer and began blowing out the dog's new Einstein do. Its pulled-back lips made the collie look like it was smiling even more than usual, which it probably was.

From mammal to mammal, he dried them and fed them and watered them, wondering what to do with them once he'd finished with them all. The houses were a total loss—flooded, frozen, structurally unsound. Once it warmed enough to thaw, there'd be mold, rot, warped floorboards, cracks where the water got in, froze, expanded, the cracks growing deeper, spreading farther.

It had been a mistake, keeping them inside. He'd been anthropomorphizing—or maybe Aspiepomorphizing. He'd projected on them his own tendencies, assuming they'd prefer the home-field advantage and being left alone. But even Dev had Diablo, and the rest—all they had were walls and waiting for Dev to bring them food and water. No wonder they'd been so free with the gratitude.

Beyond the wall, the formerly domesticated had teamed up—the dogs, at least. The cats—outside of the cheetah, he hadn't seen any. Perhaps they'd succumbed to something further up the food chain. Or maybe they really were like Dev. He'd always thought of cats as being like dogs, but with Asperger's. So maybe they were all just hiding, solitarily, wary of making themselves a bigger target than necessary by banding together like those oh-so-needy canines. They'd stick to the night and shadows, lonely hunters hooked on the element of surprise.

The dogs—they knew how to handle the cold; like hunting, they weathered the weather in packs, sharing their body heat. The cats—who knew? But they still probably had a better chance outside than in—especially now. He could leave garages and sheds open, drop off blankets, towels, throw rugs—give them plenty of places to hole up if they wanted, without having to deal with indoor skating rinks and falling plaster.

Plus, it'd be good for the ultimate safety of Devonshire. Release the hounds, right? Let fly the dogs of war. They'd be his personal security detail, howling out the approach of intruders on four legs or fewer. And so Dev propped open the doors leading to the backyards of Devonshire as the dogs of war flew and the cats of chaos catapulted. Their various exits went so smoothly, in fact, he'd begun congratulating himself on another problem solved when he remembered what he'd forgotten:

The fences. He'd forgotten about knocking them down. It wasn't hard to do, his not having mowed the grass since it stopped growing in late October. And so he just assumed once he set them free, his neighbors' dogs and cats would stick to their respective backyards. But his furry parolees had no preconceptions about where they belonged relative to fences that weren't there anymore. As far as they were concerned, it was all one big backyard now.

Except it was even worse than that. A single side gate, left open when the neighbor responsible for it died, had gone unnoticed by Dev until his newly released charges turned into a blur of fur funneling through it.

"Stop!" he tried. "Wait!" he tried. But it was too late. The big backyard he'd released them into was still smaller when compared with the rest of Devonshire. And so they chose the latter, unbound by anything, except the wall of charred trucks full of bones at the end . . .

"Oh crap," Dev said, watching as the herd charged off to what surely must have seemed dog heaven. Bone, bones, and more bones—some much longer than any they'd ever gnawed on before. He hadn't bothered locking the Devonshire-side doors, and the freeze-thaw cycle that did such damage to the houses had popped a few doors here and there. He'd tried closing them before, but the locks were pretty much shot, the doors bouncing back open no matter how hard he slammed them.

And so Dev charged after them, after making sure Diablo was safe inside. But then he stopped short. Despite there being plenty for all, the dogs had started doing what dogs do: staking their claims by peeing on everything in sight.

And peeing begot barking, and barking begot fang baring, and fang baring begat lunging at throats, chomping on ears, high-pitched yelps, and deep-throated growls. All Dev could do was stand and watch as Darwinism played out in front of him in real time—the tiny, the weak, the old and lame, torn apart in a blur of claws and teeth.

The cats, meanwhile, found tree crooks to meow down from, perhaps reaffirming the advantages of being a little standoffish.

Eventually, the killing stopped and that canine ESP that allowed dogs to hunt in packs kicked in. The survivors—the fittest of the fit—were enlisted, en masse, as Dev's "men," the ones to protect him if it ever came to that. They straddled the line between feral and civilized, licking the hand that fed them and attacking whatever it pointed to.

"Listen up, men," he'd say, hands behind his back, addressing the troops collectively. Though Diablo was the real alpha dog here, Dev was the alpha's alpha: the holder of Diablo's leash. Diablo did the translating and otherwise kept order. If a couple of roughhousing hounds got a little too rough, all he had to do was stare at them, tilt his head right, left, bare his teeth, bristle his fur, and the others snapped to.

Needless to say, Diablo was not one of the troops. He was the dog who still had a human—the one with the inside track when it came to food. The others—Dev's troops—were a means to an end if there was another end coming for him. They'd distinguished themselves by not eating their former owners; they'd further distinguished themselves by surviving the dog-eat-dog fiasco he'd inadvertently set in motion. He liked them, collectively, and would make use of their canine talents if (or when) the time came. But they were no Diablo, who'd already saved Dev, whether either of them knew it or not.

As for the cats, they were cats: softly padding mysteries, keeping their agendas to themselves. Watching from a distance, Dev realized he'd been wrong about them all along. Cats weren't dogs with Asperger's; they were neurotypical women. He could look at them all day long without knowing a thing about them, except that he admired how well they carried their indifference for him. "Ladies," he'd say, tipping an imaginary hat whenever two or more approached.

If they were hungry, they might draw closer, snake a tail around his ankle, deign to purr. But if they weren't, Dev might as well have been a ghost lost among the ghosts only cats can see. The sting of rejection never lasted. After all, Dev already had a friend, the most important dog in Devonshire—the only one with a name.

33

It wasn't fleas; it was worse. Because there was something between rats and pigs to worry about, and while fleas were a pretty good guess, they weren't the right one. The correct answer didn't reveal itself until Lucy's scratching reached her head, and her raking fingers dislodged a stow-away that landed on Marcus's arm and ended its days as a smear of bug parts and blood among dark hairs.

"What is it?" she asked.

"Was," he corrected, checking his palm for additional evidence. He almost laughed with relief, after miles of worrying about the plague. "Mosquito," he said, offering his open hand for inspection. "Tank was full, too, by the looks of it."

Marcus continued driving. "You should probably give that do of yours a good shake, make sure there aren't any others," he advised. He saw a peripheral flash of red hair being stirred on both sides by furious claws and waited for the report. Nothing. He looked in the rearview; Lucy looked like a clown on a very bad hair day, head sunk so he couldn't see her eyes, just the top of her head, flanked by shoulders, trying not to shake. Lucy herself was quiet. Too quiet, as they say in horror movies.

"What's wrong?" he asked finally.

"Can we go back to it just being fleas?" she asked, her voice tiny, her eyes jiggly with tears.

The Zika virus and the small-brained babies it led to hadn't been on Marcus's radar because the stakes were so much less for a guy, especially a virgin who was busy preparing to wage small-town jihad when the press was full of reports warning pregnant women to stay inside, to not travel to certain warmer climates, to wear deet like old women wear perfume: in copious amounts. And during her first pregnancy, Lucy was too preoccupied with ending it to give Zika more than a passing glance, even though the pope himself had given pregnant women with the virus a get-out-of-hell-free card if they got abortions under the circumstances, while also allowing birth control for a limited time only.

Irony, again.

Had Lucy known—had she been paying attention—she could have argued "special circumstances" with the pope as a character witness. It probably wouldn't have flown with her parents, but maybe the but-lady at the fake clinic would have slipped her a card for one of those "other places" that weren't so picky about the state's faith-based paperwork. But since that time, the mother-(again)-to-be had gotten caught up, reading through magazines from before in the library's periodical section while they took their little vacation from the road. Now she had all the information she needed to be scared out of her wits.

"Zika" was all she said, eyes welling, after Marcus asked what was wrong.

He tried placing the word. "Wasn't that, like, some kind of wine cooler from the nineties?"

It was Lucy's turn to try to place the reference. "Do you mean *Zima?*" she asked.

Marcus snapped his fingers and pointed. *"Yes,"* he said. "That's it!"

"No," Lucy said, shaking her mussed head. "Not Zima. *Zika.* With a *k.* The virus."

Marcus presented a passably blank face, made all the more convincing thanks to the fact he had no idea what she was talking about.

"Zika," she repeated. "It makes pregnant ladies give birth to babies with small heads."

"And you're sure that's not Zima."

"This isn't funny," she insisted.

"Neither's drinking while pregnant," Marcus said. "So if you're planning to do it, you can just forget about it."

"What makes you think I'd want to drink while pregnant?" Lucy asked. "Did you ever see me drink when I *wasn't* pregnant?"

Marcus admitted that he had not, but then pointed out that she'd sabotaged his condoms without his noticing—at least not before it was too late, along with her period.

"So just because I wanted to preserve the species," she said, "I'm pretty much capable of anything. In your opinion."

"Just calling 'em like I see 'em," Marcus said. Paused. Said: "Small heads? Like in more than one?"

Lucy shook her normal-sized head. "Like in learning disabled. Like those pinhead circus freaks."

"From a mosquito bite?"

Lucy nodded.

Marcus gripped the steering wheel and glanced at his bug-smeared forearm. "What's it do if your head's already all grown up?"

And it was a sign of the extremity of her distress that she let a straight line like that pass.

What followed were several days of hell, waiting to see if Lucy's self-diagnosis was confirmed with actual symptoms. According to what she'd read, the first signs for the mom were like a really bad flu. Thank you, diagnostic medical people. Could you be a little more ambiguous? Ebola? "It starts with flu-like symptoms, but . . ." Dengue? "It starts out like the flu, but . . ." And it was always after that "but" that the nightmare symptoms followed. Bleeding from the eyes? Check. Internal organs liquefying? Double check. Pinhead babies? And that's three in a row. We have ourselves a winner!

Lucy stayed in the truck while Marcus, in gas mask, baseball cap, and long sleeves, ran swatting at the air to a Walgreens, in search of a thermometer to check if she had a fever.

"Couldn't you find anything that doesn't need batteries?" she asked when he returned. "What about false readings if the batteries are low?"

Marcus pointed to the battery-life indicator.

"Right," she said. "What if that's the first thing to start acting squirrely when the battery's going?" He suggested they could just replace them. Nice try. It wasn't like they were making new batteries anymore. For all she knew, they were all going bad. She'd started having doubts about the ones in her watch, which seemed to be disagreeing with the windup one more and more often. The question: Which was right, and which was wrong?

"I looked for one of the mercury ones," Marcus insisted. "I think they might be banned or something. You know, because of mercury poisoning?"

Lucy figured it was probably likelier that the makers of button batteries and digital thermometers had joined forces to drive the analoggers out of business, perhaps with the help of an environmental cover story. She was also starting to think that Marcus's theory about President Bozo wondering, "What's this one do?" was probably likelier than not. Paranoia—it seemed—could metastasize even easier than cancer.

In the end, it was a lot of nothing about nothing, thank God—or whoever it was capriciously doling out miracles while also creating the circumstances under which such were prayed for. Lucy wondered if maybe she should convert to Norse mythology or something, one of

the ones with trickster gods, like Loki. The available evidence seemed to
vindicate that kind of god, as opposed to the all-knowing, all-powerful,
all-loving creator of space-time she'd been raised to believe in.

And maybe that was the problem; maybe people gave God too
many alls to juggle. The combination seemed self-canceling. Because
how could an all-knowing, all-powerful god who let babies die in earthquakes be described as all-loving? "Answer me that," Lucy demanded,
and Marcus just shrugged.

"You sound almost angry about being okay," he said.

"For the time being," she said, pointing out the bug-starred
windshield, waiting for just one more to splat before adding: "For
example . . ."

Neither the *Aedes aegypti* nor the *Aedes albopictus*—the mosquito species
that carried the Zika virus—were known to inhabit the northern states
of the US, partly because those states routinely experienced hard freezes
during the change of seasons. Though freezing temperatures were not
unknown in the American South, they were far rarer and shorter and
occurred within a far smaller window of time during the year. And so,
along with stampedes of rats, followed by stampedes of feral hybrid pigs
like buffalo of old, Marcus and Lucy had another pest driving them
precisely where they didn't want to go: north.

"But it's *cold* up there," Marcus protested.

"And sadly," Lucy countered, "that's the point. Too cold for mosquitoes carrying brain damage. Pigs? I have no idea. Here's hoping."

"But it's cold. And I come from a desert-dwelling people . . ."

"Buck up, my little nomad. I'm sure we'll be able to scrounge some
parkas and long undies along the way."

Neither had ever been above the Mason-Dixon before and assumed
the worst: a nonstop polar vortex staining the actual ground the colors
pointed to breathlessly by weather people on their maps of the country

from before, warning of snowpocalypses, snowmageddons, killingly cold temperatures—the last they imagined being like brain freeze, but all over and forever until you died. It didn't help that geography had been dropped from their curriculum, thanks to budget cuts, or that every science-denying politician hyped any snowflake anywhere as proof that "ecoterrorists hate America." And so it was a pleasant surprise when they crossed over and failed to find either *Game of Thrones* white walkers or universal arctic desolation—even in December.

"This isn't so bad," Lucy said, unzipping one of the jackets they'd scrounged along the way to let the three sweaters she wore underneath breathe.

"Speak for yourself," Marcus said, winding his scarf tighter.

"Pish-posh."

"Pish-posh?"

"It means don't be silly," Lucy said.

"I know what it means," Marcus said. "It just sounds old."

"If by 'old' you mean more mature, why, thank you."

"Whatever," Marcus said, hands in pockets, shoulders slightly hunched, as if they aimed to cover his ears from the cold.

"Think of it this way," she said. "That snap in the air?"

"Yeah?"

"Mosquito repellent."

They'd missed the explosion of color known as fall, all the trees that weren't evergreens having shed down to their bones, leaving piles and drifts of brown jigsaw-puzzle pieces behind. Lucy was especially disappointed, the pervasively gray landscape really needing a little color—a sentiment showing how far she'd come since her goth days.

"It's just death," Marcus grumbled, unconvinced that a patchwork of reds and yellows would have been adequate compensation for freezing to death. "The color changes just mean they're dying."

"Well," Lucy said, "they die very prettily—or so I've heard."

"So said the girl who never had to rake leaves."

"And *you* have?"

The answer—no—was largely due to his former neighbors' preference for evergreens and other nondeciduous landscaping options; in other parts of Oklahoma, however, leaf raking was indeed a thing. "I would have if I lived here, though."

"How hypothetically *awful* for you," Lucy said, hands clutched belle style.

"You know what I mean," Marcus said. "The boys are always the ones who wind up doing the yard work."

"Don't even start . . ."

For Marcus, these sexist observations were a brief relapse, his chauvinist caveman persona, which had been in remission ever since the father-to-be found himself thinking, *I'm going to be a dad,* whenever surviving called upon him to do something he'd rather not—like driving toward as opposed to away from the frigid north. *You're going to be a father,* he kept telling himself, *Time to grow up.*

She'd caught him trying on his new role one morning as they lay in the truck on their air mattress. He'd woken before her; the oversized T-shirt she'd slept in had bunched up around where her baby bump would be, once she started showing. She could feel his hand on her stomach, cracked an eye while still feigning sleep, and saw him staring at it like he was looking into a crystal ball that held their future.

"Hey, kiddo," he whispered in the vicinity of her belly button, which hadn't pushed out, but eventually would, as the cells inside her kept annexing more and more territory in her womb, their brains, and their hearts.

"It's Dad," the future father whispered, still imagining her asleep, letting her know without meaning to that he really was on board with this thing they'd made.

Smiling inside, she made a show of "waking," yawning and stretching as he hastily pulled his hand away. "What's new?" she asked, tugging down her T-shirt.

"Nothing," Marcus lied. "What's new with you?"

Of course, being on board with the whole baby-on-board thing didn't mean he had to like the weather being responsible was forcing on him. There was a reason the Haddads had settled in Oklahoma—in addition to its being where his dad's job was—and the reason was this: the heat. As in not freezing. And so Marcus grumbled, a lot, and waited for his baby mama to finally crack, which she did—finally—with these words:

"The weather report . . ."

He'd nearly forgotten about What Do You Miss? until Lucy initiated the latest round by mourning the loss of satellite maps and five-day forecasts. The occasion was a torrential rainstorm that came out of nowhere and seemed to have no plans to go anywhere soon. Marcus had tried driving through it until she covered his eyes, forcing him to stop.

"Let's wait it out," she said as they sat in the truck and listened to the rain moving in waves across the metal roof, counting Mississippis each time the sky lit up its nervous system, the branches of lightning making it easy to imagine the air itself was breaking up.

"It's looking a little biblical out there," Marcus said, looking at the angry green sky. Though he was no stranger to tornadoes, this seemed somehow worse, making him double down on being a jerk. "Those things can go, like, what, forty days or something?"

"Not helping," Lucy observed.

They'd driven way beyond either of their comfort zones, meteorologically speaking, into a kind of terra incognita where anything seemed possible, including fire and frogs. Fortunately, the worst they got this time was baseball-sized hail, quick and violent, out of the seaweed-green sky.

"What the hell?" Marcus said, looking up at the roof of the truck, which gonged like it was being played by a thrash-metal drummer. He looked out the windshield and saw what appeared to be translucent tennis balls bouncing off the pavement ahead of them.

"Exactly," Lucy said.

"Exactly what?"

"Hail."

"That's what I said. What the hell?" It wasn't that he hadn't seen hail before—just never this large, nor so long lasting. This stuff just kept banging the roof and piling up around them. He worried about the windshield breaking, or at least shattering in place so thoroughly he wouldn't be able to drive anymore.

"Not hell," Lucy said. *"Hail."*

Marcus heard the difference through her accent but decided to play with her, perhaps in hopes of assuaging his own fears. So: "Who's on first?" he asked.

"What?"

"Old comedy routine," he said.

"What's so funny about hail?" Lucy wanted to know.

"Ain't nothing funny about hell," Marcus said. "Especially since we seem to be parked in the middle of it."

"Not hell," Lucy repeated. *"Hail."*

Marcus shook his head, still playing dumb. She wrote the words out on the fogged windshield.

"That's quite some accent you got going there, girl."

Lucy blushed. "It's just how I talk," she insisted.

"And it's darlin'," he drawled, kissing her bright-red forehead. "Just don't let the Yankees catch you talkin' like that."

Lucy was about to object that all the Yankees were dead, to the best of her knowledge, when she noticed the smile on Marcus's face. "I shall chahm them with my Southun hospitality," she said. "Darling," she added, landing extra hard on the *g*.

34

Snow finally came to Devonshire, five, going on six months since the whatever-it-was. And it kept on coming—a big, goose-down miracle, erasing sidewalks and streets, merging with the surrounding lawns, everything blending into everything else, a universal blank slate. Porch railings and naked tree limbs were outlined white, while the branches of evergreens weighed heavy, clotted with the stuff. Canine jaws snapped at the flakes; cats brooded, annoyed by beaded whiskers. And the human, Dev, was content to watch it fall.

Minus humans, he'd assumed the snowy white, once fallen, would stay that way. And maybe it would have, if not for packs of well-fed dogs and solitary cats, pooping and peeing wherever they wanted. And thus the pristine landscape he'd been waiting for was spoiled by holes drilled in yellow- and brown-bombed craters. "Crap," Dev said, literally enough.

It wouldn't have been so bad if they'd used the oversized backyard he'd created when he pulled down all those fences. But these animals knew better than to get on the wrong side of a gate ever again. Which left the big backyard for Diablo and his human to play in when they wanted to avoid their adoring fans.

More snow fell the next day, erasing the damage out front for a while. Dev stood guard while it came down, making sure, prepared to tap the bay window with the butt of his rifle at the first sight of a squatting butt or hiked leg. "Scram!" he'd shout at those view spoilers, feeling like an old man already, railing against those darned kids ruining his lawn.

If only the picture window faced the backyard. The only damage back there was from foot and paw prints marking where Diablo and he'd played fetch just the day before. Dev didn't consider those marks damage so much as memories. But then the snow started falling again, and then stopped, perversely, once the last trace of their fun was erased—as if removing those memories had been its aim all along.

The difference in views was one of scope and convenience. The view of the backyard was located above the kitchen sink, and could be expanded only by opening the side door, which was drafty and even farther from the fireplace, which was their primary source of heat. The fireplace and a conveniently positioned rocking chair were what made the picture window the best view in the house—until some squatters spoiled it. Standing by the kitchen side as it whistled from the slightest wind required a minimum of long johns and two or three sweaters. And if Dev was going to suit up anyway, he and Diablo might as well go out and play. And so they did, until the stinging wind drove them back inside, where the alpha dog's human returned to his post, rifle butt at the ready, his trusty canine enforcer prepared to bark or bite, whatever the latest offense warranted.

Dev let down his guard once the black curtain of night fell, as the flames from the fireplace turned the picture window as blank as a slightly yellowed sheet of paper. Shielding his eyes and pressing against the window, he still couldn't see a thing, and so he curled up on the couch instead, slapping the cushion next to him for Diablo to take a seat. He then read aloud from one of the boy-and-his-dog books the boy and his dog preferred. These were usually picture books, featuring dogs of unusual hues and/or talents—books Dev would have derided as too childish if there was anyone left to catch him reading them. But seeing as the only witness now was his accomplice, he excused the simplicity of the narrative by acknowledging that the dog he was reading to—though possessed of infinite loyalty—was limited in terms of vocabulary.

"You see what he's got there?" Dev asked the evening before, pointing out a cartoon canine to the real canine beside him. Diablo licked the page—a yes as far as Dev was concerned.

The next morning as he readied breakfast, he looked through the kitchen window to where all evidence of his and Diablo's fun had been erased yet again. Not that the view he looked upon was pristine. Quite the contrary. Zigzagging everywhere he looked, there were paw prints, stopping suddenly in dents the size of golf holes to craters big enough for a baby's snow angel. Most of the prints were small and rodent-like—squirrels, rabbits maybe—but there were bigger ones too. The larger prints seemed to have thumbs, suggesting one or more raccoons had been involved.

Dev hated raccoons even more than rats. Raccoons were like those spreaders of plague, but bigger and fatter, already wearing the garb of thieves and sporting those creepy hands they kept rubbing as they plotted their evil. Plus: rabies. That's what was behind those paw prints in the backyard, circling around so furiously they had trampled the snow clean down to grass and mud. Dev wondered if maybe this was how it would start: the real zombie apocalypse, the infected not people, but animals bent on one thing: spreading the contagion. First a few, then more, then every last mammal left alive, driven frothing mad and running in circles until they all just died.

It was as they were eating that Diablo heard something, the sound yanking up on his floppy ears and dragging his head along with it. Dev had just offered him a slice of egg white, only to drop it on top of the dog's head, between hiked and vigilant ears. Dev's own head turned, drawn by the swiftness of the dog's change in alertness status. "It's him, isn't it?" he said.

Diablo didn't budge; it was all canine instincts on deck.

And then he heard it: a scream in a blender, punctuated by a chattering giggle, turned hiss, turned angry psycho mumble, then back to a scream on frappé. Diablo teleported himself from under the table to the kitchen's side door, thwacking at the wood with his nails, nosing around the drafty gap between door and jamb. The dog made noises the boy had never heard before—a low bellow of mournful excitement.

Dev leaned over the sink and saw it: an overwound windup toy, its spring sproinged, its fur flecked with frozen foam, its jaws bearded with the stuff. Its movements were aimless, darting after nothing, launching itself, all four paws in the air, landing and spinning, flinging snow and clods of dead lawn from underneath the snow. Its ringed tail moved separately from it, curling into a question mark, popping up in exclamation. The rest of the raccoon seemed at war with its tail, as if it were a snake that had rudely clamped onto the animal's rear end and wouldn't let go.

"Well," Dev announced, "that's not acceptable." By which he meant he was not going to be held hostage in his own house just because a rabid raccoon had wandered into their little refuge from the apocalypse. Not only that, but he had his "men" to think about—the ones who were supposed to protect him against something like this—but whom, it now seemed, he needed to save from being infected. Because that was all he needed—to be trapped in his own house, under siege by a pack of rabid dogs trapped by a wall of burned trucks, still full of bones, though fewer than before.

Judging from the snow tracks, the raccoon hadn't been outside the big backyard, and Dev had already closed the gate that had let the others escape before. How the thing got into the yard, especially with the aforementioned wall and his roaming troops, was a mystery at first, until he noticed a sycamore leaning over the yard's perimeter fence, its naked branches bent nearly to the ground and snowless. The sycamore's corona of branches touched the branches of other trees on either side, forming a nervous system connecting Devonshire to the world beyond the wall. The creature's madness must have carried it up a trunk on one side and deposited it in their backyard, once the limb it had ventured too far out on bent down, plopping it thusly.

Not that it mattered how the thing got there. What mattered was getting rid of it. And so Dev got his neighbor's sniper rifle, the one that had worked so nicely on the streetlights of Devonshire, the one with the laser sight to make the shot count. The fact that it also had a silencer was a bonus—to Dev's, but especially Diablo's, ears.

The bullets he loaded were decidedly overkill, the armor-piercing kind preferred in urban warfare and by suburbanites for whom the only answer to how much stopping power they needed was: more. Not that he was anyone to judge when it came to personal safety—not under the circumstances. Which is why, along with the rifle and bullets, Dev's raccoon-dispatching ensemble included his own armor of magazines and duct tape, wrapped around both legs, starting as close to the ankle as he could manage while still being able to flex. He continued layering, well past the height the raccoon seemed capable of jumping in its hyperadrenalized condition. Three pairs of pants followed, pre-apocalypse-new stiff denim. Together, the fabric and small-town-telephone-directory-thick copies of *Vanity Fair* should be an adequate buffer between his skin and the raccoon's fangs. Even if it latched on with all its might, all it would get was a sore jaw and a mouthful of glossy full-page ads. If the animal's fangs got to any of the actual articles, Dev would be very much surprised.

All the while he was getting ready, he kept an eye on Diablo, who was keeping a nose on the raccoon. "Still there?"

Diablo gave a low-throated growl that Dev took to mean yes.

And so he opened the side door, pausing with his hand on the pane of the storm door. He didn't want to make any noise, didn't want to startle the startled-enough thing, hissing and popping, just a few annexed yards away. He also didn't want to open the storm door any more than absolutely necessary to poke the barrel out while providing the laser sight a clear red shot at the middle of the animal that, unfortunately, was not offering much help in the staying-still department.

Slowly, Dev tweezed up the latch on the storm door and pushed it open just a few inches, the sudden inrushing cold making him flinch before he went back to holding steady, his hand pressed firmly against the frosted glass . . .

Then it happened.

He felt it before he even knew what it was. The pane under his palm pulled away on its own as the door swung wide. For a hopeful second, he imagined the wind had just caught it. But the unbudging snow on all those still branches said otherwise.

"Diablo!" Dev screamed the dog's name, but he was already out, already halving the distance between himself and the raccoon. *"Diablo!"* he tried again. "Get *back* here . . ."

But it was useless. The two animals met in a flash of fangs and claws. The snow grew red. A good part of one of Diablo's ears wound up in the raccoon's mouth, while part of the raccoon's tail dangled from Diablo's. With a jerk of his head, the dog flung the oversized rodent away. The raccoon rolled and hissed, plowing a trench into the snow before stopping with the laser light focused dead center. The air thwipped, and a heartbeat later, the raccoon exploded, fur and blood turning the snow into something by Jackson Pollock. Diablo, who'd begun running for round two, skidded to a stop, his big front paws sending up rooster tails of snow. He did that thing with his head, tilting it to one side, the look on his face saying, "Wha'd'ya do *that* for?"

Good question.

Diablo could have finished the animal by himself; it really didn't matter who sent the thing to hell. What mattered was the fact it had already taken its revenge. The only question now was: How long was that revenge going to take?

Every search engine he'd ever used to look up something was gone. He looked numbly at a collection of reference books he'd collected from his neighbors, his just-in-case library. But now that he needed to, Dev realized he really didn't know *how* to use the books he'd accumulated. They'd never taught him that particular life skill in school. When the topic was research papers, the focus had been on how to outline, how to write a bibliography, how to cite and attribute without slipping into plagiarism, how to judge if the source material you'd found was reliable or some crackpot's theory from his crackpot conspiracy blog. That the bulk of a student's research would be done online was just assumed. He looked at his just-in-case library, stacked wherever his arms got tired from carrying the latest haul. He looked at Diablo, bloody and panting in the snow, his foggy breath chugging like a train as he nosed around the raccoon's scattered remains.

Don't eat . . . , Dev thought.

Too late; it was already being gulped down.

He looked back at the literary remains of civilization, such as they were, and began some nosing around of his own, turning to the back of one book, tossing it aside, cracking another before running a finger down the page where the *r*-words started. But none of the books he checked had anything to say about rabies.

Dev looked out the window at his best friend in the whole wide world. Literally. And then he went back to looking for information, the before-he-was-born kind of way.

Gradually, painfully, Dev pieced together a prognosis singularly frustrating in its lack of precision. Rabies, it seemed, was a spectrum disorder itself. Not all that were bitten were infected. If the bitten had been vaccinated, infection was less likely, but still not impossible. The virus could gestate for weeks, months, even years sometimes, varying depending upon the species of the victim but varying widely, also, within a species. The virus collected in the saliva and could still infect twenty-four hours after its host died. Before symptoms showed up, the bitten wasn't contagious, but the symptoms themselves were just the sort someone with Asperger's was likely to miss: changes in the victim's mood. And even though dog faces were easier to read than human faces . . .

Dev stopped.

How did he really know that was true? He projected moods onto Diablo, just like humans had been doing with dogs ever since the two species teamed up. It was called anthropomorphizing: ascribing human emotions to animals. It was just one of the many signs of human arrogance when it came to other members of the animal kingdom—the assumption that just because we saw a grin when a dog opened its mouth to pant, it must be happy. But who knew, really? And how was Dev supposed to know, especially when his neurology was so bad with emotions, generally? Was he willing to risk frothing madness on an Aspie's hunch about how a dog was feeling?

Dev looked out the storm door at Diablo. He'd mowed his way through the bigger chunks of rabid raccoon and had become distracted, instead, by the snowflakes that had begun coming down sometime while his human was looking for answers. As he watched the black Lab standing out against the white, chasing and snapping at snowflakes, he'd have said the animal certainly *looked* happy.

That's how it was, when you didn't know any better. What was the saying? Ignorance is bliss. There, out there, was one blissful animal, if Dev had to guess—which was exactly the problem he was grappling with at the moment: guessing. Second-guessing. Looking for clues he might never see . . .

There were two kinds of ignorance, it seemed. The blissful kind and the kind Dev was facing over all these questions with no definitive answers. And it was too bad the laser made missing almost harder than not. Winding back the clock, he wouldn't have minded shooting the wrong animal by accident. At least he'd have that excuse—*it was an accident*—before pumping another bullet into the chamber and blowing that raccoon to eternity.

In the end, it wasn't like a zombie apocalypse movie, with infected friends begging to be put out of their future misery. Diablo didn't know anything about future misery. That was all on Dev's shoulders, one of which had a rifle butt resting against it as he chased his best friend in the world with a little red light as the other chased snowflakes.

The sound the silenced bullet made—*thwip*—might as well have been the sound of Dev's heart breaking. Assuming he had that mythical organ, which—judging from the pain he was feeling in his heart area—made him wonder if he was like the Tin Man, not knowing he had one until it broke. And this ticker, sad to say, couldn't be replaced with the windup kind. He'd just have to make do with a broken one, thinking this wasn't exactly like a zombie apocalypse mercy killing, but it was close enough for him.

Post-Diablo, Dev didn't like being himself so much anymore in the postpeople world. The great adventure seemed tedious without that floppy-eared black Lab to share it with. And that was the trouble with having a heart. Things got into it, and you stopped knowing how to live without them. Before, Dev was sure, he could have done solitary confinement on his head. And he probably could have. But then he had let Diablo in like a drug he was now withdrawing from.

How did neurotypicals do it? Why didn't they all just kill themselves the first time their hearts got broken, like he'd tried to when Leo—well, he certainly *hadn't* broken his heart, but made him feel stupid, which was nearly as bad? What was *in* the nerves of other people that his lacked? Copper wire? Something stronger, more resilient? And was there something he could take to make his nerves like that? A pain-killer, maybe—one he could load and aim.

Dev looked at the rifle that had done the deed. It was too long. The barrel was too long. He'd have to take his socks and shoes off—one of each, at least, and from the same foot—to pull the trigger. And how would that look, the last human on earth, his head blown off—and half barefoot? When you were the last human on earth, your death warranted a certain gravitas—certainly more gravitas than having a naked big toe stuck against the trigger of a rifle.

Not that the rifle was his only option. His ex-neighbors had constituted a well-armed militia, even if they didn't hold regular meetings to practice. He'd collected a small arsenal from them, ostensibly for self-defense against wildlife, but also for a little hunting when he ran out of the frozen meat he'd put aside before the power went out. The point was, he had guns, including hand ones because you never knew when you might need an option you could hide.

He looked out the window again, at his former friend, dead in the snow, a jet-black crow already perched on his jet-black head. He threw open the door and fired a warning shot as the crow hastened skyward. But whom was he fooling? They'd be back—the crow in question and his hungry pals. Without him to shoo them off, they'd be back. And there was no shooing off the eventual chemistry of decay. Dev knew; he'd gotten a lot of that chemistry smeared all over himself, clearing bodies.

But Diablo was too majestic an animal for that. Diablo, of all his neighbors, deserved a proper burial. And so Dev got a shovel and tried wedging it into the earth. It sliced through the snow and stopped. He shoved harder and pried up the shallowest divot and a few brown strands of dead grass. The rest was frozen solid.

Crap.

He went back to the garage and returned with bottles of lighter fluid in various stages of fullness. He traced a circle in the snow with the liquid: Diablo-sized, plus a little more. The snow fled away from wherever the fluid fell before soaking into the dirt like a sponge. There were matches in the kitchen and he got them, struck one and dropped it to the ethanol-soaked earth. The uprush of flames seemed fitting for a dog with a name from hell.

Blue tongues were still licking up from the dirt when he tried the shovel again. Much better. The blade sank halfway in this time, and when he pried up a chunk, a fireball followed as fresh vapors from the overturned dirt met flame. And onward he dug, one hour, two, following the lighter fluid down as it seeped slowly into the earth, releasing little Hiroshimas with every new shovelful until the hole was big enough and Dev stopped digging, rested his chin on the handle, and watched his breath for a while. Finally:

"Come here, boy," he said, hooking up his friend's leash for the last time. And then he dragged the body through the snow, from where the loyal beast dropped to where he would rest forever—a smear of red against white connecting the two.

35

They'd broken into various houses in search of warmer clothing because the sweaters weren't cutting it and neither was the truck's nonexistent heater. Snow tires also were not standard equipment. Seemed Marcus had managed to pick a dedicated warm-weather ride, the market for ice cream noticeably dropping once the temperature got low enough to wish your truck had a heater.

They did have a generator, of course. And since the freezer had become redundant (seeing as anything needing its services could be stored in garbage bags bungee corded to the roof), they got a ceramic cube heater, which helped keep the truck if not necessarily toasty, at least ice-free around the window areas.

Unfortunately, the extra drain on the generator meant a lot more stops to refuel. Which meant getting outside where the heater wasn't. And getting down on hands and knees on the ice-cold ground. And cursing at the chassis-to-ground icicles fanging the latest donor ride, some of which yielded to kicking, some of which required a hammer, and the thickest of which required getting back in the ice cream truck to touch bumpers before giving the other truck a little nudge. The gas donors were always trucks lately, so Marcus could do them, seeing as Lucy's condition had sidelined her in the scooting-under-things department.

"You know, when I said I wasn't sure having a kid was worth it," he said, pulling a second pair of gloves over his staying-inside pair, "I had no idea how right I was."

Marcus, of course, blamed Lucy for their having to head north to the land of ice and snow in the first place. Sure, the pigs had been pushing them in that direction, but Zika had sealed the deal, which wouldn't have been on the table even, if she hadn't taken a pin to his condoms and now worried about having a pinhead baby as a result. At least he could still feel his fingers after swatting a mosquito, as opposed to them cracking off from frostbite or whatever.

"Would you like some cheese with that whine?" was all Lucy had to say.

They might have been tempted to stay in one of the houses they broke into, especially one of the ones where someone hadn't died or left out food to rot, the more temperate climate leaving the air inside stale but not necessarily toxic. Unfortunately, what the southern heat hadn't ruined, the northern cold had. Pretty much everywhere they went it was the same story: burst water pipes, indoor skating rinks.

"I'm starting to wonder how bad it would really be," he said, breathing fog into his gloved hands, "getting trampled by pigs. At least there'd be some body heat."

Lucy ssshhhed him. They each had an armload of freshly looted winter wear—scarves, jackets, gloves, long underwear—and were on their way back from the latest ice rink when she stopped and ssshhhed him again. "Do you hear that?" she asked.

"Hear what? You ssshhhing me? Twice?" He and his freezing testicles were seriously not in the mood.

"That," Lucy said, using her head to gesture overhead.

So Marcus listened and heard . . . a lot of different things: the wind the city they were just outside of was famous for, whipping off Lake Michigan, turning the frigid air into knives. It rattled through the few leaves still clinging to their trees—either lucky, tenacious, or just stuck there by ice. But this didn't seem to be the "that" Lucy was hearing, something Marcus confirmed by asking, "You mean the wind?"

"No," she said. "Underneath the wind. Or between it. I don't know. It's a whole different frequency. Like a hum but a crackle too."

"Maybe God's enjoying a bowl of Rice Krispies."

"I'm serious."

"I'm not."

But then Marcus heard it, too, and looked up.

It was snowing at the time, and looking up into the flakes was like looking at sand funneling down on top of them from inside an hourglass. Only the snow kept coming and was somehow the source of the sound they were both hearing now: a kind of humming crackle. And though both were looking right at the actual source of the noise, it was Lucy who finally saw through their ubiquity.

"There," she said, pointing at the power lines gridding the sky overhead. "I think it's coming from them."

Turns out they'd entered a part of the country which—despite its reputation for being so cold sometimes it was hard to think—at least acknowledged that global warming was a thing and was already happening. It seemed midwestern utilities had begun experimenting with energy sources like solar and, better yet, wind. Lucy and Marcus passed billboards for NRG Energy and Dynegy, with slogans like "The Future Is Bright" and "Wind Power for the Windy City," while others featured windmills off the shore of Lake Michigan, noting that the Great Lakes were the "Saudi Arabia of Wind Energy."

Marcus, who was sensitive to the rhetorical formulation "the Saudi Arabia of . . ." whatever, made note of the first half of that factoid without fully appreciating the second half. Not until the snow started humming overhead, that is.

"Isn't the Sears Tower near here somewhere?" he asked.

"In Chicago, yes," Lucy said. "Only it's called the Willis Tower, I think."

"I really don't care what it's called. I'm just hoping it's still there."

It was—all 110 floors of it, including the Skydeck on the 103rd. The building had ventilated itself since the whatever, windowpanes tumbling out of their steel frames to shatter against the concrete below. Lucy and Marcus could feel the shards of broken glass crunching underneath the snow, the latter finding the experience of walking on broken panes a bit more poignant than the former.

"Here goes nothing," he said, pushing through the revolving doors, depositing two trapped corpses, one inside, one out.

"Don't be so hard on yourself," Lucy joked, stepping over the outside one, failing to notice that Marcus was a million miles away from a joking mood.

In a part of the country with more topography, he'd have suggested going to higher ground. In the Midwest, the area's tallest building would have to do. In both cases, the point was perspective and range. He just wanted to see as much of the area as possible without having to go door-to-door, checking for light switches that worked. Killing two birds with one stone, he could also check for smoke, because if there was anybody else still alive out there, they'd have built a fire and kept it going. That was the theory, at least.

And who knew? Maybe they'd get lucky and the Willis would turn out to be on the receiving end of those humming wires . . .

It wasn't. And so the elevators didn't work. And there were 102 flights of steps between them and that magnificent view, which better pay off or he was going to hear about it all 102 flights back down.

Speaking of which: "Not fair," she called after Marcus let his eagerness get the better of him and started taking steps two at a time. "I'm climbing for two."

"I could carry you."

Lucy crouched in the stairwell, hands on knees, trying to catch her breath. "No, you couldn't," she said. And just to confirm that this wasn't a reference to her current weight: "I wouldn't let you."

Marcus did an honest appraisal of the situation, including the state of his own knees, which were killing him thanks to the unfortunate combination of an old football injury and the brutal cold—though he'd sooner die than say so. "Have it your way," he fake conceded.

"Why, thank you," she said, marshaling her breath for another flight.

Seeing his opportunity to give his knee a rest without seeming as frail as he frankly felt, "You wanna take a break?" he asked.

Lucy nodded.

"Fifteen minutes," he said, sitting down on the nearest step, purportedly to wait for Lucy's next wind.

The view would have been breathtaking if either had much breath left. Several windows, seemingly at random, had shattered in place, thanks to the same expansion and contraction that had caused several panes already to tumble out of their frames to the street below. When their breath returned, they could see it hanging in the air, over the knit fingers they were both blowing into, trying to keep warm.

The sun was still up when they got to the Skydeck, though it had passed behind one of the Willis's second-class neighbors and was closer to setting than not. With her naked eye, Lucy couldn't tell if she was seeing smoke or not. There seemed to be a kind of fog rising off the snow, as if the entire landscape were one big ice-cube tray, steaming coldly just out of the freezer.

Marcus had brought a pair of binoculars and was training them on the gauzy scenery, looking for blips rising above the rest, suggesting an active chimney. "If we don't see anything this time," he said, still scanning, "I say we call off the search for the winter. If there's anybody else out there, they'll be doing what we need to: hunkering down and trying not to die."

"Not dying," Lucy said, rubbing her gloved hands. "Roger that." Pause. "Anything?"

He shook his head. "I'm mainly hoping for something after the sun sets," he said. "Lights, specifically. Something to show us where those wires are dumping their high-tech voltage."

"Assuming we can see them through the fog and other buildings and—" She paused. "Does that strike you as an especially large number of evergreens right there?" She pointed a gloved finger in their direction, near the horizon, green-needled tips poking up out of the blanketing fog.

"Not a lot for a suburb," he said. Paused. "Correction: Not a lot for a *rich* suburb."

"Roger that."

Once the sun set, the moon and binoculars came out, the latter pointed down at the ghost-lit landscape below. The Willis's lesser but nevertheless towering neighbors edited the available view more than Marcus had anticipated, while the sun's setting hadn't helped segregate the ice fog from active chimney smoke. But then they got lucky. Or luckier. Because out in the distance, where that unusual number of evergreens shielded the rich from the lesser so, a strange glowing arose. The fog was being lit from the inside, the light diffuse, allowing what witnesses there were to effectively see around the barrier of trees to where all that free electricity was going.

"Bingo!" Marcus declared.

"Yahtzee," Lucy countered.

"No, look," he said, pulling the binoculars' strap from around his neck and handing them to his pregnant partner.

"I stand corrected," she said, dialing the soft blur of light into a sharper blur of light. "Bingo, indeed."

Before scaling Mount Willis, Marcus had insisted they hit Walgreens for a very particular item: air-activated hand warmers, which they found a half case of in the stockroom, up in the rafters, waiting for the next winter to be reshelved, by which time the store's foot traffic had dropped off the cliff, meaning that he and Lucy were pretty much it. "Grab as many as you can," he advised. "We're going to need them."

And so they did, on the 103rd floor of the Willis Tower, with busted-out windows, a wind rarely experienced by anything other than small aircraft slicing through the cross draft. Fortunately, as the packages said, the hand warmers could get up to 130 degrees and lasted ten hours. Add a little cuddling and the couple managed to avoid freezing to death.

"How'd you know about these?" Lucy asked, appreciative but curious.

"My dad and me attempted camping once," Marcus said. "Trying to be real Americans. But my dad had to get the best price, so we stayed at Yogi Bear's Jellystone Park near Keystone Lake in the off-season, meaning November."

"So how cold does it get near Keystone Lake in November?"

"Enough to know about these," Marcus said.

They took turns keeping watch on the ghost light in the distance, to see if it dimmed or went out during the night, signaling that it was something other than the street lighting of some affluent suburb just outside Chicago, fed by the renewable part of the grid and set on an automatic timer. Not that street lighting being juiced by the sun and wind was anything to sneeze at and could probably be tapped into, even with Marcus's limited experience as an electrician.

"Light bulb, switch, dry cell," he said. "Science fair. 'What is a circuit?' Participation ribbon."

"Nice knowing you," Lucy said, patting him on the back before huddling in her corner around her little pocket sun to get a half hour or so of rest.

By sunup, the lights went out, not having revealed any evidence of human involvement in their cycling on and off. Lucy and Marcus had 102 flights to go down, which would be a lot easier, though not easy. Instead of sniping at each other, however, they killed the time imagining what they'd do with all that electricity, once they got to it.

36

It wasn't their fault they were still alive; it just felt like it. Dev, thinking, feeling—sitting in front of the living room window, watching the others as they pooped with abandon. He wondered if all the people who had died while he survived were somewhere, feeling toward him the way he felt now toward a bunch of innocent animals, doing what animals do. Had they cursed him as he hauled their bodies off to be burned? Did they collectively wonder: *Why him?*

There was still vodka in the liquor cabinet, and Dev poured himself too much. He'd be hungover for sure. Good. Hungover wasn't hung; maybe the pain would be instructive. And so he returned to the living room (so-called) and sat back in his chair, thinking of his stepfather's little sips, dragged out over an evening. He took a spiteful gulp—gagged, coughed, and then vomited. Lifting his head, he looked out at all manner of dogs playing in his front yard, their paws smearing further the already poop-smeared snow.

The next morning, nursing the hangover he had foretold, Dev decided to stop going outside. There was really no reason to anymore. Diablo didn't need to go out to relieve himself; Dev didn't need to go out to play with him afterward. Other than keeping the generator topped off, the only reason he even needed to open the door anymore was to toss out buckets of food for the roaming horde of poopers and pee-ers he'd inherited from his neighbors. That, and scooping up enough snow to melt for his various bathroom needs. Unlike his neighbors', Dev's pipes hadn't frozen, partly because he had a basement so none of the plumbing was exposed to the cold air and partly because with the fireplace and space heaters going nonstop, even the coldest part of the house was above freezing.

Post-Diablo—Dev and the vodka had decided the night before— he would be postpets. The whole notion of pet having was irrational after all. Why on earth would you attach yourself to something biologically predetermined to die before you? It was crazy. Becoming attached just guaranteed a painful amputation somewhere down the road, and there you'd be, this phantom limb in your head—this active absence— following you around, only to disappear whenever you turned around to look at it. Pets—and the acquiring thereof—was just a setup for gratuitous grief.

And why? Why would a person do that? More importantly, why would he do it twice? So Diablo the First would be Diablo the Last; there'd be no Diablos II, III, or IV—no Diablo Dynasty. His presence while it lasted had been precious, and precious things are precious because they're rare. The preciousness of Diablo would not be watered down with more Diablos.

That was the decision he'd come to, while not watering down the vodka he'd hoped would help him sleep. But even drunk, sleep eluded him without Diablo's weight on top, holding him together. While he hated being touched—especially lightly—being nearly crushed had a calming effect. The weight—the pressure—counteracted the normal chaos of feeling threatening to blow him apart. Through the simple act of lying on top of his human while they slept, Diablo had helped keep Dev's pieces together.

Around midnight, still unable to sleep or at least black out, he fashioned a Diablo simulator: a sleeping bag from his deer-hunter neighbor filled with books from his just-in-case library, the same ones that had proved useless in the one case where it mattered. Under the weight of all those useless words, he hoped to sleep once again like he had when Diablo was still alive: like a baby, albeit one who cried while awake for no reason. Or rather, one: for *one* reason.

But his decision to go petless left him with a problem—or problems, really: all the animals his neighbors had left behind. During the Age of Diablo, he hadn't been tempted to adopt any of the others. He was their caretaker; he was doing mankind's duty to those left behind. He'd not bothered to name any of them, and if they had tags or a bowl that announced what they were called, he ignored them. "Good boy" and "good girl" didn't need remembering—and were responded to as well as anything else.

Standing by the window, curtains spread for the free light, not that he felt like using it for anything, Dev looked idly outside, at his remaining responsibilities. He should have stopped feeding them when the food ran out that first time. He should have taken the Lyme scare for what it was: a warning. Looking now at what was left from that pet-food run, Dev knew he'd have to decide it, sooner rather than later. At the rate they were eating—now that food had to compensate calorically for living outside—he'd need to do another run before the winter was through.

Or . . .

Even murderers got a last meal; and those that survived their first taste of freedom were either murderers or accomplices by virtue of the fact that they hadn't been weeded out. He'd set the table one last time, and after that, they could fend for themselves. For water, there was snow. Maybe having to rely on it would make them a little more careful about where they did their business. And for food, there was what he had left—a few twenty-pound bags of dry food, a few cases of the wet stuff. He dragged the bags into the snow out front, sliced them open like bodies being autopsied. He tucked a pistol into his belt to resolve the inevitable disputes.

Within moments, the furry horde descended upon the food pile like water funneling down a drain. He just stood back and watched. When a squabble broke out, he fired, and all the chowing heads bolted up, focused on him. That's when he'd grab an open can of the wet stuff and fling it as far as he could, just to see their faces trying to decide whether to chase after it or stick with the sure thing.

More shots, more cans, more anthropomorphizing of canine philosophies, until he reached and found his hand on the last can. "Your inheritance," he announced, and then launched it, "from Diablo." He paused. "Spend it wisely," he said before stepping back inside and locking the door for the first time since locking doors had become gratuitous.

Every morning afterward, Dev would check to see if they were still there, and they were. They didn't seem to be getting thinner, nor did they crap any less. What they were living on, he didn't want to know, though he suspected it was something that could either fly over or burrow under the wall. He was pretty sure they hadn't nosed out a secret stash of preserved corpses anywhere, and the ones in the trucks that made up the wall had already donated to the cause.

He tried picking up where he'd been, pre-Diablo. When it came to talking, he did that in the morning, when he collected his eggs for breakfast, greeting and thanking his various Luckies. And then he'd start the fire if it had gone out, take a book to his chair by the window, and think about reading it, as his attention was drawn by something the animals were doing outside. There were some new ones, he noticed, runty little things doted on by what he assumed must be the mother, though right behind her was another, baring fangs at any that got too close.

He actively resisted the temptation to name—especially the newest ones, born cute as their number-one defense. Fifteen years he might get out of them, tops. It wasn't enough.

And so he'd open the book he'd taken with him, try focusing on the words on the page. Couldn't. Stared out the front window. Yawned. Wake with a start, still sitting in the chair, the shadows outside suggesting how much time had passed—along with the fire in the fireplace, having gone cold once again.

In between waking and needing to, Dev imagined what other sorts of tracks he might see in the snow someday, other than the ones that were already there. Bear and deer were possibilities, but not the ones his worried mind went to. Because there was only one kind of track he truly feared: the human kind.

He'd never been able to rid himself of the sight of that one other survivor, getting his throat ripped out by a cheetah. And so he imagined waking up one morning, business as usual, fresh snow having fallen, fresh footprints cutting a path down the center of the road. Sometimes, the imaginary maker was wearing thick-soled boots; other times, inexplicably, they were barefoot and bigger than normal, some postapocalyptic, giant mutation here to stake its evolutionary advantage by killing and replacing the last of the previous kind. Whether shod or not, these imaginary footprints always terrified Dev. Not that he didn't know what he'd do if it ever happened. He did. He just didn't want to have to. But his privacy had become too precious, and he'd already lost his quota of precious things. Luckily, Dev had the firepower to make sure he didn't have to lose anything else.

37

Lake Forest, Illinois, was affluent. How affluent? They didn't have a McDonald's. They didn't have any fast-food chains, except for a singular Burger King the couple saw later, hidden in an office park near the edge of town, presumably where the people who worked with their hands and didn't live there—the housekeepers and groundskeepers—had gotten their breakfast and lunch calories in wax paper and cardboard.

It may have been a sign of how firmly ingrained Marcus and Lucy were in their birth-assigned class—the middle one that had been shrinking all the time they were alive, right up until everybody else wasn't— that they chose one of the more modest homes to break into first. Of course, it could also have been because the homey home in question was one of the few structures that didn't show any obvious damage from frozen pipes, and its windows were neither broken nor especially frosted over.

"That's strange," Lucy said, just after they'd driven past, making Marcus turn the truck around.

"Why, yes, it is," he said, setting the brake. Because not only were the windows free of frost or ice, the building itself was surrounded by the thinnest gap between its exterior walls and the snow that covered the ground everywhere else.

"Shall we?" she asked, offering her hand grandly.

"We shall," he said, taking her hand and trying to affect a similarly royal manner.

The chicken pot pie looked like a chia pet on the counter, right next to its unzipped carton with instructions that read, "Preheat oven to 425°." And that's exactly where the knob on the electric oven was set and had been, apparently, ever since the person who set it there had died. Whatever food spatters once decorated the appliance around its four burner coils had blackened to crackling and ash, the smoke detector still pipping its distress feebly every five minutes or so. Meanwhile, the front window of the stove glowed the happiest orange either could remember seeing since they'd given up on feeling much through their fingertips until spring.

Lucy, overwhelmed by their luck, simply said, "I'm feeling like I want to kiss the linoleum. Is that weird?"

"Not if you stop at kissing," Marcus said, surprising himself by already being on his knees, facing a direction that reminded him of his more observant self from not so long ago.

The freezer they promptly raided was like Christmas for her, the end of Ramadan for him. "Look," one would say, holding up a box of frozen french fries, fish sticks, a pizza. "Look," the other would say, holding half a bag of frozen corn, twist tied closed, a Ziploc bag of hamburger patties that clattered, a package of steak.

"And for dessert," Lucy said, removing a drum of ice cream that had been hidden in the back. There were ice crystals in it, and it tasted funky, but it was ice cream and cured what ice cream cured while the two sat in front of the stove, eating right out of the container, watching the cheery, cherry-red coils glow as their toes and then the rest of them thawed out.

Once they were comfortable enough to go exploring, they discovered that the woman who'd turned the oven on had conveniently nipped off to the powder room while the stove warmed, only to die like the King of Rock 'n' Roll, with her jeans around her ankles, tipped off her porcelain throne, but doing them the added courtesy of sliding the bathroom rug up into the gap under the closed door, which had segregated the stink of her rotting from the rest of the house. Bleach, generously dispatched, took care of any hygiene issues, real or imagined, while the room's single window offered the quickest route for eliminating the source of those issues. After easing their rotting benefactress over the sill and out, they quickly gathered and chucked the various stench-absorbent articles lying about, including the fortunate rug, a set of towels and washcloths, a roll and a half of toilet paper, and a cloth shower curtain, before sliding the window shut. The tub they stopped and filled with water from melted snow they heated on the stove that had saved this place for them. The thought of sharing the bath wasn't raised by either, and so they luxuriated separately, remembering only after having it again how good privacy could feel.

And so they dug in for the winter, the ice cream truck parked out front, space heaters plugged in to heat the rooms the warmth from the stove couldn't quite reach. They'd go back to looking for others once the weather turned nice again. That's what they told themselves. They'd also keep better track of directions, so they could get back here, where they'd leave a couple of space heaters going, just in case. Just enough to keep things from freezing, to make sure that their welcome, upon returning, would be as warm and inviting as when they first crossed the threshold of the house they both thought of—though not aloud—as their miracle.

Eventually, the snow stopped falling with any frequency worth noting and started thawing instead. The frozen ground loosened, giving up its loamy scents, before making way for shoots of green pushing up and out, waking up after their season-long nap.

"We don't have to if you don't want to," Marcus said.

"Don't tempt me," Lucy said back.

"So, why are we leaving again?"

"I told you already. It takes a village to raise a child." Pause. "We need to find our village."

"And if there isn't one to be found?"

Lucy hesitated, not wanting to tempt the possibility by acknowledging it with a backup plan. But just because she was superstitious didn't make her stupid. "Then we come back here," she said, "to resume our program, already in progress."

Before leaving to find their village, Lucy charged her phone and took pictures of the miracle house: the kitchen, the bathtub, the stove, the empty freezer still rimmed with a half-inch of frost. She even took a picture of the empty tub of rocky road they'd tried to save but finished off over the course of three stove-lit evenings. There'd been more ice cream since then, scavenged from the houses and mansions with electricity that they weren't staying in because the owners had died less miraculously than their benefactress, spoiling all their tastefully curated furnishing with the stench of their messy return to the dust from whence they came. But that first scoop after the long ice cream drought was the one she remembered most fondly, ice crystals, funky aftertaste, and all.

Marcus walked in on her as she was printing the pictures out. "Um," he said, standing in the doorway. He'd spent the morning being practical, filling the truck's freezer with a collection of goodies they couldn't approximate by hunting or with something already canned. Unsurprisingly, a fair amount of it wound up being ice cream, Marcus having caught the habit from his pregnant partner.

"To remember," she admitted. "And." She paused.

"What?"

"To show our daughter when she asks where we spent our honeymoon."

Marcus blinked ever so slightly at the *h*-word, an ocular flinch. "Son, you mean," he said, as if trying to cover.

"The newcomer who'll increase the world's population by fifty percent," she offered, by way of compromise, "whatever she happens to be."

Without stampeding pigs or Zika to give them the nudge, the searchers were a little unsure of where to go next in their search. "Not back" was Marcus's not-very-helpful, no-brainer suggestion, which Lucy countered with the equally sarcastic, "And not into Lake Michigan."

"Maybe we could just hop on I-94 and see where that takes us," he suggested.

She reminded him that they had atlases that while not quite as granular as they might like, did include interstates like I-94 and where it'd take them. And so they checked, opening at Illinois, turning to Indiana, and then to Michigan.

"Anything catch your eye?" she asked.

Marcus nodded. "Anything catch yours?"

Lucy nodded too.

Neither wanted to say what it was before the other did, and so they agreed to blurt it out after the count of three. One, two, thr . . .

"Dearborn," they both said, followed by a mutual, stunned silence, followed by Lucy shaking her head before channeling her inner Jean-Luc Picard: "Make it so," she commanded.

38

Animals are animals. Formerly domesticated or not, they'll revert. Stop feeding them, and they'll revert even faster. Those claws at the ends of their paws, those fangs hanging from their jaws? They're there for a reason. Their so-called "owners" just forget sometimes, until they're playing and yank back a hand striped in blood.

Ever since he'd stopped feeding them, that very substance—blood—had joined the bodily fluids he'd see dotting his front yard and walk. The snow had pulled back, exposing the lawn on its worst hair day, dotted with fresh piles, as well as a winter's worth that had been forgotten, until the blanket covering it was removed. In addition to blood, Dev noticed tufts of fur riding the breeze, along with feathers the color of the garbage birds living on the leftovers of civilization.

But then one day, he noticed more blood spattering his walk than usual. And the feathers in the wind weren't brown, gray, or black, but white and rusty red. The white ones looked like snow blowing past the window, even though it was too late for that. But then Dev went for his morning eggs.

He could only stare at the blood, feathers, and viscera they'd left behind. The eggs he'd set aside for breakfast were smashed, their shells shrapnel stuck in slick spots where the rest had been licked clean. *They tore them apart,* he thought, the words echoing from one side of his cranium to the other. They'd even gotten the eggs he'd been incubating in hopes of future chickens and their future eggs, keeping him set until his own future ran out. But looking at the mess in front of him, he couldn't see that future anymore. He still had surplus eggs in the kitchen, enough for a few days. But after that . . .

And that's when Dev lost his mind a little, deciding to kill the whole bloody lot of them. He'd kill and eat them—some cultures did. The penalty for such theft in Devonshire—he decided on the spot—death. An eye for an eye, food for food. He'd kill them and skin them, cut through their major joints—the shoulders, hips—place the disassembled pieces into a Crock-Pot with a can of cream of mushroom soup. He'd imagine he was eating pot roast. The hearts, he'd eat raw. He'd paint his face with their blood. Make a necklace of their teeth. Clothes from their fur. He'd boil their murderous bones for broth and use their tails like Swiffers for dusting. He'd . . .

He stopped.

There really was an awful lot of dust everywhere. He could practically write his name on the mirror, looking back at himself through a gauze of his own dead skin cells, processed through the guts of dust mites. Dust—and its formation—had been a sub-*topique* of his. That's what tended to happen with his *topiques*: they branched, and the branches branched, until the diagram of his interlinking interests looked like what he imagined his nervous system looked like. Neurotypicals tended to dismiss his obsessions as random, trivial, pointless, or just plain bizarre. They weren't—not to him.

Take his obsession before the whatever: vacuum cleaners. A full and deep appreciation of vacuum cleaners wasn't just a matter of rote memorization of makes, models, and model years. To fully apprehend the concept of "vacuum cleaner" required a knowledge of physics (electronics, air pressure, suction, acoustics, the behavior of particles in a vortex), entomology (the life cycle of dust mites, especially), schools of design (from the sleek spaceships of the 1950s to the x-rayed cyborgs of Dyson), even trends in marketing (from door-to-door sales to TV to internet pop-up ads). For Dev, every *topique* was a keyhole through which, when he looked hard enough, he could see the whole world. The whole world, that is, minus people.

And so he found himself thinking about dust and dust mites, wondering which was the host, which the parasite? The predator versus the prey? Was the difference really just a matter of degrees, of who'd inherited what from whom? He'd always imagined he was still in charge, standing in as the human race's proxy. But it was the animals he was plotting vengeance against who were still making puppies and kittens. It was their DNA that was destined to outlast his—as long as it stayed out of his Crock-Pot.

And so through madness, he came to . . . *ambivalence*. What was the right move here? Sure, bloody vengeance sounded cathartic, but actually doing it? What did the planet want, based on the evidence? What was he capable of, as a practical matter? He'd killed Diablo out of necessity, and he had no doubt he could pull the trigger again, however many times it took. But each shot would make the next one harder. Not because he'd lose his stomach for it, but because they'd stop trusting him. They'd be on guard; they'd hide whenever he approached. He didn't even know how many there were, now that they'd begun breeding.

And was all that trouble worth it, just to make a point? All he really needed was for them to be gone from his sight, taking their constant reminders of everything he'd lost with them.

In a lot of ways, it was like before, with his neighbors. Once again, he was seeing how many he could cram into a truck while still being able to drive. And like before, one or two of his passengers would fart along the way. The difference this time was all the slobbering and licking and other outward signs of appreciation his passengers aimed at their former, primary food bringer. "Okay, okay, okay," he said, most of the way there. "You can stop now."

But they didn't, and Dev didn't really want them to, each warm, wet, sandpapery tongue reminding him of similar tokens of affection he'd received from Diablo. Which, of course, was just another reason for doing what he was about to do.

He had a twelve-gauge shotgun and a gallon of gas—not so much a carrot-and-stick arrangement as stick-and-a-bigger-stick. He'd have brought along some pet food as an enticement, but that was long gone. The partially thawed roast he'd used to get them on to the truck was the extent of the people food he was willing to sacrifice to get the job done. Not thawing it all the way had been a stroke of genius—or perhaps just a sign of his own impatience to get this over with. The point was: they could smell it; they could lust for it, but they couldn't quite eat it, not when their fangs hit the still-frozen part. And so he could use the same lure for the next batch, and the batch after that.

Arriving at "the gate," Dev stepped down from one cab and into the other, backing the second truck away, exposing the gap he'd left there, just in case. Once everything was in position, he fingered the key fob for the first truck, opening the doors and popping the hatch covering the truck's bed. "Everybody out," he commanded, clapping and whistling and shooing.

The animals got out but just looked at the open gate like the domesticated things they once were, milling, sniffing, cocking a leg, checking out a butt, but none seemed particularly interested in crossing the threshold between the land they knew and whatever lay beyond that gate. Needless to say, Dev could relate—not that it changed his mind. "C'mon," he said, taking hold of a basset hound he intended to make a lesson of—only to find the animal's excess flesh slipping through his fingers like some kind of furry ooze. So he switched gears and snatched up a shih tzu instead, wondering how a dog so unlikely to survive had. Holding it over his head so the others could see—and hoping it wouldn't seize the opportunity to get the drop on him by peeing or worse—he walked the animal bodily through the wall's opening and then set it down, commanding, "Stay."

The soulful eyes of the dogs stared back at him, fuzzy with animal emotions, while the electric eyes of the cats looked like they usually did: like they were plotting the perfect murder. Collectively, they all seemed to be saying, "What does this have to do with us?" while the shih tzu, echoing what it sounded like, took a dump on Dev's shoe.

Perfect, he thought, looking down. *Thanks for making this easier.* And with that, he took his gallon of gas and poured out a large semi-circle, inside which his reluctant escapees milled. The matches were in his pocket, the shotgun wedged under his arm. He dropped the match, and a wall of fire shot up.

The animals seemed conflicted, as Dev thought they might be. The fire was fire, of course, but at sufficient distance, it was warm, too, and though it had stopped snowing for the season, warmth like the fire provided was still a month or so off. And so, minus a few who got the hint, the remainder remained, perhaps remembering more pampered evenings, snug in their homes with their humans.

Time for the bigger stick, Dev thought, bracing the shotgun against his shoulder and taking aim at the transitional sun. The boom lit its own, more effective fire under all the furry butts he'd collected there. And so off they fled, in the only direction they had, through the exit he'd opened for them, bounding and leaping and darting for their lives.

As the fire died, and the sounds of animal flight with it, he hoisted himself up into the cab of the gate truck and pulled it back into place. A few more truckloads followed, and Dev didn't have to kill any of them—not personally. He imagined the shih tzu probably became a fur-ball hors d'oeuvre for something bigger a half hour out on its own. But it wasn't on him. All he'd done was give them their freedom—whether they wanted it or not.

Returning home after the (hopefully) last batch, Dev staked out a couple of white bedsheets on his front lawn to simulate snow. This would be his confirmation. If the sheets stayed unmarred, great. If not, he had some mopping up to do.

He thought about an earlier fake snow—not bedsheets that time, but tree fluff. It was the change of seasons, and the stuff was everywhere, the outside looking like a snow globe from the inside. He'd let Diablo out to play; there'd been no competition for the front yards back then. As he watched from the living room window, Diablo managed to get a tuft of the seed pod fluff stuck to his shiny wet snout and sneezed it away. And that's all it took for Dev to be off to the races, connecting the sneeze to illness to death to himself, minus Diablo.

He needed to take pictures, he'd decided. Something to remember the animal by, once he'd started contemplating their relative mortality, their inherently incompatible timelines. The pictures would be his Diablo porn, just like his vacuum cleaner porn, just like the porn of all the things he'd developed a fondness for—something for the pocket when the real thing wasn't there. And so he grabbed a charged phone, stepped outside, and started taking pictures.

In the first, Diablo was being Diablo in profile, standing point as a squirrel taunted out of reach in some branches with far fewer leaves than just a month before. After that first simulated shutter snap, though, the dog's concentration broke and refocused on where the sound had come from: his human, Dev. In that next photo, the Lab is looking right at him and the phone, his perma-grin wide, his tongue out in lieu of perspiring but still making him look like a big four-pawed goof. The next picture was more of the same, but with the head bigger, dog closer. Next, a chaotic blur followed by an unplanned selfie. In it, Dev is on his back and Diablo is beside him, the dog's tongue licking his nearly blank face, but for the slightest *Mona Lisa* grin.

He stored these to the phone's card, ejecting it before popping it into a stand-alone printer full of slots and sockets for USB, SD, micro SD, those Sony whatevers. A coffee cup's worth of gasoline ran the generator long enough to print out these memories he thought he might want someday, back before he knew how Diablo would go—and how hard remembering could hurt.

He'd hidden the pictures afterward, after burying Diablo and then burning the remaining evidence: his dog toys, his collar, the leash. Why he didn't burn the photos along with the rest, he couldn't say. Not seeing them seemed enough at the time.

But now, alone-alone, with spring on the doorstep, no chickens clucking in the garage, no dogs or cats chasing or being chased, Dev reached for the book that always made feeling alone feel especially good: *My Side of the Mountain.* He'd read the book to Diablo a half-dozen times—which was probably why his obvious mind chose its pages to act as the hiding place for those pictures he'd taken to remind himself, before the need to forget became even stronger.

Burning should have been an option, but just like he hadn't burned up the real animal, he found he couldn't burn such a detailed likeness either. He could throw them out, though, along with the SD card they'd been saved to. But not in the truck-bed garbage—not somewhere where some future, weaker version of himself could go looking. No, they'd go in the river like the other things he needed out of sight and mind, wrapped in a sheet of newsprint to keep them separate from the garbage that oozed and stank. On second thought, why not give them their own bag? By the looks of it, he could live to a hundred and still not outlast his supply.

And so Dev took the little stack of photos and folded, then double folded the *Freep*'s last front page around them, taping the edges like a gift before placing them inside a plastic grocery bag. He knotted the handles tight, blew into a hole in the bottom seam before knotting that, too, trapping both the photos and his own breath inside.

As he carried his latest beach ball to the railing at the end of the block, Dev noted how the contents flip-flopped inside, making it drum as he walked. *It's like the beating of a heart,* he thought—hoping that what he was doing now would cure him of such non-Vulcanic thoughts once and for all.

39

It seemed like a good idea: visit the Midwest Mecca, a.k.a. Dearborn, Michigan—outside the Middle East, the city with the highest number of Arabic families anywhere on earth. Not as a religious pilgrimage—the secular apocalypse had pretty much cured both of provincial religiosity—but more as a kind of ethnic validation, the sort Marcus had not found among the scarlet-necked Okies of Oklahoma. Lucy was on board with the decision, because Dearborn was also home to Greenfield Village, Henry Ford's homage to steampunk minus the punk.

"It's like a DIY kit for Western civilization," she promised.

"You know what Gandhi said about Western civilization, don't you?" Lucy shook her head, inviting Marcus to elucidate. "He said he thought it would be a good idea," he said, quoting not Gandhi so much as his handlers quoting Gandhi—ironically enough.

Lucy didn't say that dissing Western civilization was rich coming from a representative of a culture—Marcus's, not Gandhi's—some of whom wanted to bring back the Stone Age. Or the stoning age, at least. But she didn't. She simply nodded at the deepness of the observation while they drove on in silence through the leftovers of that aforementioned civilization.

Once they finally reached post-whatever Dearborn, Marcus's idea of finding his roots suffered the fate of a lot of good ideas hitting the wall of reality: it revealed itself as a bad idea. The disappointment was heightened by the fact that, at first, all the signs were as hopeful as the sun glinting off the golden onion domes and minarets of the largest mosque in the United States.

"Holy *shite*," Lucy said as they rounded a corner and the Islamic Center of America came into view. It was something she'd started doing lately: swearing in homage to her father's favorite euphemisms.

"Watch it," Marcus warned; with her accent on top, *shite* could easily have been Shiite.

"I thought this wasn't about religion," she said. "'What did you used to be?' Remember?"

"That doesn't mean you have to go out of your way to be disrespectful."

"I wasn't trying to be," she insisted. "I was just like, wow!"

And indeed, it was an impressive building. But Marcus, stung by her connecting it all back to religion, turned away from the mosque, dazzling though it was, and headed toward downtown Dearborn, the epicenter of the ethnic validation he purportedly sought.

There he found in person—well, in concrete and glass—what he'd seen on Google Street View: storefronts bearing signs in Arabic, many without English translations, leaving him to puzzle over what it was they might be selling behind those hunchbacked *T*s, backward threes, bowls, hooks, squiggles, and dots. He thought he recognized a dry cleaner, a bookstore, and a store where craftsmen made things by hand, with awls and leather, chisels and wood. There were restaurants, their menus taped to the windows, the ones with English translations not having to mention that everything they served was halal because any other scenario was unthinkable in any language. Facade after facade after facade—in the highest resolution of all: real life.

What he hadn't considered were all the dead Muslims. It was like he'd wandered into a 3-D version of his handlers' PowerPoint war porn. Knitted skullcaps lying next to actual skulls, their hair and flesh, muscles and humanity spirited off by insects, animals, and the elements. The heavy black fabric of burka-wrapped skeletons turned paisley with colorful molds and mildews. The full spectrum of Islamic women's apparel was on display, from fully Westernized moderns to medieval, dropped where they shopped, prayed, where they hurried to get from point A to B when the whatever struck. From head scarves little different from eastern European babushkas, to something that looked like a nun's habit, to full-body shrouds with eye slots some jerks back at school had once called "beekeeper outfits." Marcus had begun stepping over one such outfit when he noticed the humming and realized it had become a literal hive, buzzing with wasps that hadn't had a living human being to sting in quite some time . . .

Stepping back suddenly, he bumped into the still-living, still-very-pregnant Lucy, his hand not meaning to, but touching her bulging belly while the angry burka buzzed. And that's when it happened; his whole world flipped. His brain cross-wired itself, and suddenly he could feel the buzzing in his fingertips, as if it were coming from the child inside. He jerked his hand away, as if stung.

"This was a bad idea," he said.

He kept seeing his family—that was the problem. Every dead Muslim man was his father; every dead woman in hijab was his mother. In the younger dead Muslims, he saw himself. And among all that death, one new life, buzzing away inside Lucy's womb, threatening him in some vague way.

He thought he had talked himself into being happy about being a father, but he didn't recognize that person now. What had he been thinking? Some edited-for-TV version of parenthood, no doubt, full of bouncing knees and giggles, the tableau mysteriously preapocalyptic, as if the miracle of birth would reverse everything. But it hadn't. Wouldn't. And once the baby was born, there'd be scrounged diapers full of poop and crying jags and an insidious wedge being driven deeper and deeper into the two halves of himself: the one that was a son and the other that was a father—the two poised nakedly between cradle and grave.

He hadn't seen his own father die. Instead, he'd seen a lot of other boys and men, none related to him, dying their inconsequential deaths, collected into the catch-all "them," the vague pronoun for foreigners who'd insisted *he* was the foreigner. The empathy he'd prided himself on was a sham; he saw that now. He'd been like an anthropologist, studying a strange tribe, pleasantly surprised to find they weren't, indeed, Martians, but humans who actually had thoughts and feelings he recognized. But there'd always been that us versus them in the back of his head, a longing for all the changes that would come when he and his kind were in the majority.

Had he imagined that Dearborn would be spared the global judgment of karma just because of all its Muslimy goodness? Despite his loss of faith in the aftermath of whatever, had he harbored a secret wish that his faith would be restored, rushing back when he discovered that Allah was indeed great and had spared this little island of Middle Eastern culture in the middle of the Midwest? Though it seemed ridiculous in retrospect, the way he felt now suggested that he must have been thinking something along those very lines.

But now it was all clear. He was going to die, and being a father just hastened that reality; he'd colluded in producing—*reproducing*—his own replacement, Allah willing, a pallbearer at his funeral, no sooner than a hundred years from now, but inevitable nonetheless. The fuse was lit, the clock ticking, and there were no special dispensations for appending the adjective *Muslim*. That's what he'd felt, touching Lucy's belly: his own impending mortality, creeping ever closer, one full diaper, one sleepless night at a time.

"Let's get out of here," he said, not sure if he was just talking to Lucy or what he meant by "here."

Moving on to Greenfield Village was also a disappointment. Lucy had imagined finding the equipment and tools necessary to reboot the Industrial Revolution. What she found were stick-for-stick reconstructions of the Wright brothers' bicycle shop, Thomas Edison's lab, the storage shed where Henry Ford built his first car. There was a working farm, too, but that had stopped working when the people did, and the weeds had taken over. There seemed to be lots of mills—for cider, silk, lumber, grain. They'd even reconstructed an old-timey Main Street of shops (with signs in English, thank you) and offices: a doctor's office, a general store, a post office, a courthouse, a chapel, and a schoolhouse. All showed wear and tear, probably from a rough winter minus the tender loving care of human custodians.

Unlike Marcus, Lucy hadn't been able to dismiss the dead white Christians all around her as members of some other tribe. The dead she'd been experiencing since this whole thing happened were as personal as they could get, starting with the one inside her at the time. Her ability to see past all the dead tourists littering this museum to what used to be was hard-won: she'd simply been saturated numb. And so she focused on what other generations of the dead had left behind, while stepping over the bodies of the latest and perhaps last one.

But as he and she worked their way through the various exhibits, all she could think was: *interesting, but* . . .

But what was she supposed to do with it? Where were the instruction books for rebooting civilization? For sale in the numerous gift shops? Nope. And even if she got, say, one of the mills or the abbreviated assembly line going again, what were they going to make that wasn't as easily gotten, ready-made, in whatever store they chose to loot?

There were perishables, of course, which had promptly done what their name implied. Bread, for example. All the prepackaged stuff had turned into bags of black-and-green felt within a month. Fortunately, the ingredients had a much longer shelf life, and she'd already dazzled her traveling companion with her mad Suzy Homemaker baking skills.

But eventually, even the store-looted flour and yeast would go bad or be discovered by mice, insects, maggots, and mealworms. So Lucy put a mental pin in the grain mill, even though she hoped to be elsewhere by the time they needed it, depending on whatever else the apocalypse had in store.

"Seen enough?" she asked, flipping through a rack of pamphlets for other touristy hot spots in the Mitten.

"More than," Marcus said, joining her, looking for something that wouldn't be a disappointment in the long run.

Pure Michigan!

According to the tourist brochures they found, the state's brand message was fulfilled by things like cherries and fudge, factory tours, a couple of bridges, water (except in Flint), and the seasons. Oh, and an island where cars were banned, horse poop went unmentioned, and a grand hotel waited for guests who couldn't afford it.

None of the pamphlets said anything about the weeds, about how pretty some of them could be, once you disconnected them from the word *weed* and just marveled at how confidently they'd taken over every unpaved space. There were a dozen different kinds of tall grasses waving wherever the ground was the least bit marshy, their flagging seed heads reminiscent of wheat, tasseled corn, caterpillars, ostrich feathers, the very beard of God. There were wildflowers with these gorgeous, spiky purple and yellow blossoms that looked like floral fireworks, surrounded by twiggy, thorny bushes exploding with berries so round and red they were almost certainly toxic. Standing outside the ice cream truck in the midst of all this, Lucy and Marcus didn't speak but just listened to crickets sawing their legs for love; dragonflies buzz-zipping on cellophane wings through stems and stalks, hovering over lily-padded ponds while songbirds in the tops of gold-lit trees at sunset tweeted up a storm, ignoring the character limit.

"You'd think they would have said something about this in the brochures," Marcus said finally in the deepening dark, his tone hushed, reverential, as if they'd gone into that mosque after all.

Since the world ended, they'd spent their time under an assortment of roofs—houses, stores, vehicles mainly, a library. Their options had been limited by the ambient stench of death, extremes of temperature, viruses, rats a-paw and hogs a-hoof. As a result, they hadn't spent a lot of time outside, enjoying the simple pleasures of a warm—not hot, not freezing—breeze, minus the aforementioned stench of death. But it was springtime in Michigan, minus the people, minus the traffic, leaving just this star-spilt oasis of pleasantness behind.

"Maybe they were worried about crowds," Lucy said.

40

Before the massacre, he'd built up a modest reserve of eggs he kept in a wicker basket on the kitchen counter. Eggs didn't need to be refrigerated; he knew this from his research before, when he'd decided to get into the egg business. And during the warmer seasons, he didn't. Unrefrigerated eggs were good for about two weeks, while refrigerated ones would stay good for up to three months, but once refrigerated, that had to stay that way, lest condensation promote bacterial growth. Pickled, they'd stay good without refrigeration for months as well, but pickled eggs started out hard-boiled—not his favorite way to cook eggs—and the pickling solution changed how the eggs tasted. For an egg to be an egg, it should be poached, soft-boiled, over medium, or basted. He liked his yolk slightly runny, so he could dip a slice of toast into it, though crackers were the best he could manage nowadays, his attempts at baking being closer to brickmaking than bread.

Before the massacre, he thought the biggest threat to breakfast would be running out of crackers. He'd already worked out a list of dipping alternatives, beginning with fried Spam, running through various jerkies, and ending with his pinky, though unlike the others, this last would merely be licked. There needed to be a line, after all, and autocannibalism seemed a good place to draw it.

But the massacre changed everything. The half-dozen eggs in his strategic egg reserve were effectively all the eggs left in the world.

Rationing was a must. And so he went from two eggs a day to a half, scrambled one at a time with lots of powdered milk added and stretched over two days. He'd hard-boiled the last two so he could quarter them, but his first attempt was disappointing. He'd rested the egg on its side and cut four slices—one of which, the tip of the small end, held no yolk at all. The last he held big end down and then cut it from top to bottom twice, in the shape of a cross, each grinning slice with a happy bit of sun inside.

And after that, there'd be no more eggs. No more eggs, no more breakfast, as strictly symbolic as that meal had become in its final days. No breakfast, and there went any reason to get out of bed, which would become the final resting place of the human species, as its (maybe) sole surviving member belligerently starved himself to death out of force of habit.

The robins were returning now that it was spring in Michigan. And his portion control had become so extreme by the end that a fried egg the size of a quarter might very well have seemed filling. But there was a problem with robins and sparrows and even the garbage-picking seagulls and crows: unlike chickens, when they flapped at the sight of a human, they actually took flight. He knew; he tried, felt stupid doing it. And as far as raiding one of their nests, they built them inconveniently high, so when they caught you stealing eggs and started pecking at you, it'd be a miracle if you just hurt your leg after falling, instead of breaking your neck. Dev knew; he'd tried; he'd started up the refrigerator to make ice to put on it.

He tried imagining the post-Dev world. Couldn't. Remembered a line from *The Shawshank Redemption* instead: "Get busy living, or get busy dying."

Okay, he thought, *the latter.*

And so, feeling sorry for himself, he laid his body out on the couch next to the fireplace, a sleeping bag full of books weighing him down as he looked up at the ceiling, the paint meant to hide the cracks pulling away in spots. He thought about writing a note, in case there were others, in case they found his dead needle in the world's haystack. But all he could think to say was the truth—"Ran out of eggs"—which seemed too stupid for an epitaph, even to its author.

Luckily, starving yourself to death out of sheer bullheadedness proved harder than it seemed. The level of difficulty was roughly the same as trying to suffocate yourself by holding your breath, a method of self-removal Dev had tried and failed at, a thousand years ago, in his fallout shelter. He could puff out his cheeks, bulge his eyes, sweat and squirm desperately—even go as far as pinching his nose and covering his mouth—but passing out was the best he could expect. And once that happened, his fingers would unpinch, his hand would fall away, and those autonomic bellows, his lungs, would go back to sucking air.

What the autonomic response to starvation was, Dev still didn't know. As it turned out, he didn't even get as far as passing out. He was imagining what it would be like to starve to death, picturing his stomach shrinking until it touched his spine, his rib cage vacuum-wrapped in skin. His body would slowly eat itself until it finally ran out of him just like he'd run out of eggs . . .

But then a spurious thought flitted like a butterfly across his mental landscape of personal ruin: *I could really use a cookie.*

It didn't even sound like his voice, frankly; it sounded smarter. And so Dev took its advice and got up. He mixed some powdered milk and unclipped a sleeve of stale but acceptable Oreos. As a rule, he didn't eat sweets that often; the only reason they were even in the house was because of his late stepfather, the vector through which all things sugary entered the Brinkman estate. But just like a pregnant woman can find herself suddenly needing smoked herring and ice cream, the quasi-starved Dev found he suddenly *needed* lard whipped with confectioners' sugar sandwiched between chocolate cookies. Following the memory of his stepfather's preferred approach to cookie eating, he dunked his into a glass of reconstituted milk.

Not bad, he thought. *Not bad at all . . .*

The milk undid the cookie's staleness, helping it dissolve in his mouth, the texture surprisingly buttery against his Aspergerian tongue. He fished out another, dunked it, and was struck by how familiar the motion felt, though he'd never been a cookie dunker before. His muscles remembered it, remembered doing something just like this every . . .

And then his database kicked in—all the images he'd stored and sorted, like with like: dipping toast in egg yolk, cookies in milk, doughnuts in coffee, chips in dip; basted egg yolks, Jell-O jiggling, chilled chicken drippings all a-jiggle; piercing the yolk, breaking the ice, peeling back the skin on chilled pudding. He remembered a science experiment from school, where they'd been blindfolded and had their noses stopped, to see how much sight and smell contributed to taste. The astronauts aboard the International Space Station experienced something similar, using hot sauce on everything just to taste it, because smell molecules got messed up in zero gravity. He thought about virtual reality and how it reminded him of how he watched TV as a kid, with his nose pressed to the screen as if he might pass through it into another world . . .

And the more he thought about it, the more convinced he became that he could deconstruct the experience of breakfast into its gestures, its textures, its sensations edited, pulling forward some, pushing back others. Maybe it wouldn't be the same breakfast from before, the sort he looked forward to and savored, but he could get close. Close enough to get past the mental block he'd erected, to check off "breakfast," and get on with the day. He could at least simulate having breakfast with a cold. And considering the alternative, having breakfast with a stuffy nose wouldn't be so bad.

And so: he found a professional photo of his dream breakfast in one of his mother's glossy magazines, shot it, saved it on his phone, and strapped the phone to a pair of goggles like a VR headset. His nostrils he plugged with toilet paper. Egg whites he simulated by using some of the unflavored gelatin his mom used to make her nails stronger, adding lots of salt to trigger those taste receptors on his tongue. A dollop of vanilla pudding, also salted, and chilled until it skinned over, became the yolk.

It looked ridiculous and tasted like a slightly salty nothing. It was all textures. Mouthfeel. But it was better than nothing, this salty nothing, and it would do. It had to.

41

While Lucy collected edible flora, Marcus was charged with killing something that could be served fresh. They'd been living off the land to the extent they could, and when they couldn't, they'd eaten what they'd found in the walk-in freezers of Lake Forest. It was Lucy's doing. She wanted to stay away from food that came in cans because she'd heard they were lined with BPA, which she figured was bad because chemicals that hide behind initials usually are (with the exception of DNA, of course, which she was pretty sure BPA messed with). Plus, all the baby stuff they'd shoplifted was labeled "BPA-Free," which suggested maybe she should be, too, especially in her current condition.

And that's why Marcus was hunting when it happened. He'd been charged by his baby mama to kill pretty much anything but another rabbit, several of which still clattered in the freezer whenever they moved things about, looking for something else to thaw for dinner. They'd been avoiding these "blue bunnies" because along with abstaining from "robo-food," as Lucy'd taken to calling canned goods, she'd also developed an aversion to rabbit meat, the distaste either hormone or repetition induced.

It was time to aim higher. "Like geese," she suggested, having noticed them scissoring across the sky—though *suggested* might be too polite a term. If Marcus recalled correctly, she'd said something about turning him into a eunuch if she had to choke down one more bite of pan-fried Thumper.

"Shoot something else," she insisted. "Something with feathers."

"Emily Dickinson said, 'Hope is the thing with feathers,'" Marcus noted, feeling a need to remind her that he had a brain as well as a trigger finger.

"And Plato said that man is a featherless biped," Lucy countered. "So I guess that means men are hopeless." She paused to let the gratuitous swipe at his gender sink in. "So why don't you prove them both wrong by not being so hopeless, okay?"

It was the pregnancy talking; the hormones had her raging for two—or so Marcus told himself. And speaking of two, he was rather attached to the pair he'd been born with and preferred to keep it that way. So while Lucy foraged, the male of the species followed goose poop.

He'd noticed it earlier—quite a lot of it, actually, as evidenced by the bottoms of his shoes, which were puzzled with squished green logs looking like moldy cigars. He followed the poop he hadn't stepped in (yet) down to a river of assorted grasses as tall as he was, seed heads shaking and shushing in the breeze.

Nosing a few stalks aside with the barrel of his shotgun, Marcus nearly stepped in what the river of grass had been hiding: an actual river. He paused midstep and was preparing to reverse course when an entire flock of geese lifted into the air on huge, pumping wings. The sight was enough to freeze him in place as he marveled at their size and labored disregard of gravity. They seemed to have gotten especially large on mankind's leftovers; their flight, while still majestic, seemed a little sluggish, their huge wings pulling them up to the sky like fat men climbing ladders.

Remembering what he had on the line, Marcus rested the butt against his shoulder, tilted his head back, and sighted along the barrel.

He drew a bead on the biggest one, following as it rose, preparing to squeeze the trigger when—poof!—feathers. Tipping the barrel out of the way and unsquinting his eyes, he saw the bird drop out of the sky.

Had he fired without realizing? he wondered, cracking the shotgun to check. Nope. Two chambers, both loaded, the primers set in the brass heads looking back at him like a pair of strange yellow eyes. No smell of cordite in the air. No report echoing in his ears. His shoulder didn't feel sore from recoil. Nothing. Just a bird apparently shot—and not by him.

He stood there for a minute, feeling his testicles pull up into his body cavity, apparently as unsure of this new development as their owner was. Given the goose's size, he guessed it could have had a mid-air heart attack, but then there'd been that puff of feathers. It had been hit by something. Assuming it wasn't a meteorite, that meant Lucy and he had company. *Armed* company.

The thing that troubled him most was what was missing: the gunshot. The goose was there one second and falling the next, webbed feet over head, limp neck flailing in a tug-of-war between gravity and wind resistance, contrail of spiraling feathers following behind. As soon as he saw it, Marcus started counting Mississippis as reflexively as he did whenever he saw a lightning strike. But this time, the count just kept going up, followed by nothing louder than the insects scritching in the weeds.

If there'd been some sound, he could have gotten the shooter's direction and gauged how far away he was. So either said shooter was so far away the blast got lost in the distance—unlikely—or a silencer was involved. But what kind of rifle comes with a silencer? Handguns, sure, but the only rifle he could think of that might come with a silencer was military-grade and used by snipers—hardly a reassuring development.

And what was the point of being quiet? Was the shooter worried about scaring the rest of the flock? Maybe. But no other birds fell from the sky. One and done, so who cared if the others heard? Clearly, whoever shot the goose didn't want company. Meaning his original impulse—to fire his own gun as a way of saying hi—had been rightly second-guessed. For one thing, who says hi with a bullet? A psycho with a gun, that's who. So he returned silence with silence, wondering if he was already being watched, perhaps through a sniper scope.

But why hide? Lucy and he hadn't. They'd been through several states with and without each other. When they finally hooked up, it wasn't a problem; it was the best thing to happen to either since that worst of all days. So what made this new stranger different? More importantly, what did the shooter have to hide?

It occurred to Marcus that all the other others either he or Lucy had found, had been found dead. Accidents and suicides—or so they thought.

But why kill other survivors? There was plenty for everybody; no need to defend the local stash. So what else was there? What resource was still worth fighting over? What, in a vacated world full of plenty, would somebody kill anybody else over? He ran through the three *F*s of survival: food, fuel, and fortification. And then he thought of a fourth *F*.

Marcus kept the shooter's existence to himself. Likewise, he saw no need to inform Lucy of her postapocalyptic status as potential bargaining chip. He *was* curious, however, about what sort of harem the shooter might be hiding. And truthfully, Ms. Abernathy hadn't been his type when they hooked up—other than being alive and female and agreeable to the whole hooking-up thing. Plus, he had to admit, ever since she'd gotten pregnant, her less attractive features had become more obvious, starting with the castration threats, which seemed to be coming with far greater frequency than seemed healthy in a relationship. And speaking of castration . . .

He still hadn't caught his nonrabbit, noncanned, made-out-of-meat something to please the mother of his child and self-appointed castrator. He'd come *that close* to scoring a goose, but now that was out—along with using the shotgun. It wouldn't be a good idea, broadcasting their location to a possibly homicidal, definitely antisocial maniac, whether or not he happened to be hoarding a herd of humanity's last breeders.

Behind him, the cattails shushed like a room full of librarians as the wind came up, as if scolding him for such chauvinistic thinking. Turning, Marcus watched the corduroy-covered corn dogs waving at him, wondering if they might be edible and, if so, how best to prepare them. But then the wind died, and he heard what he'd missed before: a piping-chirping-burping noise, punctuated by the occasional plop and splash.

As a culinary backup plan, frogs came with one big advantage: he didn't need to shoot them. All he needed was a reasonably straight stick he could sharpen to a point, which he proceeded to find and whittle, already imagining his return bearing a kind of frog abacus: spear one, slide it behind his fist, spear another, slide, repeat. Since they'd only be eating their legs, he figured they'd need several each.

"I bought a different vowel," he'd say, presenting his frog kebab. "Ribbit for rabbit." Lucy would laugh at that (he hoped). They didn't laugh enough—not since she'd become the self-appointed vessel of the future. Maybe laughing more would help. Marcus hoped so.

But when he parted the curtain of cattails, there was a different and more pleasant surprise waiting for him: a nest full of giant eggs. From the geese, no doubt, and at least three that he could see, more than enough for both of them, given their size.

Imagining omelets the size of medium pizzas, Marcus let go a breath he didn't know he'd been holding. Between the eggs and the frogs, they had enough food for several meals, not a shot fired, not a ball busted. Now all he had to do was keep it that way—on both accounts.

At first, Lucy was just happy for some fresh protein that didn't remind her of Easter. Not that eggs didn't run the same risk, but between the two, eggs were the novelty, so . . .

"I never realized how much I missed these before," she said before moaning her approval over the next several bites.

"Cool," Marcus said, hastily and hushed. "You mind keeping it PG, though?"

"I thought you liked it when I moaned," she said, a dab of yolk on her chin. "Not that I've had much occasion to," she added, an unsubtle allusion to his recent drop in libido. A drop that correlated disturbingly with the expansion of her waistline—or so it seemed to her.

"I don't want to hurt the baby," he said. "I know the books say that's not a problem," because Lucy had told him they said that, every time they had this argument. It was easier for her; she had a direct line to the kid and the kind of jostling it was subject to. Marcus, on the other hand, just felt like he was returning to the scene of some vague crime he'd be paying for for the rest of his life.

But in the end, Lucy recognized a convenient excuse and accepted it, albeit reluctantly. After all, barring a significant change in circumstances, the man serving her giant fried eggs was pretty much it from here on out.

Pee.

Ever since getting pregnant, she'd had a thing about it—hers, specifically, but the urine of pregnant women more generally as well. She couldn't say where in her stash of trivia it came from, but she was convinced there was something in the excretions of pregnant women that attracted wild animals.

"Why would that even make sense?" Marcus objected. "From an evolutionary standpoint, I mean. Pregnant ladies—as you're fond of pointing out—are the future of the species. So why ring the dinner bell every time one of them squats to take a leak?"

"You're thinking like a human," she countered. "Maybe it's something that evolved in the *predators*, making them better at tracking down inconveniently hobbled prey."

There was no point in arguing the point, of course. The decision re peeing, and where she did it, rested with Lucy. And as long as she was pregnant, her preferred peeing places would involve running water, based on the assumption that doing so would disperse whatever predator-attracting pheromones might be contained therein.

Fortunately, as they learned from one of the tourist pamphlets they'd picked up at Greenfield Village (a.k.a. the Henry Ford), among its various nicknames, Michigan counted Water Wonderland, thanks to its eleven thousand inland lakes, rivers, and streams. And that didn't include the Great Lakes that surrounded the Mitten on all sides except the one they'd entered from. Bottom line: Lucy's bottom had plenty of places to choose from, whenever her spirit or bladder was so moved.

And it was because of this preference re peeing that Lucy found herself along the banks of the Ecorse River not too long after her partner made his discovery and kept it to himself. Since that day, he'd also kept them moving, never staying in one place for more than a night. Though he was curious about what the shooter might be hiding, he was in no hurry to be shot—a possibility he further deferred by observing radio silence as they drove.

"Why aren't you playing the weasel anymore?" she asked as they sped away from the latest campsite like they were fleeing a bank robbery. It was not the first time they'd so sped, nor was it the first time she'd asked the question.

"Saving the battery," he'd said the first time she asked. "Driving me crazy," he replied the next time, which was true enough, but not the whole story. "Don't want to scare the food away," he tried yet another time. By the time they parked along the banks of the Ecorse River, he'd stopped even trying to come up with excuses, just shrugging his shoulders as he bent over the steering wheel, hell-bent on being some-where else.

This predisposition for movement did not sit well with Lucy's incli-nation to sit tight—especially not since she'd shown a liking for the Ecorse River. It was prime peeing real estate, after all, and promised to last her for a while, based on how far the pale-blue squiggle ran along the pages of her atlas—nineteen miles, give or take, winding through a dozen cities from before until it branched, north and south and met again, before spilling into the Detroit River.

Off the page and in the real world, the river was shielded for most of its length by trees growing on either bank, their branches touching in a canopy overhead. The trunks were further stitched together by a dense tangle of woody vines, so that the river flowed through perpetual shadow, sparsely dappled here and there, wherever a coin of sunlight managed to drop through. Berms of concrete and railings of galvanized steel had been installed during the before time, the barriers running flush with the grid of side streets and overpasses that sat above the river in its modest valley. Following the slanting earth to the water, Lucy felt like she'd entered a large tunnel, overgrown on the inside with ivy. She liked the feeling of her little bower, especially given the preciousness of privacy in a world boiled down to a population of two, going on three.

"Gotta tinkle," she announced after lunch, before rising and wad-dling off that fateful afternoon. Usually, these trips seemed too short to have done much of anything in the way of relieving one's self—at least based in his personal experience. And so it was worrying when she hadn't returned right away. So worrying, he'd fetched the shotgun and was about to go after her when Lucy suddenly came quick-waddling back, holding her stomach against bouncing. She was out of breath, and her eyes looked as excited as they had the first time they'd met—maybe even a little more excited.

"Come," she demanded, grabbing his arm with surprising ferocity.

"Careful," he complained, but she ignored him, tugging harder, lifting him until he was half-standing before heading back to the river. He kept tripping, just trying to keep up.

"Just say what it is," he demanded, stopping and refusing to take another step.

Lucy wheeled on him. "No spoilers," she said before resuming her quick waddle to whatever perishable thing she'd found.

42

While he knew, intellectually, that the season had changed from winter to spring, Dev didn't take it personally until it pooped on his head. Looking up to get a better look at his aerial assailant, he saw them: geese returning from their whirlwind tour of elsewhere. Bringing his hand back from his head, he called after them. "Happy spring to you too," he shouted, flicking his spattered hand in disgust.

He thought he'd taken care of sneak attacks after the raccoon incident, taking a chain saw to all the low-hanging branches he found reaching inside his fortress against the world. He'd also filled jars with predator urine—*his*—and heaved them over the wall of charred trucks, to pop against the street on the other side. The pee and broken glass, he hoped, would keep even rabid quadrupeds at bay. But what was he supposed to do when his attackers could fly? And that's what it was, he decided: an attack. Biological warfare, specifically, because who knew what sorts of poultry-borne diseases would be raining down on him once word got out that you could crap on the human with impunity?

In retrospect, he probably should have kept a dog or two, murderers though they were. Having practiced, they'd be more than up to this new challenge. As it stood now, it looked like it was up to him. And so he went back inside and returned with the rifle he'd used on the raccoon—the one with the laser sight and silencer. On the bright side, he figured, he could take care of two problems with one bullet. His frozen meat supply had gotten dangerously low over the winter.

The clearest message was to go for the goose at the tip of the V. Give them a sneak peek at what messing with (but especially on) Dev Brinkman got them. Keeping the lead bird in sight was tricky, but the laser's red dot helped a lot, as did the silencer when his first two shots fell somewhere between the legs of the V. The third time was the charm, as his target stumbled in midair and then gave itself over to gravity.

He was about to cheer his own marksmanship when the V broke open like a hinge. One leg flew out front while the other fell in behind, the birds ranking themselves like troops before banking and heading his way. They looked like Indians—the Native American kind—storming over a hilltop in some cheesy Western.

If he'd been the sort to swear, he would have right about then. Instead, he just yelled, "Crap," which the geese seemed to take as a command. "Crap, crap, crap," he continued, shielding his head as he ran for the safety of home sweet home. Slamming the door, he turned to the window just as the line of charging geese deployed their landing gears and stepped lightly as a group onto his front lawn where they proceeded to mill about like angry, honking villagers outside Frankenstein's castle.

"Happy spring, my butt," he whispered from the safe side of the glass.

A cooling-off period was in order. And even though to the outside world this "cooling off" might look like hiding, it wasn't. He was cooling off, hoping the geese would do likewise, after which they could fly their bladders elsewhere and Dev could go out and appreciate the spring weather. He might even take the opportunity to restock his stash of frozen meat with some protein that couldn't get the drop on him anytime it wanted. Maybe a few of the rabbits that had turned Devonshire into a golf course during the winter.

By next morning, the plan seemed to be working. Checking the front and back yards, he judged the coast clear and decided to set out his laundry to dry. The summer before, he'd taken to using the dead service line to the house to dry clothes on, his shirts, pants, and towels all whipping in the warm breeze like flags at a used-car lot. He hadn't done a load of laundry all winter, gradually relocating all the Dev-sized clothing from the neighborhood into a pile filling his otherwise unused bedroom. But now that he was in hiding—he meant, *cooling off*—he might as well use his time productively, especially since his aerial tormenters seemed to be cooling off as well.

Wrong.

As he set his laundry out to dry, the birds' sphincters must have tingled. All that flapping fabric suddenly became an excrement magnet, not a scrap of cloth spared from this new, aerial assault. They left green, purple, and gray asterisks bleeding on every flapping shirt and struggling pair of jeans. The towels, made for absorbency, were a total loss. Not that Dev didn't have more; he had a whole neighborhood of more. But there was a principle here. *He* was the human. He held dominion over nature. It wasn't supposed to be taking a dump on his clothes, especially not when he had just washed everything.

And that's when he knew what he should have done when they were all just there, milling about, honking on his front lawn. He should have opened the window and shot the bunch of them like the sitting ducks they (almost) were. Teach them that on this piece of ground, under this particular square of sky, death awaited. Maybe then they'd leave him alone.

But there they went again—a great big V of judgment—honking and pooping with abandon. The sound of them made him feel like he hadn't since the people went away: like he was being laughed at. He'd survived a Michigan winter on his own, something he could be proud of—but this undid all that. Suddenly, he was the little weirdo everyone picked on again.

"Crap."

The more he thought about it, the less sense it made, how the geese seemed to be targeting him. Was it revenge for shooting their leader?

Maybe, but that was stupid. How did they know he wouldn't slaughter them all? He'd thought about it—still was—even though he knew in the end it didn't make sense. Not if he wanted a steady supply of poultry for dinner. A couple of burps from a semiautomatic would do it, but he'd just be wasting ammunition and good protein. Once dead, the clock started ticking just like it did with all dead things. And there was no way he could get them all dressed and frozen before the vast majority started to rot.

He looked at them, milling there again: a pair of pink flamingos that had grown into an infestation. Maybe they were smarter than he thought. Maybe they understood the safety their numbers provided. But why risk even a few if they didn't have to? They literally had *the whole rest of the world* to honk and crap over. Why pick this nowhere in the middle of nowhere to make their stand?

He wondered whether the geese had some instinctual need to defecate near people. If so, their targeting him confirmed what he'd already come to believe: he really was the last one left. He wondered what they did when they were down south for the winter. Did they hold it? No, there must be people down south too. If they'd been holding it for months, that first dump would have been much bigger—up to his ankles, at least.

Not that crapping was the worst of it. And it wasn't being chased every time he stepped outside either. It wasn't their honking—not *just*—or their webbed feet paddling after him as they flapped their wings, trying to make themselves seem even bigger than they were. And he didn't run because he was afraid of being hit by a couple dozen ten-pound fluff balls. Even collectively, it wasn't like they could do much damage with their feathers.

Dev ran because of the beaks. He ran because of the cobra-like necks the beaks were attached to, darting and stabbing at his soft parts, grabbing hold of his pinchable flesh and leaving painful marks behind. Even when they missed latching on, just being struck was bad enough.

Their beaks, while blunt, were hard. And those necks were all muscle-wrapped bone. When they struck, it was like being hit by a rock—*dozens* of rocks—pelting him from all sides. It was like the geese were stoning him—a fittingly biblical execution, tailor-made for the apocalypse.

So he ran.

He ran every time he'd thought the coast was clear and been wrong. He ran as fast as he could, leaping the front porch steps and then slamming the door as Hitchcock's *The Birds* played out on his front lawn. And as he held his breath, holding on to the barely parted curtain, yellow flippers shuffled, cobra necks bobbed, and a vengeful flock bided its time.

Trying to sit it out, he endeavored to think like a bird. And what Dev the Bird wanted to know was: Why weren't they afraid? Humans had killed them—many of them, hunting season after hunting season. He himself had shot their leader right in front of them. But still, they showed no fear. Why? Was it because all geese look alike, even to each other? Did losing one here or there just not register? Plus, those (literal) bird brains probably didn't help. Maybe there wasn't enough room in there for the idea of death to stick. Maybe they all had bird amnesia and just forgot they could die.

Pain, on the other hand . . .

Pain was an excellent teacher. Because flesh and bone remembered what a bird brain might forget. A bruise or a broken bone was its own reminder, and even a bird—or its muscles—would know enough to stay away from whatever had caused it.

So Dev got a baseball bat. He opened the door and offered himself up for pecking. And when they came charging at him this time, he tapped a few (instructively) on their little bird heads. He didn't hit them hard enough to send those heads soaring over home plate—though he was tempted. Instead, he hit them just hard enough to knock some sense in, let them know the human wouldn't be pecked at with impunity.

It took a few turns at bat, and a lot of goose bells got rung, but eventually the flock understood. Eventually, all Dev had to do was rap the sidewalk with the bat before venturing out. He'd drag it across the pavement on the way to wherever he was going, the flock putting air between themselves and him.

And when he got a hankering for poultry, he'd leave the bat at home, take his rifle instead, and wait.

And then one day he noticed a pair of geese waddling in the distance—a mother in front, a father behind—with a string of fuzzy goslings padding in between. Despite the scraping bat, they hadn't burst into flight. Couldn't—not while guarding their babies, which were still too young to fly. Belatedly, he felt a twinge of nostalgia for the time he'd had parents—the real one and even the fake one. It was nice to have someone looking out for you—and somebody else watching your back. The lead bird and rear guard turned in sync at the sound of Dev, looked right at him, and then looked away again, picking up the pace of their waddle. The heads turning and turning again were like a slow but definitive *no* in stereo.

"Don't even think it, human . . ."

He imagined answering the imaginary warning: "I'm not interested in your babies," he'd say if he spoke goose. But then he stopped. Imagined something else. Did the math. Belatedly.

Momma bird plus daddy bird equaled baby birds. But before the baby birds . . .

Bingo! Somewhere in Devonshire—or very near Devonshire—there were nests *full of goose eggs*. And given their size, they weren't likely to get away with the sorts of hiding places favored by robins. Something hidden away, but closer to the ground. Or so he hoped.

And so, for the second time that spring, he found himself thinking like a bird. If he were one, where would he build his nest, assuming there was a problematic human with a baseball bat in the area? Well, someplace the human *wasn't*, obviously. Of course, the most obvious place Dev wasn't was on the other side of the wall, which he'd preemptively bombed with his own urine and salted with broken glass—more or less stacking the deck against nesting there.

Of course, the wall was just three sides of the perimeter that defined Devonshire. There was still the river, blocked off by a steel guardrail beyond which the land dropped off suddenly to the water below. He'd almost forgotten it was there because a funny thing had happened over the winter: the Ecorse River stopped smelling like embalming fluid. The surface had frozen over, which was apparently all it took. Allowed to sit still for three, four months, unstirred by hot industrial spillage or its own current, the crap that made the river a toilet settled out, dropping to the bottom, where it silted over, out of sight, out of the ecosystem. The water flowing there now wasn't brown and didn't stink. It sparkled in the sunlight dappling through the branches and leaves spreading over the river from either bank. The water seemed to giggle to itself—apparently delighted at this posthuman second chance. Dragonflies hovered like little helicopters while other, smaller insects traveled in clouds over the water, the surface broken now and then by hungry fish, helping themselves.

And here was the missing piece that answered the question of why the birds had chosen his neck of the woods. It wasn't Dev. And it wasn't even the woods. It was the river flowing past the former and through the latter. Geese were *water* birds. He'd forgotten about the water because it didn't stink anymore. And so the waterfowl came because the water wasn't foul anymore.

Leaning over the railing, Dev looked in the direction of the current, then turned and faced upstream. A beaver had started a dam with some fallen branches but must have been driven off by its new neighbors—the ones that let their beaks do the talking. Their nest rested in the crook of a lightning-split tree, out of the way of ground-dwelling scavengers with plenty of other options, now that the river was back. From where he stood, Dev could see four eggs, each large enough for two breakfasts without compromising his preapocalyptic expectations re portions.

He returned with some rope, some Bubble Wrap, and a pillowcase. He'd take two and leave two, counting on their bird brains not being very good at counting. He'd find the other nests, rotate, taking no more than enough for a few days at any given time. There was a fairy tale he vaguely remembered, something about geese laying golden eggs. He could attest to that; they were quite golden inside, surrounded by white, and even tastier than the chicken kind.

Happy spring, indeed.

43

"I'm not crazy, right?" Lucy said as the two stood next to the river where a tree had fallen across and around which a few dozen plastic grocery bags bobbed. Many of them were still knotted and full of what the one she'd torn open was full of: garbage of varying degrees of freshness wrapped in pages from a newspaper whose singular date suggested the pair might have company after all.

Poking through the spilled contents with a stick, Marcus did his best to tamp down her enthusiasm. "It's somebody's garbage," he said, the big whoop silent but implied.

"Check out the newspapers," she insisted. "Check the dates." She paused, corrected herself. "The *date*, I mean."

He did but really didn't need to. "Oh," he said, feeling more caught than surprised. "Wow," he added, trying to make it sound like he meant it.

"I know, right?" she enthused. "People!" The word itself spun her, albeit awkwardly in her condition. "*Still-alive* people. *Finally . . .*"

"Wow," he echoed hollowly as his heart sank, gasping for air.

"It's a morning edition," he tried. "This could all still be from before."

"Who wraps up garbage in a newspaper from the same day?"

"Speed readers?"

Lucy folded her arms above the globe of her pregnant stomach. "Why are you peeing all over this?"

"I thought that's what you did," he said, a lame rejoinder, but he didn't seem to have much else.

Lucy smacked her forehead. "I forgot." She gestured for him to turn his back while she stepped to the other side of the fallen tree. "I was so excited," she said, tinkling into the flowing water.

With his back to her, Marcus tried thinking of other reasons to dismiss her discovery, only to find himself regretting that girls didn't pee as recreationally as guys did. Because barely had he put two thoughts together when there she was again, tapping his shoulder.

"So?" she said.

"So?" he echoed.

"What do we do?"

He wanted to say, "Act like it never happened" or "Tiptoe away," but settled for stalling, instead. "The only way to know for sure," he said, "is to see if another one comes in."

"You mean *when*," she said, as buoyed by her discovery as the bags themselves.

He didn't quibble; he already knew she was right. It wasn't a matter of if but when. And so he helped her fish the bags out, clearing the way for the next one, hoping he'd know what to do by the time it showed up.

Lucy set up camp by the river and waited. Spring had most definitely sprung in southeast Michigan, and the canopy overhead was thick enough to shield her from the lesser storms that blew through, just as it kept scavenging seagulls away from the buffet of trash she'd stumbled upon. Walking up the river earlier, she'd found that the bags that hadn't survived intact had snagged on low branches as they rafted down the river or been nudged to shore by others that came after them. The usual vermin had helped themselves to whatever they could reach from shore, turning the newspaper into confetti, splintering poultry bones for their marrow, licking the dregs from an unhealthy number of eggshells. Styrofoam trays from packaged meat had been nibbled into a flurry that still stirred among the ground clutter when the wind was right.

As she sat vigil, Lucy wondered what was making Marcus so skittish. It was almost as if he was looking for excuses *not* to find the others she now knew were there. But the more she thought about it, the more she saw they might not agree about the desirability of her discovery. She could see where he might feel threatened—the whole alpha-male thing. As far as she was concerned, though, the more the merrier. Unlike the apocalypses of fiction, in this world, their enemies wouldn't be other people; their enemies were nature and time. Whatever others there were would welcome them because the commodity of value wouldn't be stuff, per se, but people themselves and what they could bring to the community.

Needless to say, the most valuable people would be the people who could make more people—a thought that made her smile as she rested her hand on the passport in front of her, stretching out her waistband: another person on preorder. What Marcus could bring to the party, he'd already brought (see waistband and the stretching-out thereof). What other services he might render, well, that was up to him.

Of course, if their new neighbors were Amazons (the female kind, not the online retailer or rain forest), then there *might* be more interest in her traveling companion. Good for him. But if she knew women—and being one, Lucy figured she did—she knew this: even Amazons would be suckers for babies. And bingo! Another win for Team Abernathy!

Frankly, the only downside she could see was if the people on the other end of all this garbage turned out to be serial killers or something. Man, it would suck being a serial killer nowadays. But what were the odds? Using regular statistics, not great, but using the ironic kind . . . Still, even serial killers would probably defer to a pregnant lady, if only in hopes of building up a victim pool for later. Plenty of time to win them over with her charm or—you know—kill them first.

As she waited, Lucy wondered how much you could tell from a person's garbage. On those CSI shows, they could practically reconstruct a person's head from a wad of gum. Herself, she'd already figured out the most obvious conclusion: whoever it was was a wee bit anal. Why else bother wrapping your garbage before throwing it out? She just hoped whoever it was fell on the Martha Stewart, not Hannibal Lecter, end of that spectrum.

While she waited, she began poking through the garbage she'd unpacked, looking for evidence of a personality. Would there be doodles on celebrity faces—blacked-out teeth, an arrow running from temple to temple, gratuitous stitches across flawless cheeks? Would there be mysterious psycho scribbling, full of archaic symbols and sixes? Would they have answered all the trivia questions, filled in the crossword, completed the relationship quiz? Perhaps they'd scribbled snide comments next to the horoscopes destined to fail epically or run a line through the five-day forecast . . .

Nope. No marks, remarks, or marginalia. No good or bad guesses. No defaced faces. Nothing but the stained pages of the really final, final edition of the *Detroit Free Press*, full of stories rendered meaningless by the afternoon of the day they'd been printed. There wasn't so much as a fingerprint or ink smudge left by anything except for what had been wrapped inside. It was a little creepy, in fact, how much nothing she found.

And then she hit the jackpot: a separately bagged bundle of digital photos, helpfully time-stamped, post-whatever, came floating down the river like a PS to all that other anonymous garbage. The pictures were of a Labrador retriever, jet-black, except for the last one, which featured a selfie of the photographer—a boy around her age—lying next to the dog. She imagined showing the picture to Marcus—finally, proof positive—but then paused. She looked at the picture again. Thought about Marcus. Folded the photos and slipped them into her pocket.

Whether he'd see what she saw in the stranger's face and feel threatened wasn't clear. Of all the things humans can empathize with, the sexual attractiveness of their own sex—assuming they aren't already attracted to their own sex—seemed especially elusive. Take the coked-out anorexics that once graced fashion magazines—she didn't get that. They looked unhealthy. Not necessarily the same sort of unhealthy she'd affected in her zombie-goth days, but she'd been making a statement about the death of culture (or innocence or whatever); *her* unhealthy appearance was decidedly *not* the byproduct of a fashion-friendly drug habit.

But all the boys she knew except gay Max drooled over those pencil-thin blond waifs. Max, on the other hand—discounting their one, mutual lapse—would probably agree with her about this handsome boy waiting to be found somewhere upstream.

"Swipe right before I do," he'd say. "And that heart thingy. Make like Astaire and tap that bad boy."

And so Lucy did, or would have, if they still lived in a world where Tinder was a dating app as opposed to something gathered for the setting of actual fires. As it was, she just patted her pocket and thanked her dead friend for his sage advice.

The next bag of forensic trash came bobbing down the river shortly thereafter, cementing the conclusion she'd already drawn that the photos had been separated on purpose, though what that purpose might be, she had no idea. She intended to ask—in person—when she returned them to the handsome boy who'd taken them in the first place.

Later, Marcus joined her and poked through the contents of the latest one. Same old, same old: not-old garbage wrapped in a now-old newspaper knotted in a plastic bag that had been inflated, he assumed, to facilitate its journey downriver. He recognized the bones of a goose in that one but didn't say so, bits of uneaten meat still fresh enough to be pliable. He kept poking instead, looking for an excuse to dismiss the confirmatory evidence he himself had stipulated as his condition for following these bread crumbs to their punch line. If he backed out now, she might finally claim the testicles she'd been threatening, even though they'd become largely decorative since the pregnancy.

"Well, it's not like there's an address or anything" was the best he could come up with.

But Lucy was way ahead of him. "It's practically as good as," she said, pointing out the eastward flow of the current and how the banks on either side were as good as train tracks leading from point A to B. All they had to do was follow the shore upstream until they came to . . .

"What?" he asked, a little hastily.

The cute boy, she thought, but said instead, "I'm kind of hoping it'll be obvious once we get there."

Marcus—remembering the silencer and all it suggested about the shooter's desire to remain unfound—didn't say a thing.

There were no paved roads running alongside the river, meaning they had to drive the ice cream truck down the grassy incline between railed-off dead ends. Turning the wheel slowly as they approached the nearest shore like they were preparing to parallel park, Marcus negotiated the not-enough space between the river and the trees growing next to it on shore, the truck riding at a slant with the driver-side wheels splashing in the shallow water while those on the passenger side rolled along packed mud. Lucy had to cling to her door handle to avoid sliding across the bench seat into him as he steered reluctantly toward his appointment with a silent bullet.

He could have confessed his concerns, except doing so would mean telling Lucy how long he'd known without telling her, which was unlikely to turn out well for either him or his testicles. Better to get shot by a sniper, he reasoned; at least he wouldn't hear it coming. There was nothing stopping him from pointing out the obvious, however.

"You found that garbage *by accident*," he said. "It wasn't some kind of invitation. There weren't any flares at night. No sweeping spotlights or beep-boop-beeping over loudspeakers like in *Close Encounters*."

"No signaling." Lucy nodded. "Roger that."

"Which means they're *hiding*," Marcus said. "They're not *trying* to be found."

"Which also means they're not trying to lure us into some kind of ambush," she countered.

True, he thought. "But . . . ," he said.

"Go on," she prodded. "But what?"

"But," he repeated, "why *don't* they want to be found?"

"Maybe they just gave up looking. Or maybe there's enough of them that they don't need to find more people."

"But how many is enough?"

"More than two, definitely." Pause. "Probably an even number, at any rate. If there was an odd number, they'd probably want to make it even, so they'd keep on looking."

"What if they're hiding because they've got something worth hiding?"

"Which would make them worth finding."

"Which would make them fight to protect it."

"Or share, if we're nice," Lucy said, "and contribute to the greater good."

Marcus didn't know what to say to that kind of naïveté. He was pretty sure he knew what she imagined her worth to be: she had a womb. She could make copies. But what did he have to offer? Bomb making and ball throwing, neither of which seemed especially useful in this egalitarian paradise she imagined they were driving toward. He could contribute his seed, he supposed, but he was pretty sure they'd have that base covered. Not that he was sexist or anything, but it was clear the shooter was male. It just was. She'd probably argue with him— "Women can shoot too"—which was just another good reason for keeping his mouth shut about the iper-snay.

They followed the riverbank through a series of switchbacks and straightaways, hairpins, and long, slow curves, the last of which hid what they were looking for until they reached the other side of it, and there it was: the Great Wall of Devonshire, just ahead and above them, perched on the crest of the valley they'd been driving through for the better part of a day. They would have gone more quickly had they not needed to stop every few yards to hack through generations of dead vines gone woody, some as thick as Marcus's thumb. But now that they could see where they were headed, it was just a matter of throwing the truck in reverse and easing back up the incline diagonally, steadily, steadily until they reached street level and scraped both sides—driver's, passenger's—squeezing the cab through the gap between concrete berm and steel guardrail.

"So much for the paint job," Lucy observed as Marcus, on pavement once again, executed a series of left, right, lefts until they were facing the Great Wall once again, this time on a level playing field and close enough to touch.

It had rained while they skirted the river under the canopy of vines and leaves; they'd heard the pattering overhead. The wall hadn't enjoyed such protection from the elements, and the pavement around all that rendered fat had foamed to the point that it looked like someone had just washed the trucks and been called away suddenly while hosing them off.

"I'd be okay with turning back," he offered, looking at the world's least welcoming welcome mat. "Let sleeping dogs lie . . ."

Lucy shook her head. "We've come this far," she said. Paused. Added, "That sounded like something they'd say in a slasher movie, didn't it?"

"I wasn't going to say that," he said, totally missing her teasing tone, "*but . . .*" He reached under his seat, making sure the shotgun was still there.

Lucy almost patted his shoulder and told him not to worry—she was that sure of herself and her secret—but decided to keep teasing instead. "Wouldn't *that* be ironic," she said, playing Marcus's paranoia like a harpsichord, "the last people on earth running into the last serial killer?"

"A serial killer would have definitely included his address," he observed, straight-faced.

"Or *her* address," she added.

"Well, ex*cuse* me," he said. "I didn't mean to *imply* that *women* couldn't be *homicidal maniacs* just as well as men."

"And yet you did," Lucy said. "Chauvinist . . ."

Marcus shrugged. Was it his imagination, or was she getting mouthier the closer they got to finding somebody else?

Meanwhile: "Do you think we should knock?"

"Where?" he asked, looking down the line of burned-out vehicles for some way to get in.

Lucy stepped aside so he could see the single uncharred SUV she and her pregnant profile had been blocking from view. "Ta-da!"

Great, he thought, looking at the truck like he was looking at a wedge of cheese in a supersized rat trap. *Just great.*

Lucy hoisted herself up into the SUV, preparing to move it. Marcus spoke up before she put the truck in gear: "I don't like this. It's like a mansion with the door left open. It feels like a trap."

Lucy turned off the ignition. "A pretty bad one," she said before assuring him he'd been right: a serial killer would have included an address. "I mean," she continued, "let's say *I* was a serial killer trying to lure victims. I'd advertise everything from gourmet cooking to free Wi-Fi. You wouldn't be able to go *anywhere* without tripping over blinking arrows showing the way. And when the people showed up, there'd be a gingerbread house because, well, you know."

Marcus wondered who he was supposed to be in this fairy tale of hers: Hansel or Gretel. Under the circumstances, it was starting to look like the latter.

Lucy, meanwhile, slid back the seat and let out a sigh of relief. "Well, that's one thing we know," she called out, checking the rearview, where Marcus was heading back to the ice cream truck so he could move it once she'd cleared the way.

"What's that?" he called back without turning.

"Our killer's not pregnant," she said, giving the engine more gas than was strictly necessary.

PART FOUR

44

He'd heard the tune in his sleep: "Pop Goes the Weasel" looping over loudspeakers . . .

Except this wasn't a dream. There really was an ice cream truck out there, with a malevolent-looking guy (though Dev could be projecting) and a pregnant girl dancing around the dot of laser light he'd trained on first one, then the other, trying to decide: Which, both, neither?

Weighing the options, he found himself thinking back to that English class where they'd read about Gregor, the guy who turned into a bug. They'd read a lot in that class, precious little of it involving vacuum cleaners, though the teacher *had* said something that caught Dev's attention, and it came back to him now: the name Chekhov. When his teacher had dropped the name in class, Dev had stopped his doodling of assorted parts from a disassembled Dyson Animal and raised his head expectantly. Could it be they were finally going to discuss the much overlooked and underrated original *Star Trek*, about which he had theories related to who was evolutionarily superior, humans or Vulcans?

Sadly, such was not to be; the Chekhov in question turned out to be some Russian playwright, first name Anton, who had something to say about guns not unlike the one he found himself holding and couldn't decide whether or not to use. Apparently, this Russian was of the opinion that guns, once written into a play, had to have a purpose.

His point, which seemed painfully obvious to Dev, was that if you showed a gun at the beginning, it better go off by the end.

And so he used it.

The jock looked like he was about to spring into action, and so, drawing a bead on the guy's leg, Dev pulled the trigger and exchanged one red dot for another. The silencer was superfluous under the circumstances, as there was a pane of glass between it and said leg. When Dev pulled the trigger, the window blew out a split second before his target buckled in pain, hitting the sidewalk hard with both knees.

"*Shit!*" the target yelped, repeating the word among several colorful others as he rolled around on the ground, holding his wounded leg and painting the air blue with profanity.

Dev let go of something he didn't know he was holding—a breath, maybe, a grudge—something invisible but with a kind of weight that left him feeling relief in its release. The feeling was the opposite of how he'd felt when Diablo was at the other end of a decision to shoot. It was as if with one bullet, he'd avenged himself against all the bullies who'd ever bullied him.

Minus the glass, with the curtain billowing around him, Dev could hear the target screaming, swearing—not unexpected, but a little ungrateful, considering where the bullet could have gone. The woman, meanwhile, was making what he'd come to think of as pregnant-lady noises, trying to decide between taking care of her sperm donor or charging the house. In the end, she decided to stick with the inseminator while she shouted instead.

"What is *wrong* with you?" she demanded at the top of her lungs.

It seemed a fair question, and so he tried to answer it. "Asperger's," he shouted back.

The target stopped his yelping just long enough to ask: "Did he say *ass* burgers?"

Perhaps it's how I'm pronouncing it, Dev found himself thinking.

Later, in the middle of providing aid, Dev tried correcting the impression that he'd been trying to kill the guy he learned was called Marcus. What part of shooting him *in the leg* didn't they understand? Not that his logic did much to stop the rain of fists the pregnant girl delivered to his back while he was still assessing the damage. Perhaps if he could fix this, they'd be on their way.

"That's not helping him," Dev pointed out to the one he learned was called Lucy.

"It's helping *me*," she said through gritted teeth, still hammering away.

The one called Marcus had passed out by this time, as Dev ripped away the bloodied pant leg, starting at the bullet hole and continuing until the rip met itself, coming around from the other side. He slipped off the injured leg's shoe and sock, noting how cold the limb felt before pulling the bottom half of the pant leg off. The bullet had not been kind to the flesh, but also hadn't overstayed its welcome, exiting through a complementary wound on the other side before continuing into one of the ice cream truck's tires, flattening it. It was just dumb luck that the bullet missed hitting bone, passing through nothing but meat and muscle, proving, as Marcus would later say, that he hadn't wasted all that time building up his legs for football.

Looking at her lover's leg, Lucy composed herself long enough to admit there were better things she could be doing than hitting Dev. Boarding the truck, she thought about grabbing the shotgun but hesitated. If she shot the shooter, who would tend to Marcus? A zombie-loving goth, Lucy was nevertheless no fan of for-real gore—chalk up another point for irony. And so she grabbed the box of emergency medical supplies they'd collected along the way.

"Will any of this help?" she asked.

Dev singled out the hydrogen peroxide, some gauze, and a bottle of antibiotics.

Lucy shook her head at the last of these.

"No?" Dev translated.

"Allergic," Lucy answered.

"How bad?"

"Very," she said, "apparently."

"Crap," Dev said, not using that exact word for the substance in question.

By the time they were through with Marcus's leg, they'd made use of his two favorite shopping items from whenever they shopped together, not counting condoms: duct tape and an extra-large zip tie. The latter worked well as a tourniquet, while the former kept the wads of blood-soaked gauze from falling off. Marcus roused near the end, a hand reaching for his leg, making sure it was still there.

"That looks awful," Lucy said.

"Feels it too," Marcus said. Though everything below the zip tie was tingly, the trauma of being shot was still echoing around his nervous system, lighting up every place where bone rode bone with radio waves of pain.

Fortunately, Marcus was not allergic to painkillers. Doubly fortunate was the fact that, during their pharmacy raids, Lucy had gotten "the good stuff," based on her recollection of what Max had told her the good stuff was. When she'd asked him how he'd come by that particular knowledge, Max had joked that obviously, he was in a lot of pain. At least she'd thought it was a joke at the time.

Now that her only other lover had been patched up so he wasn't leaking all over the place—and Lucy had gotten over not being welcomed with open arms of the embracing sort—the two relocated to Dev's place, moving the victim into the senior Brinkmans' bedroom to recuperate, while Lucy inherited Dev's old bedroom, along with the mattress full of ghosts. Compared with the truck's air mattress, it was a step up.

Dev, too, had improved his situation. Now that he had guests—invited or not, recuperating from his having shot them or not—he had to admit he'd gotten low on some supplies he'd been reluctant to make a run for: things like toilet paper, toothpaste, soap, shampoo—things they all agreed would make life together easier if restocked. Fortunately, one of his guests—the unshot one—had no qualms about making a quick dash for some toiletries as well as anything else that might come in handy under the circumstances. And so Lucy borrowed the Miata after securing Dev's assurances that he wouldn't shoot Marcus again while she was gone. His insistence that he wouldn't because it would be redundant wasn't exactly all she'd hoped for in a guarantee, but it would have to do.

Once it was "just the guys" and Marcus had been placated with one of the better painkillers they had on hand, Dev explained why he'd had to shoot him. "I needed to level the playing field," he said, resorting to another bit of sports terminology he'd inherited from his late stepfather, along with *the home-field advantage*.

"You know," Marcus said, doing his best to rise up on an elbow, an attempt thwarted by the memory-foam mattress into which the elbow kept sinking, "when they talk about handicapping somebody, they don't mean it literally."

"Literally works better," Dev pointed out.

"I guess that depends on who's doing the handicapping," Marcus said, "and who's being handicapped."

They were quiet for a while, Marcus waiting for Dev to say something in the way of an apology, Dev wondering how soon the other would be well enough to leave. Neither was destined for satisfaction, though Marcus opted for the next best thing. "Um," he said, after clearing his throat. "Can I have another one of . . . ," he said, lifting his chin toward the bottle of painkillers, just out of reach.

Marcus, it turned out, really enjoyed the good stuff and, when he wasn't knocked out by it, got chatty under its influence. Too chatty. "I've got something I need to say," he said once they were all together again, he in bed, Lucy and Dev to either side. He'd had something to say for quite some time, he said. This was also true of Lucy, and Dev, too, though of the three, Dev hadn't had a human audience since the whatever-it-was. It seemed they'd all been harboring the same secret, the other thing they all had in common other than being alive.

Marcus cleared his throat and then said what he had to say: the part of his just-before story he'd left out before. He prefaced his confession by saying he'd had *this*—meaning his being shot—coming.

Lucy's face went from light to dark and all the gray emotions in between as her lover and the father of her child spoke. Finally, when he was finished, the words came out of her:

"Like *blow-yourself-up* up?" she asked. "Like with *a bomb* and everything?"

"Like with a bomb and everything," Marcus confirmed, the drugs that warmed his blood adding a little reverb, making the words sound profound as opposed to what they described, which was still all kinds of stupid.

"So you're, like, a terrorist, then?"

"Was," Marcus corrected. "Would-be."

"I don't know that I like that," she said, touching her stomach reflexively.

"Join the club."

"No, *seriously*," she insisted, her anger trumping any sympathy she may have felt for his being shot. "Does *stupid* run in your family or something?"

"I don't—" Marcus tried before being cut off.

"Is there, like, some *gene* for gullibility?" she wondered aloud. "Because I've got to be honest with you: I can't imagine what anyone could say that would make blowing up myself and a bunch of other people sound like a good idea."

"It's complicated," Marcus said. "*Was*. Was complicated."

"Well, *that's* the understatement of the millennium . . ."

"Like you never did anything stupid," Marcus tried.

Cue Lucy.

"Not that being stuck between an unwanted pregnancy and my best friend's suicide is on quite the same level as waging global jihad," she said once she'd finished.

"But planning to *kill* yourself?" Marcus said. "What part of two wrongs . . ."

"At least *I'd* be the only victim . . ."

"Plus one," Dev said, making the others turn.

"Do you have something to contribute, Mr. Hotshot?" Lucy asked, wheeling on him, spoiling for a fight.

Cue Dev.

"Hmmm," Marcus mused after their host had finished. "What are the odds?"

In typical Aspie fashion, Dev had done his research before executing his plan, including looking up suicide statistics in general, the current thinking on neurochemical causes, and how those causes expressed themselves differently based on age, sex, and location on or off the spectrum. Also in typical Aspie fashion, he couldn't help but share the results of that research.

"Before, about one hundred and seventeen people killed themselves in the United States per day," their host said, not realizing until he was doing it again how much he missed showing off. "The rate for nonautistic adolescents was roughly twelve percent versus other age groups. That made about fourteen successful teen suicides in the US per day. On average, there are—*were*—about twelve attempts per successful suicide. So that's one hundred and sixty-eight attempts for our age group per day."

"Fascinating," Lucy said. "So what's that tell us about what happened?"

"I'm still thinking it through," Dev admitted. In fact, until his visitors' confessions, he'd been hoping that being inside the fallout shelter had saved him, with the one cheetah-mauled survivor perhaps having been somewhere else especially fortified when it happened—like a bank vault, maybe. "But if our age and suicidal thoughts are what saved us, we're looking at a few hundred survivors at best, spread over slightly more than three million square miles covering just the continental United States. If those survivors kept on moving—like you two—it's a small miracle you found each other, much less me. Plus, I know for a fact that not all the initial survivors . . ." Dev paused for an uncharacteristic moment of tact, trying to choose the right word before concluding with, "Persisted."

Lucy and Marcus both nodded at this last observation. To lighten the mood, Marcus called attention to how dark it had gotten. "And that, ladies and gentlemen," he announced, "was just about the most depressing story problem in the history—"

Lucy cut him off. "But what makes suicidal teenagers different from all the ones who died?"

"Our brains are different from the ones the whatever-it-was targeted," he said—guessed. "My stepfather was a pharmacist, and there was this one side effect that drove him crazy: 'May lead to suicidal thoughts in teens.' Had to do with how the drugs interacted with hormones or something. And the brains of teenagers already having suicidal thoughts are even more different from everybody else's."

"How could they *know* something like that?" Marcus asked, rising halfway up from the bed. Ex-Muslim or not, he still harbored the hope that he might have a soul to go somewhere when he died—despite the overwhelming evidence to the contrary. "How can they know what's in a person's head?"

"It's a kind of MRI," Dev said. "It lets you see what parts of the brain light up when you're thinking something. And when teens are thinking about suicide, it lights up different areas than it does when adults are thinking about the same thing."

"So, like, what," Lucy said, "they stick a kid in this giant metal tube and ask her to think about offing herself?"

Dev shrug-nodded.

"That sounds awfully triggering," Lucy observed, which struck her traveling companion and baby dada as suddenly—almost unbearably—funny.

"What?" Lucy and Dev said together, donning their "What?" faces for emphasis.

Finally: "Somebody should sue," Marcus wheezed before gesturing for another one of those painkiller thingies.

45

The pregnant one could bake bread, so there was that. And the ex-terrorist (once he was sufficiently medicated) treated Dev like a peer, but more interesting—so there was that too. These traits served as the couple's visas to Devonshire. How temporary those visas would be, only time—and their host's atypical nervous system—would tell.

But a funny thing happened on the way to Dev's deciding how to handle his intruders: he became popular. Without meaning to, he became the one the others sought out—the one they wanted to be alone with. Lucy and Marcus *wanted* to talk *to* him—not just *at* him. Instead of being mocked for his eccentricity, he was consulted for his outside-the-box wisdom. And what was the source of this popularity? Dev's not being the other one.

"She tricked me into getting her pregnant," Marcus complained. "I didn't say, 'No kids,' but—you know—*condoms*. Hel*lo?*"

"He thinks I'm disgusting because I'm fat," Lucy theorized. "I'm not fat; I'm *pregnant*—with *his* child."

Dev's resting blank face was as good as a magnet when it came to drawing them out whenever either got him alone. Not really paying attention to the substance of what was being said—which, as nearly as Dev could tell, was almost always some neurotypical emotional mountain manufactured out of a logical molehill—he'd make a comment about something that was going on in the real world, like, "Aren't those flowers huge?" or "Do you remember it always being this hot in the summer?" But instead of taking these as literal observations about what was literally going on in the world around them, Lucy and Marcus inevitably took them personally, reading them like some sort of Zen commentary on whatever they'd been blathering on about.

"So you're saying I should appreciate the things I have?" (or) "Tomorrow really *is* another day, isn't it?" (or) "It's just that simple: let it go, reboot, and start again . . ."

Invariably, they'd conclude with "I'm glad we had this conversation," as if they'd actually had one.

Lucy was the one who helped establish the pattern, though it was Marcus who was the first to talk to Dev alone—at Lucy's prodding. She'd suggested it, mainly, to get away from her "significant other" for a while, which had been easy enough while he was bedridden, but became slightly less easy once he started using a cane. Among the latest things to drive her crazy—in addition to realizing she was carrying a would-be terrorist's child—was his increasing tendency to talk to said child through her belly button as if she weren't there. It was during one of these Lucy-excluding father-kid talks that she pushed Marcus away, saying, "Go play with Dev."

"What?"

"You know what I mean," she said. "Bond, or whatever."

Marcus looked at her the way he had ever since she'd become undeniably pregnant: funny. "You're sure you'll be okay?" he said, this apparently being the day for him acting like he cared.

So Lucy nodded and began counting off. "Keep breathing," she said, ticking off one finger. "Don't get myself killed," another. "And, oh yeah, don't lift anything heavy," a third and a pause. "That about cover it?"

"Sure," Marcus said, leaning on his cane, "ridicule me for caring . . ."

Precisely, she thought, but said, "Just teasing, sweetie," like he was a diabetic for whom sweetness could be deadly.

And so Marcus tried to be buddies with Dev, to the extent that either was capable of being that with or for the other. There were some stumbling blocks, of course. For Dev, there was his Aspergerian conviction that the needing of friends was a kind of weakness he'd fallen prey to in the past, to his peril. Marcus, on the other hand, was a natural friend maker—something that had also cost him much (nearly all) in the past.

But Dev was a challenge, even for the other's natural empathy, and knowing about his location on "the spectrum" didn't help. Marcus understood the condition, intellectually, but he couldn't get the feeling of what it was like not to have feelings—which was *not* what Asperger's was, he knew, but he couldn't help himself from still thinking about it like that. Looking at Dev, trying to figure him out, the phrase "the feeling of no feelings" drowned out any more productive reactions to (as he spoke of it to Lucy later) "the whole *Dev* situation."

To the world's single female, "the whole *Dev* situation" wasn't anything new. It was just how all boys were about feelings, scaled up.

"I've come to the conclusion that the male of the species are not *really* social animals," she said. "You're all sociopaths. You *play* at being sociable to the extent it might help get you laid, but . . ."

"That's harsh," Marcus said, "but . . ." And he was about to say, "I know exactly what you mean," when, sensing this, she cut him off.

"And yet, accurate," she concluded, with all the feminine certainty on the subject of male emotions that made guys clam up on the subject—inadvertently confirming the diagnosis.

"But if we're such bad guys," Marcus tried.

"So you're talking for Dev now?"

"I mean *other* guys . . ."

"*What* other guys?" Lucy asked. Because that was the trouble with everyone else being dead: all generalizations suddenly became very personal indeed.

Lucy: that was the key. Marcus realized this right after she pushed him to "go play with Dev" for the second time. He and the Martian could bond over the real alien in their midst: Lucy.

"You know how she . . ."

"Like when she . . ."

"Women." "People."

Dev looked at the one who said *women* while Marcus looked at the one who said *people*. And that's when Marcus got the tiniest inkling of what life was like for the only other male left standing. Dev was like the only guy living in a world full of women (emotionally speaking). Everybody of either sex was inscrutable to and prejudging of . . . *him*.

Marcus tried putting his new understanding into words. "So," he said, "being around people for you is like holding a fart on a date that never ends."

Dev thought about that. He wasn't sure Marcus was right, but he wasn't sure he was wrong either. What he suddenly saw with blinding clarity, however, was what he needed to do to make Marcus *think* he understood, thus forging a bond that would make living with his new guests easier in the long run. And what he needed to do was so simple, so primordial, he was surprised he hadn't thought of it sooner.

He farted.

And Marcus nearly tipped over with laughter, finally sitting down before he didn't have a choice. And from that position, with his butt cheeks splayed on a surface that promised amazing acoustics, he let one rip. "Am I right?" he asked, looking at Dev for a reaction.

Dev pinched his face—and less visible parts—eventually producing a sustained flatulent response he capped thusly:

"You took the words right out of my mouth."

After that, whenever they saw each other without Lucy around, they exchanged farts just like saying hello. They'd laugh just like that first time, boys being boys, regardless of their more nuanced neurological wiring. And after that, they'd get down to whatever business needed getting down to, which was usually just walking, exercising Marcus's leg, complaining about Lucy, checking the perimeter to make sure all the things they hoped to keep at bay were.

"You did this all by yourself, eh?" Marcus commented, surveying the wall of death once again, this time with less trepidation, seeing as the worst had already happened.

"Well," his host said, in an uncharacteristic moment of modesty, "the inherently flammable quality of gasoline helped."

Marcus hesitated before fobbing Lucy off on Dev, even though he really needed a little Marcus time. The trouble—of course—was that Lucy was a girl and Dev was a boy. And Marcus was the boy who'd had sex with Lucy more recently—that more recently being a thought that needled him constantly, now that the girl presumably had options.

He needn't have worried. Even before, when there were so many more possible partners—including ones as weird as he—Dev couldn't imagine having sex. His fantasies were decidedly PG, mainly consisting of scenarios in which he and some mystery woman were in the same room together—at a restaurant table, say, or, even sexier, a kitchen table set for breakfast. They wouldn't be having sex in these fantasies—just talking, Dev doing most of it and (the fantasy part) actually being listened to with something like interest. Now he found it even harder to imagine experiencing romantic love, given the radically reduced options when it came to finding a willing partner. Lucy wasn't an option because, well, she was Marcus's. And even though Marcus complained about her often, Dev didn't read that as his chance to insinuate himself into the situation. If there ever came a time when the two fought over Lucy, the only thing he could imagine it being over was her bread baking. He'd really gotten used to having toast with his eggs again; he'd hate giving that up.

Bread.

What farts appeared to be for Marcus and Dev, bread was for Lucy and Dev. "You need to knead it," she explained, suggesting that his own failed attempts were due to the lack of this important step—in addition to his having left out key ingredients, like baking powder or yeast. "You try it," she said, removing her doughy hands from the lump she'd been working over like a fat man's back on a massage table.

And so Dev did, touching the dough tentatively at first, with his index finger, like he was poking a potentially dangerous animal. He couldn't help but view the lump as somehow alive, thanks to her explanation about the importance of fermentation, meaning bacteria were involved.

"It's okay," she said. "Dig in."

So Dev did, first with one hand, then, once it appeared he deemed the overall texture tolerable, both.

"I'll tell you something else that needs needing," she said, not spelling out her poignant pun, letting the tear that rolled down her cheek do that.

"What's wrong with your eye?" he asked, pointing at the one that was leaking with a dough-covered finger.

Lucy wiped it away. Sniffed. "I think Marcus hates me," she said.

"Why?" Dev asked, his hands back in the dough, working away. He seemed like he was actually starting to enjoy the feel of it, squishing it between his fingers, rolling it out like a snake.

"Because he said so," Lucy said. Paused, then qualified her statement. "Not in so many words, but . . ."

"How do you say something without using words?" Dev asked.

"You know," she said, "the way you can mean something by what you *don't* say," thinking, *Like, "I love you."*

"Isn't that like the movie *Minority Report*?" Dev asked.

"You mean, arresting people for things they haven't done yet?" Lucy asked, wondering if that's really what she was doing with Marcus—considering him guilty until proven innocent.

Dev shook his head. "Mind reading," he said.

"Oh," Lucy said, interpreting Dev's response as telling her that she shouldn't be angry at Marcus because he couldn't read her mind. "I don't think I've even seen him read a *book* all this time," she said, continuing the thought she'd begun, aloud.

"Who?"

"Marcus."

"Tell him to try *Minority Report*," Dev advised. "It was a book before it was a movie. Philip K. Dick." He paused. "Excuse me," he said.

"For what?"

"I used the *d*-word."

Wow, Lucy thought. *Wow, wow, wow.* "You really are different, aren't you?" she asked.

"Yes," Dev said, and left it at that.

46

Marcus thought he was getting better until it occurred to him suddenly that he wasn't. And then he *really* wasn't. He asked Lucy to feel his head.

"You're burning up," she said.

"Don't exaggerate," he said back.

And so Lucy got the thermometer they'd used to clear her of Zika. She inserted it between his reluctant lips like she was checking his oil with a dipstick—a comparison she now knew to make, at the cost of one fried Sonata, and everything else that followed.

"You're burning up," she said, presenting him with the thermometer as proof. One hundred four degrees Fahrenheit. He'd been scratching his leg—the shot one—for days, had complained of feeling light-headed and had thrown up a few times, but hadn't mentioned, or maybe even noticed, the darkening veins underneath his already dark skin, crawling slowly but inexorably toward his organs.

When he was still bedridden and didn't have much say in the matter, they'd changed his dressing regularly. But ever since he'd been caning it, Marcus had been more cavalier in the area of basic prophylaxis. Still able to stand (with help) after a through-and-through gunshot wound, he had figured his time would be better spent getting his muscle strength back to where it was supposed to be. No pain, no gain, and all that crap.

The problem with equating pain with progress is that it might not necessarily be the kind of progress one is hoping for. In this case, for instance, the pain in Marcus's leg was a sign of sepsis progressing—a diagnosis they all suspected the second they removed the soiled dressing and recoiled from the stench that arose from the wound, a smell they all recognized from having smelled it all around them, afterward.

"He who smelt it dealt it," Dev said. The others remained stony, which he took as his cue to fetch the *Physicians' Desk Reference* he'd used to get a heads-up on what to expect from Lyme disease, so they could confirm this less ambiguous diagnosis of sepsis. Proper diagnosis was important because Marcus's only hope was if it was something *other than* blood poisoning. That's because the treatment for sepsis, a.k.a. blood poisoning, was—and here Lucy's ironic universe was having its way once again—massive doses of broad-spectrum antibiotics, the use of which would also kill Marcus.

"How bad is it?" he asked, his eyes closed.

"Bad," Lucy said.

"But *how* bad?" he asked again.

"As bad as it gets," she told him.

By the time the end came, the only nonstupid thing about the whole stupid affair was the lesson it taught the remaining two: the only thing they had to fear was being stupid. That and the fact that stupid was all around them, just waiting to take its advantage. For Dev, this was not news, and his behavior didn't change much from the way it had always been. Lucy, on the other hand, took the news kind of hard, seeing the world now much more cautiously, through eyes grown justifiably paranoid about—well, just about everything.

"After, you know," she confided, meaning after the whatever, not Marcus's dying, "I felt lucky, I guess. Special, like I'd been chosen. It was like the world said, 'Her. Let's spare her.'" She paused, sniffing back some snot. "But it didn't last, that feeling. Now it feels more and more like I was saved, but just for later. You know, like for dessert?"

"Seems about right," he said, as bad as ever when it came to telling the comforting lie.

But then, on second thought: "At least you got to say goodbye," Dev said, probably quoting some plum of wisdom he'd heard on TV. Instead of finding it comforting, however, Lucy just remembered all the others she'd lost without having a chance to say goodbye, magnifying her grief proportionally. And so she cried—for Marcus, for Max, for her parents and brother, for her baby's unborn brother or sister, even for Sir Sheds, goddamn it . . .

And Dev just stood there, watching, waiting it out. It couldn't last forever, this eye-leaking and noise. That's what she found herself thinking, on Dev's behalf. Finally: "You can't stop being you, can you?" Lucy asked, trying to recalibrate her expectations re her latest last man on earth.

"Not so far," Dev admitted, avoiding her eyes as automatically as a bad smell. "Nope."

"Cremation," Dev suggested, being an old hand at that form of body disposal.

Lucy shook her head. If it was up to her, burial was what she'd have chosen; even though the Catholic Church had lifted the outright ban on cremation, it still insisted the ashes be buried afterward. The reason had something to do with the dead rising on Judgment Day, as if our earthly bodies were just seeds for the next life. Lucy had liked thinking about it that way, before: burial as a kind of planting, hopefulness implied. She'd soured on the idea since then, mainly because there still hadn't been a mass resurrection, despite the apocalyptic body count. This lack had led her to conclude that whatever happened, it wasn't *the* apocalypse: a hopeful thought, in Lucy's world of diminished expectations.

"We should do it the way Marcus would have wanted," she said.

"Explosives?" Dev asked, making her flinch. He really did have a knack for saying the precisely wrong thing.

Shaking her head, "No, he wanted his body to be"—she hesitated, resorted to euphemism—"returned to nature."

What he actually told her was that he wanted to be fed to animals. And maybe that summed him up: he was the kind of guy who, while cuddling in the afterglow of making love, talked about what he wanted done with his body when he died. Lucy, who'd been staring at the ceiling of the ice cream truck, imagining the stars on the other side of it, rolled over to face him. "Is that some kind of Islamic thing?" she asked.

"It's a *me* thing," Marcus said. "I want to go out being ripped apart by something wild. I want to give myself back to nature . . ."

"You can give yourself back to nature by being buried," Lucy insisted. "Plants are part of nature. Wouldn't you like a nice tree growing out of you?"

Marcus looked down as his nakedness stirred, taking himself in hand, literally. "Oh, I've got a tree for you, all right," he said.

Lucy slapped him, in the angry-fond way that lovers sometimes do. "I'm serious," she insisted.

"So am I," Marcus insisted right back.

"About?"

He glanced down. "But the other thing too," he said. "About the wild animals. Being torn apart. It's not like my body will be doing me any good by then."

Lucy wondered if he'd changed his mind since being shot. If he had, he hadn't mentioned it. Then again, he'd been busy building muscle tone, trying to wring whatever good was left him in that body.

"We need to leave him outside," she announced, deciding it. "On the other side of the burned-up trucks," she added. "Somewhere away from here, where the animals can . . ." She trailed off.

". . . eat him," Dev said, completing the thought.

Lucy nodded.

"Yeah, he told me," Dev admitted.

Lucy looked back over Marcus's dead body, wondering what else he might have spilled the beans about. Just thinking about it made her blush. And so she went on the defensive. "So why'd you suggest burning him if you already knew what he wanted?"

"I don't think we need to advertise that people are still on the menu."

It was a fair point. But as Dev would say, Lucy was a neurotypical with a baby on board, meaning she had at least one and a half votes and no pressing reason to be strictly rational. She was also the closest thing Marcus had to family; if she wanted to use his body for bear bait, so be it.

But before they did this thing, Dev insisted on going back to get a gun, which he said had been his policy for going beyond the wall ever since there'd been a wall to go beyond. "Just in case," he said, dipping his head through the gun's strap, letting it hang over his shoulder, business end pointed skyward.

Lucy didn't bother asking, "In case of what?" Whether it was packs of wild dogs, or rabid unicorns, or Judgment Day itself, ever since whatever happened, happened, she refused to be surprised by surprises anymore. Instead, she held out hope that whatever the next surprise was, it would be a happy one for a change.

Dev pulled back the SUV blocking the exit just far enough for them to pass through with Marcus's body and left the engine running. Hopping down, he headed for the body's shoulders just as Lucy grabbed his feet.

"Should we take his clothes off?" she asked, holding on by his pant legs, which had grown far too slack, once he'd stopped eating.

Dev began lifting but stopped. "Why?"

"To," she said, moving her head in a complicated way that meant nothing to her audience.

"Use words," Dev suggested.

"Make it easier," Lucy said finally, "for the animals."

Without meaning them to, Dev's thoughts drifted in a pornographic direction he'd later blame on having met Lucy and Marcus, a couple his own age who'd indisputably *done it*. "Is that *really* the reason?"

Lucy shook her head, seemingly confused. "What other reason would there be?"

Dev didn't know how to put it politely, so he put it the other way. "To get a last look."

"One last look at *what?*" she asked.

"At a naked guy," Dev said, going there. "At his sex . . . *stuff*."

Lucy dropped her end, letting Dev hold up all of Marcus's dead weight. Emotion stained her cheeks a bright red.

"Well?" Dev prompted.

But Lucy remained silent. She picked up her share of the corpse, shoving a little as if to indicate her desire to get this over with, in silence preferably. Which was fine by Dev. For him, the silence between them was as welcome as it was golden.

Much later, while Dev was readying the couch and Lucy had closed what was now the door to her room, she opened it again and walked right up behind him. She stood there, radiating, until he turned and she said what she had to say: "So you've decided already?"

"Decided what?" Dev asked, fluffing a pillow.

"The future," Lucy said. "That there isn't going to be an 'us.'"

"We're already an 'us,'" Dev said, borrowing her tone. "You're not going anywhere, are you?"

Lucy blushed again while blaming Dev for his selective opacity. Though she couldn't tell for sure from that blank face of his, she'd swear he was enjoying this: forcing her to say things that were too embarrassing to say out loud—and wouldn't have to be, with a normal person.

"You know what I mean," she bluffed, and blushed harder.

But Dev just shrugged. "Not a clue."

The words marshaled themselves on her tongue, awaiting instructions from her brain. They kept waiting. Her brain, unfortunately, was busy sending more blood to her cheeks and forehead. Her mouth opened, but nothing came out.

"Trying to catch flies?" Dev asked.

Lucy's mouth closed. Her face felt incandescent. Trying to get through to him suddenly felt as unlikely as the atoms in a wall getting out of her way just by her shouting at them. "Never mind," she said, taking her and her crimsonness back to the bedroom that was now hers and hers alone.

47

It wasn't fair—that was the gist of what she wanted to say. It was the gristle of what followed that made things so hard. Because what followed was about sex, their obligation to have it, and what it meant that Dev had preemptively decided they wouldn't. That's what his comments about "last looks" and "sex stuff" had been about. But the ramifications went beyond just him and her, especially if that's all there was: just him and her. She'd had a lot of hope when it came to finding others—hope that had been punctured again and again, each time she found another survivor who'd stopped surviving. Marcus had been the solitary bright light in that search, until they found Dev. But it was like the world couldn't handle more than one last man on earth. So Marcus had to die. And now his replacement wasn't willing to help her reboot the species . . .

Of course, even with his cooperation, the biological math wasn't very promising. It seemed some degree of incest or incest lite was bound to be involved. Which got her thinking about that part of the Bible that had driven her nuts ever since she'd realized she hadn't been delivered by stork—the way Adam and Eve had two sons and (magically) *then there were more.*

How did that work? Even if Eve had a few daughters the Bible didn't bother mentioning, how was it *not* incest? Did God pluck a few more bones from Adam's rib cage? Or maybe one each from Cain and

Abel? When exactly did people stop reproducing via ribectomies? And if Eve really came from Adam's rib, how was she *not* the genetic equivalent of his daughter or, really, a female clone? No wonder she couldn't follow the simplest shall-not: the woman was an inbred idiot! And the sad generations that followed were just her idiot children . . .

Lucy felt a kick from inside, as if in protest to this particular line of thought. "Not you, my little snowflake," she whispered. "We've got big plans for you . . ."

But what were those plans? Restarting the human race? How did that work? If she was carrying a boy, they'd need a girl for him—and *not* his own mother. Lucy had no interest in starring in some Oedipus/*Chinatown* mash-up. Plus, she'd be in her thirties by the time that was even biologically possible, which was practically menopausal—not to mention way too young to be a grandmother. Or whatever a woman doing double duty like that was called.

The thing was, unless she happened to be carrying fraternal twins—which was too messed up and mythological to even contemplate—she and Dev needed to have a kid or two if humanity was going to survive based upon the available evidence. Regardless of what she had this time, the species needed another of the opposite sort to hook up with her firstborn. The fact that they wouldn't have the same father helped take a little of the incestuous stink off it, but just barely.

Or if her firstborn was a girl, then it wouldn't have to be incest at all—just really creepy in a Woody Allen/Soon-Yi Previn kind of way. Sure, that was just kicking the incest can down the road. The point being, if humanity's family tree was going to be anything but all trunk, she and Dev still needed to have kids.

Which didn't mean they had to have sex, she assured the Dev she imagined objecting in her head. If he didn't want to or couldn't get past his aversion to being touched, turkey baster *in vitro* was an option. But . . .

But what if Dev was attracted to her?

What if he was just too shy—or too Aspergery—to make a move? Did Lucy want him to? She'd saved his picture for a reason—and not as more proof if Marcus demanded it. It just got complicated once he shot Marcus and turned out to be, you know, *Dev*. There was potential— she'd admit that—had been, at least, back when she tucked that photo away. And if she was being honest with herself, she had to admit, his not wanting to be hugged triggered an equal and opposite reaction in her. The more he resisted, the more she wanted to just grab him. It was like being told to not think about elephants. Every time she saw him, a part of her wanted to wrap him in her arms and rock him back and forth while he flinched and trembled. And the harder he did, the harder she'd hold him, until he cried out and began sobbing great, racking sobs . . .

. . . and still she'd hold him, rocking him back and forth while he cried all the Asperger's away. And that's when the crying would stop, turned down like a light on a dimmer switch. That's when the knot of muscles pressed to her breast would let go, his shoulders settling back down to where shoulders belonged. That's when Dev would look up, his face still wet with tears, but looking her straight in the eye—her Pinocchio, a real boy at last.

Or . . .

Once they fixed the flat on the ice cream truck, there was nothing stopping them from picking up where she and Marcus left off, looking for others. If there was even half a chance of not having to play genetic roulette to reboot the species, they owed it to the future to try. Right?

"I said, right?" Lucy repeated.

"But I don't want to," Dev said. "I like it here."

"You're *stuck* here," she said. "You've *settled* for the familiar and the path of least resistance. But there's a whole world you haven't seen. A whole world that might still have some people in it."

"Have you *met* people?" Dev asked. "I have; they suck."

"They suck—*sucked*—because there were so many of them they took each other for granted," Lucy said. "You may have noticed, things have changed."

"Don't care."

"What's wrong with checking? We can always turn around and come back."

"The number-one mistake everyone makes during a zombie apocalypse," Dev said, making it sound like he was carving the words into stone as he spoke, "is giving up *the home-field advantage*."

"You're just scared."

"Yes," he agreed, adding a nod for good measure. *"Exactly."*

Lucy blinked, speechless. What was she supposed to do with that? Every boy she'd ever accused of being scared rose to the challenge to prove her wrong. It was kind of fun, being able to manipulate someone bigger than she so easily.

Not that guys didn't know how to push her buttons in return. It was just that her buttons were more like sliders on a soundboard, leaving it to the individual guy to figure out the right balance of sexual objectification versus intellectual seriousness. The thing was, when they got it right, they got her, whether she wanted them to or not. She'd wondered before if boys resented their programming as much as she hated hers. Now she missed the ease with which a guy's emotions could be hacked, leaving her feeling as unarmed as the *Venus de Milo* when it came to convincing Dev they needed to move on.

And she *did* need to convince him—and before his "home-field advantage" took advantage of her weaker moments when just settling seemed the easiest way to go. Because Dev wasn't wrong; it could be dangerous out there. Not that there were zombies lumbering around, but hordes of hybrid pigs and Zika-carrying mosquitoes were nothing to sneeze at. Well, maybe the latter was, but . . .

The point was, the chances of a mother and nursing baby making it out there without some backup were grim. At the very least, she needed Dev to kill stuff while she was busy taking care of the miracle of life.

"*Shite,*" she said, exasperated at how quickly her options came down to getting an autistic to do something he didn't want to do. "*Shite* and onions . . ."

"You okay?" the source of her exasperation asked, confused by the tonal shift after they'd just come to an agreement on the fact that he was scared.

"Baby," Lucy lied, wincing, a hand on her belly. "Guess nobody ever told her about the home-field advantage."

Dev blinked.

"I mean she wants out," Lucy explained.

"Marcus said it was going to be a boy," Dev observed—stating a fact, not necessarily trying to start another argument.

But Lucy gritted her teeth anyway. "Then I guess Marcus should have stuck around," she said, waddling away before he could raise another quibble she wasn't in the mood for.

It wasn't that Lucy wanted them to leave the safety of Devonshire right away. That's not what she was suggesting. She was just thinking about the future. That was a side effect of being pregnant, she'd found—right up there with throwing up and weird cravings. And the future as she saw it—the *immediate* future—was this: she'd have the baby; she'd nurse the baby; she'd wait until the baby could walk, talk, and follow directions . . .

Lucy found herself smirking at her own train of thought. That last criterion—good luck with that. If she waited that long, they wouldn't be leaving Devonshire until her kid was older than she was when she had it. So she clarified—*old enough to* understand *directions*—and crossed her fingers about the rest.

According to her watch—the LCD one with the month and day—she had about a month to go before meeting her baby. What remained of the baby's father would have traveled through the guts of assorted wildlife by then, giving back to the earth in the form of fertilizer. With any luck, he'd wind up with a tree growing out of him anyway: score a point for Lucy.

The original plan had been for Marcus to be there when the time came. Dev hadn't had a problem with that plan. "Whatever," he'd said, "just keep it down." It was exactly the same position he'd taken on the prospect of their having sex in his parents' bedroom: he was okay with anything, just so long as he didn't have to hear it.

Circumstances had changed since his original acquiescence to the miracle of birth happening right there in Devonshire. Surely he knew the plans had changed now that Marcus wasn't around. He *did* know that, right? They'd not discussed it in so many words, but . . .

Okay, they'd not discussed it in *any* words, but he had to realize . . . *right?*

"You know I'm going to need you there," Lucy said, broaching the subject she'd assumed didn't need broaching—until she remembered whom she hadn't broached it with.

"Where?" Dev asked. "I already told you I'm not leaving. We both agreed; I'm scared."

"The *there* I mean is really not a place so much as a time," Lucy tried.

"You mean like Einstein?"

Lucy looked puzzled, but then got it. "No, not the space-time continuum," she said. "Though it *is* about relatives."

It was Dev's turn to look puzzled.

"My baby," she explained. "My kid. We'll be related. You know, like relatives?" She paused. "Get it?"

And slowly—*painfully* it seemed—Dev did. "You want *me*," he said, "to be in the same place as *you* when you're having the baby?"

"Yes," Lucy said, exhaling the word with a sigh.

"Um," he said, "can I think about it?"

"What's there to think about?"

"Lots," Dev said, bolting away as if from a bomb ready to explode.

Trying to explain how Dev chose his *topiques* was like trying to explain love at first sight. Something he'd seen and ignored a thousand times before would suddenly grow sticky in his imagination. He could try brushing it off on a pant leg or passing it from finger to finger, trying to flick it away like a stubborn bit of snot, but eventually he had to admit it—like a Band-Aid, it was stuck on him, and he was stuck on it.

Take vacuum cleaners, for instance.

One day it was just another plugged-in thing he had to avoid tripping over on his way to and from his room. But the next day, he saw the way the light from the window fell along the curve of its handle, as sensuous in its way as the neck of an upright bass. He'd noticed— *suddenly*—how thought-out the thing was: the way the handle fit into a hose and could be removed from it, making room for attachments, each for some specific, vacuum-related task—a tool for sucking crumbs from along the piping around a couch cushion, another to remove the same from deep-buttoned upholstery. There were hooks top and bottom, placed there for winding the cord back up, and which his mother never used, preferring to gather the long wire in a sloppy loop she draped over the handle and dust canister. There was a lever at foot level you stepped on to release the handle, dropping it until it was nearly horizontal, the better to vacuum under tables and beds. The canister was made of clear plastic, like a cloud chamber for creating lab-sized tornadoes he could study now for hours, learning about vectors, wind shears, the cyclonic force behind dust devils and spiral galaxies . . .

Vacuum cleaners were his last, pure *topique* since before everything changed. After that, he'd tackled what needed tackling to stay alive until he ran out of things to tackle. And then he started looking for something new to fall in love with. And there it was, the old stickiness, heralding his next obsession, the words in the air, coalescing around it:

. . . I'll need you there . . .

. . . when the time comes . . .

. . . the baby . . . the baby . . . the baby . . .

Delivering babies, obstetrics, parenthood: these would be his latest and most pressing *topiques*. And unlike the others—except maybe the survival ones—the clock was ticking.

Loudly.

And so Dev ran. Of course he did. He had a lot to learn and not a lot of time to do it. Unfortunately, while his neighbors' porn collections had provided an amateur's understanding of gynecology, he'd found only one DVD of a live delivery preserved by a couple that had been middle-aged by the time Dev knew them. Judging from the clamshell, the DVD was actually a transfer from a videocassette shot sometime in the 1980s, judging from the chunkiness of the doctor's wristwatch and the hefty videographic gear the dad was shouldering when he took an old-school selfie by shooting himself in the mirror before swinging around for the money shot. The good news for those long-dead parents was the delivery went smoothly; the bad news for Dev was *the delivery went smoothly*.

Smoothly was not what he was looking for. He wanted to know what could go wrong. The complications. The avoidable mistakes. The things one might do just before, just during, or just after that would misshape a life, or cut it short. These were not new questions. The mysterious ways that birth and early life could go wrong had been the subject of much debate in the Brinkman home, all coming back to the same, extremely personal themes:

What happened to make Dev Dev? And whose fault was it?

If he'd had an e-reader and the infrastructure to make it work, he'd have searched online, read reviews, zeroed in on exactly what he needed and been reading a minute or two later. As it was, Dev had already collected all the books worth collecting in Devonshire. If it wasn't in his just-in-case library, it was fiction and untrustworthy on its face. That was the situation inside the wall. Outside, however, there was an actual public library a few miles away. Dev hadn't been there since—well, ever. Didn't need to. The internet had been enough to get him through grade school and as much of high school as he'd had before class was dismissed forever. But what choice did he have now?

He could send Lucy, he guessed. She had a vested interest, after all. And maybe he'd get lucky—two birds with one cheetah . . .

Dev shook his head. No. He'd not shot her when he had the chance, and he hadn't because of the baby. None of this was the baby's fault. Maybe with Dev as its default stepfather, the kid could be raised to be a more humane human, unlike the jerks he remembered. The baby deserved a chance at least. And that chance started with not being miscarried or stillborn or strangled by its own umbilical cord: all possibilities Lucy had mentioned while they made bread together—possibilities he needed to prepare for now that Marcus was dead.

And so he gassed up the Miata and grabbed some firepower for when zoom-zoom wasn't enough. He thought about telling Lucy where he was going, but the where would demand a why, and he didn't want to worry her. Dev was doing enough of that for all 2.875 of them.

Lucy felt a wave of fear pass over her, watching the last man on earth getting into a midlife-crisis car. "You can't leave me!" she shouted, running as best she could with a bowling ball strapped in front of her.

Dev stopped to let her catch up and catch her breath before saying, "Have to," before adding, "It's imperative."

"Abandoning me?" Lucy said before touching her stomach and changing course. "How is abandoning *us* imperative?"

"I'm coming back," he said. "I've just got an errand to do."

"An errand?" Lucy said. "Yeah, right." It was obvious he didn't go out beyond the wall, because he hadn't—except to help her drag Marcus's body out. And as a fellow, onetime sufferer, she could feel the anxiety coming off him that time. So what was it about the act of giving birth that was scarier than everything else he was already scared of?

But before she could ask, he was already gone, leaving her to walk back to the house alone, her legs as bowed as a cartoon gunfighter, heading for a rendezvous with high noon.

The sight of all that information, bound and shelved, made his Aspie heart leap—to the extent it could. Here was the internet in printed form. It was bulky and clunky and harder to search, but not bad for the generations that came before the generation that didn't need buildings to house what it knew. It was a shame he hadn't brought something bigger—a Hummer, say, or a mobile home. He'd gladly have filled either with books like he'd once filled similar gas guzzlers with his neighbors' dead bodies.

But he was driving a two-seater with a strictly decorative trunk, and he had no intention of making another trip. Along the way, he'd noticed that the world had entered its dog-eat-dog phase—literally; he thought he might even recognize a few of the remains from back when they'd been under his care. The bodies from before had rotted or been chewed down to bone, disassembled, scattered, used to build things by the animals that built things—beavers, mainly. The other rodents of note were the rats, which had become noticeably larger, looking more like possums now. Seeing the world come to this made him congratulate himself all over again for building his wall—and fueled his desire to get back to the other side of it.

He started with the medical reference section, focusing on obstetrics and gynecology, carrying stacks to the Miata and piling them on the passenger seat. Next, he headed to the parenting section and pulled down anything with the word *difficult* in the title. He fit as many of these onto the driver's seat as he could while still being able to drive—low enough so his head missed hitting the roof at every pothole, but not so high he couldn't compensate by adjusting his mirrors. He balanced a couple of the larger tomes on the gas and brake, to make up for the extra distance between his foot and either pedal. And then he headed back to Devonshire, his reading list set from now until the fat lady sang—so to speak.

To say that Lucy was surprised to see him return was an understatement. As she'd run after him before, she ran to meet him now, a semiquick, bowlegged waddle that would've been funny if Dev hadn't had a car full of how unfunnily things could go in Lucy's condition. Before he could even get out of the car, she was there: a great, looming pregnant lady bending over the open door, taking aim at Dev with outstretched arms. "Thank you, thank you, thank you," she said, punctuating each thank-you with a temporary tightening of the hug she was inflicting upon him while Dev grew stiff as a board—and not in a good way.

"You're welcome," he said through gritted teeth. "Please don't touch me."

"Sorry," she said, relinquishing his shoulders. "I forgot." She stepped away from the car, carving out a Dev-sized slice of personal space, her hands reaching around and bracing her lower back. "What's that all you got there?"

"Books," Dev said.

"What kind of books?"

"Thick ones, thin ones, paperback, hardback . . ."

"I mean, what are they *about*?"

Dev looked at her belly, as big and round as the whole world. "That," he said, pointing.

48

The baby was born at night, next to the fireplace for warmth and to boil water because somebody always boiled water for delivering babies on TV, though why, he had no idea. It wasn't for sterilizing the assortment of baby-delivering equipment he had assembled: a variety of scissors, clamps, twine, and gauze, all of which he sterilized in a bucket of rubbing alcohol. He'd developed a kind of tic as they timed contractions, plucking various instruments out to test them, though for what, Lucy had no idea. The truth was he loved the cooling sensation of the alcohol evaporating off his skin. It contrasted nicely with the buffeting warmth from the fireplace.

For light, while the flames added color and a certain ambiance, the real star of the evening was the full moon. Throwing open the curtain to let the light in, Dev pulled the air mattress from the ice cream truck to the center of the lit floor. This auxiliary source of lighting was so convenient the mother-to-be suggested it might be an omen.

"It's like God is saying he approves," she said. "Like we've got his blessing to reboot mankind." Yeah, she'd begun talking like that—like her mom—the closer she came to becoming a mother herself. Seemed it was hard to be a nihilist once your stake in the future grew by a generation.

As far as Dev was concerned, the moon was no big deal. Had it not been around, he'd have used flashlights or the garden lights or run the generator. It was convenient, was all—not a sign from God. As far as Lucy's lesser claim that it was romantic, he'd just have to take her neurotypical word for it.

Not that he did so without challenging it, starting with, "You mean the moon?"

Lucy nodded during the latest sweaty calm between contractions.

"It's just a rock with sunlight bouncing off it . . ."

"So why are you always looking at it with your telescope?"

"Because it's a rock with sunlight bouncing off of it," Dev said calmly, "*in outer space.*"

Lucy was about to say that that made a lot of sense, but winced instead. Whether it was from a contraction or the thought of spending the rest of her life having conversations like this, she didn't say. Whichever it was, that was that for the romantic talk that evening.

The rest of the talk wasn't even talk so much as animal noises: screams and cries; groans and growls; hard, rapid panting; and a mixed medley of *there*s and *okay*s from the one who wasn't giving birth, just encouragement, to the extent he was able. That, and a hand to hold, which was to say *squeeze* until the knuckles cracked and the fingers became so slick with sweat Dev had to clamp his other hand over the top to keep them from slipping free, which he wouldn't do until . . . *there*:

A bloody, slimy baby-doll head coming out all smushed and close lidded, its shoulders hunched around its ears, its skin a pale blue that reminded Dev of the corpses he'd seen, before they got much worse. But he'd read all about that; he wasn't scared about that—not yet.

The rest came sliding out in a fraction of the time it took to deliver that big-brained head, so fast that Dev barely had time to get his hands freed and under it before the body was already in them, the umbilical tumbling out after it like the intestines of some of the game he'd dressed. He used dental floss instead of suture, tying it fore and aft before cutting in between, dividing being from being by sliding steel against steel:

Snip!

He cleared the mouth with a rubber suction bulb, wiped around it with a warm, wet cloth. He didn't hold it by its ankles to smack out its first breath, but pinched the baby's robin-egg rear end as its slick, slack face hole became a yawn that grew into a scream as the pale blue thing turned pink, then red—a squalling, bawling ball of red rage tensing its hands, feet, whole body into fists shaking at being push-pulled out of its warm amniotic bath into this other place. It cried for days—or minutes—before facing reality, or at least accepting the fact that it had to breathe for a living now, as opposed to just kicking back and letting life happen in a womb of its own.

Calmer, its red, raw skin settled into a mottled, marbly pink as its black lizard eyes blinked open and looked right at him—Dev was sure—even though there wasn't enough white to really tell. Lucy, her own eyes raccooned with broken blood vessels from the strain, looked at Dev, too, searching his face for any news about what was going on down there, on the other side of her hiked and curtained knees.

"You were right," he said.

"It's a girl?"

Dev nodded, sweat slipping from under his hairline. *We're all wet,* he thought—not a judgment, just an observation. And indeed, they were: from sweat, from tears, from amniotic fluid—a slick-haired trio, becoming in their wetness, and at that instant, a family.

"Let me see her," Lucy said, wrung out but with enough strength left to reach, to hold, to cradle.

And that was when Dev felt something he'd never felt before, at least not toward a fellow human being. He didn't want to let go. He didn't want this squirming mass of muscle, skin, and bone to leave the shelter of his hands. Somehow, it had attached itself to him in a way he couldn't describe but one that threaded through his heart and into his brain, linking the two like they'd never been linked before, even at the thick end of a *topique*.

He looked at the baby. He looked at Lucy, opening and closing her hands: the gimme gesture. He looked at the baby again. "Oh," he said, the first syllable of "okay," but he was stuck on it, like an amoeba reluctant to split. "Oh," he said again, still clinging to this Velcro feeling inside, the one making a ripping sound only he could hear as he handed over the baby and finished the one-word sentence he'd begun twice:

". . . *kay.*"

"Say that again," Lucy said, looking at her baby but talking to Dev. "What you just said."

"Okay?"

"Yes," Lucy said, "but slower, like you did before."

"Oh," Dev said, counted a second, two, three. "Kay," he concluded.

"Kay," Lucy announced. "That's going to be her name."

"Kay?" he echoed, but as a question. It wasn't his first choice for a girl, which was Electra, short for Electrolux. But what did it matter, really? It wasn't like they were going to get each other confused. And so after a moment's pause, "Okay," he agreed, not that it mattered whether he did or not.

Lucy, meanwhile, had continued her train of thought re naming. "Maybe Kay can be her middle name," she said. "Her first name should start with an O. That way her initials can be OK." She paused. "O. K. Abernathy. Sounds like a writer."

Dev didn't point out that there weren't a whole lot of people left to write for. He was getting a little bit better about not giving all his thoughts air.

Lucy, meanwhile, looked at her baby's face like she was trying to read something off of its forehead. "How about Olivia?"

Dev shrugged. It didn't seem special enough, but then again, he couldn't come up with a name that was.

"Of course, we'd still call her OK," Lucy continued, returning to her original theme, "for short, that is."

"Well, she is that," Dev observed. "Short, that is."

"She's the other thing too," Lucy said, rubbing her nose against the baby's nose. "Okay, that is."

Dev thought about saying, "So far," but didn't—another unaired thought. It was a slow process—that learning—but he was doing it all the same.

Having the necessary equipment for child feeding, child everything else largely fell to Lucy while Dev killed or gathered or grew things and just stood by watching as a third of the world cleaned up after the natural byproducts of having fed her little Okeydokey. It didn't seem exactly fair, this division of labor, postlabor, and Dev—who'd gotten off easy—said so.

"Can't I help?" he asked. And Lucy acted like she was thinking about it before shaking her head no.

He wondered if she was worried the baby might catch his Asperger's and tried reassuring her. "I don't think I'm contagious," he said.

Lucy smiled a weak smile. "It's not that," she said, playing catch and release with her pinky and her daughter's gimme-gimme hands. "It's how you hold her."

"How do I hold her?"

"Like a bomb that's about to go off."

Dev looked at her, his resting blank face as blank as ever, leaving Lucy to fill in the blank as she tried to take it back. "It's endearing, really," she said, "but I don't think all that anxiety is good for the baby."

"So I'll stop being anxious."

Lucy looked back at him, a former, fellow sufferer. "That sounds wonderful," she deadpanned. "You let me know how that works," she added over her shoulder, patting Olivia Kay's back as she walked away.

They'd always been there in his stepfather's closet. No need to go to the library to assemble a collection of books about the one subject he'd avoided all his life: himself. Or his condition, at least. Easier to formulate theories about evolutionary next steps and neurological superiority than read what people who'd made autism not just their *topique du annum* but *pour la vie* (for life). He'd known they were there—books by researchers and Aspies themselves—but Dev didn't want to know.

Now he did. Now he needed to. And so he went to his parents' bedroom and opened his stepfather's closet, pulled down the boxes of books with their one-word, black Magic Marker-ed labels: "Dev."

He unfolded their flaps. He took out the books, the xeroxed articles, his stepfather's notebooks of observations. Stacked and totaled in feet and inches, they were taller than he was. And though it was no way to measure information, he hoped the stack's height was a good sign. Dev didn't think he could trust something shorter than he was to explain him to himself. Even though, in the end, that was exactly what happened.

Diving into the books, he read about something called mirror neurons, the nerves that light up in an MRI the same way when someone performs an action as when they merely watch someone else perform the same action. They'd been mentioned—briefly—in his suicide research. Evidently, these neurons were believed fundamental not only to how children learn through mimicry, but could also explain the human capacity for empathy. Conversely, defective or poorly developed mirror neurons were suspected in everything from the reflexive parroting of words known as echolalia, to the stickiness of certain tics in Tourette's, to the empathetic impairments of autism spectrum disorder.

He thought about his mother and all the time they'd put in, Dev looking at the faces she showed him, trying to translate the cards into the emotions they portrayed. They'd been looking at only half of the problem—the recognition of certain emotional states as an intellectual exercise. She'd been teaching him pattern recognition, but not empathy.

Dev and his resting blank face stayed blank, blinking rarely, while his brain sorted through its Rolodex of x- and y-coordinates for plotting the shape of lips. Smile, frown, grimace—guess correctly and get a reward.

But he had never felt the emotions he was statically decoding. He had never tried to make the faces they were making. If he had—if they'd introduced a mirror into the game so Dev could practice the lip shapes he saw—how much closer would he have gotten to feeling what they felt? At the very least, he'd have learned what the facial muscles felt like when they made certain expressions. If he held them long enough, would the physical sensations turn into something deeper? Did the doing become the being—the expression become the emotion the expression expressed?

Dev tried explaining what he'd read to Lucy, asked her the questions he'd been asking himself. She nodded as he spoke and spoke when he stopped. "Act as if you believe until you do," she said.

"What?"

"It's something they told us in Catholic school, before I got yanked out due to 'economic conditions' beyond my parents' control," she said. "If we found ourselves doubting some article of faith, we should act as if we believed it anyway, and the act, with grace, would become a reality." She paused. "They've got a bumper-sticker version for AA: 'Fake it till you make it.'"

"Can you just *do* that?" Dev asked. "Fake emotions?"

Lucy nodded. "Sure," she said. "It's called acting." She paused, thought about saying something about fake orgasms. Didn't. Smoothed the wisps of Olivia Kay's hair as the child crinkled her nose and squinched her lids, her toothless mouth forming a reflexive smile.

Dev watched OK and her lively face. He'd always been better with children's faces, though his prior encounters had been inherently fleeting, lasting as long as whatever line he was in did. And then, after that, it was back to looking at his shoes to avoid the chaos of older faces.

Maybe he could learn emotions from Olivia Kay. She could be his time machine, giving him a glimpse at how a neurotypical's emotional-empathetic palette developed from the ground up. They could be empathy buddies, she and he. He could watch her eyes as they looked at their mother's face, learning to mirror it, smiling when she smiled, frowning when she frowned. "Let me try," he'd say, and Lucy would turn. Smile. He'd look at the mirror, or imagine one inside his head, one in which Lucy was Dev, smiling back at himself.

"Up," she'd say, twitching an index finger upward, pointing at one corner of his mouth. "Up a little on that side," she'd say. "Good. And now the other." And Dev would smile.

"Good," she'd say, and smile, too, Dev and she, a mirror facing a mirror, their smiles going on forever in both directions.

49

Even though they probably had two years or more before the baby known as OK would start asking questions, Lucy and Dev saw no reason to wait. And so they started asking each other, on her behalf. What would they say happened to her father? Or would Dev step in and be a father for her?

"Huh," he said, thinking about it. "I never made that connection before."

"What connection?"

"Stepping in," he said. "That's what a stepfather does. He steps in. Get it?"

"O-kay," she said, understanding but not thinking much of it. Of course, she had a real father before, so . . .

"I think I should just be Uncle Dev," he said, preferring to keep things flexible—in this area, at least.

That he could pass as the baby's actual, biological father wasn't discussed, but it was there. They could see that for themselves. Though she'd come out Caucasian pink, as the lizard wrinkles smoothed in that mysterious process of a baby's moving from an anonymous lump of protein that pooped and made noise to a stand-alone individual with a personality of her own—as that process progressed, her complexion caramelized, acquiring the pigment bequeathed to her by her father's DNA. While she'd never be as dark as either Marcus or Dev, she'd also

David Sosnowski

never be as cadaverously white as her Scottish mother. No, her mother's contribution would be a pair of emerald-green eyes and the slightest hint of auburn in her otherwise black hair, visible only in certain angles of sunlight, while it was setting and cicadas shimmered in the trees.

Perhaps more important—or at least in more need of explaining— was where all the other stuff came from. The houses. The cars. The light bulbs, books, and DVDs. The people, spoken about and seen in the latter two. How had the world in those become the world out here? Obviously, her mom and Dev couldn't have made all of it, gods though they'd be in her emerald-green eyes. How were they supposed to explain it without scaring her? How were they to explain what happened when all they had was theories about hormones, suicide, and irony?

So what was the kid-friendly version of doomsday? Aliens? Gods? Elves? They needed a maker myth in which the makers came, made, and then went back to wherever, maybe another planet, to go and make stuff there. Anything that didn't end in the deaths of billions of people.

It was Dev who suggested they just say they got everything from Amazon.

"But what happens when she asks what Amazon is and where it got everything?" Lucy wanted to know. "We'll still be stuck walking backward to the big bang and left shrugging when she asks what came before that."

"The *ylem*, actually," Dev said, going back to when astronomy had been his whole world, so to speak. "The primordial egg. That's what there was before the big bang. It's the thing that went bang."

"You know what I'm saying," Lucy insisted. "Every vague, pat answer leads to more specific questions."

"You mean like God. How old were you when you asked what came before God?"

"I didn't," Lucy lied. "Not until everybody died, when I was sixteen. And even then, the question wasn't what came before God, but what was coming after."

408

"So you didn't question God before?"

"No." Another lie.

"Why not?"

"It's a sin," she said. "*Was.* Kind of."

"So we just make it a sin."

"What?"

"Not believing in Amazon," he said. "Questioning its existence."

"So you want to make up a whole new religion just so a kid will stop asking questions," Lucy said.

Dev nodded. "That's what religion was for, wasn't it? That, and tax exemptions."

Once the baby was weaned—and Dev had made progress in not handling her like she was a bomb—Lucy began trusting him with Olivia Kay more and more often. "Here," she'd say, plopping her daughter down in front of him. "I've reached my quota. I'm all peekabooed out." Dev, for his part, had no quota when it came to repeating whatever OK wanted him to repeat; apparently, a touch of OCD wasn't necessarily a handicap when it came to proxy parenting.

In exchange for childcare services, Lucy did the shopping. She didn't have nearly the qualms Dev had about going beyond the wall, plus Olivia Kay was the primary reason they needed more supplies in the first place, from diapers to baby food to whatever else caught her new-mother's eye. She used one of the high-riding SUVs Dev hadn't torched and brought along a semiautomatic assault rifle with extra ammo, just in case. Having learned just how easy it was to die in this germ-crudded, rusty new world of theirs, she also made sure to take along a first aid kit that was at least as well-stocked as a drive-through urgent care unit for the very good reason that that's where it had come from, having been liberated during her first shopping trip post-Marcus.

During that first trip solo outside the wall, she'd also hit an army surplus place called Harry's off Telegraph and gotten a couple of field-grade walkie-talkies and extra batteries. Like everything else she took with her "out there," the walkie-talkies were for just in case. Not that she imagined Dev strapping the baby on and coming to her rescue should a just-in-case occur out there. The just-in-cases she envisioned all had to do with the other side of the channel and involved child-related crises such as diapers needing changing, a belly needing filling, or a broken heart in need of fixing only a mother's voice could provide.

As it turned out, what she got was the equivalent of a baby monitor, listening in on the contented coos of a daughter apparently oblivious to her absence. Other than that, there were the sounds Dev made, especially once he stopped paying attention to the live mic and fell into playing with the baby to the exclusion of all else.

He seemed to become a different person with Olivia Kay—a more personable one, a sillier one, one she could almost imagine not just procreating with for the good of the species but maybe loving. The most striking thing about his interactions with her daughter was how seriously he took OK as a fellow human being. He didn't stoop to baby talk, but had one-sided conversations with her, asking her questions and supplying what he imagined her answers might be.

"So what do you think about being the first in the next line of human beings?

"You're frowning. I guess that means you don't think much of it.

"I agree. It's just a label. An accident of timing. If I hadn't been born when I was born, I would have been something other than what I turned out to be. I don't know if that would have been better or not. Probably not. Being on the spectrum got me a lot of special handling, I guess.

"A title? Yes, a title would be a lot better than a label. I suggest we call you OK the Queen of the Future.

"I take it from your giggling that you approve."

And so on.

Lucy wondered if she should allude to any of these conversations, maybe ask how the Queen of the Future was behaving while she was out. But she didn't want to break the illusion—didn't want to remind them they had company, listening in. So instead, she'd ask, "Was she any trouble?"

"Nothing but," Dev would say, a practice smile on his face while OK squeezed his pinky, laying claim to it and everything it was attached to.

Time passed, and Olivia Kay's baby fat got reallocated into making all of her bones longer, into making her baby's brain brainier, leading to first words, including the usual suspects, like *mama*, of course, and *deh*, which could have been *death*, but Lucy assured Dev it was probably *Dev*.

And like Adam in the garden, naming was a way of taking possession, which is exactly what OK did with deh, a.k.a. Dev. And so he busied himself, introducing her to words, her acquisition of language his latest *topique du annum*, except this *topique* spread over more than one *annum*, the so-called formative ones, as Lucy and Marcus's daughter became a real person, with thoughts of her own, and an active participant in the formerly one-sided conversations Dev and she had while Mommy was out shopping.

And then one day, on just such a trip, Lucy had to break in on playtime, interrupting Dev, who was hiding the "nose" he'd stolen behind his back as little hands slapped at him. "Um, I'm going to be late," she told them over the walkie-talkie. "I've got a little trouble here."

"What kind of trouble?" Dev asked.

"Rats," Lucy said, a sense of déjà vu making the word echo in her head.

"Light them up," he advised, borrowing Lucy's own expression for whenever she needed to resort to firepower.

"I don't have that many bullets," she said, still echoing.

"How many are there?"

"Um, bazillions," she said. "Give or take."

Dev's end of the conversation went silent.

"Hello?" Lucy said. "You still there?"

"I don't like rats."

"Join the club," Lucy said back before clicking off.

So this was it; the end of the break that driving to the land of ice and snow had afforded them. Because it was obvious what these rats foreshadowed. It was the same thing she and Marcus had run from, the same thing that drove them together and pushed them as a couple north, to Dev and Devonshire. Though neither liked the winters the north promised, they'd hoped the pigs would hate the cold even more. The pigs, that is, and the mosquitoes bent on turning unborn little OK into not OK at all. They'd been right about the mosquitoes but wrong about the pigs, apparently. Perhaps the porkers were the victims of their own success as a species, having grazed and rooted themselves out of options. Whatever the reason, they were here or very soon would be, eating everything in their path, except for anything inconveniently wrapped in concrete, say, or maybe charred SUVs.

Once the tide of rats had ebbed to the point where she could actually plant her feet on pavement without stepping on one or more of them, she headed back. Stragglers still hightailing it after the pack had no interest in her, scurrying around her moving feet like little test drivers. Her tires splattered a few of these when she turned on the ignition and started rolling, slowly, fatally through their numbers as she caught up with the others, not aiming at them per se, but not going out of her way to miss them either.

As she got within eyeshot of Devonshire, she noticed that Dev's broken bottles and SUVs were having the desired effect, the surging sea of rats parting like the red one in the Bible, the flow split in two, passing on either side of the barrier and underneath the railing bordering the river, where they borrowed the water's current to carry them faster and farther away. By the time she was outside the gate, all but a few had ridden the slope down, the river now so full of rats the only water left seemed to be the shine on their wet and matted backs, their tails pointing straight back in staggered rows while they swam themselves ahead of their own overwhelming wet-fur stink.

"They're coming," Lucy announced upon her return.

"Who they?" Dev asked. "The rats?"

Lucy shook her head. "Something much, much worse."

They decided they needed more glass. And screws and nails and anything sharp and piercing they could add to the broken bottles on the other side—whatever it took to keep the inevitable stampede from coming too close to the wall of charred trucks. The wall had been enough when all it had to keep out were deer, cheetahs, a bear or two. There'd been elephants in the Detroit Zoo, Dev remembered from past school field trips, but they'd never made it from Royal Oak to Devonshire, leading him to suspect they'd either died in their cages or been run down by one big cat or another. And none of the other animals—exotic or domestic—had the sheer weight needed to do much damage. But a stampede of thousands of wild hybrid hogs, anywhere from five hundred to a thousand pounds each, might shake the ground enough to jar apart a truck here, a truck there. And next thing they knew, the flimsier walls much closer would start coming down, no match for the battering of giant, tusked, porcine heads.

So yeah. Broken glass. Screws. Nails. And beyond that, loose bullets scattered like little land mines. And beyond that, rags soaked in motor oil and gasoline. And beyond that—with any luck—a lot of pigs learning a valuable lesson about getting any closer to the world's most unwelcoming welcome mat.

The sound of squealing traveled faster and farther than the earth-rumble of hooves, and OK's young ears, still fresh to the highest frequencies humans can hear, heard them first. "What's that?" she asked, looking up from the dictionary she'd turned into a coloring book.

Neither Dev nor Lucy had heard them yet but were on standby, waiting. The rats had given them fair and early warning—about a day's worth—during which the bigger two of the world's three humans busied themselves breaking glass, scattering bullets, soaking rags, trading off babysitting duty and trying to act like they weren't terrified.

"What's wrong?" OK asked Dev, who said nothing.

"What's wrong, Mommy?" she tried with Lucy, who didn't fall for it.

They'd agreed to make up something when the fact that something was up was undeniable—perhaps when the walls were caving in—but had opted for denial in the meantime. When the time came, Dev planned on saying ground thunder, a hitherto unexperienced weather phenomenon OK had no reason to fear (he hoped). Lucy thought she might try out God or, you know, Amazon—also a hitherto unexperienced phenomenon on the child's part—but with the same punch line: fear not, little one.

Unfortunately, they'd forgotten all about the rest of the pig sounds, beyond the trampling hooves. They'd forgotten about the squealing and grunting and how far they might carry, multiplied over a thousand times. But then OK asked her question and they remembered just before they could hear it too. "Is that pigs?" the little girl asked, and they wondered, fleetingly, before they remembered the See 'n Say they let her play with to their regret at the time and even greater regret now. They'd heard what the cow says, the horse says, and, yes, what the pig says until their dreams smelled of manure, but at least she wasn't playing with matches.

So yes, the child knew what pigs sounded like; there was no tricking her on that account. But as far as what they were capable of or even how big they were, all she had was that little pink Porky on the See 'n

Say, the one that could be any size at all. The one with nary a fang nor tusk nor appetite for little girls named Olivia Kay.

"Yes," Lucy admitted. "It's pigs."

"Can I see?" the little girl asked, springing up from the floor where she lay like something spring-loaded.

"Let's hope not," Dev said as the squealing got louder and his body iced slowly around his joints.

Books fell, and crashable things crashed, though in an eerie, noiseless way caused by the louder, enveloping noise of stampeding hooves. Lucy's mouth made mouth shapes in her daughter's and Dev's directions, and their mouths made mouth shapes back. Ground thunder would've been a good description of the general din if anyone could hear Dev say it. As it was, the noise sounded like being inside a crack of thunder, slowed down and amped up, recorded and played back on eighteen tracks at different speeds, over and over. The sound became one with the shaking, with the squeals on their own separate track, riding high overhead.

And then a sound like popcorn popping slowly, just about done, the popping kicking up the squeals even higher into a kind of tornado of squeals. Followed by a sound like pigs on fire, which is exactly what they were.

OK faced it all with an innocent kind of awe. The experience of something bigger than her wasn't new; that's what her mom and Uncle Dev were. But the experience of the pigs—even at a distance, even held successfully at bay—was bigger than her whole world until that point. Not being able to see them as they shook the house that had heretofore protected her from everything and seemed immovable—the very anonymity of all that power bestowed on it a kind of mystery that (but for the nonbelievers who fed her) could have easily morphed into its own religion, headed by a pigheaded god who shook your house when you failed to worship him in the manner to which he was accustomed.

Which is where the word *just* came in handy. As in, just pigs.

"It's just pigs," Lucy assured her daughter once said pigs had dwindled to the point of allowing conversation again. She'd said it because she recognized in OK her own gullible girlhood, Bible-polluted and impossible to live up to.

But the seed was planted. Whether there were pig gods or not, one thing was absolutely clear to the child, now that the pigs had come and gone: there was something enormous out there, on the other side of the don't-go-there place, the one with all the bones, just like inside her, just like inside everyone, meaning, so far, her mom and Uncle Dev.

50

Olivia Kay stayed OK for as long as it took her to learn how to misbe-have. That's when the wisdom of a nickname that was synonymous with permission showed its dubious side, as demonstrated in exchanges like:

"Can I go shopping with you?"

"No, OK."

Followed by the predictable disobedience, followed by the even more predictable, "But you said it was *okay* . . ."

And there Lucy was, turning the truck around and heading back to home base before advising Dev to use duct tape if the kid got within ten feet of any door that led outside.

"I believe the cattle prod will suffice," Dev would say, winning a wide-eyed, slack-jawed "Mo-*om* . . ." every time.

And so OK became just plain Kay. She also became a world-class asker of why, first about the ever-growing number of rules that only she had to obey, but then about the rules that everyone and everything had to follow as well.

"Because of gravity," Dev would answer.

"Because you've got blood underneath your skin, and when you scrape it, blood comes out.

"Because you don't want germs in your cut.

"Because it stings when the germs die.

"Not yet. Not for a long time. I hope.

"No, not her either.

"Because she's a big girl and she has a big gun.

"Because Uncle Dev knows the importance of the home-field advantage, that's why."

It was after this and similar barrages that Dev decided to teach Kay how to read as soon as possible. It wasn't because he wanted her to leave him alone; it was because (with the exception of going beyond the wall) he was prepared to give her the world that (as long as they weren't going beyond the wall) could be found in books. He started with alphabet blocks and some of the baby books Lucy picked up while shopping. He pointed to concrete things—his eye, her eye, a tree—and then arranged the blocks to spell out the name of the thing, sounding each letter out as he handed it to her and having her sound it out as she handed it back. He'd then flip through the baby books and have her pick out instances of the word she'd just learned.

It was slow going at first. But Dev was dedicated like only an obsessive can be, and Kay was motivated too. Her uncle had already promised her that the answers to all her questions were in the books her mother had collected on a shelf under a sign Dev made that read: "Kay's Library."

By the time she was four, she was making her own words out of blocks and quizzing Dev on them. Soon, the words started getting longer and less and less likely to have come from any of the books set aside for Kay's Library. "Where'd you learn that?" Dev asked, after being surprised by the words *focal point*.

Kay handed over a book on astronomy he hadn't noticed was missing from Dev's Library. "Those are pretty grown-up words," he said.

Which was all he needed to say, of course, to send her ripping like a buzz saw through whatever reading material she could find. And the more she read, the more she began wondering about the circumstances of her existence with her mom and Uncle Dev in this world she routinely walked to the edge of, beyond which, her mother assured her, there were monsters, though that didn't stop her mom from going.

Dev's response to Kay's interest in things astronomical was a strategic mistake. He simply took her out one clear evening, wheeled out his telescope, and showed her some of the things that had fascinated him when he was a child. "Do you see those circle things on the moon with lines spreading out from them?" he asked.

Kay nodded.

"Those are from meteorites like the one we saw making a line in the sky earlier. They're like rocks, but in outer space, and when the earth gets in their way, they burn up in the air. The moon doesn't have any air, and so the rocks just hit it, leaving those marks."

Kay kept nodding as Dev explained, and he thought he'd done it: preemptively cured her of wondering what was beyond the wall, once she'd outgrown the tiny world she'd inherited. There was, after all, a lot of sky they could work through, certainly enough to distract her until he, himself, was dead.

This illusion was short-lived, however, coming to an end with four little words: "Can we go there?"

"Where?" Dev asked, though he already knew and regretted bringing it up.

"The moon," Kay said.

And that was the perversity of astronomy to a citizen of a world only a handful of blocks from end to end: it implied much bigger worlds that, alas, you couldn't get to, no matter how hard you tried. Instead of satisfying her curiosity, he'd focused it into a desire to be elsewhere.

"I *did* say there's no air up there," Dev said, trying to salvage it.

"I can hold my breath," Kay said before proceeding to demonstrate.

"Stop that," Dev said, taking hold of her shoulders. "Breathe," he said.

Kay shook her head, cheeks bulging.

"Lucy!" he finally called as the little girl flapped her arms, either trying to fly or to just not pass out.

"Miss Olivia Katherine," Lucy said, deflating the girl's cheeks by pressing them from either side, forcing her to take a great, gasping breath, "what on earth are you doing?"

"Getting ready for the moon," her daughter said as Lucy looked at Dev and just shook her head.

The more she read, the more curious she got about all the stuff that was in the books that wasn't anywhere she'd looked within the handful of blocks that made up the known universe. "Where is everything?" she wanted to know.

"What everything?" Dev bluffed.

And though the object of her curiosity varied every time, it was usually something conspicuous enough to make hiding it difficult if her circumscribed world really was all there was. Things like: the Eiffel Tower. The Statue of Liberty. New Jersey. All the people . . .

"What people?" Dev asked back.

Kay opened an encyclopedia and started pointing out names.

Dev tried bluffing again, this time by suggesting they were the ones the skulls belonged to in the wall at the edge of the world.

Yeah, right. Kay had counted the skulls, and she counted proper names in the encyclopedia. Not even close.

"Well, um." Dev hesitated. "Why don't you ask your mom?"

Lucy tried suggesting that everything in the books was made up—a hard sell. Once again, Kay did the math and found it hard to believe that there were more made-up things in books than there were real things in the world. One obvious question: Why would *anybody* make it all up in the first place?

"To entertain us," Lucy said. "So we won't get bored."

"What does *bored* mean?" Kay asked. Interestingly, the subject of boredom was not often addressed in books—perhaps because it was boring. And other than Lucy and Dev, books were Kay's primary source of information.

"Um, you know. 'There's nothing to do,'" Lucy said, using her whiny-kid voice. "'I'm bored.'"

Kay didn't get it and said so, so her mother tried again. "Say you're counting your toes. And you count them. They're all counted. Bored is why you counted them and how you feel after you have."

"Oh," Kay said.

Whether she recognized it as the nuclear option for getting her way with Uncle Dev or not, that's how Kay used it, the very next time Lucy left to go shopping. "I'm bored," the little girl announced, flopping down on the couch like her strings had been cut.

Dev suggested they read something. Kay had read everything in Devonshire and even though more was available at the library he'd raided prior to her being born, both Lucy and Dev were reluctant to feed a curiosity that was rapidly outpacing their ability to make up answers.

And so Dev suggested they play a game.

"A board game?" she asked, setting him up.

"A *video* game," he replied, not falling for it. So they tried *Mortal Kombat,* but the things that made it exciting in the world before were all wholly outside her experience. She had never physically fought anybody and had never seen anybody else do it. It really didn't make a lot of sense. Killing, yes, she was familiar with that; Uncle Dev killed stuff for dinner. But the winner never ate the loser in *Mortal Kombat,* and so, again, what was the point?

"I'm bored," Kay announced as her avatar had its spine ripped out.

"Um," Dev said, turning off the game, wondering what to try next.

By the time Lucy returned, they had a vacuum cleaner in pieces and spread across the living room floor. She took one look and said one word: "No."

"She was bored," Dev explained.

"Nope," Lucy said. "No way. Living like this is bad enough. You're not turning my daughter into a weirdo . . ."

"What's a weirdo?" Kay asked, another subject not broached in the books she'd read.

Lucy looked at Dev. Dev looked at Lucy.

"Who wants ice cream?" Lucy tried.

"What's ice cream?" her daughter asked on top of Dev's, "Where'd you get ice cream?"

"That's just what my mom used to say when . . . ," Lucy began.

"You had a mom?" Kay said, eyes wide.

"*Shite,*" Lucy said, as Dev just looked away.

51

He was being counted on. He'd been on the planet for how long now? Sixteen years before, going on six years after, and in all those years, he'd never been counted on—not by anyone but himself, that is, and before, not even then. Before, he'd been something to be taken care of, tolerated, taken for granted and, eventually, taken for a fool. After, he'd done what he did to survive. There'd been Diablo and his lesser—and it had felt like he'd been counted on back then, but not really. Once he'd removed the man-made barriers between the animals and their self-reliance, they took care of themselves, including helping themselves to his chickens. But now, with this little human in his life, talking and full of needs, Dev Brinkman, previous waste of protein, was being counted on to make decisions in someone's best interest other than his own.

Sure, the human also had her mother. But there were decisions to be made—decisions that tangled the three of them together, that couldn't be made without affecting every thread in that knot. And one of those decisions threatened to upend one of the most fundamental tenets of his survival thus far: Dev's comfort zone, a.k.a. the home-field advantage.

It hadn't even been a question before. If you had the home-field advantage, you kept it. Wandering about for no good reason was how survivors became *ex*-survivors. The loophole—and Lucy showed every sign of exploiting it—was that no-good-reason clause. Suddenly, it wasn't a question of staying or leaving, but what would make a good enough reason to go.

And here's where Dev was being counted on. Kay—they needed to leave Devonshire because of Kay. That's what Lucy said. They needed to find others—"for Kay." They needed to find friends—"for Kay."

"I never had any friends," Dev tried. "Not real ones, at least."

"And how'd that work out for you?"

Dev wanted to say, "Just fine," but he'd become enough of a "real human" by then to know that Lucy and he had totally different opinions about how he'd turned out. "I just don't want her to be weird," she continued.

"You were weird," he pointed out. She'd said so herself.

"Yeah," she admitted wistfully. "So I know what I'm talking about."

Dev had been accused of being weird so often he started wearing it like a badge of honor. Lucy had, too, until everybody died. She'd told him that after that, the only thing she ever wanted to be was normal. Dev had been useful back then; he had the power to make anyone seem normal in comparison. Now all he could do was make her daughter as weird as he.

"Listen," she said. "Being weird has to be a choice. If it's your default setting because you don't know what the options are, it doesn't count." Pause. "What I'm saying is, she can decide to be antisocial, but she's got to have the option of being social first."

"So your argument is she *should* talk to strangers."

Lucy blinked. "Um," she said, "kind of?"

"What happens when she gets kidnapped?"

"I think we're getting ahead of ourselves here," Lucy said. "I just want to find out if there are any strangers out there to worry about."

"Cheetahs," Dev said. "Bears. Deer with Lyme disease . . ."

"I meant *people* strangers," she said. "Prefriends. For Kay's sake."

And so it went, round and round, Lucy advocating expansionism, Dev solidly in the isolationist camp until that day when Kay added her two cents with the weapon of mass distraction her mother had taught her:

"I'm bored."

It didn't help that she put her whole little body into those two nuclear words, shoulders slumping, knees buckling underneath her as she tipped backward to plop onto the couch, the soft cushions of which threatened to envelop her, close over, swallow, then burp. Her head hit the back cushion, bent, chin resting on clavicle. Her head looked like a chubby-faced sun, setting below the horizon of the rest of her.

"Bored . . . ," she repeated.

If it was an accusation—and it stung like one—it was aimed at Dev, and she, this little human named Kay, was counting on him to do something about it.

Until that point, he'd been convinced they had everything they needed in Devonshire to survive. He looked around now, confronted by the sameness he'd collected around himself and rigidly enforced. The books had been read, the DVDs watched. The board games—despite the sound-alike name—had been fun. Until they played them a hundred times and lost some vital pieces.

He'd tried teaching her chess, but the game wound up suffering from missing-piece syndrome—a case of it that he suspected was really *hidden*-piece syndrome. He'd allowed the charade partly because he'd realized it was just that—thanks to how poorly the kid lied.

Her lying had been one of many important moments on his journey of discovery to the higher human emotions. Sometimes a bad example is better than a good one. Thinking about his bad liar, Dev wondered if she'd ever get better at it with only her mother and him to practice on. How important was lying in the development of a nonweird human being? Judging from how poor he himself was at it, likely very.

So Lucy was probably right, but for the wrong reasons. Kay did need other people around, not to be friends with, but to lie to. To get practice lying to people with varying degrees of BS-detection abilities. Maybe then she could build up her own. And then, if she decided she needed friends, she could make sure they were the real kind.

"So how are you going to find these strangers?" Dev asked. "Or should I say, prefriends?"

Lucy shrugged. "Like how I found Marcus," she said. "Like how we found you. Drive around."

"Drive around? That's your plan?"

"You got a better one?"

He hesitated. But he was being counted on. "If it were me," he said, "knowing what we know about who survived and who didn't . . ."

"What we *think* we know," Lucy corrected.

"I'd look for suicide-prevention call centers," he said, finally sharing an idea that had occurred to him some time ago. "See what calls came in on the day of, especially just before. I'm sure everything got recorded with all the metadata, including addresses. They'd have to keep that stuff just in case."

Lucy's eyes widened, and she nodded. "That makes sense," she said, considering it. "Almost every robo you called back then would tell you they were recording 'to ensure sound quality' or some such BS. What they really should have said was 'We're recording this to cover our ass . . .'"

"Language," Dev said, ever mindful of young ears in need of protecting, "but yes. Exactly."

But then Lucy's excitement deflated. "Except, Google's dead. How are we supposed to . . ."

And then, evidence that this conversation had been more premeditated on Dev's part than he'd let on. "Here," he said, handing her a slightly yellower copy of the yellow pages from before. "It's under *S*."

Okay, it was a long shot, but it was for Olivia Kay. Sure, some of the callers could have gone through with it. Sure, some of the survivors could have stopped surviving along the way. And those who were still surviving may have set out like Lucy and Marcus rather than staying put like Dev. But it was something, and if enough somethings started pointing to the same somewhere . . .

"You know," Dev said, having second thoughts and naming them, "on second thought, this seems like a total long shot."

"It's better than the no shot we've got staying here," Lucy said while Kay helped her mark suitcases in chalk—"Mom," "Kay." A gratuitous gesture, or maybe just a sign of their hope that one day there'd be enough others to warrant the labeling of things.

"*Better*'s a relative term," Dev said, thinking about how he'd thus far evaded death, despite the many times he'd believed it imminent. Leo's making a fool of him hadn't killed him. Driving on the freeway at nearly freeway speeds hadn't killed him. The cow stampede hadn't killed him. The cheetah, deer crash, and Lyme disease scare had all left him shaken, but not dead. Diablo's death came close but still fell short. He'd even failed at willing himself to death when the eggs ran out. Perhaps he wasn't the best judge of what would kill him after all . . .

Dev remembered a conversation he'd had with his mother—a monologue, really—when she'd learned that the reason he'd stopped talking for a day and a half was because he'd overheard someone he considered his inferior refer to him as "slow." When she'd stepped into his bedroom and sat on the edge of his bed, he'd fully expected her to try to make him feel better by explaining what an idiot the other child had been and telling him to ignore such talk—the usual. But it wasn't the usual rah-rah you're-perfect-just-the-way-you-are speech. After a heavy sigh, she'd begun:

"I know it's not politically correct to say it, sweetie," she'd said. "But think of it this way: you've got a developmental disorder, *not* a static condition. *Slow* doesn't mean *stopped*. It doesn't mean *stuck*. You're fast—you're *very* fast—when it comes to intellectual intelligence." Here she'd touched him on the head even though she knew he hated being touched. "But you're a scooch slow when it comes to emotional intelligence." Moving her hand to his chest—the presumed home of this latter kind of thinking. "But you'll catch up, one of these days."

A lot of days had passed since then, and the people he'd needed to catch up to had largely disappeared, not that he'd cared for them much anyway. But "largely" wasn't all. And the ones excluded—the ones he found himself caring for—were preparing to leave, luggage now waiting by the door. And Dev could let them. Or he could try to catch up.

"Wait," he called as mother and daughter bent for their suitcases, Olivia pausing and turning to check on whether he was coming or not.

"I'm not packed." Dev stalled.

Lucy tapped Kay on the shoulder—a cue, apparently. "Already done," she said, and each lifted a suitcase out of the way, like curtains parting. Behind stood two more suitcases, the name "Dev" scrawled across them in chalk.

"You don't have to leave your comfort zone," Lucy said, revealing that knack Dev envied: the seeming ability to read other people's minds.

"I don't?"

"Just make it portable," she said, casting a downward glance at her daughter, the one whose only baggage was wholly literal and came with its own handles.

"But what if it's all a waste of time?"

"Good thing we got plenty, then."

The odds were long, he'd thought, but maybe not. In about a year, three survivors who'd persisted had found each other, and they'd each found at least one of the other kind of survivor as well. And if there were other pockets out there like theirs, who'd survived long enough to create even one more human life half as precious as the one Lucy and he were raising . . . Well, the odds could be getting better every day. Not for Dev—the Wizard of Odd, as his stepfather once dubbed him—but for the ones who'd survive the original survivors: call them Generation Clean Slate or—even better—Generation OK, the one for whom the end of everything was just the beginning.

"Okay," Dev said, echoing the most hopeful sound to cross his mind lately.

"Yes?" the girl with the optimistic initials said before grinning a mischievous five-year-old's grin.

"Can you hold my hand?" Dev asked, holding out his own.

Kay could. She did.

"After you, O Queen of the Future," he said, as Her Highness led the way.

ACKNOWLEDGMENTS

As many writers know, writing a book can often be the easy part, especially nowadays in the ever-changing world of publishing, which is why those of us who are exceedingly lucky have found agents to take on the heavy lifting. I count myself luckier than most because my agent, Jane Dystel, has not only been a tireless champion for me, my career, and the book you now hold in your hands, but whether she knows it or not, she was also instrumental in giving me the push needed to have a book to sell in the first place. It's easy to lose steam when working on a long project; it's easier still to never get up a head of steam to begin with. For a long time with *Happy Doomsday*, I was content to entertain myself by jotting down notes and the odd scene here and there, holding off on the actual writing because it's difficult to reject an unwritten book. But when Jane heard about the idea I was toying with, her enthusiasm combined with my total faith in her judgment helped crank up the heat, got my butt in the chair, and got this book written. And for that, Jane, and for everything else you have done, I am forever in your debt.

And then there are the people who said yes: the excellent team at Amazon Publishing, first among them Jason Kirk at 47North, whose enthusiasm for and faith in this project helped fuel my own. As acquiring editor, Jason not only "got" my book in the sense of the sale, but he also "got it," at a level that writers dream of when they dream of the ideal reader, one whose enthusiasm becomes advocacy and—best of all—contagious.

Which brings me to LAM, a.k.a. Leslie Miller, CEO/COO of Girl Friday Productions, one of the people Jason "infected" with his love of the project. LAM's guiding editorial hand and thoughtful suggestions helped make the revision process every bit as fun and exhilarating as the initial creative spark that led to the first draft. Like Jane, and then Jason, LAM "got it," which in turn helped me get the story to where it needed to be.

I'd also like to thank everybody else at Amazon Publishing who had a hand in bringing this dream to life, including Kristin King, who made the publishing process both welcoming and fun; Laura Petrella, who made sure I kept my facts and inventions straight; Tim Green and Faceout Studio, who were responsible for the book's overall look; and Marlene Kelly, Haley Kushman, Colleen Lindsay, Kyla Pigoni, Brittany Russell, and Kelsey Snyder, who made sure the word got out to those wonderful creatures we're all indebted to: the people who buy (and read!) books.

Finally, but with no less gratitude, I'd like to thank the others who helped along the way, with encouragement, editorial advice, or good old-fashioned moral support, both on this side of the mortal divide and the other one. Among these champions, I count Miriam Goderich, Jim McCarthy, and everybody else at Dystel, Goderich & Bourret LLC; Josie Kearns (my earliest reader and most honest critic); my late friend Mark Schemanske for haunting me as I wrote; my parents, Eugene and Florence Sosnowski, both of whom have passed but whose influences are with me every day; my fellow survivors in missing our parents: my sisters, Susan Dudek and Kathleen Rodriguez, and my brother and fellow artist, Mike; and, lastly but certainly not least, the fans of my previous books, *Rapture* and *Vamped*, for emailing and friending and asking (always politely though not always patiently) when the next one was coming out. Here you go, guys: The Next One. Out. I hope it was worth the wait.

ABOUT THE AUTHOR

David Sosnowski has worked as a gag writer, fireworks salesman, telephone pollster, university writing instructor, and environmental-protection specialist while living in places as different as Washington, DC; Detroit, Michigan; and Fairbanks, Alaska. In a novelistic twist, David currently lives in a Michigan home previously owned by the sixth-grade English teacher who inspired him to write. A winner of the Thomas Wolfe Fiction Prize, David has had his short fiction appear in numerous magazines, including *Passages North*, *River City*, and *Alaska Quarterly Review*. He is also the author of the critically acclaimed novels *Rapture* and *Vamped*.